THE SPARKS OF DISSENT

THE SPARKS OF DISSENT

BEING THE SECOND PART OF

THE SPARKGAZER SAGA TRILOGY

BY
DAN F. SWINNEN

COPYRIGHT © 2025 BY DAN F. SWINNEN
All rights reserved.

No part of this publication may be reproduced, distributed, or transmitted in any form or by any means, including photocopying, recording, or other electronic or mechanical methods, without the prior written permission of the publisher, except as permitted by U.S. copyright law.

For permission requests, contact dan.f.swinnen@gmail.com.

The story, all names, characters, and incidents portrayed in this production are fictitious. No identification with actual persons (living or deceased), places, buildings, and products is intended or should be inferred.

Editing by Sarah Grace Liu
Illustration by T Studio @ Shutterstock

Book Cover/Layout by Benoit Vangeel

First edition 2025

For Janne,

whose courage never fails.

***

For Fons,

whose curiosity was infinite.

CHAPTER 1

nce, Doorstep's Ditch had been a cesspit of human depravity; now it was an open-air prison. Less than a year ago, the Ditch's nighttime streets had been home to brawls, stumbling floaters, and murderous robbers. Tonight, they were silent.

Brina Springtide pressed her back against the alley's wall, her black hood drawn deep over her burning eye. A patrol of darkhelms, the empire's goons with black helmets shaped liked raven heads, shambled past. There were half a dozen of them, dragging their boots through a thin layer of snow.

Brina shuddered. Not because she was afraid. If it came to it, she'd dispatch the lot of them without breaking a sweat. It was the sheer unnaturalness of it all. The empire and its citizens dwelt within Mallion's Depth's city walls, while banished thieves, beggars, and inconvenient thinkers were left to fend for themselves on the outside. Or so it had always been. Now the church wouldn't even let them have that.

No time to worry about that now. There's more urgent business to attend to.

She crept down the alley, trudging past one boarded-up window after another. Here and there, the weak shimmer of candles escaped through the cracks. Most houses still bore the marks of the ravenous fire that had swept through the Ditch last winter. Sometimes, when things got too quiet, Brina could still hear the horns wail as hordes of Skullbeard mercenaries stormed up from the beach to sack and burn the village.

Blackened walls, soot-stained windows, and missing roofs covered with scraps of old sails and jute sacks lined the alley. Brina spat in the snow, a familiar rage rising in her throat. It hardly ever left her these days. Everywhere she turned, the church was there, looming over her like a giant scarecrow.

When she reached Wicket Row, the main street of Doorstep's Ditch, Brina pushed herself up in the narrow space between two houses and flung herself onto a shingled roof. Crouching, she peered over the edge into the slush-covered road. Icy wind lashed her face, making her missing eye weep.

The flesh surrounding the empty socket had become hard and numb, but the socket itself remained sensitive to the elements after all these months.

Here and there, stone towers jutted out above the sea of ramshackle roofs like sharks' fins in the lull between waves. Every time Brina counted them, there seemed to be more of them. They were reverse cages, shielding the darkhelms from the vermin outside the wall. Though the scepter had repressed the outwalled for centuries, they still feared them. *A good sphinx tamer never forgets the beast's claws.*

Brina closed her eye, searching her memory for the power she had stored there. A rainbow formed in her mind's eye as close to a dozen power shapes lit up inside. She seized on *Leve*, pulling her hood further over her eyes to block the emerald glare as the teardrop-shaped rune lit up her good eye. A hollowness swelled in Brina's bones as her entire body grew lighter. She smiled.

Time to move.

Brina ran toward the ruined roof of an adjacent house. She leaped from wooden beam to wooden beam, feeling like she was dancing on a giant's ribcage. When she reached the roof's end, she flung herself forward. For one glorious moment, she hung in the air, cloak flapping in the wind. Then she was already charging across the next roof.

She glided through the night like a bat. Weightless, silent, invisible. She let the newer towers glide past. They tended to be manned by jittery crews of new recruits. Which meant that they were still on high alert, clinging to their weapons like a babe to its mother's chest. Too much hassle.

Complacency, that was the ticket. A crew of grizzled warriors who felt untouchable surrounded by the outwalled rabble. Soldiers whose nerves had been deadened beyond fear. Soldiers who were relaxed enough to cut corners.

There it is. Brina skidded to a halt, cursing as a handful of loose shingles tumbled off the roof's edge to the street below. They hit the ground with a series of soft thuds, their impact muffled by the fresh snow. Brina crouched down and crawled to the far side of the roof.

Across the narrow street, two shadowy figures leaned back against the tower's reinforced front door. Their raven helmets reflected the pale light of the two chariots racing across the firmament above. Brina touched *Auris*. She winced as the night grew deafening in her ears. Loose boards rattled in the wind, doors squeaked on rusty hinges, and across the street, clear as day, she heard the guards' annoyed voices.

"Gernich has it made," the tallest of the two muttered. "First sign of snow, and he vanishes into the city to deliver yet another 'report.'"

CHAPTER 1

The other guard snickered. "What do you suppose he even writes in them?" He put on a high-pitched, sycophantic voice. "Filthy criminals are still filthy, Your Purity."

"I knew I should have applied for that promotion." The tall guard shook her head. "If they're making morons like him sergeant, I could be the bloody cardinal by spring. Sometimes it seems like the whole church is one big—"

"Karris, please." Her colleague held a finger to his lips, then pointed up at an open window on the tower's third story. "Don't let her hear you."

"It's past midnight. She's asleep," Karris snapped, though her voice shrank to a whisper.

Brina's eyes lingered on the open window. A smile blossomed on her face. Sometimes they just made it too easy. She let go of *Auris* and burned *Rhetoris* in its place. Psycho-sigils weren't her specialty. They required too much subtlety to be used to their full effects. Why manipulate when you could just poke a dagger in someone's face and tell them exactly what you want? Luckily, Brina only needed a little edge of credibility.

"Help!" she shouted, her voice infused with artificial panic. She pried a shingle loose with her fingers, then flung it into the wall of an adjacent house to simulate a struggle. "Get off me. Get. Off. Me."

Neither of the guards stirred. Brina cursed under her breath. Of course, they wouldn't lift a finger while an—admittedly fake—woman was attacked right in front of them. They were here to contain, not to protect.

"Not my jewelry. Please, it's all I have."

And there they go. Brina watched in disgust as the darkhelm duo glanced at each other before marching across the street and into the alley. She resisted the temptation to spit on them. *Eye on the prize, Springtide.*

With effortless grace, she burned *Forte*, and used the surge of strength to launch herself into the air. At the apex of the jump, she switched into *Leve*. It was like flying a kite. With a rush of tingles in her belly, she shot upward and soared across the street. Her fingers dug into the cracks in the tower's wall. Aided by *Forte*, she felt like a spider as she climbed her way to the third-floor window.

Boots squelched in the mixed snow and mud on the street.

"... must have gotten her," Karris said.

"Shame. Could have been a nice bonus."

Brina glimpsed the pair returning to their post right before she squeezed herself through the tiny window.

The inside of the tower was dark. Brina burned *Lux*, forcing her eyes to adapt to the gloom. Four bunk beds stood against the circular walls, while a small round table took up what little space remained in the middle of the room.

A grunting snort yanked Brina's heart into her throat. She reached for the dagger in her ankle holster before she noticed the rising and falling chest of a woman sleeping in the bunk to her right. The darkhelm's armor and clothes hung from wooden hangers clipped to the back of the bed. Brina remained motionless for a few deafening heartbeats. When she was satisfied the darkhelm was asleep, Brina riffled through the clothes, turning pockets inside out and running her fingers along the seams. *There we go.*

She grabbed the large jute sack she had brought and threw in a dented silver pocket watch, a pouch containing a handful of sapphire and emerald gem shards, and a set of golden hairpins.

The wooden floorboards whispered under Brina's feet as she made her way toward the wooden staircase on the opposite side of the room. As she tiptoed past the sleeping darkhelm, the woman turned over, revealing a scroll of parchment with a blood red seal clasped in her fist. Even though the wax had been torn, the rectangular scepter symbol imprinted in it was unmistakable. *From the Cardinal himself.*

Brina's gaze drifted from the scroll to the woman's face. Her mouth hung open, the skin around it sagging with age. A crop of short gray hair framed a harsh face with a short, hooked nose like a beak. With every shuddering breath, the darkhelm's jowls quivered. *Senior officer, letter from the Cardinal, do the math, Springtide.*

Brina extended her hand, then withdrew it as though she'd burned it. It was too dangerous. Food and weapons, that was what she needed. In that order. People in the Ditch were starving and counting on her to help them. Was she willing to risk that for a piece of parchment? After all she had been through over the past year, all the times she had barely escaped a one-way ticket to God's Maul, it would be beyond stupid to—

She grabbed it. In one fluid motion, the scroll slipped from the darkhelm's limp fingers. Brina dropped it into the sack, resisting the urge to read it right there and then.

"You. Where did you come from?"

The darkhelm sat bolt upright, her eyes wide. Veiny hands skittered across the mattress, reaching for a dagger tucked away under the woman's pillow.

It was over in a single heartbeat.

Brina's own dagger sank into the officer's neck up to the hilt, her other hand

CHAPTER 1

clasped tight over the woman's mouth to stifle a scream that never came. The darkhelm gurgled. Blood seeped through Brina's fingers like water bursting from a spring. The officer's green eyes locked on to Brina's. Hatred, fear, or both, it was impossible to tell.

Brina gazed back as the darkhelm's life ebbed away. She had killed before. In battle, steel versus steel. Or when she'd rained down firebombs on an entire fleet of redsails. It had never been like this. She was close enough to smell urine mixing with metallic blood as the darkhelm's bladder gave up. A hint of iron coated her tongue. Her fingers were smeared with blood, snot, and spit. The darkhelm's face was wrought in a perpetual grimace, inches from Brina's own.

There was a wet crunch as Brina pulled her dagger out. She tried to wipe it on the gray bedsheets, but it was no use.

The most shocking thing of all, however, was that Brina found she didn't care. There was no sadness, no disgust, no guilt. She had done what needed to be done, and that was that.

She grabbed the officer's ornate dagger from under her pillow and threw it into the sack, along with the rest of the stuff she'd stolen. Pushed forward by adrenaline and the knowledge that she would have to be as far away as possible when the body was discovered, Brina inched down the stairs.

The second floor was divided into two sections. The first was a kitchen with a tiny hearth, above which a series of shiny steel pots and utensils hung from a wooden rack.

Brina considered taking them, but they were too heavy, and all that steel clanking together as she leaped across the rooftops would make her a laughably easy target to track.

When she opened the door to the second room, Brina's mouth watered. *Praise the Seven.* Though the pantry was small, it contained enough food to feed a dozen people for a week. Twice that, if need be. Two smoked hams hung from ropes tied to the ceiling beams, spreading their delicious odor through the pantry. Three quarters of a wheel of cheese lay wrapped in a cloth on top of a closed cabinet, and a few loaves of bread were stacked in a basket beside the door. Brina dumped everything into the sack, then opened every drawer, cupboard, and cabinet she could find.

She grabbed a few small, unopened bags of dried oats. The sacks of flour were too large to carry, so she sliced them open with her dagger and let the fine powder spill everywhere. Clouds formed in the room, coating everything in a fine white mist.

With her sack filled to bursting, Brina sprinted back up the staircase to the third floor. If the guards outside heard her thumping footsteps, all the better. By the time they got up here, she would be long gone. She bumped into the round table that stood between the bunks as she made her way to the window, and a delightful, familiar tinkling sound greeted her. A wild grin pulled at Brina's face. They sounded full.

She sank down to one knee and found two full bottles of kelp rum standing beside one of the chairs. *Don't mind if I do.*

Right on schedule, a voice called out from below.

"Is that you, lieutenant? Everything alright?"

Brina ran for the window, brushing her fingertips against one of the straw mattresses as she went. She burned *Gnis*, and the straw smoldered at once.

"Fire! Help. Fire!" The fit of coughing she followed up with was genuine as thick smoke filled the room.

The heat intensified behind her as she squeezed herself through the window, burning *Forte* to keep her balance with the heavy sack slung over her back. She took a deep breath, flared the shape as brightly as she could, and made the jump to the nearest roof. She held still for a moment, but as she'd expected, nobody had noticed a thing.

Morons.

With the rustle of her cloak brushing against wooden shingles, Brina slid off the roof and into the alleyway below. As usual, she was getting away scot-free with yet another sack of provisions to hand out to those living in the Ditch's muddy streets. Reaching into the sack, she tore a loaf of bread and tucked half of it away in her cloak's pocket. It would be just enough to get her through the day. Tomorrow night, she would do it all again. Brina liked to stay at least a little hungry at all times. It kept her sharp.

As she put the other half of the bread back into the sack, her hand brushed a sharp edge. *Oh, right. The scroll.* In the afterglow of watching the tower go up in flames, she'd all but forgotten about the scroll she'd stolen from the sleeping officer.

Might as well see what those bastards are up to.

She unfurled the scroll and burned *Lux* to amplify the pale moonlight.

CHAPTER 1

"Be advised, commanders of the Enlightened Watch,

Upon the thawing of winter's frost, a full withdrawal of your regiment from the wastes outside the stoneward shall be ordered. Upon receiving the official summons, you are to report to Reynziel General Denbrook on Keeper's Square, where you shall receive instructions for the part your unit is to play in the approaching campaign to subdue the untamed sections of the province of Bior. We trust you will undertake the necessary steps to prepare your crew for this assignment.

May the Keeper's light shine upon us.
Writing in the name of the Cardinal August De Leliard,
Reynziel Medina Khayin
Assistant to the Cardinal throne."

Brina's stomach dropped. An anxiety far beyond anything she'd felt as she struggled with the darkhelm officer flooded her system. She had stumbled upon something huge. They had a chance to get one step ahead of the church. With any luck, the fire in the tower would look like an accident. They might never know the orders had been stolen.

Her eyes flashed from one end of the alley to the other. It had never been this important for her to not get caught. This information needed to reach the right ears as soon as possible. A groan escaped Brina as she realized what this meant. She'd finally have to visit headquarters. Her skin crawled as she imagined the looks she would get walking into that place.

CHAPTER 2

Brina watched from a distance as long tendrils of flame burst from the windows of the guard tower like a leviathan's tentacles grasping for the sky. Satisfied that every darkhelm in the area would be distracted by the inferno she had started, Brina slid down from the roof, landing in one of the countless muddy alleys that characterized Doorstep's Ditch.

Once, she would have avoided nighttime excursions through this labyrinthine network of claustrophobic paths and crooked shanties at all costs, but these days she moved with the confidence of a spider in its own web. As long as she kept her power stores full, no one here could touch her. Not the gangs, not starving opportunists, and certainly not the darkhelms. There was only one adversary who could have taken her in a fair fight: the eyeless priestess. Acheron had given his life to ensure she would never be a problem again.

Brina moved with slow deliberation, sneaking through the Ditch's backstreets with the satisfying weight of a sack full of food and valuables pressing down on her shoulders. With any luck, the fire would take the tower out of commission for weeks. Though there would be no stopping the avalanche of surveillance and repression streaming forth from Mallion's Depth, Brina was going to hinder the darkhelms at every step. She would make sure those bastards slept with one eye open.

Mud sucked at Brina's boots. The overwhelming stench of human waste mixed with the acrid smoke to form a nauseating cocktail. She pulled her tunic over her nose and broke into a jog. Minutes later, she spotted a wooden hatch on the ground between two barrels of rainwater. The trapdoor was suspiciously devoid of snow. Brina glanced over her shoulder, then lowered herself into a low earthen cellar. As soon as the hatch thudded shut behind her, darkness swooped in.

Lux. Brina took a deep breath and willed the magical sigil to appear in her mind's eye. The blazing star flashed to life in the darkness, like a spark

CHAPTER 2

dropped in a pile of thatch. She blinked and found herself standing among dozens of stacked crates holding empty bottles of kelp rum. Peeling yellow labels read "Old Martin's Original Kelp." Glass tinkled as Brina's cloak brushed past the bottles.

It took longer than it should have to locate the splintering red crate Baron Don Lonzo De Malheure had mentioned in his letter. "Always welcome to join our parleys," he had written. "We could do with someone who has your street smarts."

Brina had politely ignored the message. The last thing she needed was more talking about rebellion. Every minute spent debating and plotting was one less minute to be out there in the night, taking action. That was why she had left the safety of the rebel citadel on the Isle of Metten. But now, she didn't have a choice. The scroll of parchment in her inside pocket had changed everything.

"These safe houses are getting ridiculous," she muttered to herself as she slid a stack of red Old Martin's crates aside, only to find a solid brick wall. She gave it a shove. Of course. Rock solid.

She rapped her knuckles against the stonework. It sounded hollow.

With a sigh, Brina burned *Forte*. Darkness wrapped around her as she relinquished *Lux*. Being able to burn only a single shape at once was one of the most frustrating limitations of being a sparkgazer.

She took a step back and landed a fortified kick on the brick wall. Dark cracks tore through the cement. The second kick did the trick. A handful of bricks crumbled away, leaving a hole.

"Wait, wait," a high-pitched voice whined on the other side. A beam of lantern light appeared through the opening.

With a series of metallic clicks and pops, the section of wall retracted and slid aside, revealing a potbellied man who looked like a walrus crammed into a velvet doublet. He raised his lantern to inspect the damage Brina had done to the door, shaking his head.

"Why the brute force?" Baron De Malheure yammered. "Always the ruddy violence."

"Old habit," Brina said, stepping over the threshold. "Besides, it's war out there in case you hadn't noticed. Violence is the name of the game these days."

"Yes, yes. I am well aware, Miss Brina, well aware indeed."

He closed the hidden door behind her, attempting to shove some bricks back into the gaping hole Brina had left. Deep grooves had formed in the baron's face since she had last seen him. His usual cheery, booming voice sounded diminished, strained. Even his masterpiece of a nobleman's belly had suffered. He wore an emerald doublet with gilded thread that was coming apart at the seams. The ends of his sleeves were frayed, with gold thread sticking out in all directions like a mop of unruly blond hair.

De Malheure led her down an earthen passage that opened into a vaulted room.

Brina stepped back when a dozen thin faces appeared from the shadows. Then she noticed the makeshift mattresses and bloody bandages.

"It's Springtide," one of the wounded muttered in awe. Brina could feel their eyes on her skin like a rash. After a lifetime of trying to stay out of sight, she hadn't quite gotten used to her newfound fame.

"I heard she killed a griffin with her bare hands," a boy no older than fourteen whispered to his friend. Both of them had suffered multiple wounds to arms and chest.

"And she just walked into God's Maul to break her father out," the other boy said. "Elias told me none of the darkhelms survived. She slaughtered every last one of them. By herself."

Brina snorted. If she could do even a quarter of the stuff the rumors attributed to her, she could have taken down the empire solo months ago. *Not that I haven't been trying.*

"They look up to you, you know," De Malheure said, eyebrows raised. Brina sighed, but took the hint.

She kneeled down beside both boys, who drew back in surprise as though they had only just realized she was not a figment of their imaginations.

"What are your names?" she asked, doing her best to soften her usual harsh tone.

"Theo," the oldest of the two replied. He gestured at the other boy. "This is Gideon, my little brother."

Brina nodded.

"How did you get those?" She pointed at the thick bandages around Gideon's shoulder.

"Got hit with a quarrel," Gideon muttered. "We tried stealing a basket of bread from the darkhelms, but one of them had a loaded windup ready. Theo tried to drag me away, but they got him too."

"Good thing the idiots thought we were dead," Theo said, putting on a brave smile that did not quite hide the pain in his eyes. "They just left us there. That's when Mr. Fortuyn brought us here. He saved us."

Brina almost choked. "Mr. who?"

"Mr. Fortuyn," Theo repeated. "Don't you know who he is? He's here right now." The boy pointed toward a door at the end of the room.

"Oh, I know who he is, alright," Brina said, repressing a grin. *Mr. Fortuyn. Unbelievable.* "In fact, I was just on my way to pay him a visit."

She waved an awkward hand and followed De Malheure.

A flood of light and heat engulfed Brina as she stepped into a small cellar with a vaulted ceiling. A round table stood in the middle of the room, littered with maps, ledgers, and half-empty bottles of Old Martin's kelp.

"I've told you a thousand times, Crook," Mattheus Fortuyn shouted at a middle-aged man with a gray beard and mustache who sat across from him. "If we had rations, we would gladly distribute them. But I can't wish them into bloody existence, can I?"

The man named Crook made a brisk gesture, as though throwing something over his shoulder. A serious insult in these parts. Crook might as well have told Mattheus he was a walking sack of horse manure.

"Easy there, Mattheus." Brina chuckled as the man's face flushed with anger. The sapphire studs on his leather armor glimmered in the pale light of a jelly lantern. "Tomato red doesn't go well with those golden locks of yours."

Crook chuckled.

"And who's this boor?" She pointed at the graybeard.

Crook opened his mouth to respond, then seemed to realize who she was and shut it again.

"Impressive." A woman with a tangle of black braids grinned at her from the opposite end of the table. "You've managed to insult two out of three before so much as touching a chair."

"I learned from the best." Brina sat down beside her. "I'm surprised to see you're alive, Mahrovia," she went on, reaching across the table for a full bottle of rum. "Zot seems to think otherwise."

Elstaka Mahrovia's face twitched. Even now, Dimimzy Zot's name was enough to scare the most hardened gang members in the Ditch. "You're not going to tell him, are you?"

Brina shrugged. "He's all the way across the Sundered Isles in Port Merkede. I'd say you're in the clear for a while."

"Nobody's ever in the clear where that man's concerned." Mahrovia took a large gulp of kelp and shuddered.

"Enough with the niceties," Crook barked. "We were discussing actual problems of the here and now. My brawlers are growing tired of snatching coals out of the fire for you lot while their stomachs remain empty and their throats dry."

"Oh." Mahrovia feigned surprise. "You should have said something. My crew has been feasting on turkey legs and drinking fine Hawqallian spirits every night." She snorted. "Everyone's going hungry, you dunce."

Crook jumped to his feet. "This. This right here is why the Bladefin have never tolerated being in the same room as you Auctioneer scum."

Mahrovia's chair clattered to the floor. "If you don't want me to point out your whining, there's a very simple solution."

Mattheus shot Brina a *do-something* look.

"Easy, friends." Brina raised a hand and burned *Consol*. A smooth, calming quality seeped into her voice like honey into freshly baked bread. "We're all worried. We're all hungry. Let's not add wounded or dead to that list, shall we?"

Both of them glowered at Brina.

"What are you doing to me?" Crook said, though he sounded more interested than alarmed.

"I'm helping you clear your heads," she said, holding on to the shape. "Now, let's sit down and think of solutions instead of insults."

Both of them did so. Brina relinquished the shape.

"I didn't care for that, Springtide." Mahrovia gave her a reproachful look. "We're not puppets, you know."

"I've told you that makes people uncomfortable," Mattheus said, clearly still anxious to prevent a brawl from breaking out under his nose.

"Didn't you stab me last year?" Brina asked. "My apologies if I don't care about your opinion on what makes people uncomfortable."

Mattheus's pale cheeks flushed. "You're not letting that one go, are you?"

"I think I'll hold on to it until the scar fades." Brina pulled up her nose at him, then threw the scroll with the Cardinal's orders onto the table. "Here. If you're looking for something to argue about, I've got just the thing."

Crook reached for the scroll on the table, unfurled it, and read.

"Doesn't concern us." Crook shrugged and handed the document to Mattheus. "The more of the Cardinal's troops are away from the Ditch, the better, I say."

Mattheus scanned the letter.

"Bior's our closest ally," he said, frowning at Crook. "If they fall, what do you think will happen to those shipments of dried fish we've been relying on?"

"They're not enough, anyway." Crook made a throwaway gesture.

Mahrovia drummed her fingers on the table.

CHAPTER 2

"If the empire controls all of Bior, you can bet your last nib they'll force enough Skullbeard crews into their ranks to take over the rest of the isles within the year. Remember the last time a single crew of theirs paid us a visit?"

Brina's jaw worked. She hadn't forgotten the flames and the slaughter. She supposed she never would. The Biori weren't traitors, but they were warriors first and foremost. They would go wherever the promise of fighting and looting took them. If the rebellion was to succeed, they needed the Biori on their side.

"The first thing we've got to do is warn them. I'll take care of that," Brina said. "Next, we'll have to organize a defense. They'll need all the help they can get if they're to withstand the full might of the church knocking at their front gate."

"Based on this letter, we have four months, five at most, to prepare a defense." Mattheus's hand closed around the scroll as though he were strangling a goose. "We'll need to act fast."

"I don't think any of you were listening." Crook shook his head. "Come on, Mahrovia, you at the very least ought to understand how fickle our position can be. Power is no more than the promise of a stuffed belly and a full flask. A hefty purse doesn't hurt either. Take those things away, and my ability to inspire my lads and lasses to storm into the breach becomes lackluster."

Mahrovia's jaw worked, but she didn't contradict the man. Even Brina had to admit he had a point. Hunger was an old friend to her, and she knew that when you were in its grip, little mattered but that next bowl of stew. Besides, what could a bunch of famished mercenaries in scavenged armor do against legions of fully trained and armored darkhelms?

"We'll have to fix that." She looked at Mattheus. "Think you can handle it?"

"Why not? If you can steal from the darkhelms, I don't see why I couldn't." Mattheus sat back in his chair, blue eyes trained on Brina. "What about you?"

"I'll leave for Metten tomorrow." Her muscles stiffened at the words alone.

"You're really going back there, huh?"

Brina stood up and walked toward the door.

"I'm afraid I don't have much of a choice."

CHAPTER 3

etten was a fossil. A dusty reminder of a forgotten age. *At least we have that in common.*

Abrasax sat on a toppled pillar in what had once been the citadel's panoramic gallery, fifty feet above the jungle floor. In summer, the gallery's roof would be a welcome shield against the oppressive heat. Now it created a wind tunnel. An icy stain of shadow among the rapidly diminishing pools of winter sunlight between the trees below.

A chorus of shouts rang out below as a band of about fifty new recruits armed with makeshift spears followed Bron, the Biori warrior, onto the sandy training pitch. They shuffled awkwardly, as though they expected to tumble into a pitfall trap at any moment.

Bron raised a horn, giving one short blast, followed by a second longer one. The skulls woven into his wild ginger beard tinkled in accompaniment.

A few of the trainees lowered their spears into fighting position. The others followed suit in twos and threes as they realized what they were supposed to do. It was like watching a drunk sea urchin raise its spikes one at a time, more comedic than frightening. Abrasax's chest tightened. They were as good as dead. As soon as the empire's hammer came crashing down, those brave, bumbling recruits would be slaughtered down to a soul. It was as inevitable as the tide itself.

"This is how your brothers and sisters die," Bron shouted over the clattering of spears bumping into each other. He ran between the soldiers, correcting postures and picking up dropped weapons. "The spearhead formation is a ship's hull. Every board needs to fit just right, or the whole thing sinks like a brick."

"You." Bron pointed out a slender woman with dreadlocks down to her hips and a spear made of a kitchen knife tied to a long branch. "Pick five of your fellows and show these bastards how it's done."

The woman nodded. A smirk tugged at the deep lines in her face. She

CHAPTER 3

assembled her team with the mere flick of a finger.

Bron shoved the horn into the hands of a pimply teenager, who took the instrument with trembling hands. Bron squared up with the team of six and beckoned for the teenager to repeat the signal.

Bu buuuut.

Six spears flicked down instantly, one right next to the other, creating a triangular formation. Bron charged straight at them. His war cry echoed off the gallery's mossy walls like an erymanthian's roar. Five out of six took an instinctive step backward, but a command from the woman with the dreads made them hold their formation.

Bron raised a wooden training sword and swung it at the woman's head. It whizzed a good two feet in front of her nose. She didn't flinch.

Abrasax smiled to himself. The Biori wasn't much of a talker, but there was a teacher buried inside him.

Bron sidestepped and swung at one of the spears this time. The weapon was knocked aside, creating an opening in the line. Before he could exploit this weakness, another spear jabbed forward, forcing him backward.

"Excellent," he barked. He threw the training sword to the ground and gave the recruits a thumbs-up. "That's what the spearhead is all about. Total coverage. Our most potent shield is our comrade's spear."

As the Biori began dividing the trainees into practice groups, footsteps echoed in the gallery behind Abrasax.

He turned to see Saphara Al Noor striding toward him. Her venom-green robes stood in stark contrast to her dark skin and short black hair. Even from a distance, she looked regal. It was something about her gait, Abrasax thought. The straight back, the raised chin, and the graceful, yet swift pace gave one the feeling that there was not one step this woman took without purpose. A crisp perfume of fig leaf and juniper accompanied her arrival.

"They are progressing well," she observed, joining him on the fallen pillar. "Though I would love to put slightly more solid spears in their hands. They need experience with the real thing."

Abrasax squirmed. He loved nothing about the scene unfolding below.

"I thought the goal was to put the power of sigils into their hands," he said, trying not to sound accusatory.

"It is." She gave him a sideways glance. "But we don't have enough scripts to train new sparkgazers in meaningful numbers. We only have one or two copies of most of the essentials, and I will not risk them being damaged or, worse, stolen."

"I see." Once, that statement would have outraged Abrasax. Back when his band of rebels roamed the Sundered Sea, hindering the empire's march to dominance wherever possible, he too had envisioned a future where magical sigils and the immense power they held were available to all.

That had been before he'd spent over a decade in God's Maul, the empire's harshest prison. Since Sabrina and her friends had helped him escape a few months ago, Abrasax had discovered that the old fire had died in him. Gone were the passion, the anger, the hope. All of it. It was like his insides had shrunk over the years, leaving a hollow in his chest that would never be filled.

Some of what he had been thinking seemed to have appeared on his face, because Saphara frowned.

"I am taking two apprentices soon," she said, eyes scanning the training group below. "But I need to take my time in deciding who is most worthy."

"Every one of them came here out of their own free will. They believe in your cause. Does that in itself not render them worthy in your eyes?"

"My cause?"

Abrasax closed his eyes, praying that she would have vanished by the time he reopened them. Instead, her hand clamped down on his shoulder.

"It is not me they follow, *Viper*," she whispered. "The news of your escape has reached all ears in the Sundered Isles and beyond. People have seen that the scepter is not untouchable. Hope has been rekindled.

"Do you not see them craning their necks to get a better look as you walk by? Do you not hear the whispers or see the look in their eyes as they pass you?"

"Don't call me that." Abrasax folded his arms to hide his trembling hands. The gallery seemed to expand around them, a vast chasm of emptiness. The daylight burned in his eyes, dizzying him, but he didn't dare close them. If he did, he would be back there, trapped between those blackened walls. "I am not a martyr. I am not a leader. I am not a fighter. Not anymore."

"Then fake it," Saphara snapped at him. Her eyes were wide and alert. "You are the symbol of this revolution, and you will play the part."

She stabbed a long-nailed finger at the training pitch below, where the recruits were running laps, dodging obstacles as they went. "They sweat and bleed because they believe. They believe that a better tomorrow is within our grasp. It was you who told them that all those years ago."

Abrasax took in their faces, contorted with exertion, rivulets of sweat cascading down their cheeks. They were giving all they had and then some. *How long has it been since I felt that alive?*

CHAPTER 3

"I don't know what I believe anymore," he said, refusing to look at Saphara.

"It doesn't matter what you believe. What matters is that we keep going, that they keep going. There is no turning back now, Viper. Cardinal De Leliard cast the die when he sent his fleet across the Sundered Sea last summer."

"I won't allow anyone else to die on my account." There was a finality to Abrasax's voice that shocked even him. As though all of it was just now sinking in.

Over the course of his years spent in the deep dark of God's Maul, he'd prayed every day for an opportunity to see daylight just one more time. He'd imagined the moment over and over again. It had been a lifeline to him. Now he was coming to realize that his newfound freedom might just have been the worst thing that had ever happened to him.

Acheron, his dearest and very last friend, had given his life to save Abrasax, completing a process that had begun eleven years prior. All of his friends had died because of him. All twelve of them.

Now dozens, soon maybe hundreds, were preparing for outright war against the empire, and Saphara was using him as bait to lure them in. *Sabrina trusts her,* he reminded himself. *Brina's instincts are good. Perhaps better than mine ever were.*

That thought brought him some solace. It had been she who had wanted him free, not for political reasons, but because she loved him. It was a love he didn't deserve, but one he cherished. After she was born, he'd dreamed of a time when they could move to a distant atoll somewhere to live in peace, far away from the danger and the violence.

We could still leave, a voice told him. It was a small one, thick with the tremors of panic and cowardice, yet it sounded reasonable to his ears. Even though Sabrina had left Metten to jump into the action in Doorstep's Ditch, some part of him believed that she could be convinced to leave it all behind in pursuit of a simple, but free life.

He was drawn from his spiraling thoughts when Saphara sprang to her feet beside him.

"We need you, Viper," she said, her back already turned to him. "We follow in your footsteps, and if we—if *I*—have ever had need of your wisdom, it is now."

He watched her stride down the gallery, waving at the trainees on the training pitch who greeted her with an enthusiastic chorus of war cries. She smiled and pointed one long finger back at the place where Abrasax sat.

Dozens of eyes turned toward him. His heart rate spiked.

"Long live the Viper," they chorused. "Death to the empire."
They clattered their spears together in a rousing rhythm.
Saphara looked back at him, a coy smile lingering on her lips.
Without a word, Abrasax turned and walked in the opposite direction.

CHAPTER 4

Zot tugged at his silver and emerald doublet. The velvet was itchy against his sweaty skin, as if he had rolled around in honey and then lain down on an anthill. It smelled of dust, mold, and times gone by. The sheer humiliation of being seen in such a rag was only surpassed by the fact that no one seemed to recognize him. Last year, these plebeians would have bowed.

Merkede was a greenhouse. A sweltering mix of humidity and heat carried across the sea from the Hawqallian desert to the west. Square buildings of white sandstone crowded around them, creating patches of much-needed shade. Dozens of marketgoers pressed up against Zot, sapping away the last remnants of breathable air. It took all his might not to scream.

Beside him, Harrod Wane strolled through the sandy street with a look of wonder on his face, eyes darting from a snake charmer playing a thin wooden flute to the colorful canvases of the market stalls squeezed in on both sides of the road. The boy's short-sleeved tunic was much better suited to the environment. Furthermore, the boy was already a head taller than Zot, allowing him to look out over the throng of people. His curly brown hair hung down to his shoulders, swaying in a sparse breeze.

"So," Wane began, hesitating as if he were about to light one of Oppen's grenades, "do you think this one will remember you?"

"She will." Zot gritted his teeth, trying not to snap at the boy. "She better."

For two decades, Merkede had been a focal point of his life. It was where deals were struck, mercenaries hired, and exotic, less-than-legal substances acquired. Zot's name had been currency here for much of that time. Dimimzy Zot had always made good on both his promises and his threats. As a result, he had been respected and feared in equal measure.

Until the previous summer, when a band of Skullbeard warriors had looted and burned his warehouses to the ground, stealing one of his prized galleons. A gang leader with an empty purse was much like an innkeeper without kelp rum, unable to keep anyone around.

His return to Merkede had only emphasized that notion. First, White Dronx, an old Biori warlord turned mercenary, had had his crew chase Zot and the boy halfway across town because of unpaid services. They had escaped only because of the boy's brilliant idea to jump down a sewer grate.

Afterward, Galari Mekton, a Hawqallian smuggler who had been working with him for fifteen years, had outright pretended he had no clue who Zot was. It had been like trying to chat up a rusty anvil.

That left only the shamanka on his list. She was the last straw he could think of grasping. Although he had sworn off selling cloud, he had made no such vow regarding other addictive substances. If he could only borrow a handful of bricks of wakeroot, he would finally have some capital to rebuild what was rightfully his.

"Maybe we should just take jobs as fishermen for a while," Wane said. "We promised Saf and Brina we'd return with food and supplies. Maybe we can teach the recruits how to fish for themselves?"

Zot made a noncommittal grunt and dragged the boy into a narrow alley. The houses on both sides leaned against each other near the top, forming an arch.

"Fishing," he scoffed. The only way he would return to that was if someone were to use his corpse as bait. He regretted ever accepting this responsibility. It had been pride more than anything else that had led him to promise that a few months in Merkede would be enough to return with weapons and provisions to sustain the growing resistance movement gathering on Metten.

A bell chimed as they squeezed past a lime green curtain into Sachrya's shop. Clouds of licorice, dried lavender, and cinnamon made Zot's eyes water. Tall clay jugs filled with herbs and spices from every corner of the known world cluttered the earthen floor.

Zot aimed a slap at Wane's outstretched hand as the boy reached for a jar of ominous black seedpods.

"Touch nothing, say nothing, do..." He sighed. "Actually, why don't you wait outside? I'll only be a minute."

The boy shook his head vigorously. "I want to see the shamanka. I've never met one in real life."

"Then today's your lucky day, my boy." Sachrya stood in the doorway leading to the living quarters behind the shop. As always, she took Zot's breath away. Seven feet tall, slender as a grapevine, and adorned in purple and golden robes that wouldn't look amiss on the empress of Hawqal. Her

CHAPTER 4

skull was entirely hairless, which amplified the effect of her emerald eyes as they peered into his own.

"Sachrya," Zot called out, trying to emulate some of his former swagger and charm. He sauntered over to her and kissed her hand. He didn't need to bend over to reach it. Behind him, Wane followed suit.

"What brings you to my humble apothecary, Dimimzy?"

One of Wane's eyebrows lifted at the mention of Zot's first name.

"Business. Of the urgent variety."

"Word around town is that you don't do much of that anymore." Her wide smile wasn't enough to offset the disdain in her voice.

"Rumors," Zot exclaimed, throwing up his hands. "You know how it is. Things get exaggerated, taken out of context, and so on and so forth."

"Are you insinuating that I am so gullible as to believe the first piece of gossip a drunk halfwit whispers into my ear?"

Zot's foot tapped nervously against the base of a pot filled with stark white fruits the size of his thumbs.

"I am insinuating no such thing," he replied, fighting against the old anger welling up in his guts. "What I mean is that you don't have all the facts."

"And I'm sure you will present them to me right now." She crossed her arms. Wane's feet shuffled nervously, his eyes darting from Zot to the shamanka and back.

"I need some capital to pay off a handful of debtors I've accrued over the past couple of months. Once that's over with, it will be business as usual." His sneer didn't have quite the same zing it used to.

"How much?" Sachrya picked up a bundle of palm leaves and fanned herself lazily. *Oh, how very quick their attitudes change,* Zot thought bitterly. The woman hadn't even offered him a drink.

"Five bricks of wakeroot." It was a lot to ask. Too much.

"In exchange for?"

"I will pay you back in full after they've sold. I'm not asking for charity; I'm asking for a loan."

Sachrya's smile deepened, but the expression didn't reach her eyes. She bent down, drawing level with Wane, who gave her a sheepish grin.

"And you, boy, who are you?"

Zot gave the kid a warning look, but he didn't seem to catch it.

"My name's Graydon Zealous, mistress shamanka." Wane bowed.

Good, at least he remembers the cover story.

"How long have you been working with Dimimzy here?"

Damn it all. That question hadn't come up when they'd briefly plotted out the boy's false identity.

"We met last summer. Mr. Zot hired me for my agile hands." He held out a fist and opened it under Sachrya's nose, revealing a small leather pouch with a gilded drawstring.

The shamanka straightened herself, feeling at the waistline of her dress. A tinkling laugh escaped her as she took back the purse the boy had stolen from her.

"Very good, boy," she said. "Very good indeed."

She tucked the purse back into an inside pocket and looked down her nose at Zot.

"I can't help you," she said. "I deal with clients who pay up front. Not beggars who stumble in here looking for a handout."

The insult was too much to bear.

"I pulled you out of the muck," Zot shouted, pointing a gnarled finger at her. "When I met you, you were peddling cures for venereal diseases at the docks."

"My dues to you have been paid many times over," Sachrya said. She took a step forward and actually had the audacity to poke him in the forehead with her index finger. "And you would do well to remember the wide variety of poisons I have mixed for you over the years. They work on everyone."

Zot laughed. It was a maniacal laugh, born out of anger bordering on madness. He put a hand on Wane's shoulder and began steering him out of the shop.

"Come on, boy. A wise man knows when he's wasting his breath."

He was about to cross the curtain into the street when Sachrya called after him.

"There might be another way for you to purchase those bricks."

Zot turned, one eyebrow cocked. "What do you want?"

"The boy." Her smile turned into a leer. "I have need of one his size with quick wits and quicker fingers. If you leave him here, you can walk out with those bricks right now. Once you've paid me back, the boy will be free to go."

Zot's heart sank. A minute ago, he thought he would do anything for the chance to make a fresh start, but Sachrya had found something he wasn't willing to give.

"I'll do it." Wane stepped forward.

Fool. Sweet, brave fool.

"Out of the question," Zot snapped. "We have a mission to accomplish, remember?"

"I do. This changes nothing." Wane stared straight ahead, avoiding Zot's gaze. The boy's face tightened into a look of resolve, but he couldn't hide the trembling of his hands.

Sachrya's tinkling laugh echoed across the apothecary.

"Perfect," she said. "I am sure we will get along splendidly."

Zot let out a deep sigh. Every fiber in his body screamed that this was a terrible idea. Sachrya was a scorpion of a woman. Even if the boy walked away from her unscathed, he would never be the same. Zot couldn't allow that to happen.

You've lost your edge. That's why nobody respects you anymore. Zot's fingers clenched into fists. Fury rose within him at the thought of all those mocking faces he'd been forced to endure over the past months.

Moments later, he walked back out into the bustling market, carrying a heavy chest of wakeroot.

CHAPTER 5

By the time Brina reached Barrow's Perch, a distant halo of light was appearing at the horizon. She had to make it quick.

With a brief flash of *Forte*, she forced open the heavy steel door to a barrow at the far end of the hillside. The rustle of feathers greeted her as she stepped inside. Brina smiled and reached out into the dark. Something soft brushed her hand.

She burned *Lux* and found Razorwing's massive head inches from her own. The griffin's eyes reflected the starburst hues of the sigil right back at her. Its steel beak was flecked with fresh spots of blood.

"Hope you were done with that." Brina reached down and grabbed a mostly eaten goat carcass by the leg. As she dragged it outside, Razorwing followed closely behind her. The creature tore idly at a few loose strips of muscle while Brina gathered up a spare cloak, tunic, and a pair of trousers.

Before she closed the barrow's door, Brina cast a wistful glance at the broken urns and vials Acheron had left behind last year. They were the last physical reminders that the man had existed. That he had actually roamed these hills and made his home in the very grave she was standing in. She shook her head and pulled the double doors shut behind her. It was trash, no matter who it once belonged to.

A sinking feeling overcame her as the gap in the steel narrowed, sealing the barrow—perhaps forever. With a sigh, she stooped down, grabbed a shard of pottery off the floor, and put it in her pocket. A smile tugged at her lips, but only for a moment. She was growing sentimental. *I'll have to watch that.*

"Come on," she snapped at Razorwing, who was still gnawing on the goat's bones. "We've got a long way ahead of us."

***

"There it is at last. You did well, Razorwing." Brina stroked the griffin's

CHAPTER 5

feathers. "Not far now."

In the distance, a small green dot was growing amid a swirling tapestry of blue. Spires of blackened rock littered the water surrounding the island of Metten. They made it all but impossible for sailors unfamiliar with the area to reach the shoreline, forming a natural line of defense. It was one of many reasons the rebellion had chosen Metten as its base of operations.

Brina winced. The day-long journey on the griffin's back had taken its toll. She was so tired and cramped that she lay rather than sat on Razorwing's neck. It was a miracle the beast's wings hadn't given out yet.

On their journey to Doorstep's Ditch, Brina had made sure to find multiple stops along the way. There was no time for such luxuries now, however. The sooner the scroll in her chest pocket reached Saf, the better. She would know what to do. Brina loved and hated that about her in equal measure.

The thought of Saf's sleek face and penetrating gaze stirred up a dangerous mix of emotions. Brina hadn't exactly left things on a positive note. *Guilt can wait*, she reminded herself. *First, we have to stick the landing.*

Guided by Brina's gentle tugs on its feathers, Razorwing gradually descended until they were flying a mere twenty feet above the sea surface. The griffin arced around the island's shore until the familiar sheer cliff face on the north side came into view. Atop fifty feet of solid granite stood the towering Citadel of Metten.

Its white walls were covered in vines, making it difficult to see where the jungle ended and the fortress began—another layer of natural protection. From the outside, the citadel looked like nothing more than a ruin. On the inside, the stone walls stood as tall and strong as ever.

Over the past year, every gap had been filled in and every crumbling section rebuilt. The small rebel army wouldn't be able to fend off a full-scale assault, but at least they'd make the darkhelms' lives difficult. That was more than enough for Brina.

Brina considered landing on top of the citadel's central donjon, but at the last second, she couldn't bring herself to commit. They glided over the tower. *Just a few more moments of peace before I have to face her.*

They touched down near the waterline, at the bottom of the steep path that led to the citadel's white gate. Stretching her legs would do her good. Besides, she needed the walk to build up her courage.

"Go rest. You deserve it." Brina touched *Consol* as she spoke, and Razorwing's posture softened at once. The beast was tired. Its wings hung low to the ground, and its chest rose and fell like a smith's bellows. "Go on ahead. Bron will give you something to eat."

Brina watched as the griffin's feathers sparkled in the setting sun. Razorwing flapped toward the citadel's courtyard, then dove. It was like seeing a rainbow in motion. Once the griffin was out of sight, there were no more excuses.

Brina forced herself to put one foot after the other. The trek up the hill had never felt so steep. With every step, she felt like she was dragging a millstone behind her. She was back in the place she'd been so desperate to leave, and it was weighing her down already.

She'd made it halfway to the gate when a dark figure appeared on top of the citadel's wall in the distance. It shot up into the air, arcing over the citadel and landing on top of the gatehouse. With another flash of speed, it sailed straight toward Brina.

Saf thundered to the ground, striking up a cloud of dust around both of them. She righted herself, brushing wayward black hair out of her face. Her venom-green robe suited her narrow frame well. Saf's eyes caught Brina's. It was like staring down a sheikan.

"Look who deigned to show up." Saf's voice was a string approaching its breaking point. "Miss Springtide, what an *honor*."

"Oh, come on," Brina said, "I would have told you I was going away if—"

"But you didn't, did you?" There was a deep sadness in Saf's face. It was the first time Brina had ever seen Saf make that face, and that realization hurt far beyond words.

"Fine. I deserved that. I shouldn't have left the way I did, but if I'd told you, you'd never have approved."

"Since when do you need my approval to do anything?"

Brina swallowed. How could she explain something even she herself didn't fully understand?

"It's just..." Brina's mouth went dry as she tried to speak. Saf raised her eyebrows. The rest came out in a single breathless ramble. "I knew if you asked me to stay, I wouldn't have had the strength to refuse you."

Brina's face burned. No one had ever made her feel this way. Guilt, happiness, excitement, and fear warred inside her as she looked into Saf's eyes. Somehow, Saf had found a weak spot in the armor Brina had so carefully built up over the years. That was dangerous.

Saf's posture deflated. For a moment, the two of them stood in silence. Then Saf said, "If you were unhappy, you could have told me. We could have given you different responsibilities. Or no responsibilities at all, if it's a break you needed."

CHAPTER 5

She reached for Brina's hand and held it in both of her own. "I know you've had a hard time after what happened to Acheron, but slinking off into the night isn't the answer."

A single tear formed in Brina's good eye. She let out a bark of a laugh. There was no joy in it. "I couldn't stand it," she muttered. "The looks. The whispers behind my back. They treat me like some sort of demigod. Don't get me wrong; I appreciate the free rounds of rum, but I am human, Saf. Human. I am not Sabrina Springtide. I am Brina. Just Brina."

"And that is exactly what makes you so legendary in their eyes." Saf smiled.

"That doesn't make any sense."

"Let me put it this way," Saf said. "What makes you different from them?"

"Nothing. That's my point."

Saf's smile deepened. "And therein lies the seed of their admiration. You aren't some mythical heroine blessed with infinite power. Or a freak of nature incapable of suffering. You are perfectly, wonderfully ordinary.

"And yet, your choices have changed the course of history. You have shown them it doesn't matter who they are, as long as they know what they stand for."

Brina shrugged. Eager to drop the subject, she strode past Saf and began walking up the hill toward the gatehouse. "So, what have you been up to down here? Same as usual?"

"What we do here is important." Saf's eyes narrowed. She caught up to Brina in a handful of long strides.

"I know it is."

"Do you?"

Brina bit her lower lip. She could feel the old frustrations churning in the pit of her stomach. She didn't want to start off her return to Metten with a fight on the very first night. So instead, she simply watched the sun sink beneath the horizon.

"New recruits have been arriving almost weekly recently," Saf said. "We've had to expand our sleeping quarters, and we've long ago run out of weaponry to hand out. I know you think we're just sitting around doing nothing, but we're building an army here, Brina. A real army, capable of things we as a small group could only dream of."

"That's what we're calling it now, an army?"

Saf's eyes sparked. "Why would you, of all people, have a problem with that? I thought you wanted to see the empire fall just as much as I do?"

"Armies imply commands." Brina kicked a rock and watched it tumble down the hillside to the shoreline below. "Ordering people to die is what the church does. We're different."

"You have to face a painful truth, Brina. If you want to fight the empire, if you want freedom, it's going to come at a cost. Every movement needs leadership. And leadership means accepting that some sacrifices will be necessary along the way."

"Sounds a lot like saying the ends justify the means."

"That's because sometimes they do." Saf's eyes glowed purple, betraying the burn of *Consol*. She didn't speak, however. Brina realized with a stab of embarrassment that Saf was using the shape internally to calm herself down. So much for avoiding a fight on the first night.

"Why did you even come here if you have such a problem with the way I am running things?" Saf asked after a few tense moments had passed.

Brina slapped a hand on her forehead. She'd all but forgotten the scroll.

"I stole this from a sleeping officer in the Ditch. Thought you'd want to know."

As Saf's eyes traced the squiggly lettering, they once again took on a purple hue.

"We need to deal with this quickly," she said. "Go rest up. I'll arrange a meeting first thing in the morning."

Without another word, Saf crouched down and launched herself into the air, leaving Brina coughing in a cloud of dust. She trudged up the hill toward the gatehouse alone.

CHAPTER 6

Just after dawn, Brina exited the citadel's gate and made her way down the steep slope toward the tree line below. The chilly morning breeze made the hair on her arms and neck stand up, but at least she was alone. With any luck, she'd be the first one to arrive at the high temple. *A few moments of peace before the blathering begins.*

When she reached the foot of the hill, a narrow trail of flattened plants and dirt pulled her into the thick jungle. The smell of moss and dew hung in the air like a soothing blanket. Some of the tension immediately left Brina's body. All too soon, the path opened into a seaside clearing where a square temple with a domed roof stood.

A thin layer of hoarfrost coated its white walls, adding a sparkle to the otherwise drab sandstone facade. Vines snaked their way up cracked pillars, and patches of tall grass obscured the low set of stairs leading to the inner sanctum.

Inside, emptiness reigned. Brina's footsteps echoed off the domed ceiling as she strode toward the circular pit in the center of the room—the well of offerings.

She hadn't been back here since Acheron's funeral. Though there hadn't been a body to deposit into the sacred tunnels below, Brina shivered as she peered into the dark hole.

Those depths seemed to call out to her. Though neither of them would have ever admitted it out loud, not even with a thousand windups pressed to their heads, Brina and Acheron had shared a special connection.

Acheron had been her godfather, and though he had taken up the role in his own, unorthodox manner, he had taught Brina everything she knew about sparkgazing and even more about life in general.

He had been cynical, borderline cruel, and downright rude. But most of all, he had been right. Brina saw that now. Thinking of yourself as the good guy only set you up for a rude awakening once reality kicked in. There was no moral high ground to be gained when you were rolling in the muck with the likes of Cardinal De Leliard. Blood spilled with good intentions clung to your soul just the same as blood spilled indifferently.

Tearing her gaze away from the abyss, Brina turned aside and sat down on one of the stone benches that spread out in circles from the center of the room. During meetings, the inner ring was reserved for officers and those with "elevated responsibilities," as Saf so eloquently put it. Brina sat down in the very last row, with her back to the outer wall. She'd be damned if she was going to sit in front of the recruits as though she were better than them.

A cough rang out in the empty temple. Brina whipped around to find an unusually tall, sinewy woman with sharp Hawqallian features and waist-length dreads standing in the temple's doorway. A smile lingered on the woman's face.

"Miss Springtide," she said with a nod. Her gaze briefly strayed to the thick scar tissue surrounding Brina's dead eye. "We meet again."

"Erm..." Brina's brain froze. She'd never been good at small talk. "Sure."

The woman marched up to her and extended a brawny hand. "My name is Ak-Zul. I was on the galley that fished you and your father out of Mallion's Bay last year."

Brina shook Ak-Zul's hand mechanically. *How does Saf do it? All the smiling, the handshaking, the polite conversation. Gives me a headache.*

"Thanks for the ride."

"It was an honor," Ak-Zul said. "Is this seat taken?"

Brina shook her head and tried not to groan out loud as Ak-Zul sat down.

Luckily, a group of twenty-odd recruits chose that moment to lumber into the temple with the subtlety of an erymanthian in heat.

They were nervous. Brina could smell it in the room, could see it in the wideness of their eyes, the poorly disguised tremors in their hands.

Though they had no way of knowing what was coming, they had clearly speculated among themselves enough to figure out that trouble was afoot.

"We've missed you here," Ak-Zul said. "Some of the other recruits were whispering that you had abandoned us. But I knew that couldn't be true. You are his daughter, after all."

She nodded toward the temple's entrance, where her father stood surveying the scene, looking rather lost. He still hadn't cut his overlong black hair and beard. On the contrary, he looked even more like a wild man now than he had on the night Brina had broken him out of his cell at God's Maul. Even at a distance, his eyes looked bloodshot. Before Brina could call out to him,

CHAPTER 6

he sat down on a deserted row at the very back of the temple. Did he even know she had returned?

Brina wondered which was worse. That he hadn't been there to welcome her back, or that she hadn't bothered to knock at his door either. She was spared the effort of coming up with a suitable excuse by Saf, who rose from her seat on the inner circle of the temple and held up a fist to call for silence.

All the air was sucked out of the temple. The only sound left was the rushing of waves breaking on the beach outside. "I am sure you're all wondering why you have been summoned here at this early hour." Saf sounded calm, yet decisive.

That voice. Brina felt it tug at her own emotions. *She doesn't even need to burn a sigil.*

Mutters of assent rippled through the assembly.

"The hour upon which the empire seizes what little freedom remains in the Sundered Isles draws near," Saf went on.

To Brina's surprise, Saf retrieved the scroll of marching orders from the inside of her purple robes and held it out for all to see.

"This is a message from Cardinal De Leliard himself. Sabrina Springtide risked her life to acquire this, and I believe it is your right to hear every word of it."

Brina sank lower in her seat to avoid the dozens of eyes that roved the temple in search of her.

Saf read the letter in a deep, sonorous voice. With every word, the mood among the recruits grew grimmer. They turned to look at each other. Some with hard expressions, anger and determination etched into weathered faces. Others looked as though a chimera had just landed in their laps.

When she was done, Saf tucked away the scroll with a flick of her wrist.

"Bior lies right there." She pointed a finger southward. "Who among you hasn't seen its sandy dunes rise up from the waves on a clear day?"

Muttering followed this pronouncement. They had all seen it. In fact, Bron had taken to wandering the beach at dawn, just to stare at his homeland in the distance. The empire's hammer stroke would fall very close to home indeed.

No longer was the threat of invasion just a concept, an abstraction somewhere between a campfire tale and a history lesson. It was right here, approaching like a stampeding herd of pronghorn.

"Once Bior falls..." Saf didn't need to raise her voice to cut through the murmur. "...where do you think the darkhelms will come next?"

"Nobody knows we're here," a short, stocky man balked. He looked like a cross between a bulldog and a graying wolf. There was fear in his watery brown eyes. "You promised us when we arrived that this island was secret. Unfindable unless someone tells the darkhelms where it is."

"Coward," Ak-Zul muttered beside Brina. "Idiot couldn't hold a spear if it was dipped in glue."

"This is true, Max. It will remain true until one of us tips off the empire, whether that be intentionally or not."

"Then what's the problem?" Max replied. "You don't think one of us is going to turn coat, do you?"

Bron stood up, heavy jaw working underneath his thick ginger beard. Dozens of intricately wrought metal skulls were woven into his beard, tinkling together like sheep's bells.

"The problem is that Bior is the last island in this bloody sea with warriors worth a damn." He glared at Max, as though daring him to disagree. A vein pulsed in his temple. "Without my brothers and sisters, who is going to storm the mighty stoneward at Mallion's Depth? You?"

Saf raised a hand.

"What Bron is trying to say," she said, her tone soothing, "is that Bior will be a key ally in the years to come. Without them, no other island realm packs a big enough punch to dent the Cardinal's forces."

"If they're our allies, where are they?" Max snapped, waving an arm at the assembled crowd. "Where are the pale-skinned bastards now? I haven't forgotten Doorstep's Ditch. I was there when it all went up in flames."

Brina groaned. She'd been afraid this would come up. The Skullbeard mercenary crews that roamed the waves, selling their spears to the highest bidder, were Biori by blood, but that was where their loyalty ended. For many in the isles, the sight of those blackened sails and the stench of death and fire they left behind was the first and last time they saw a Biori in the flesh.

Max's words rattled around the temple, causing a ripple of shuffling and whispers.

Bron aimed a jagged dagger at Max. "We have been keeping the empire off our doorstep for generations, you pigheaded, water-gutted—"

"Enough." Brina had never heard Saf raise her voice. It was like an avalanche. She gave Bron a look that could have withered a flower, then turned to Max and the growing cluster of like-minded recruits around him.

"The Biori have needed every man, woman, and child to contain the empire's foothold on the island to the Bay of Bones. But rest assured, they are on the same side as we are in this conflict. They have cause to hate the

CHAPTER 6

Cardinal just as much as we do."

"Hear, hear." Ak-Zul stood up, fist raised. "Any breathing soul that stands against the darkhelms is our ally."

"Hear, hear." A chorus echoed as recruits stood up throughout the gallery.

"We want to fight," a lanky woman with sinews of steel and short black hair said, "but how can we turn the tide of battle? There's only a few hundred of us."

"You make an excellent point," Saf replied with a faint smile. "That is why I propose to send emissaries to all remaining independent nations in the Sundered Isles. They have been under constant pressure, and they stand to lose a great deal should Bior fall. If we can build a united front to face the church's legions, we can stop them."

Brina raised an eyebrow. They were doing politics now? *Better Saf than me.*

"But who will go?" Ak-Zul asked. "If that letter is correct, we only have a few months' time. Who could unite enough people under our banner in such a short amount of time?"

"Let the Viper go," someone shouted. "They'll listen to him. No one has withstood more than him."

A roar of agreement went up all around Brina. On the opposite side of the room, Abrasax shrank in his seat.

"Viper! Viper!" A chant went up, accompanied by the stomping of spear butts on the stone floor. Saf's lips curled into a smile. She waited for the chant to die down, then addressed Abrasax directly.

"It seems your people have a great deal of faith in you," she said. Her voice was slippery, like a patch of ice on a mountainside. "What do you say?"

Abrasax lowered his face into his hands. Silence stretched on for so long that people began craning their necks and standing up to see what was going on. When Brina's father finally spoke, his voice was low and hoarse.

"I'll do it. I'll go."

Applause exploded all around Brina, drowning out her groan.

CHAPTER 7

After the meeting, the temple emptied like a leaky bucket. It took forever for the last clusters of recruits to trickle through the front door. News of the impending invasion had rattled the greenest of them and awakened a hunger for glory and vengeance in others. Both groups' prattling annoyed Brina. It was just more talk. Brina couldn't wait to get out of there, grab Razorwing, and return to Doorstep's Ditch to continue what she'd started.

Once the recruits were gone, Brina's eye was drawn to the gaping hole in the center of the temple. It seemed to expand as she stared at it, a boundless darkness that threatened to swallow everything around it.

Wells of offering had once been believed to provide a direct connection to the very bowels of the earth, where the original gods themselves had grown from great cosmic seeds. Every settlement, from tiny hamlet to towering city, had a well of its own, where the citizenry brought sacrifices whenever a major life event took place. Birth or death. Prosperity or privation. Fitness or frailty. Each was marked with an appropriate sacrifice.

These days, the church's ban on every religious practice they deemed heathenism had all but erased the wells from public memory. Every well the darkhelms could get their hands on had been filled up with rocks and leveled, destroying centuries of memories. *But they won't get this one.*

A great sigh hissed through the temple like a winter wind, startling Brina. She jumped up, only to exhale with relief when she spotted the sound's source. Hunched in one of the back rows of benches with his head in his hands sat Abrasax.

Outside, the sun stood high in the sky, illuminating one of the clearest days they'd had all week. Outlined in the distance, the Isle of Bior rose from the ocean like a breaching whale's hump. Brina wondered how many of the recruits were staring out at the horizon, watching those same jagged, rocky mountains. It seemed close. So close that Brina felt the mad urge to reach out and pluck it from the sea before the church could do so.

"I'm fine," Abrasax grumbled, finally acknowledging Brina's presence.

"Is that so?" Brina raised her eyebrows. "Then why are you just sitting here like a boulder gathering moss?"

"Because sometimes I feel like I'm still a prisoner. Except now I'm locked up behind other people's expectations, instead of iron bars." He rubbed his forehead with bony hands. "I don't even know what freedom is anymore."

Brina sat down on the stone bench beside him. Cold seeped into her legs at once.

"Then why didn't you just say you didn't want to go?"

Abrasax shrugged. "What could I have said? Refusing to go would have been a slap in the face to all those people who came here because they were sold a fairy tale with my face on the front cover."

Brina's eyes narrowed. "What's that supposed to mean?"

Her unease turned to concern. Abrasax's skin was smattered with beads of sweat, and even though he had been eating better in the months since his escape, his limbs were thin and gnarled. A decade in God's Maul had atrophied his muscles to those of an elderly patient with sheikan pox. His ragged hair had grown longer since his escape, tangling with an unkempt, curly beard that made him *look* like one of the seven patron saints of the outwalled.

It was hard to see the man he had once been through this vision of weakness and misery.

Brina thought of Versa and how their stay at God's Maul had shaken their identity. Moving on after that experience had required them to change everything about themselves and build a new person from the ground up. Was her father going through the same process right now? He seemed volatile, like a wild animal backed into a corner.

Tears welled in the corners of Abrasax's eyes.

"What have I done?" he wailed. "Oh, Sabrina, what have I done?"

He rubbed his face in his hands.

"I started something that can only end in death."

"You stood up for yourself and others," Brina said. "Screw how it ends. You showed people they didn't have to take the abuse any longer."

"How I envy the young." A watery smile appeared on her father's face. "Things used to feel so much simpler in here." He pointed at his head. "And in here." He tapped his chest. "All I foresee these days is more suffering, more destruction, more families torn apart. It's hard to see how all of that will be worth it in the end."

"Then what would you have us do?" Brina asked. "Nothing?"

"I would have us live a normal life while we still have the chance."

Brina looked over his shoulder at the narrow beams of sunlight floating in through the temple's tall windows. "What do you mean, a normal life?"

"We could do it, you know," he said. His fingers combed through his beard. "Between the two of us, we have more than enough skills to disappear. The empire would never find us. Even if they did, we could get away. The sense surgers will give up eventually, and things will go back to normal. We could find an island somewhere, build a hut, cultivate some roots and grains, dig trenches to harvest crabs. It wouldn't be much, but it would be a peaceful life. Our own life."

"And give up on freedom?" Brina asked. "We would be hunted for the rest of our lives. The Heilinists would overrun the Sundered Isles. All the island nations would fall and turn into one gray mass of church territory. Everything that doesn't fit with their view of the world would burn. Is that the world you want to live in?"

"Give up on freedom?" Abrasax laughed out loud. "What freedom is there in this? Will it free you to die on the battlefield? Will it free you if, after all that violence, we oust the Cardinal from his throne and are then forced to replace his tyranny with our own?"

It was all Brina could do not to lunge at him. "How could you say that after what you did to Estav? After the entire Signum died trying to break the church's dominance."

"Many deaths are on my conscience, I admit it. But tell me, what freedom will you, personally, have once the church falls? An entire empire will become rudderless. Will you seize the wheel and shape thousands of people's futures? Will you spend the rest of your days quelling Heilinist insurrections, battling famines, and bartering trade deals?"

His casual tone pulled at Brina's nerves. He didn't seem to notice. "I once thought I was up to that life. I thought there could be no nobler thing than to spend my life behind bars in protest of all the injustices we have suffered, but now that I can breathe fresh air once more and feel the smooth sand of a beach under my bare feet again, I find that my priorities have changed."

Brina rubbed at the scars in her left eye socket. She hadn't thought of that. Over the years, she had learned that no plan survived its brutal collision with reality, so she'd ceased worrying about anything beyond next week. What *would* she do if the rebellion was successful?

Surely others would step forward to claim positions of power. Saf probably already had it all figured out. Maybe some of the other island leaders would step up to steer things in the right direction.

But who would you trust, a voice in the back of her head murmured? *To whom would you hand the power to control tens of thousands of lives?* The dilemma grew in Brina's mind until panic threatened to consume her.

"We have time enough to worry about that later," she snapped. "The church must fall. The darkhelms must be disbanded. Their crimes have gone on too long."

"You want revenge," Abrasax said with that same maddening matter-of-fact tone.

"So what if I do?" Brina's jaws tightened.

"There is no shame in it," Abrasax said, "but know that the drive for vengeance limits our vision."

"Isolating yourself on this island has the same effect," Brina said. "You should go on that mission. It'll be good for you to see what the darkhelms are getting up to out there. You just might rediscover your anger."

"Will you come with me?" He avoided her gaze. "Please. I can't do this alone."

Brina's heart sank. Diplomacy was the last thing she wanted to get involved in with all its fancy banquet halls and extensive rules of decorum. But her father needed someone by his side to harden his resolve. Too many people depended on reinforcements showing up in time to save Bior.

Besides, what if he was right and death was on its way? What if this was her last chance to spend time with her father?

She put a hand on his shoulder. "Fine. I'll come."

CHAPTER 8

olana woke up screaming. Her head felt like it was being crushed under a boulder. Every bone in her body ached, and what little remained of her muscles screamed for nourishment. As soon as she thought about eating, her stomach roiled, and a spray of saltwater erupted from her mouth.

As she reached out into the darkness, her hands brushed an improvised mattress of reeds spread out over a sandy floor. She turned her head but found that her echolocation abilities had given out. She was floating in the night sky, adrift in an endless canvas of black.

Solana recoiled as a cloth brushed against her lips and chin.

"Take it easy," a soft female voice whispered. "It's going to be okay. Better out than in."

"Where am I?"

"Funny," the woman replied. "This is the third time you've woken up without remembering our prior conversations, and each time, that is your first question. Why do you think that is?"

"Do I look like someone who has time for philosophical games?" Solana pushed herself into a sitting position, and a fresh wave of saltwater forced its way up out of her stomach.

There was a chuckle from the woman beside her.

"I thought we'd gotten the last of it already, but it looks like the sea really pushed you around. If the waves hadn't spat you onto my little island, I shudder to think what would've happened."

"My prayer book," Solana said. "Where is it?"

"Everything you had on you and everything that washed up alongside you is on the bedside table to your right," the woman said.

Solana's fingers reached out into the darkness, brushing against the coarse side of a wooden crate. Her hands skittered across what little of her possessions the unknown woman had retrieved. It wasn't much. There hadn't been

CHAPTER 8

much to begin with.

For the past few months, she'd been hopping from island to island, building improvised rafts, swimming across narrow channels at low tide, doing whatever she could to make her way back to something resembling civilization.

But the constant lack of food, chronic dehydration, and lack of sleep had gotten the better of her when she tried to swim a narrow channel between two island clusters.

She remembered screaming as a rogue wave lifted her a dozen feet from the ground before slamming her into the sandy seabed.

She remembered fighting against the weight of the water as it bore down on her, holding her under. Her hands clutched at handfuls of sand on the bottom as the current rolled her over and over and over. Then... nothing. How far had she drifted? It couldn't have been far.

Renewed panic flared up inside her chest. It wasn't here. The prayer book wasn't here. She threw aside a length of improvised rope she'd made from a patch of tall grass, pushed her worn-down sandals off the crate, desperately searching for more. Then she felt it. The smooth lettering on the inside of the wooden cover, the reassuring heft of the prayer tablets stacked against each other, held together by metal rings. "Heil be praised," she muttered.

Solana clutched the prayer book to her chest. She needed privacy to pray to Heil, to heal her deteriorated body. She couldn't let this stranger know the value of what was right under her nose. Good people had made bad choices for far fewer shards.

She pulled herself up on the crate's edge and staggered forward. She bumped into something that might have been a table, careened sideways, and hit her head against a wall.

"The door is to your right," the woman's voice tinkled cheerfully, "but I suggest you lie back down. Getting overzealous will only prolong your suffering."

Solana's fingertips brushed the wall until they found the door. She yanked at the handle and felt the cool outside air wash over her. *Farther,* she told herself, *until I'm out of sight.*

Dropping to her knees, she began crawling along the sandy ground. She could hear the rush of leaves to her left and feel a breeze that suggested a vast open area around her. She was still on the beach. The sound of saltwater spray in the air almost drove her to vomit again, but her stomach was painfully empty. Struggling to put one hand in front of the other, Solana crawled in the opposite direction, away from the water's treacherous grasp.

She couldn't have gotten far before a tingling numbness spread from the tips of her fingers and toes throughout her limbs. Her body became heavy and unwieldy.

Have to put my head down. Just for a moment.

"No," she yelled out loud. "Have. To. Keep. Going."

Every word burned in her throat. If she allowed herself to slip into unconsciousness again, she would be doomed. It would all be over.

The stranger would steal her book of prayers and leave her to die. She was sure of it.

"Are you done?" The woman's voice echoed from a distance behind her. "I didn't drag you out of the water just to see you succumb to the elements. There are snakes in there, spiders too. Pretty sure I've seen about five species of scorpions. Not to mention the larger creatures that wouldn't pass up a tasty morsel falling asleep on their plate."

"I'm fine," Solana muttered. "Leave me alone. I'm free. Free."

And with her lips still parted, she sank into the black. Gentle arms closed around her, and she felt herself being lifted off the ground.

"Who said you weren't free? If there's anyone out here who knows the value of freedom, it's me."

CHAPTER 9

rina held the bottle above her head and watched a thin stream of kelp rum splatter into her tin goblet. Beside her, Sneak tried to stifle a giggle as droplets sprayed everywhere. The thin man leaned back in his chair, arms folded behind his head.

"Would you two knuckleheads focus?" Saf snapped. She and Abrasax were bent over the long granite table, studying a frayed map of the Sundered Isles. The square chamber near the top of the donjon had become a war room of sorts, filled with Saf's collection of maps and tomes, tucked away on secret shelves behind huge, fraying tapestries depicting ancient wars. The tall, narrow windows, crafted from delicate leaded glass, gleamed as though they'd been installed only days ago—Saf's doing, no doubt.

"Morassia, here," Saf said, poking at the map with a long nail, "and Onderheem, here, should be our prime allies in this matter. Both of their peoples have managed to retain some independence, and while their economies have suffered under recent trading restrictions, they should have enough resources left to put up a fight.

"The Morassians have always relied on trade with the Biori. They can't afford to lose their primary source of outside goods. Meanwhile, Onderheem has been selling large quantities of ore to Bior for generations. With any luck, they too should realize what they stand to lose should the church occupy the island."

"What about Barangia?" Abrasax asked, combing his fingers through his beard. "Their library hosts one of the largest collections of pre-Heilinist manuscripts in all the Sundered Isles. The scholars there have a broader view of history than anyone. They remember what life was like before the Heilinist revolution."

"Not an option," Saf said. "The city has been consumed by the church. The Doge has been secretly replaced by a covert Reynziel, and everything that enters or leaves the harbor is searched."

"That's a shame," Abrasax said, drumming his fingers against the tabletop. "They used to be one of the most free-spirited cities around. A sparkgazer's paradise.

"There's a secret order of scholars who dwell in the lower sections of the great library. Only the universe knows just how many manuscripts they have kept safe from destruction."

"I'm afraid we'll have to consider those lost," Saf said, pursing her lips. Her eyes lingered on the windows. Outside, great tendrils of fog reached down from the heavens to seize the land. "My sources tell me a purge was held in every institution of the city. If the organization you speak of still exists, it must have gone underground."

"Still," Abrasax argued, "it couldn't hurt to send someone down there to make contact. Those manuscripts could prove a tremendous boon in the future. If we could reproduce them, anything becomes possible."

"Like I said, they are almost certainly lost." Saf's eyes narrowed. "Let's consider our prime candidates more closely. King Krocht has ruled Onderheem for thirty years. He's been a staple in keeping his people as independent as possible, given the pressures they face.

"That includes some compromises made with the empire, but he's a sly fox. He knows how to maneuver himself so that the cards fall in his favor. If you want to get in his good graces, you'll have to pay exquisite attention to etiquette.

"The Heemians have many elaborate customs and rules, all of which you must follow to the strictest possible degree. It is imperative that you do not offend the king, his family, or his nobles.

"When you arrive there, be careful not to upstage the local nobility. If they see you as trying to place yourselves on a moral pedestal, or as trying to impress the king by demonstrating superiority, they will turn on you in a heartbeat." Saf glared at them as though they'd already violated the rules she was laying out.

"Make sure your attire is neat at all times, but it should never be more ornate than that of your hosts. Ensure that they do not see your presence as a challenge to their own status.

"If you can make them think that rushing to Bior's aid is their own idea, they will take to it twice as fast."

"Shouldn't be hard to appear less fancy than a bunch of nobles," Brina said. "By then, we'll have been on the open sea for weeks. They'll smell us from a hundred miles away."

CHAPTER 9

"Also," Saf said, a hard undertone in her voice indicating she didn't appreciate the interruption, "if all goes well, the king will invite you to a bond-dance."

"A what now?" Brina choked on a gulp of rum she was working down.

"It's a formal dance," Saf said. "It symbolizes the union between host and guest. Get your mind out of the gutter, Springtide."

"Hey, look," Brina said, raising her hands, "let's just hope the old coot doesn't want to take the whole union thing too far."

"Are you going to be like this all day?" Saf asked, cocking her head sideways and surveying Brina.

Brina smiled and nodded. "It seems likely."

Sneak snorted, and a fountain of rum sprayed from his nostrils.

Saf gave Brina the sort of glare that had been reserved for Acheron in the past. The brief burst of pride Brina felt at that thought was rapidly overshadowed by grief. Even with her eyes open, she could see Acheron's body sailing over the battlements of Locktower A before plummeting toward the rocks below. Over and over, she was forced to relive the moment, especially during the quiet hours of the night or when she was forced to sit still.

Brina shook her head like a wet dog, as if she could shake the horrible vision out through her ears. It didn't work. She refilled her cup and downed it in one.

"Anyway," Saf continued, a hard edge to her voice, "Heemian miners have had a tough time since the church established colonies on their land.

"They haven't been squeezed with direct taxation, but the empire has become increasingly demanding about tributes in raw metals. There's only so much they can produce every year, and the deeper their mines get, the harder it becomes to find enough ore to satisfy both the church and their own needs.

"With any luck, you'll find some of them very receptive to your message."

"That's an optimistic analysis," Abrasax said. "The Heemians have lived under that mountain for as long as history remembers. They don't care about what goes on above ground, let alone what occurs hundreds of miles from their doorstep.

"Their politics are just as conservative as they are complicated. I've met with Krocht before. He doesn't seem like the type of man to roll the dice on a crate of beer, let alone the precarious peace he has brokered with Cardinal De Leliard."

"Krocht is one man," Saf countered.

"Maybe, but he is the man on the throne."

"You, of all people, should know how easily those are replaced."

"I know how easily bad is replaced with worse." Abrasax's eyes drifted toward the windows on the opposite side of the room, where they lingered on the rippling tapestry of the mist-shrouded jungle.

Saf scowled. Before she could respond, Sneak jumped in.

"What about those other people you mentioned, the Morassians?"

"Honestly, I know little about them."

Brina sat up in her chair. Had Saf just admitted to not knowing something? Sneak frowned. "How come?"

"They move around," Saf said. "From what I gather, Biori merchants announce their presence on the island by burning a pile of dried herbs on the beach. Then they wait until a Morassian trading party emerges from the swamps to greet them."

"So we're supposed to go there and burn herbs?"

"I don't care what you do, as long as you convince the Morassians that joining our alliance will be their best chance at a free future," Saf said.

"We'll find them," Abrasax assured her. "They used to be quite hospitable back in the Signum's heyday. Archdruidess Caldessa's husband was detained by the darkhelms and sent off to slavery. Ever since then, she's been looking for any opportunity to thwart them."

"Head over there as soon as logistically possible." Saf rubbed at her temples. "We don't have a single day to waste. Spring will be here sooner than any of us would like."

"How will we get there?" Brina stifled a belch. Her nostrils burned as the rum vapors forced their way out.

Saf shook her head at Brina, though her eyes belied amusement.

"Captain Samok will take you. He's done a lot of work on his *Chimera*, and he's been dying to take her out to sea."

Brina shrugged. "Tell him to bring rum."

CHAPTER 10

*hree hundred.* Zot sat back, staring at the three piles of sapphire, emerald, and ruby gem shards on the small table in front of him. A smug grin curled his lips. He still had it.

After all these years since he'd last walked the streets slinging product, he'd still sold a brick and a half of wakeroot in just over a week. By himself. No network, no dealers, no enforcers. Just him and his quick tongue.

Unfortunately, the achievement came with its price. The sickly-sweet stench of the resin clung to his skin and fingernails, staining them an incriminating green. Though he had washed his hands as often as he could, the damned substance had seeped into his flesh like water into a sponge.

Combined with the metallic, dusty stench of gem shards that had passed through too many pouches and hands, the smell was almost unbearable.

Until recently, Zot's entire world had smelled of sandalwood and cinnamon. Every room he entered had been perfumed to his liking. The stench and filth of the real world had been a concern of the past for him. Now he was stuck in a cramped, filthy room on the second floor of the Boar and Barrel inn. He was forced to bear the stench of beer and mediocre stew boiling up through the loose floorboards, filling his room like poisonous gas. Though his stomach grumbled, he was sure he wouldn't be able to keep down a single bite of the innkeeper's slop.

No, his time was better served continuing the work he had started. The sooner the boy left the shamanka's presence, the better. Though he didn't think Sachrya would physically harm the boy, who knew what that hag was teaching him. No matter how much he himself might resist the notion, Wane was just a boy. He was vulnerable to Sachrya's wiles in ways he wouldn't even be able to understand.

Not that Zot's own company was much of an example. Still, at least he *tried* to teach the boy proper skills to make it in this ruthless world.

Only one hundred more shards, and it'll be over. Once the half brick stuffed in his coat pocket was gone, he'd return to the apothecary to buy the boy's freedom back. After that, the third brick the shamanka had given him would be all profit. Another potential two hundred shards, right into their pockets. *Into the rebellion's pockets,* he reminded himself. By itself, the two hundred wouldn't be enough, of course. Not even close. It'd hardly hire them a crew for a luxurious journey back to Metten.

But it would be starting capital. Enough to do business the old-fashioned way. The legal way. Well, maybe semi-legal.

Zot trudged down the creaky stairs and entered the common room. He nodded at the half dozen foul-smelling fishermen who lay slumped against the bar. Their cheeks burned with bad kelp rum.

Some of them groaned greetings as he passed. Before he exited the inn, Zot cast a sly glance at the innkeeper. He was a young man, no older than thirty cycles, with short black hair and a lazy eye. Something about his face spelled trouble.

When Zot had entered the Boar and Barrel yesterday, he'd been sure that this lad had recognized him. Or perhaps he'd heard about Zot through the grapevine. Whatever the case, the innkeeper smelled money. He stared at Zot the way a shark traces a seal's movements.

The innkeeper winked at Zot as he exited the inn. Zot smirked. As soon as Zot was out of sight, the man would rush up to his room to ransack it. He would find nothing of value. Except, perhaps, one of the dozen sleepthorns Zot had hidden in strategic places. One prick and the innkeeper would sleep for two days, allowing the other patrons to rob him blind while he slept.

Zot laughed out loud as the door closed behind him. Sometimes his own ingenuity scared him.

***

Stepping out into the nighttime streets of Merkede was like kneeling above a kettle of boiling water. The sweltering moisture in the air, combined with the heat that blew over from the nearby Hawqallian desert, made the island's climate all but unbearable. Within seconds, beads of sweat began trickling down Zot's skin underneath his heavy coat.

Though he would love to take it off, he could scarcely carry a brick and a half of wakeroot and a bulging pouch of shards openly in his hands. Besides, the double layer of quarter-inch leather provided at least some cursory protection against glancing arrows or a jab with a blunt knife. It wouldn't do

CHAPTER 10

any wonders in a full-on battle, but at least he wouldn't get taken out by a blow dart to the armpit.

He walked his usual route toward the dock district, peering left and right into alleys to ensure he wasn't being followed. Over the past week, he'd developed a solid routine. In the late afternoon, just before dusk, most of the workers and sailors on the docks were nearing the end of their shift. They would be tired, but craving the excitement and release of a night out in Merkede's inns. Wakeroot gave them that extra push to keep going. Zot had even garnered a small roster of daily clients who split their day's wages with him in exchange for a sliver of the good stuff.

As he passed the edge of the town center, a steep hill rose above the roofs of surrounding houses. On its summit, an abandoned lighthouse looked out over the bay. Zot swallowed. That place had haunted his dreams for years. Over and over, he would watch himself dig deeper and deeper, his hands stained black by the soil.

Digging up what he'd hidden there would be an easy way out. But he wasn't prepared to walk those few hundred yards and start digging. If he did so, it would say something about the course his life had taken and just how sad his state of affairs had become. He wasn't ready to admit that to himself or anyone else yet. He was Dimimzy Zot, and he would handle business as he always had. The lighthouse was off-limits. It was a symbol of all he had yet to accomplish.

Zot's feet left solid ground as he stepped onto the first ship. He nodded at a bald sailor whom he'd met with every day this week. The man perked up, walked up, and put two sapphire shards in Zot's coat pocket. Zot retrieved a pre-cut sliver of resin from his pocket and slipped it into the man's hand. The entire transaction was over in a handful of heartbeats.

Zot threw a look over his shoulder, checking the nearby docks for patrols. The trade of illicit substances, though rampant on the island, was subject to harsh punishments. Even tiny quantities were punishable by up to a year of hard labor in the Hawqallian desert.

To his satisfaction, no constables were near. All who remained on the docks now were those doing hard labor; no captain or officer would bother standing watch all night as their men scrubbed, cleaned, and repaired nets. He made the rounds of the dock, making sure he took a different route each night. His movements ought to be as unpredictable as possible. When he neared the *Saint Mary*, a trading vessel all the way from Mallion's Depth, a man whistled and beckoned.

Zot turned around and recognized a long-haired fellow he had traded with a few nights ago. So far, the man had only requested modest amounts of root, but he had tipped well. He seemed like the sort of fellow who had money enough to buy whatever he wanted, but was smart enough not to be caught with too many valuables on his person.

As Zot approached, the man climbed down over the ship's railing and landed on the dock with a heavy impact. The tips of his boots reflected the setting sun.

"So," the man said, "here to do business again?"

Zot nodded, annoyed at the obvious statement. If he'd wanted his every move narrated out loud, he would've hired one of those useless poets from the Merkedian Society for the Fine Arts to write a play about him.

"Excellent," the man replied, eyes glittering. "Me and the lads want a little more than usual for the return journey to Hammerstroke. Prices being cheaper here and all."

"How much do you need?" A pit of excitement grew in Zot's stomach, but he couldn't let that show, or the guy would know he had leverage to wheedle the price down. Instead, he let his shoulders slump, as though the request was a burden.

The man shrugged, scratching at his nose. "There's about two dozen of us chipping in. Let's say all of us have a handful of shards to spare. How much would that buy us?"

Zot smiled as the man lifted his stained white shirt to show a full pouch hanging from his belt. There must be a hundred shards in there—enough for Zot to get the boy back straight away. The kid wouldn't have to spend another night with that awful woman.

"I could give you about half a brick for that," Zot said, holding apart two fingers to illustrate how much that would be. The sailor gave a satisfied nod.

"That should hold us over for a while. When can you get it to us? Our ship sails in two days."

"When can you get me the money?" Zot replied, keeping track of the man's eyes. There was a shifty quality to them. *Nervous buyer or nervous scammer?* He wasn't with the constables. That could be ruled out. Two nights ago, he'd sold the same man a slice that could have landed him in prison for the rest of his days already. An undercover agent would have pounced then and there. No, whatever this guy's problem was, it was something else.

"Well, it's all right here," the man replied. "So if you can hand me the root, I could pay right here and now."

CHAPTER 10

"I can deliver, but not here." There were too many eyes watching Zot from the decks of the moored ships. He was drawing attention to himself, and he didn't like it. One loose-lipped person could be the end of him, and by extension, the boy. "Meet me in the alley behind the Barrel and Boar in about half an hour."

The sailor gave the briefest of winks, then climbed back onto the ship from which he'd come.

As Zot walked back to the inn, he made sure that the hand-off would happen on his own terms. He checked and triple-checked the alley for any windows from which he could be seen. He loitered around, noting when patrols passed. From his observations, he estimated the same patrol circled the block every half hour. That gave him a sizable window to work with.

When the sailor arrived later that night, Zot clutched the hilt of his dagger inside his sleeve. *Pull it together, man; you're acting like a green-behind-the-ears schoolboy.* The sailor untied the leather pouch from his belt and held it out to Zot.

"Count it. Out loud." Nothing could go wrong. Not now. He needed every shard to be there.

The man gave an annoyed sigh. "Look, man, there are constables about..."

"Count. It." Zot's palms were slick against the smooth metal of the dagger.

With a shrug, the sailor began counting out shards by the dozen, handing them over to Zot. A wave of euphoria grew inside Zot with every handful he deposited in his pocket. What better sound in the world than the clatter of gems?

"There. One hundred." The sailor scowled, glancing over his shoulder. Zot pulled a random sapphire shard from his pocket and bit it. His teeth ached as they clamped around the harsh crystal. He held it up toward the nearest oil lamp illuminating the street at the end of the alley. No scratches or dents. Clear coloring. Genuine. With a practiced motion, Zot tossed the half brick of wakeroot wrapped in a religious pamphlet at the sailor.

The man pocketed it without opening the parcel. Amateur. That was good. Zot preferred dealing with amateurs—less to worry about. He waved a hand, dismissing the sailor. The man gave a curt semi-bow and scuttled out of the alley, his hand tucked in his pocket where the chunk of wakeroot had disappeared.

Zot chortled, his fingers rustling through the pile of loose gems in his pocket. "May the Seven bless you, sailor." In one swoop, he'd gathered enough money to buy the boy's freedom. From here on out, every ounce he sold would be pure profit. And he would have the boy to watch his back. Zot swaggered out of the alley and up a short section of wooden stairs toward the inn's front door.

The common room was deserted, save for the glow of embers clinging to life in the hearth. All the jelly lanterns were covered with their cloth hoods. There was no sign of any patrons, nor of the innkeeper. A handful of mugs stood on the bar. Still full. Zot stiffened, drawing his dagger as fluidly as he drew breath. Perhaps the trap he'd laid for the innkeeper had worked too well.

He kneeled before the fire, picked up a branch from the pile of firewood, and held it in the embers to create a makeshift torch. Dim light washed over the scene. Zot tiptoed to the bar. There was a squelching noise as the sole of his boot landed in a patch of thick, drying blood. It ran down the groove between two floorboards like molten steel.

Zot leaned over the bar and sighed. The innkeeper lay slumped against the liquor cabinet, crimson blooming on his chest. He'd been cut from his collarbone down to his sternum. Whoever had done it had rampaged like an animal, stabbing and ripping at random. Zot knelt beside the innkeeper and shook the man's shoulder. To his surprise, the man's eyes flickered open for the briefest moment, locking on to his own.

"You," he whispered. "Why... Why did you..." He let out a groan, and Zot heard the familiar rattle as the final lungful of air exited the man's body.

Panic was setting in. He stood up, downing half a mug of the beer still standing on the bar to clear his head. Whoever had done this couldn't be far.

He wanted to go back to his own room and collect the spare clothing, business ledgers, and whatever else he had left there, but something told him not to. It was better to just leave. A small voice in the back of his head told him it was cowardly to leave without checking on the patrons who might've been asleep upstairs.

"Not my business," he told himself out loud. *The boy's my priority*. He threw his torch into the hearth, and slipped out of the back door of the inn, back into the alley he had come from.

"Halt!" a deep voice called behind him as soon as he set foot across the threshold. Three blades pointed at his neck, one of them caressing the sensitive skin underneath his chin. "You are being arrested on suspicion of murder, robbery, and unlawful imprisonment." Zot turned his head gingerly, so as not to cut himself on the blade pressed against his throat, and found himself face to face with three uniformed constables of the trade union.

His heart sank. As he looked down, he noticed his shoes were covered in

CHAPTER 10

blood, as were his hands from touching the innkeeper. He was being framed.

Zot held up his hands. "I had nothing to do with it," he said. His voice was embarrassingly shaky. "I just went in there to retrieve my things. I was on my way to inform the nearest constable of what I'd discovered."

A slap rang out in the night. Zot crumpled to his knees from the force of the blow.

"Shut up," the constable said. "You have been found at the scene of the crime, with the victim's blood all over you."

"And what's this?" the second constable, a thin woman with eyes the color of ice, said as she patted his pocket, which jangled with the incriminating sound of a few hundred shards in ill-gotten gains. Zot shook his head.

"I'm innocent. The killer is still inside. I saw footprints. I ran because I was scared."

The third man chuckled. "Nice story. Keep it up for when we arrive at the jail."

Before he could protest further, they forced a leather hood over Zot's head, and the constables dragged him out of the alley.

CHAPTER 11

"Yep," Brina said, scowling at the increasingly deep mud sucking at her boots and the thorny bushes catching on her trousers. "This is officially the worst trip ever."

They had left the ship and its crew in a nearby lagoon, surrounded by palm trees and craggy sandstone cliffs. From down there, the island had seemed a lush paradise, complete with idyllic vistas and clouds of colorful birds rising and falling in azure skies. Now that they were undertaking a harsh trek up the rocky hillside, Brina's feelings about the place were turning sour.

"Embrace the hardship," Bron said, muscled arms outstretched. "It'll do us good to be back out in the wilderness instead of stuck behind cozy walls and gates."

Despite his tough talk, the Biori lifted his feet comically high to keep himself from sinking into the wet soil. Bron hated getting dirty. Brina grinned at the thought of what he would do if he fell into one of the slimy green puddles that surrounded them. "Whatever you say, drill sergeant Brokenspear."

"And you're sure you can find the Morassians? I thought Saf said the Biori burned herbs on the beach." Sneak looked at Abrasax, flapping his arms at a swarm of mosquitoes. "It would be a great look for the rebellion if we traipsed around in circles for two weeks, only to end up with nothing but bug bites to show for our trouble."

"Yes." Abrasax didn't look up. "I've visited them more than once. Though it's been years since those days. The tribe may have moved quite a distance in that time. They don't stick around in one place for too long if they can avoid it. Their canoes and folding huts allow them to set up and disband camps in a single day. The entire forest is their home."

"The only reason the church hasn't driven them out yet," Bron grumbled. "Nothing lasts long once those bastards know where to find it."

Brina knew what he was thinking. As they had sailed around the island's shore, looking for a place to moor the ship, they had spotted multiple ruined

CHAPTER 11

and abandoned settlements. Blackened huts surrounded by piles of ash and debris. Near the last one they'd passed, dozens of bodies swayed from ropes along the tree line. The memory of the sight made the hairs on the back of Brina's neck stand up.

"But what if the church has gotten to them, and we just don't know yet?" Sneak asked. "Wouldn't that mean that we might never find them?"

"The Morassians are fine," Bron assured him. "We Biori trade with the swamp dwellers. Medicine, dried snake, messenger toucans... We would've noticed if those stopped coming our way. Some of us would've gone looking."

He sniffed the air as though he expected to find the Morassians by scent alone. "They're out here; just a matter of picking up their trail."

They crested the hill and found themselves on the edge of a dark swamp. Streams of murky water snaked in between gnarled tupelo trees like the tentacles of a beached leviathan. Overhead, a spider's web of branches stretched out as far as the eye could see, shielding the forest floor from sunlight. Temperatures dipped as they trudged onward into this strange, shadowy world.

The oppressive stench of rot and damp crowded in around them. Wafts of sulfur stung Brina's nose as bubbles of swamp gas disturbed the water on both sides of the path.

Before Brina's eyesight had adjusted to the gloom, the path disappeared, turning into a network of fallen trees connected with planks. Most of the wood was rotten and crusted with lichen and moss. A single false step would be enough to tumble into those murky waters.

Brina had spent enough time in the swamps on Hammerstroke to know how disastrous that could be. There would certainly be one or more quetzal nearby. Those feathery predators loved hiding in trees, ready to pounce on unsuspecting prey that meandered their way. Not to mention snakes, crocodiles, or any of the other slimy creatures that thrived in these muddy depths.

She broke a branch off a nearby bush. Step by step, she poked the wooden walkways in front of her, looking for weak spots. Brina made it a point never to trust anything she hadn't built with her own two hands. The constant testing made progress slow, but it was better than ending up as chum in the water.

"So," Sneak asked, his high-pitched voice grating against the silence, "you've been here before, have you?"

Abrasax nodded, eyeing Sneak, as though he were worried the lanky young man was about to ask him for money.

"What are they like?" Sneak's eyes lit up. "I heard that during the solstice they sacrifice and eat one of their own babies."

Abrasax let out a low chuckle. "Can't say I've witnessed any such thing in my time here. The Morassians are like any other people. Sure, they like sticking to themselves, but they can be quite hospitable if they see you mean no harm.

"Most of them spend their days tending to the forest. They harvest what needs to be culled, and rekindle that which threatens to fade away. They are of the swamp and the swamp is of them."

Sneak was about to launch into another question when Brina held up her hand.

"Shh," she hissed. "Something's wrong."

Her eyes traced a series of suspicious bubbles that had been sprouting up in the water beside them for the past few minutes. It had taken her until now to realize what had bothered her about them: they were traveling upstream.

She stooped down and drew both of her daggers from her ankle sheaths. Behind her, the others shuffled on the log, making it sway like a ship on stormy seas. A glimmer of red touched the surface to Brina's right before disappearing back into the depths.

"It's a mud lizard," Brina said, taking a deep breath. "Keep walking behind me. Don't make any sudden movements."

The others fell silent. They inched across the log after her, ignoring the growing stream of bubbles that followed them.

When Brina reached a small island—which was to say, a clump of trees whose roots stuck out high enough for all four of them to stand on—she helped the others off the log.

"Draw your weapons." Brina positioned herself between the others and the water's edge. The bubbles remained stationary in a spot only six feet from the base of the roots. *It's watching.* The rustle and clinking of weapons leaving sheaths felt ominous in the silent forest. "It'll be on us as soon as I strike."

Brina picked up the largest floating branch she could reach, heart hammering in her chest. With one swift motion, she stabbed the branch into the stream of bubbles as hard as she could.

The bubbles stopped. Brina prayed she'd hit an eye or a nose and the lizard would get spooked and decide this wasn't a battle worth fighting.

No such luck.

A thunderous roar echoed off the trees as the lizard crested the surface. Scaly red skin rose from the water. It was a juvenile, only twelve feet tall, but no less dangerous for it. Moss encrusted the creature's thick armor like fur. Its slimy head looked like a boulder with two rotting coconuts for eyes. It

CHAPTER 11

reared up on its hind legs, leaving four clawed arms to swipe at the air.

"There we go," Brina yelled.

Let's do this, you ugly bastard.

Brina flung the branch at the lizard. The beast didn't even blink as the branch bounced off its head with a hollow *thunk*. Squeezing the hilt of her dagger, Brina burned *Gnis*. Within moments, her hand burned as hot as a smith's furnace. When the metal gained an orange halo of heat, she whirled around on the spot, using her momentum to launch the dagger straight ahead. The moment it left her fingers, she knew her aim was true. The weapon flipped over thrice in the air before plunging straight into the creature's chest. There was a sizzle of flame against flesh. The lizard let out a deafening screech, rearing up as the glowing metal singed its insides. Beside Brina, Sneak whooped in excitement.

For a moment, it looked like the creature might back off. Then it rallied. It leaped forward with a furious roar. Razor claws swept down at Brina. She dodged, causing the claw to rake across the bark of one of the nearby trees, leaving deep gouges in the wood.

"Oi, ugly, over here!" Sneak yelled. He jumped up and down, waving his arms to draw the creature's attention away from Brina. It worked. The lizard lunged forward. Its jaws unhinged, opening wide enough to swallow a pony whole. A wave of sour, rotten breath almost made Brina gag. Sneak's eyes flashed emerald as he burned *Leve*. In one fluid motion, he jumped ten feet straight upward and pulled himself onto one of the tree's lower branches.

When the lizard snapped at him, Bron hit it in the stomach with a jab of his spear. A deep gash appeared in the creature's belly, oozing black blood. It swayed on the spot as though hypnotized.

"Nice one, we got it!" Brina thumped her fist into her forehead in a Biori sign of respect. Bron grinned back at her. A vast shadow swept over Brina. The lizard's long tail swooped down at her. Too quickly. There was nothing she could do. Brina felt her feet leave solid ground. She clawed at tree branches as she went flying. Her fingers skidded across slippery moss. Then she was submerged in the icy river, her vision gone. The murky gray was like trying to look through ground-up tea leaves. She tried to swim up, but her left boot was stuck in the mud on the riverbed. The more she fought, the higher it crept up, consuming her leg one inch at a time.

Horrible visions of unsavory creatures nibbling on her trapped corpse forced their way into Brina's mind as panic took hold. Her lungs burned, contracting with the desperate need for air. *I'm going to drown on the very first day like an idiot.* Bubbles escaped her mouth as she barked out a maniacal laugh. That was life. You spent years fighting to make your mark in the world, only to get sucked into a rising tide of mud and filth when you least expected it.

White lights popped behind her eyes as her consciousness grew dim. Shadowy figures danced just beyond her vision. She heaved, causing the last air to abandon her lungs in a spray of bubbles. Then, just as darkness threatened to consume her, she saw them again—crystal clear. Dozens of emaciated, naked Morassians dangling from frayed ropes at the forest's edge. The burned shacks of Doorstep's Ditch, collapsing on their trapped inhabitants. Acheron tipping over the edge of the tower at God's Maul, then falling. Falling... Screw them. A sudden rush of anger exploded deep inside Brina, drawing forth a reserve of strength from nowhere. She writhed, kicked, and bucked with all her might. As she fought against the tide of sand, powerful arms closed around her torso, pulling upward.

Together, Brina and her unseen helper pulled her boots free from the soil. Brina breached the surface with a gasp. Her senses were flooded with the sulfuric stench of the swamp, the lizard's roars, and bright rays of sunlight poking through a hole in the foliage above. Her vision cleared just in time to watch Bron sidestep the creature's razor teeth as it tried to swallow him. With a powerful thrust, his spear pierced the creature's neck just behind the boulder-sized head. A good two feet of the weapon disappeared into the flesh. With a lurch, the lizard jerked itself away from the spear, screeching.

A fountain of black gore jetted from the wound in slow spurts. It stepped backward, then sank back underneath the surface from whence it had come. A trail of bubbles vanished across a bend in the river, accompanied by clouds of black in the water. Brina looked up at her savior. Abrasax's eyes glittered with the faint blue of *Forte*. His clothes and beard were sopping wet and muddy, but a wide grin covered his face. "Figured I owed you one for the whole preventing-my-imminent-execution thing," he said.

Brina coughed up a mouthful of water. "Look who woke up. Glad to see your old strength is returning."

CHAPTER 12

rina awoke to a hiss in her ear and a sharp edge pressed against her throat. "Don't move," a high-pitched voice whispered, "or I'll gut you like a bog eel."

Brina seized *Lux* and found herself surrounded by a dozen pale figures, each armed with a shimmering silver sickle and clad in long robes of woven reeds. Their hair hung in elaborate braids, interwoven with twigs, flowers, and dried leaves. Wincing, Brina turned her head as the razor-sharp weapon her captor held sliced into her skin.

Bron, Sneak, and her father all had sickles pressed against the hollow beneath their jawbones. One tug at the weapons would be enough to sever every major artery in their necks.

"It's okay," Abrasax said. "My name is Abrasax Springtide. I'm a friend of the archdruidess. We're here on important diplomatic business."

"Lies," the woman holding Brina snapped. "Abrasax Springtide has been locked up in God's Maul prison for over a decade."

"Aha!" a tall man with broad cheekbones cried out, eyes blazing with triumph. "I told you, Chief. These landwalkers are up to no good."

"Right you were, Silas. Our caution pays off yet again." Brina's body tensed. What were they about to do to them? In one flash of silver, their blood could be spilled into the dark water of the bog. Brina's fingers reached for the dagger hidden in her boot, but Abrasax gave her a furious headshake.

"Don't resist," he said aloud, glancing around to make eye contact with the others. "They'll see their mistake soon enough."

Brina wished he didn't sound so shaky.

"You've got some nerve," Silas said. "You've been found trespassing on sacred grounds. Yet, it is we who are in the wrong here?" Silas's hand shot up, a glimmer of moonlight reflecting on his sickle. Without hesitation, it swung downward. Brina screamed. Just before the blade severed Abrasax's neck, the Morassian leader let go of Brina and grabbed Silas's wrist. She gave him a menacing look.

"We are not the judge here," she said. "We shall take them to the archdruidess. It's up to her to decide their fate."

Silas spat onto the ground in front of Abrasax, his eyes full of hatred.

Abrasax nodded at the woman. "Yes," he said, "please, take us to the archdruidess. All shall become clear there. No one needs to get injured over this unfortunate misunderstanding."

"I wish I shared your optimism, landwalker," the leader said. "Evana is not known for her mercy, especially after these last few years."

A strange twist played on Abrasax's features at the mention of the name. Brina couldn't catch his eye to gauge what their next move should be. If they were going to fight, they would all need to move at the same time, or the Morassians would execute them at once.

Right now, it was four sparkgazers against a dozen lightly armed Morassians. It was a dangerous gamble, but one that had a reasonable chance of going their way. If they allowed themselves to be taken deeper into the forest, however, escape would become nigh on impossible.

Even here, half a day's march from the edge of the swamp, Brina wasn't sure that her navigational skills would get them back to the ship. If the Morassians took them deeper into the dark, those odds would become awfully slim. They would be trapped in an endless cycle of traversing the bog, surrounded by enemy scouts.

Brina tried a second time to catch her father's eye, but Abrasax seemed transfixed by his own shoes, as though he were reading scriptures engraved in the leather. After a tense silence, he stood up and presented his wrists to the leader. He did not flinch as they bound him and shoved him into a nearby boat.

A glint in Bron's eyes told Brina that he was having a lot more trouble accepting this scenario. Making a split-second decision, Brina put her trust in the man who had given her life and done his best to raise her for what few years they had spent together.

She stretched out her arms and allowed herself to be bound. Never had she felt so vulnerable as when the rope's coarse fibers wrapped around her wrists. She was giving up control, and she hated it. It took everything in her power not to bite Silas's hand when he pushed down on her shoulder, forcing her to sit down next to Abrasax. The boat wobbled as Bron and Sneak were pushed into it after her. Four of the Morassians hopped aboard, while eight others got into a second boat.

CHAPTER 12

With smooth grace, two of the Morassians began paddling. The boat slid into motion, and they were carried off into the dark depths of the swamp.

***

The first tendrils of daylight snaked their way through the dense branches and leaves above as the claustrophobic swamp opened into a lake. Brina had no idea how long she'd been staring off into the distance, but it must have been hours. At first, she'd been alert, making note of every characteristic tree trunk and bend in the river, but memorizing their route had proved an impossible task. Everything looked the same, and the river split into so many different branches that Brina wondered how the Morassians themselves could navigate so confidently in the dark.

The water passing underneath the boat turned from mossy green to crystal as they neared a makeshift dock. It consisted of floating logs tied together with a pattern of intricate knots. The white ropes dug into the dark bark like tendons on a fresh carcass.

Silas pulled Brina from the boat. Her shoulders and bound wrists ached from the uncomfortable position she had been stuck in for hours. The rope chafed at her raw skin, drawing blood.

"Out you go," Silas said, shoving her toward a flimsy rope bridge. "Don't bother with any tricks. There's nowhere to run."

As they were herded across the bridge, Brina's mouth fell open. In the middle of the lake, a white spire that looked like it had once belonged to a grand cathedral jutted up from the surface like a dragon's fang. Clustered around it were dozens of pontoons constructed of empty barrels and logs, atop which stood wooden huts topped with roofs of dried reeds, bobbing in the morning breeze. The village looked like a giant spider's web of rope, with the sunken spire sitting in the middle.

Dozens of eyes followed their slow march, peering out from cracks in doors standing ajar. They were clearly an unexpected spectacle to the swamp folk.

"I guess the old man didn't lie when he said these were very different people," Sneak said, rolling his eyes. "The reception here is on par with an all-inclusive package at the God's Maul dungeons."

"Shut up," Silas said, holding up his sickle in a warning gesture. "If I hear so much as another whisper before you are spoken to, I will silence you for good."

"'I will silence you for good,'" Sneak repeated in a childish, mocking tone, pulling a face. Silas smacked him with the flat of his sickle.

They were led to a rough opening in the spire's side. It seemed a recent, much less masterfully constructed addition. There was no door, only a crimson and emerald curtain that rippled in the morning breeze.

The chief beckoned for her scouts to wait as she entered the room beyond. Mere minutes later, Brina and the others were shoved through the curtain and into a circular room flooded with sunlight streaming in through huge stained-glass windows. The entire room was a kaleidoscope of red, yellow, and emerald sunbeams. It was like standing inside a rainbow.

Thin mats of woven fibers covered the floor, which insulated Brina's soaking wet feet from the icy cold of the marble beneath them. The relief was instant. An herbal scent, reminiscent of Huygen's Apothecary in Doorstep's Ditch, hung in the air.

At the far end of the room stood a man-high throne carved out of a single piece of beechwood. Its armrests and sides were decorated with carvings of distorted human faces, screaming in what could have been either despair or ecstasy. They seemed like ghosts, rising on the surface of the wood, trying to force their way back into the realm of the living. Atop this ghastly throne sat the smallest and most intimidating woman Brina had ever met.

Archdruidess Evana wore a long robe of golden thread, beset with beads of amber in a floral pattern resembling the lilies and hyacinths that blossomed upon the lakeshore outside. Her ashen hair was braided with green vines, making it look as though a dozen snakes sprouted from the woman's scalp. Her emerald eyes shone bright against the unnatural pallor of her skin.

"Step forth," Evana commanded with a flourish of her hand. Brina moved forward at once, subconsciously willing to obey. Here was a sheikan of a woman: all-seeing and ready to pounce.

"My scouts tell me you were sneaking through our territories under the cover of dark." Evana's voice was ice. Unbending, rigid, and yet brittle in a way. "You have thirty heartbeats to explain yourself."

"Mistress of wood and water," Abrasax said, falling to his knees, "my name is Abrasax Springtide. I have been a friend to your people for over two decades, and I come bearing grave warnings."

"You lie." The druidess's face remained impassive, though her sneer was lost on no one present. "I have never seen you in my life. Abrasax Springtide has been behind lock and key for the better part of a generation."

"These lands are sacred. We protect them and everything that dwells in them from the trampling of boots and the clinking of iron. That is our duty as stewards of the forest."

CHAPTER 12

A flicker of panic rippled over Abrasax's face at these words. Brina's teeth ground together. A lump the size of a millstone was swelling in her chest. Had her father misjudged the Morassians? Eleven years was a long time to be locked away in a world where alliances could be forged at dawn and broken at noon.

"Your predecessor, Caldessa, and I were on excellent terms in her day," Abrasax insisted. Desperation leaked into his voice. "I came here out of concern for your people. Grave perils are assembling close to your shores. It is paramount that you hear us out with an open mind.

"The world is changing, and soon even these remote parts will not be safe from the storm that is brewing to the north. Caldessa was aware of this danger years ago. Will you not honor her memory with a mere ten minutes of your time?"

The archdruidess's mouth twitched. *Doubt*. Her shoulders shifted, eyes darting from Abrasax to the troop of scouts that lined the walls of the chamber to prevent the prisoners from escaping.

"There is only one way to settle this." She turned to the scouts surrounding them. Her face had become a mask. Hard. Immovable. "Take them to the totems."

Whatever that meant, Brina was sure she wouldn't care for it. She jumped up, hand reaching for a dagger that was no longer there.

Icy steel prickled against her neck at once. Silas. "Stay still."

To Brina's left, Bron and Sneak also tried to break away from their captors, but when they saw the sickle at Brina's throat, they raised their hands in surrender.

"It is not up to me to pass ultimate judgment upon you," Evana said. She stared straight ahead as though she couldn't bear to look upon them a moment longer. "That responsibility lies with Argul-Khan, the seer of the forest."

The druidess waved a hand, and the scouts dragged Abrasax and the rest of the group back toward the curtain through which they had entered. "Should the seer deem your hearts true, I shall listen with open ears for as long as it takes for you to state your case. For now, may the spirit of the land be with you."

"You swamp crawlers better have my spear ready and polished by the time we get back," Bron grunted, glowering at the Morassian who had relieved him of his weapons. The woman cracked a smirk and leaned on the weapon as though it were a common walking stick.

"After Argul-Khan is done with you, I think I'll keep this as a trophy."

CHAPTER 13

 A crowd gathered on the pontoons that made up the village of Sunken Spire as Brina and the others were dragged back toward the same boats they had arrived in.

Pale faces watched from the rope bridge as their captors paddled them toward a series of wooden poles that protruded ten feet above the surface of the lake. Like the archdruidess's throne, they were carved with grimacing faces. Two rusty metal rings were attached to the top.

Brina's heart hammered in her throat. They had lost all control of the situation, and now they would be fed to whatever slimy creature the Morassians called "Argul-Khan."

She thought about the dozens of contracts she'd fulfilled in places just like these. Their prognosis was grim. Things that lived in the deep gray of swamps tended to have far too many teeth, far too many eyes, and the empathy of a mossy stick.

Tension grew palpable as more Morassians streamed out of their huts to watch what would happen to these strangers who had invaded their lands. Brina had sensed the same atmosphere in Doorstep's Ditch countless times. It was the tightening of the bowstring before the arrow flew. It was the inhale before the scream. The glint of the knife before the arterial spray.

The Morassians wore tattered rags. Many wore bandages covering wounds to heads and torsos. Too many cheekbones stuck out too far from hollow faces. These people had suffered over the past few months, maybe even years. They would be eager to see their misfortune compensated in black-and-white punishment. An ounce of blood in the water for all that they had lost.

Brina looked over her shoulder, desperate to glimpse the others. Was this the time to fight? Their captors outnumbered them five to one, and they would not hesitate to cut their throats at the first sign of trouble. No sigil could save them from bleeding out. If they were going to try something, it would need to be coordinated perfectly.

CHAPTER 13

"Eyes forward," Silas barked.

He thumped Brina in the head with the handle of his sickle. A lightning bolt shot through her temple. Brina had half a mind to headbutt the man.

As though he had read her mind, Abrasax muttered, "Relax. We're going to be okay. Trust me."

He sounded as though he was talking to himself more than anyone else. His face was sallow again, his eyes dead. Little remained of the strength he had shown in fighting the bog lizard. It didn't matter. Brina had no choice but to have faith. Even if they miraculously freed themselves, they wouldn't make it far in this claustrophobic death trap of a swamp.

The boat tapped against the first totem pole.

Two scouts hoisted Brina from the boat and tied her wrists to the rusty ring. Coarse fibers dug into her skin, cutting off the blood flow to her hands. The rope burned like a firejelly tentacle closing around her arm. Another scout kicked Brina's feet off the edge of the boat. She fell down with a jerk, the tips of her boots kissing the water.

The full weight of her body pulled the rope unbearably tight. Brina bit her lip to keep herself from screaming. They could kill her, but they would never get to see her break.

She closed her eyes and activated *Leve*. Lowering her body weight eased just enough of the strain to allow her to think clearly.

A commotion rang out across the water. Bron was struggling against five of the scouts as they tried to force his hands above his head to tie him up.

"You traitorous, bastardous, cowardly, good-for-nothing, pale-faced, swamp-smelling..."

His eyes flared blue. One of the Morassians went sailing through the air before splashing into the lake. The others backed off, hands straying toward their sickles.

"No!" Abrasax waved his bound hands up and down. "Do not resist. Trust me."

The Biori stuck out his jaw proudly; his ginger beard rippled with sunlight. "Bron Brokenspear has never cowered before any enemy."

"I'm not asking you to cower. I'm asking you to have faith."

Bron looked sideways at Brina. There was a silent question in his eyes. Brina took a deep breath, then nodded. What else was there to do? They were too deep in the swamplands. Without a Morassian by their side to lead them out, they were doomed.

There was a metallic click as the scouts kicked Bron out of the boat to dangle by his wrists.

When all of them were tied to the poles, the scouts paddled away. They seemed eager to put as much distance as possible between themselves and the totems.

The Morassians on the surrounding pontoons began an eerie chant, led by the archdruidess, who had arrived on an ornate palanquin, held up by heavily muscled warriors with painted faces and exposed torsos. Symbols made up of red, yellow, and green stripes gleamed on their bare chests.

For a moment, nothing happened. *Maybe it's not hungry,* Brina thought.

Her hopes were dashed when three crimson dorsal fins breached the surface. Bubbles the size of human heads rose less than thirty feet away, followed by a monstrous shadow the size of a submerged house.

"What is that thing?" Sneak said. His voice shot up about two octaves. "Cap'n, you're the expert here. What do we do?"

Mossy green scales broke the surface. Brina's heart stopped. Even before the first head sprang up at them, she knew what it was.

"It's a hydra." She lifted her feet away from the water, careful not to disturb the surface. "Don't look into its eyes. Don't make any noise. It's as good as blind. If we go limp, it might not realize we're here."

"Go limp?" Sneak yelled. "Go limp and turn into Heil-damned fish food?"

He wriggled violently, causing the rings near his wrists to clatter like a dinner bell. Ominous ripples spread around the totem he was tied to.

The beast's first head sniffed at the air. It was covered in obsidian scales with bright yellow eyes. Bone spikes ran from between its eyes all the way down its spine.

Immediately, eight more heads, each the size of a fully grown ox, sprang up around them. Its eyes glowed in the early dawn. An overwhelming stench of rot and seaweed spread from its gaping maw. Rows upon rows of jagged black teeth gnashed furiously. The hydra sniffed, nine noses hell-bent on detecting the free snack it had undoubtedly learned to expect whenever the wooden totems vibrated.

On the shore, the swamp folk sank to their knees. Their chants swelled as the beast revealed itself. "Argul-Khan, Argul-Khan, Argul-Khan..."

Brina looked to the side. Abrasax's eyes were closed. He was muttering to himself as though praying. He seemed lost in his own head. She called out to him. No response came.

When one head was close enough to Brina that she could have touched it, she activated *Consol*.

CHAPTER 13

"It's okay," she said, voice low and soothing, "we're not food. We're poisonous. Look at all those other snacks behind you. Wouldn't they make a much better meal than my scrawny bones?"

The beast sniffed and shook its slimy head. It seemed confused for a moment. It obviously couldn't understand the common tongue, but Brina's tone gave it pause in the same way a snake dances to a flute.

Just as Brina was gaining influence over the beast, a high-pitched squeal tore across the roiling water. Two totems over, one of the hydra's noses was pressed against Sneak's forehead. He looked ready to throw up and cry at the same time.

The hydra's neck cocked back, mouth open to strike. A single gulp would be enough to swallow Sneak whole.

A loud clank resounded. Bron, eyes burning blue with *Forte*, broke free from his bonds and fell into the water. The hydra's head, triggered by the sudden motion, abandoned Sneak and snapped toward the place where Bron thrashed in the water.

The Biori's muscular arms closed around the creature's log-sized neck, just behind the scaly head. He clung on for dear life as the hydra tried to shake him.

Sneak blinked as though waking from a nightmare, then swung his feet up. He kicked another head right in the eye as it rose from the surface. There was an earth-shattering roar as all nine heads jerked upward.

Making use of the beast's distraction, Sneak activated *Forte* and broke free. The hydra was ready for him. It reared back just in time to avoid Sneak's grabbing arms. One of its heads slammed hard into his side. Sneak went sailing through the air and landed in the water between the nine enormous necks.

One head dove after him like an eagle spotting prey. A cloud of bubbles burst to the surface, making Brina's guts churn. She turned to Abrasax.

"Do something. Help him."

He looked back at her, bloodshot eyes wide with panic. She yelled at him again, and he gave a feeble moan. His face contorted with effort. For a brief moment, his eyes flickered purple. The sigil went out as soon as it activated. Abrasax's head slumped.

"I can't do it," he croaked. "I just can't. Not after..." He shook his head, unable to get out more words.

Fewer and fewer bubbles rose from the place where Sneak had vanished. Brina prayed he'd gotten a lungful of air before he'd gone under. Time was running out. Brina seized *Forte*, snapped the rope binding her wrists, and lunged for the nearest of the heads. Using the totem behind her as a platform to launch into a fortified jump, she was carried sideways by the momentum. In midair, she switched to *Leve* to increase the distance.

Brina's arms locked around the hydra's neck, just behind the head. She switched back into *Forte* and pummeled the hydra's head. It was like punching stone. Her knuckles tore against the hard scales, spattering blood everywhere. Growing desperate, she jammed her thumbs into a tiny hole she thought might be the creature's ears. If the hydra felt it, it didn't care.

"Over here. Come get me, you oversized trout."

For a moment, another head locked eyes with her. Then it snapped at her. Brina jumped from one neck to the other just in time to see the head she had been clinging to plummet into the water, severed. A fountain of black blood spurted everywhere.

"Don't hurt it," Abrasax yelled. "It's sacred to the Morassians. If we kill it, we're dead."

"If we kill it?" Bron roared, clinging onto one of the beast's necks. "If we kill it? How about right now, you idiot? We're one chomp away from the beyond realm."

Brina's eyes searched the water for any speck of motion that might indicate where Sneak had vanished. One of his arms flailed above the surface. He came up gasping for air, kicking and struggling to get as far away as possible.

He scampered up the nearest totem and climbed until he stood on top of it, shivering. "Thanks," he yelled at Brina, "that thing was trying to drown me."

"It still is," Brina said, waving vehemently as the hydra bucked and weaved under her vice grip. "Get away from there."

The head Brina was clasping onto lunged downward at Sneak. A second head dove for the same target. They collided with a dull thump. Brina, caught in the middle, let out a stifled scream as her body was squished between both vast skulls. If it hadn't been for *Forte*, her rib cage would've shattered like an old teapot. She tumbled, head-over-heels toward the murky surface of the swamp.

The last thing she saw before the water enveloped her were three sets of monstrous eyes swooping down after her.

"Stop!" Abrasax's voice exploded across the lake. It was deep as an earthquake and loud as thunder. A single stroke took Brina back to the surface. She looked up to find the hydra's heads circling around Abrasax, who stood atop his totem with outstretched arms. His eyes flared so brightly that his face was obscured from sight.

CHAPTER 13

The hydra ceased its thrashing. Abrasax let out a low whistle that cut through flesh and bone, striking straight at Brina's heart. A bizarre, wonderful calm came over her. Everything would be all right. There was no need to fight anymore. Peace was within reach.

Abrasax beckoned, and one of the hydra's heads lowered itself toward him. He reached out and stroked the creature's massive jaw. His mouth moved as he whispered to it, words lost in the wind.

Sneak let out a yelp as one of the hydra's heads swooped down toward his feet.

"Get on," Abrasax called out. "Don't worry. It won't hurt you."

Brina felt something slippery brush her legs as another head scooped her up out of the water. The creature stretched its neck, lifting Brina far above the surface.

A twinge of anxiety returned. If Abrasax lost control of the creature, they would all be very close to a set of teeth the length of spears. Brina glanced at her companions, who looked equally nervous.

Abrasax's eyes never wavered from the hydra's largest head as he continued to whisper soothing words, his voice resonating with the power of *Consol*. The hydra responded, occasionally releasing a low, guttural sound, as if conversing with Abrasax.

With slow, deliberate motions, the hydra began carrying them toward the pontoons where the Morassians were watching. Some looked horrified, others awestruck.

With every twist and turn of the creature's neck, Brina felt her heart leap into her throat, her trust in Abrasax's control of the creature pushed to the limit.

Sweat beaded on Abrasax's forehead, his face contorted with concentration. The hydra's heads began to sway and undulate, as if struggling against his control. Brina felt a growing sense of unease, her grip on the slippery scales tightening.

With a sudden jerk, the head tipped sideways, and Brina fell onto the pontoon. She spluttered as the wind was knocked out of her, her already bruised ribs exploding with agony. Sneak and Bron rained down beside her.

All three of them got up and tried to back away, only to bump into Archdruidess Evana's guards, who were insistent on keeping them in place, evidently hoping the hydra would change its mind.

With bated breath, they watched as Abrasax's eyes glowed brighter, and the hydra's movements calmed once again. One by one, its heads disappeared below the surface, until only the creature's vast shadow could be seen receding toward the center of the lake.

"Argul Khan has reached judgment," Abrasax told Evana. The second his eyes returned to their regular shade of amber, he crumpled. Brina rushed forward to support him. She glared at Evana, who seemed dumbstruck.

Evana stared at them for what felt like hours. Then she shouted out, "Judgment has been reached. Argul Khan has deemed our visitors worthy."

The Morassians burst into a renewed chant of "Argul-Khan…"

Evana bent low so only Brina and Abrasax could hear. "You got lucky. I know your kind. Get yourselves cleaned up. You reek of swamp and death."

CHAPTER 14

olana shuffled along the overgrown jungle path, exhausted but satisfied. Her strength was returning. Heil hadn't abandoned her just yet. She ducked a low branch and smiled. Her echolocation was as good as it had ever been. Whether it was the constant practice in dense foliage or the fact that Lypsa fed her three square meals a day, Solana had recuperated faster than she would have believed possible.

The smell of salt and seaweed drifted on the air as she emerged from the tree line, heading straight for the lone dune upon which Lypsa's shack stood. As she approached, bare feet sinking deep into the loose white sand, the rich scent of frying seafood greeted her nostrils. Her stomach rumbled. She hadn't eaten since she left the cabin that morning. She'd been too entranced in her prayers to have room in her mind for anything else.

"Look what the leviathan dragged in," Lypsa said with a grin as Solana closed the door behind her. "I thought I'd lost you. What do you even do out there every day? There are safer and more pleasant places to go for a walk than this spider-infested tangle of a jungle."

Solana shrugged. "It's good to be in nature. Makes me feel closer to…"

She had almost said Heil's name out loud for the first time since she'd woken up in Lypsa's hut. So far, she had done her best to keep her connection to the church secret. The way Solana saw it, there were only two outcomes such a revelation could have. Neither appealed to her. Either Lypsa was devoted to the church, in which case she'd wonder why a Reynziel like Solana found herself this far away from Mallion's Depth and the Cardinal's command. Or Lypsa was a heathen, in which case she likely had more than one grievance with Solana's former employer.

Lypsa let out a laugh somewhere between a bark and a howl, amused by Solana's discomfort.

"Oh, come on," she said. "You think I haven't figured out what you are by now?"

Solana's fingers crept to the prayer book tucked away in the inside pocket of her robes. "What do you mean, what I am?"

"I may be old and stranded on a forsaken mound of sand, but old Lypsa used to be more than a hermit. Years ago, I traveled my share, and saw and experienced more than enough. I knew what you were when I dragged you out of the water."

"Then why did you save me?" To her embarrassment, Solana noticed a guilty undertone in her voice. As though she were no longer proud to have served the church with all her soul for many years. *Heil forgive me. I will never renounce you.*

"For one, because you would have drowned. Where I come from, leaving people to die is considered poor manners. Second, I figured if someone in your position could grow so thin and weathered, you were either on the run, or they had abandoned you. In either case, I didn't think you would turn me over to that scepter-waving lunatic in Mallion's Depth."

Solana opened her mouth to defend the Cardinal's honor, then closed it again. She had wasted too much breath on that man. Wasn't the fourth tenet of Heilinism that one should not lie or obscure the truth with sophisms and deceit?

Lypsa stirred her pan of frying squid. She added a dash of sea salt and fresh lemon grass, then cast a sly glance over her shoulder. "So, which of the two is it?"

"I don't know," Solana admitted. In a sense, she was on the run, but hadn't the church abandoned her first? It had been sheer luck, combined with her own indomitable will to live, that had carried her to this very moment. For months, she had survived off roots she dug up with her bare hands and fish trapped in tide pools. Not a single person, not one red-sailed ship, searched for her.

"It hardly matters one way or the other," Lypsa said. She grabbed two bowls from a cupboard above the fireplace and scooped a generous helping of boiled roots, baked potatoes, and fried squid into each. Two wooden spoons thumped against the kitchen table. "What matters now, dear girl, is what you will do next. Have you figured out that much? Or is that why you spend all your days isolated in the depths of the jungle?"

Solana remained silent, scooping spoonful after spoonful into her hungry mouth. She hadn't realized she'd been starving until food was right in front of her. It was delicious, and for a moment, all else disappeared from her mind.

Afterward, as she stared into her empty bowl, a hollow feeling filled Solana.

CHAPTER 14

What would she do? Her first thoughts went to her mother, who she hadn't been able to contact since her supposed death.

Then she thought of Everberg and Brother Wilhelm. He'd been good to her in the short time they spent together. Even though it had been he who had removed Solana's eyes, forever altering the course of her life, he had guided her through every step of the process and had made her into something far more powerful than she had ever dreamed she could be.

Those days were gone. Neither Everberg nor her mother could ever learn that she was still alive. As soon as Cardinal De Leliard found out, he would accuse Solana of desertion, withdraw the mandatory martyr funds that her mother received every month, and Solana would spend the rest of her living days in God's Maul. She was certain of it.

Even though her love for the Keeper hadn't waned for a single moment, the church had put her in an impossible position. Not even Brother Wilhelm could protect her from the Cardinal's wrath. The Cardinal had used her as a puppet and discarded her. Once he figured out that she was alive and had neglected to return to him, his anger would be fearsome.

"I have nowhere to go," Solana said, breaking the icy silence that had formed in Lypsa's shack. "I have no one."

As she heard those words out loud, something inside her broke. She had known the true nature of her situation for a long time, but it wasn't until this moment, until another living soul heard the words from Solana's own mouth, that she accepted the reality of it.

"Oh, I doubt that's true," Lypsa said with inappropriate cheer. She got up, gathered their bowls and spoons, and dropped them in a bucket of saltwater in a corner.

"How could you possibly know that?" Anger bubbled up in Solana's voice. "I might as well be dead for all the chances I have of getting back my old life. Who I was then can never exist again. Too many people would suffer. So please," Solana snapped, her face growing hot as her sadness turned to fury on the way out, "tell me what I missed, stranger who knows nothing about my life."

"I know," Lypsa said with a smile, "because the Keeper kept you alive. She isn't done with you.

"So, you serve a purpose. One that may only become apparent in the future, but if there's one thing I have learned in my time, it is that Heil, as we call her, Argul-Khan as the Morassians call her, or the Mountain Mother the Heemians worship, never acts without forethought. She strives above all to keep life on this strange and mysterious plane in harmony. She strives for balance."

Solana frowned, unsure of what to think of this. Lypsa spoke like one educated in the finer points of Heilinism, and yet she put Heil's holy name into one sentence alongside the idols of the heathens. It was a strange juxtaposition. One that would have had any scholar outwalled from Mallion's Depth in a heartbeat.

Still, there was a grain of truth buried somewhere in those words. Solana could feel it in the same part of her that had opened its eyes when Brother Wilhelm had exposed her to the transcendent fumes at Everberg Abbey.

For a single moment, she had seen everything and known everything. Before she had had the chance to grasp this knowledge with both hands, it had slipped away again like water receding at low tide. But, just like the ocean shapes the beach, the receding of that knowledge had drawn deep grooves upon her soul.

"Even if you are right, and the Keeper has spared me to fulfill some higher duty to her creation, where would I begin?"

Lypsa nodded. "It's not easy, I admit it. Ask yourself this: Where does your love for the Keeper and her creation reside?"

"I don't understand," Solana said. "It's not a physical thing, not something I could keep strapped to my back and carry with me throughout the world. It isn't anywhere."

"Is it born out of thought?" Lypsa looked at her, and for a moment, Solana was sad that all color was absent from her vision of the world. She could only make out a rippling outline of a head.

"No," Solana answered after a moment. "I don't think it is. It is not some philosophical proof. It could not be dissuaded by rational thought. It's deeper than a theory someone could subscribe to, only to cast it aside once disproved. Thought is of the material world, rooted in the limitations imposed on us by our own minds. My devotion to the Keeper runs deeper."

"Then is it a matter of the heart?" Lypsa seemed to be enjoying herself now. She leaned closer to Solana, drinking in every word of her replies. Solana's fingers ran across the scar tissue in her hollow eye sockets. She tried to find the words to explain.

"I don't think so," she said, hesitant. "It is love in a way, but not in the way one loves a friend or a lover. It is not passion, not something that flares hot and can then grow cold the very next day."

"The heart is easily wounded, and through it, we wound others. My devo-

CHAPTER 14

tion to the Keeper is more stable than that. It simply exists, every moment of every day, in every situation. I feel it in the sun setting over the Sundered Sea. I feel it in the breaching of a pod of whales, and I hear it in the song of birds as I march through the jungle."

"Then where does it originate?" Lypsa urged, pushing Solana to the inevitable conclusion.

"My love for the Keeper is of the soul. It exists in my very being. If I were struck down by a mace, shattering every coherent part of my mind, I would still love her. If I were tied upside down to a tree to await the gallows, and she did not lift a finger to save me, I would still love her. Because it is through her that I exist."

"Exactly." Lypsa's chair creaked as she leaned back. "Now, if I were you, I would begin looking for my purpose in the place where that feeling is at its strongest. Where you feel most at peace with the world. Life has a way of illuminating the path one step at a time. It's only a matter of taking that first step."

Luna. A harsh claw seized Solana's heart as the face of her sister appeared in her mind's eye. Unlike the world of vague gray she inhabited these days, this image was full of color and life. She watched as the two of them went cliff diving together. Only children, desperate to experience the thrill of the free fall. Then the scene turned to horror, when she remembered how she'd all but murdered her own blood last time they'd come face to face in Doorstep's Ditch. Luna had been unrecognizable, but her voice had been the same. Solana hadn't been able to get it out of her head since. It was the most grievous sin she'd ever committed. Acted out under direct orders of the holiest man in the physical world. Only now did she realize just how deeply she had wounded not only her sibling that day, but herself.

"I see you've thought of something that makes you feel close to Heil's light," Lypsa said. "I'd seize that feeling with both hands if I were you."

CHAPTER 15

ane was beginning to learn that being a hostage was boring. He'd spent most of the past week in a dusty attic room above the shamanka's apothecary, with nothing but a stack of Sachrya's old books for company.

At first, these guides on exotic herbs and plants had been fascinating. Wane had spent hours upon hours researching deadly poisons made from common and unassuming weeds. After that, he'd delved into the love potions the Hawqallian rulers brewed for their lovers.

After a few days, however, even that novelty had worn off. Wane found himself staring out of the small window of his room into the busy street below, craving the excitement, noise, and fresh air that only the outside world could offer.

He played a game with himself, trying to see how many pickpockets he could spot in the street below. Today, he was up to seven, though he might have counted a small boy with thick black hair twice. All of them had sloppy technique. Wane's fingers itched with the urge to show them how it was done.

Just as he was fiddling with the lock on his window, gauging how hard it would be to pick, the door to the attic room swung open.

Sachrya stood in the doorway, her shaved head gleaming in the sunlight. Her face was radiant as always. His heart skipped a beat, and not because he had almost been caught trying to escape.

The shamanka's eyes flickered from the padlock on the window, which was still swaying back and forth suspiciously, to Wane. An amused smile curled her lips.

"I have need of your skills, boy," she said. Her voice was light but authoritative, like wind whipping across the sea, pulling ships off course. She beckoned him to follow and turned on her heel. Wane heard the receding thunks of her heels on the wooden staircase.

Wane slid off his bed, jolted into action by the prospect of a change of

CHAPTER 15

scenery. He had too much energy to be locked away for long. He was built for running the streets and filling his own pockets with the contents of others'.

So far, he'd been allowed to join Sachrya in the shop below every day for dinner. Given that he wasn't so much a captive as a voluntary piece of collateral, she had shared her meals with him. Those few hours they spent together each night had been highly informative.

Wane suspected Sachrya was involved in much more than the mere procuring and selling of herbs. For one, she had a keen interest in the lucrative underworld of Merkede. Over the past week, cloaked figures had crossed her doorstep on an almost nightly basis.

Wane had overheard tantalizing fragments of conversation but never enough to piece together anything concrete. His fingertips tingled at the thought of learning more. That the job she had for him might be dangerous only added to the thrill.

He descended the stairs and stepped into a small sitting room behind the store. It was sparsely furnished, with two leather sacks resting on a fine rug. A small table stood against the wall, holding a wooden rack filled with scrolls of parchment. Wooden shelves lined the walls, displaying dozens of glass and clay containers filled with various poisons, herbs, roots, and fungi.

Sachrya sat down on one of the leather sacks, which seemed to melt away beneath her, taking the shape of her form as she sat. She reached for a teapot on a spindly table beside her and poured two cups of a magenta liquid that smelled of flowers. She extended one cup to Wane, who took it and sat down across from the shamanka. Although he had little desire to sit after being locked in his room all day, he had to admit the sacks were comfortable.

"I gather you are adept at sneaking around. Is that correct?" Sachrya's eyes narrowed as she stared at him.

Wane nodded. Anything was better than another night stuck with the moldy books in the room upstairs. Besides, whatever business the shamanka was involved in was bound to be fascinating. He took a sip of his tea, which tasted like rosebuds and almond.

"Excellent," Sachrya replied. "You are a sharp boy. Undoubtedly, you have by now realized my dealings are not limited to the confines of this shop." She gave him a meaningful look over the top of her glasses and sipped her own tea. Wane nodded once more.

"Last week, an associate of mine by the name of Octavian Drago saw fit to betray me. A shipment of delicate goods meant for both of us disappeared from under my very nose. Though the imbecile denies any involvement, I know it was him. No one else would know what to do with them."

Wane took a nervous gulp of his tea. This business sounded more high-stakes than what he had in mind. Snatching a pouch of coins was one thing. Involving himself in a criminal rivalry was sure to put a target on his back. Once again, however, his curiosity got the better of him. "What do you mean, 'do with them'?"

"I had ordered half a dozen freshly caught scolopendrae from the desert for a very special client who commissioned them from me."

"Scolo-what?"

"Scolopendrae." Sachrya's nostrils flared. "A large, fast, and venomous species of centipede."

"Centipedes?" Wane made an involuntary face. "What on earth would anyone want those for?"

Sachrya raised her eyebrows. "A good businesswoman doesn't ask. A good client doesn't tell."

She grabbed a scroll from the nearby table and unfurled it on her lap, revealing an intricate map of the city of Merkede. Every building in the city was marked. It must have taken hundreds of hours to create and even more shards to purchase.

Sachrya's index finger landed on a section of the city that was no more than a ten-minute walk from the apothecary. Did she expect him to steal back the scolopendrae? The hairs on the back of his neck stood up as he imagined scooping up a handful of centipedes and sticking them in his pocket.

Some of his concern must have shown on his face, because Sachrya shushed him. "Don't worry, boy. I don't expect you to return them to me. I've already ordered replacements. All I need is for you to be my little twist of fate."

Her eyes lit up with sudden anger, and a malicious smile curled the shamanka's lips. Wane's heart raced. "Scolopendrae need to be kept in a solid glass container. Tonight, one of Drago's henchmen will forget to seal the container after feeding. *Oops.*"

"You want me to set them free?"

Sachrya nodded. "If you do it right, no one need ever know it wasn't an accident."

"But what if those centipedes sting someone?"

A tinkling laugh echoed through the sitting room. "What they do after you leave is not your concern."

Wane's mouth had gone dry. He'd been looking forward to a bit of sport. Some spying or thieving would have been a nice change of pace. But this?

CHAPTER 15

Sachrya believed those scolopendrae would wreak havoc once they escaped. Setting them free would be as good as murder.

"What's in it for me?" To his surprise, his tone sounded firm, almost professional.

Sachrya's eyebrows lifted. "For you? You entered my service willingly."

Wane shook his head. "I agreed to stay here as collateral. It seems to me that if you're going to involve me in business that could get me sentenced to hang, there ought to be an extra incentive."

Sachrya let out a tinkling laugh. "My, my. The boy is a businessman. Go ahead, what were you thinking of?"

Wane closed his eyes. He hadn't expected to get this far. "How about I get to keep your book on poisons? The one upstairs."

Sachrya raised a single eyebrow. "Taking an interest in the poisoning arts, are we?"

Wane shrugged. "Never hurts to be prepared."

Sachrya extended her hand, which he shook. "Deal. Now go, but be warned. If you get yourself caught, I won't know who you are."

Wane stood up, his whole body buzzing with a strange mixture of adrenaline and dread. Was he really going to do this? It was almost unbelievable to think that he would be able to walk out of here with nothing but Sachrya's trust that he would come back. His hand closed around the door handle. He was almost free.

"Oh, and by the way, boy."

"Yes?"

"That tea you just drank was laced with a slow-acting poison. A recipe from that book you love so much. If you don't return to me within forty-eight hours, your hair will fall out, followed by your fingernails, until your heart stops on the fifth day. If you're interested in receiving this antidote"—she held out a small crystal bottle containing a blue liquid—"you'd better do as you promised. But I'm sure that won't be a problem."

"Of course," he stammered, "not a problem at all. I wouldn't dream of betraying your trust."

As he snuck out into the nighttime streets of Merkede, Wane cursed himself. He should have asked for more than that stupid book.

Between the risk of capture, death, and the lethal poison that was seeping into his veins, he was pulling more weight than could be compensated with a pile of parchment.

Though he was in a tough spot, he noticed that the feeling in his chest wasn't quite fear. It was exhilaration. This wasn't the first time he had come to this realization. It was one of the main reasons he had become such a good thief in the first place.

Where other kids his age felt panic or sadness in a dangerous situation, Wane had always felt strangely energized. As though the prospect of injury and punishment was just as much of a reward as the reward itself.

He made his way down to the dockyard, dipping into side alleys, the hood of his cloak drawn deep over his face. Even though most Merkedian pickpockets were sloppy idiots, those who were bad at stealing pouches in silence often resorted to violence at the end of an unproductive day. With a small five-foot-three frame, Wane would seem an ideal target for any coward with a knife in his pocket and hunger in his belly.

As he passed one of the sailors' inns, close enough to the dock front to smell the silt of the sea mixing in with the stench of urine and excrement, a woman no younger than fifty waved a wrinkled hand at him, beckoning him in for a good time. He lowered his hood, showing her his youthful face. The woman shrank back, a blush appearing on her face. Wane chuckled. It always tickled him when he could toy with people.

He reached his destination at the end of the darkest, dirtiest road in the entire city. It was the last warehouse before the terrain turned into the hillsides of the mountain, atop which stood a crumbling lighthouse. Wane shuddered as he took in the warehouse's boarded-up windows and mossy facade. The roof groaned eerily in the breeze coming in from the sea, as though the building was greeting him.

CHAPTER 16

n oil lantern shone in Zot's eyes, blinding him. He sat on a splintering wooden floor. His hands were tied to a metal hook attached to the floor, forcing him into an uncomfortable hunched position. The place smelled of rank sweat and moldering straw.

The beam of light turned aside, and Zot could make out the profile of the two constables as they made their way back to the other side of the room.

"Hey, wait!" he shouted as the last of them was about to close the door, leaving him in the dark. "Where am I? Why am I here?" He didn't expect a genuine answer, but their reaction would give him at least some hint as to whether his suspicions were true.

One of them strode back into the room and slapped him in the face. Though the blow stung, Zot forced himself to look the man straight in the eye. He had an unusually scruffy beard for a lawman. Thick scars on his face told Zot this man was no stranger to a knife fight.

It was possible that the local constabulary had hired a man with a reputation for being a skilled street fighter, but no officer he knew would allow a subordinate to wear his uniform so sloppily. Buttons were missing on the man's vest, and his trousers were caked in a layer of white mud that had seemingly been building up for weeks.

The man kneeled down, holding up the lantern in Zot's face. The heat seared his forehead, forcing his eyes shut.

"You will wait here until our chief returns." His voice was a low slur, as though he'd suffered one too many concussions.

"And who might that be?" Zot demanded. "My name is Dimimzy Zot, and I think you will find that you have made a big mistake. A very big mistake, indeed."

"Oh no," the oaf replied, shaking his brutish head. "I don't think so, Master Zot. The chief was very specific about who he wanted."

Zot swallowed. Was this unknown chief someone who Zot had wronged in the past? Or a new party hoping to squeeze a few last drops of blood out of his dry carcass?

"But the innkeeper... why?" The soles of Zot's boots were still sticky with the man's blood.

"We need to make our profit as well, don't we? The chief won't mind, not as long as we got his prize alongside our own."

A high-pitched chuckle came from the second man in the doorway. He sounded like a rat who'd learned to speak the common tongue. *These buffoons are not constables.*

"Come on, Rufus," Ratman squeaked. "Let's celebrate."

With one final slap around Zot's head, Rufus stepped away. The door slammed shut behind them, and darkness engulfed Zot. Nausea churned his stomach. Wherever he was, the Merkedian constabulary had nothing to do with it. There were no laws to protect him, and he had no funds left to negotiate his way out of this mess.

The complete darkness made loosening the knots around his wrists harder. He rubbed them against each other, trying to find weaknesses. They might as well have been blocks of obsidian.

Zot groaned. Just when he thought he had it all—money to buy the boy's freedom, an entire brick of wakeroot left to sell for his own profit, and the foundations of a new network—everything had been snatched away from right under his nose.

Even worse, there was no doubt in his mind that whoever had ordered his capture had unsavory plans for him. Zot himself was no stranger to having a rival snatched up off the streets with a bag over their head. Those occasions had rarely ended well for the kidnapped party.

With desperation setting in, Zot twisted his limbs into an uncomfortable knot to get his teeth close enough to the floor to chew at the rope around his wrists. He had to get out of here while his limbs were still firmly attached.

After a few minutes, his jaw was cramped and tired, while the rope remained unaffected by his gnashing. He spat a mouthful of irritating fibers on the floor and took a deep breath. It had been decades since he'd allowed anyone to scare him, and he wasn't about to relapse into old habits.

Anger fueled his renewed efforts. He jerked the rope back and forth between his aching teeth, picking at the smallest fibers he could bite. Slowly, he made just enough progress to move his wrists, allowing him to use his fingernails to give his teeth some rest.

He thanked the seven patron saints of the outwalled that the men who'd

CHAPTER 16

picked him up were morons. Anyone in their right minds would have used iron manacles, from which escape would've been impossible.

A few frantic minutes later, Zot felt the satisfying snap of the rope between his wrists. There was a bright tinkle as the metal ring clattered to the floor. His heart skipped a beat. That had been loud.

Zot got to his feet, tiptoed across the room, and put his ear against the door. On the other side, all was silent except for the occasional thump of clay mugs on a wooden table. *Good.*

The flickering light entering through a crack under the door illuminated a pile of crates in the corner. Zot lifted the lid off the top one. It was empty, save for a peculiar sour stench that wafted from it, like flatulence escaping a corpse.

Anxious to keep the smell from spreading, Zot was about to replace the lid when he hesitated. He positioned himself with his back to the wall beside the door, clutching the heavy wooden lid in both of his hands.

Given his small stature and slender limbs, he wouldn't amount to much in a fight. The comfort of always having hired soldiers to take care of his business had made him soft. Zot leaned back against the wall and waited.

CHAPTER 17

ane crouched behind a barrel underneath one of the warehouse's drainage pipes. The muddy alley he was in smelled like a public latrine, which it probably was.

Now and then, he mustered the courage to peer over the barrel's edge toward the double wooden doors that marked the warehouse's entrance. A drop of icy water plunked down on his forehead. He dropped back down onto the ground, heart pounding. For a second, he thought they'd caught him.

Being locked up in Sachrya's warm, safe attic didn't seem as bad as it had only an hour or two ago. If he had to choose between boredom and death… well, maybe the choice wasn't so clear-cut after all.

He'd just have to be silent. That was all. If he could sneak in and out unseen, everything would be fine. If blades came into play, he was a dead boy.

A dead man, he reminded himself. This was a grown man's business, and if he was going to stick his nose into it, he'd better start thinking of himself as one. Just as he was feeling at ease, squelching footsteps broke the silence. Someone was out there. Though he didn't dare look over the barrel to see who it was, the clinking of metal on metal and a pair of low grunting voices formed the picture of two armed goons in his mind. Thunderous knocks against the shabby wooden doors resounded in Wane's chest.

A muffled yell came from inside the warehouse.

"Right, right, the password. The bloody password," a woman's voice barked.

"What are you looking at me for, then?" the second voice, male, asked. He sounded almost insulted, as though his colleague had inquired about the length of his trouser snake. "I don't got a clue, do I?"

There was a sigh, a few moments of silence, then the woman's voice rang out into the night: "The blunt blade's edge."

With a groan of rusty hinges, the wooden doors opened. Wane leaned sideways, stealing a glance around the corner. Two men stepped outside, holding the doors as the visitors hurried inside. The two guards cast hasty

CHAPTER 17

glances left and right before slamming the doors shut again.

Deadbolts rattled into place, followed by the clicks and pops of the lock. There was no getting in that way. Not because of the locks, but because of who was behind them. There were at least four of them now.

Over the years, Wane had gotten into a few scraps with the other children at Madame Arturia's home, but those had been fought with fists, never sharpened steel. This wasn't the time to practice. He would have to find some other way to get inside.

As yet another icy drop of rainwater splashed on top of his head, an idea trickled down to the small of his back.

The drainpipe rattled as he grabbed hold of it. It had come undone from the main wall about halfway up, causing the lower half to wobble back and forth when he pulled on it. One false move would be enough to break it.

The fall itself might be survivable, but the racket he would make as he cascaded to the ground would ruin tonight's plan. He would have to return to Sachrya with bad news. She didn't seem the type to take that kind of disappointment in stride.

Wane looked over his shoulders at the distant glow of lights in Merkede's bustling center. Mere minutes away, people were drinking, singing, carousing, fighting, and having an all-around great time.

And here he was, one mistake away from being discovered by a group of armed gang members. The idea of what they could do to him made the hairs on the back of his neck stand up.

He'd been a kid on the streets of Mallion's Depth for too long not to know that being killed would be the very best outcome he could hope for. Then again, what choice did he have? Sachrya's poison coursed through his bloodstream. His heartbeat was a clock in his chest, ticking away the hours he had left.

If only he knew where to find Zot. He'd know what to do. He had a thousand connections in a thousand shady places, and if there was anyone who could get his hands on an antidote in time, it was him.

Wane gritted his teeth and grabbed the drainage pipe with both hands. He rolled his shoulders one last time, then made that mental click that he had been practicing for years. Everything went quiet.

The alley dissipated around him. No thought of the bandits or their shiny, sharp weapons could reach him. He was in action mode.

With slow, deliberate movements, he pulled himself up. The tips of his leather boots inched into cracks in the masonry. The pipe groaned and tilted as he pulled himself up, but it held.

When he reached the roof's edge, he grabbed hold of the copper gutter, legs wrapped around the drainpipe. As he let go, trying to swing one leg up onto the roof, his left hand caught behind a rusty edge. He bit his lip to stifle a scream. Hot blood splattered down his forearm. His slick palm slipped away, leaving him dangling forty feet above the alley by a single hand.

The gutter tilted forward with the squeal of bending copper. Wane reached up, forcing himself to close his wounded hand against the dirty metal. He had to act while the adrenaline shielded him from the worst of the pain.

With a mighty heave, he flung his heel upward into the gutter and rolled himself onto the roof, where he lay panting, inches from the edge.

He let out a relieved chuckle. Looking down made his head spin. The alley below was just one thread of a spider's web of black shadows in the illuminated nighttime city. Countless roofs stretched out before him in a pattern of squares and rectangles. Here and there, large patches of shingles were missing, exposing the wooden beams below like the ribs of a decaying beast.

That gave him an idea.

He crawled along the top of the roof, taking care to only put his weight on the supporting beams holding the mossy clay shingles. When he reached the top, he pulled himself forward until he was right above the door where the two men had entered.

His fingers trembled as he pried loose a shingle. He laid it down beside him as though he were handling a bomb. If he dropped it, it would be as good as a warning bell announcing his presence. A hole opened up in the roof as he repeated the process. Soon, a dusty attic came into view.

Lantern light drifted up through slits between the floorboards. Raucous laughter exploded on the warehouse's ground floor in sharp bursts, intermingled with the clanks of mugs slammed into wood.

Wane burned *Lux* and stuck his head into the attic. Coils of damp rope lay rotting in one corner, while the other was taken up with cobwebbed crates. In the center of the attic, the top of a ladder protruded through an open trapdoor.

Wane chipped away at the hole in the roof, piling up the loosened shingles behind him. When it was just large enough for him to squeeze through, he reached for the nearest support beam with his good hand. He swaddled his bleeding right hand in his sleeve, trying to stem the flow of blood so as not to leave a trail of spatter that could lead back to him later.

As he lowered himself into the hole, his bloody hand slipped, causing his

CHAPTER 17

body to swing off balance. He tried to cling on with his good hand, but he could feel the fibers of the wood splinter under his fingertips as he was carried sideways. He crashed into the dusty floor with a thud.

The noise from the gang members below died.

"What?" an annoyed voice barked. "What's it this time, Atticus? I told you, lay off the cloud. It makes you paranoid, man."

"I heard something," Atticus replied. "Up there."

Heart racing, Wane crawled as silently as he could toward the other end of the attic, away from the ladder that would lead the gang members straight to him. Piles of rat droppings littered the floor, squishing and smearing underneath his weight as he crawled along. Wane gagged.

The stench was overwhelming, and it was all over him. He locked his jaw to avoid retching, forcing himself onward.

"Of course you heard something, idiot. The loft is swarming with vermin. Rats, owls, geckos. When we swept the place, we even found a fox's skeleton up there."

"This was different," Atticus insisted. "Sounded heavier."

"Everything sounds different to you; it's the drugs getting to your already tiny brain."

There was a round of howls and hoots from the group, and the man named Atticus fell silent. Moments later, the sound of drunks playing cards swelled again.

Wane let out a sigh of relief. *Dimwits. Bunch of marvelously, beautifully moronic buffoons.*

If they'd bothered to check the attic, he'd have been cornered. But over his years as a small-time thief in Mallion's Depth, Wane had learned that those drawn to a life of criminal servitude tended to take little pride in their work.

They were the type to live from one payout to the next. Once they'd been paid, they couldn't help but drink, whore, and gamble away their handful of gems at record speeds. Rinse and repeat.

Wane reached the far end of the attic and was delighted to find a second ladder that led to a dark landing on the second floor. A flight of wooden stairs to Wane's right was illuminated with flickering lantern light from the room below, while a single wooden door straight ahead led into the rest of the second floor.

Wane slipped down from the loft like a shadow. He kneeled beside the keyhole, but his *Lux*-fueled eyes could only make out a series of thick cobwebs hanging in the four corners of the rooms, and the outline of a pile of boxes in the far corner. They were too far away to see if they bore the triangular rune he was looking for.

He withdrew his tools of the trade from an inside pocket, his hands slippery with nervous sweat. Technically, they were Sneak's tools. The experienced thief had spent many an afternoon with Wane last year when they had been trapped in De Malheur's castle north of Barrow's Perch. He had taught Wane how to open simple locks. Wane had taken to it quickly because of the boredom of being holed up in a dusty castle for days on end.

He'd been delighted when he'd unlocked the first padlock Sneak had given him as a practice project. It was an exhilarating feeling, like solving a puzzle someone else had left for you. Of course, there was the additional enticement of the knowledge that, usually, treasure lay beyond.

That had been a year ago, though, and Wane was all but sure that his fledgling skills could help him unlock this.

To his delight, however, a few seconds of poking around inside the keyhole with the lock pick revealed that the lock was an old and cheap one. It could be unlocked with any object that had three prongs.

He fidgeted inside the lock, triggering each of the three cylinders in turn. Then he pulled on the lock, and with a sigh of satisfaction, Wane pushed open the door.

He stepped inside, and as he tried to silently close the door behind him, something heavy hit his shoulders. There was just enough time to register the top of his head exploding with white-hot pain. Then everything faded around him. The last thing Wane felt was his knees hitting the wooden floor with a crack.

CHAPTER 18

"Ba, got him." Zot looked down at the limp form of the unconscious goon with satisfaction. His plan had worked.

He kneeled down beside the guard's slim form and ran his hands through the man's pockets. The guard was a small man, with a slim build for someone hired to perpetrate kidnappings.

To Zot's dismay, the guard carried no weapon. The only thing he found, still clutched in the man's hand, was a set of lock picks.

A queasy feeling spread across the bottom of Zot's stomach. He wedged the tip of his boot underneath the man's shoulders and lifted. When he saw Harrod Wane's face, he slapped a hand to his forehead.

A million questions forced their way to the front of his mind at once, clamoring over each other like beggars fighting for a stray coin. He slapped the kid in the face. Wane didn't stir.

Footsteps thumped up the stairs outside the door.

"I told you," someone yelled. "I told you I heard something."

Zot panicked. In the split-second he had before the door swung open, he did the only thing he could think of. He lifted Wane's body so that the boy's face was pressed into his chest. Holding one of the blunt lock picks against the boy's neck, he took a few steps back. As the door burst open, a now unmasked man with a face that looked much like a crab froze in the doorway. He clutched a shiny but bent dagger in his right hand.

"Drop it," Zot barked. "Or your man is as good as dead."

Crabface looked from the back of Wane's head to Zot's determined eyes, back over his shoulder, and back again. After what felt like an eternity, the dagger clattered to the ground with a clink.

"Now kick it over here." Zot emphasized the point by prodding the lock pick into Wane's neck. Crabface kicked the dagger, holding up his hands. Zot stooped to pick up the dagger and slid the lock pick back into his own pocket.

"Go on. What are you waiting for?" a low voice barked at Crabface. A broad-shouldered man shoved his way into the room, pushing Crabface aside. "What in the…?"

"He's got one of ours," Crabface bellowed. "Don't approach him."

Broadshoulders' face turned to rage. "How can he have one of ours? All five of us were downstairs, weren't we?"

"I guess so," Crabface said, his eyes blank.

"Then who can he have? It's a trick, you idiot."

A flash of anger crossed Crab's pointy face as he realized he'd been played. "Oh, that is not so nice. I can't believe you did that." He looked up at Zot with genuine disappointment.

As Broadshoulders and Crabface approached Zot, the other goons charged through the door.

Oh, crap.

Realizing that the jig was up, Zot dropped Wane and moved into a fighting stance. His chances of winning were as slim as walking back into Mallion's Depth and claiming the Cardinal's throne for himself, but if he could break just one more nose before his untimely demise, it would all be worth it.

Broadshoulders was the first to lunge. Zot's subconscious took over. He sidestepped the lunge and swiped his dagger across Broadshoulders' forearm.

The man let out a bellow and turned, attempting to jab his own dagger at Zot's back. It was only through sheer luck that the man skidded on a piece of hay at the last moment, causing the strike to go wide. Crabface was next, enraged by the fact that he'd been deceived.

Zot dodged the man's first punch aimed at his temple. Before he could make use of the temporary opening in the man's defense, two more of his captors surrounded him, leaving only one way to go. Backward.

Zot's heart rate spiked. He was getting too old for this. On the bright side, it didn't look like he would get much older. He kicked at Crabface's chin and connected. A loud snap was followed by a howl of pain as the man doubled over, clutching his face.

That still left three muscular, angry goons approaching. Zot took a step backward and felt his back hit the wooden wall. His heart sank. He raised his hands, dropping his dagger in surrender. He was cornered.

"I'm sorry," he said. "Escape instinct and all that. You guys understand. I bet all of you have been in jail, right?"

It was the wrong thing to say.

"What, you calling us some kind of criminals?" Broadshoulders asked, his dim eyes focused on Zot, filled with watery rage.

CHAPTER 18

"Well, no," Zot stammered, looking for a way out. "You are very distinguished fellows, to be sure. All I was trying to say is..."

***

Wane's head felt like it had been used as a doorstopper in a busy inn. He opened his eyes and saw four shadowy figures on the other side of the room. All of them had their backs turned toward him, except for one—a small man in the corner with his hands raised, pleading for his life.

Wane burned *Lux*, and when he recognized Dimimzy Zot's sharp features, his heart dropped into his stomach.

He crawled away as quietly as he could. There was a slap of flesh on flesh as a woman punched Zot in the side of the head.

The small man went down, and the three goons ganged up on him. Wane wanted to get up and fight, but he had no weapon, and faced with three grown fighters, he'd get knocked about like a sheet of parchment in a storm.

Wane's hands closed around a clump of hay, a thick layer of which lay strewn across the floor as some sort of improvised bedding. He knew what he had to do. It would be risky, but time was running out. Grabbing as much of the hay in both of his hands as he could, he summoned what little concentration he had left and tried to focus on the triangular rune that made up *Gnis*.

The hay smoked in his hands, then caught fire. The light was blinding in the gloom of the warehouse. He threw the hay into the opposite corner, as far away from himself as he could. Smoke filled the room.

"Fire!" Atticus yelled. "Fire!"

The others turned around, momentarily forgetting about Zot as they tried to stamp out the growing fire with their boots. Wane jumped up, reached for Zot's arms, and pulled him toward the door.

They were all but invisible in the smoke, and it would be a matter of minutes before the entire warehouse would be engulfed in flames. Zot and Wane sprinted down the steps and into the warehouse's main room, where the gang members had been playing cards.

They rushed toward the door, and with a jolt of relief, Wane saw the giant steel key that unlocked the front doors was still lodged in the keyhole. As the doors creaked open, he heard Atticus call out.

"Stop! They're getting away through the front door!"

Without a backward glance, Wane and Zot sprinted into the night, weaving from one alley to the next, circling back, and taking different routes to confuse anyone trying to follow them.

They didn't rest for a full hour. By the time they felt comfortable enough to sit, both clutching at stitches in their sides, they had reached the edge of the city on the opposite side of the warehouse.

As they trudged up a wooded hillside, they could see the large plume of smoke that had once been the warehouse. Wane prayed the flames wouldn't jump from one building to the next, catching innocent victims in their wake.

"We're screwed, huh?" Wane asked Zot, not daring to look at him.

"I think we were screwed a good while ago, kid," Zot panted, shaking his head. "A little more or a little less can't hurt. I think it's time to concede that our time in Merkede is over, wouldn't you agree?"

Wane's stomach contracted. He would love nothing better than to sneak on the first ship back to Metten and forget all about that had happened here. But he couldn't. With Sachrya's poison circulating in his veins, it was only a matter of time before he dropped where he stood.

"Yes," he said, "we should leave." He didn't want Zot to end up in the hands of those kidnappers again. If it meant his death, so be it.

"What's that tone?" Zot asked, his eyes shrewd.

"There's no tone," Wane said. "It's just been a long day, that's all."

"She did something to you, didn't she?" Zot wasn't asking; he was making a statement. "That witch is as trustworthy as a hungry serpent. I knew I should've never left you with her. Come on. Out with it. What did she do to you?"

Wane's resolve crumbled under Zot's gaze.

"I'm dying," he said. "There's nothing we can do about it." It was true. Sachrya's scolopendrae had gone up in flames right alongside the warehouse, and he had been the one to light the fire.

"What are you talking about?" Zot asked, his tone sharp, almost angry. "You're just a kid. You're not going anywhere."

"The shamanka..." Wane mumbled. "She offered me some tea..."

"Don't tell me you drank it," Zot said with a groan. Wane's silence was answer enough. To his surprise, Zot put an arm around his shoulders.

"How much time do you have?"

"How do you know that's how it works?"

When asked, Zot shook his head. "Me and Sachrya go back a long time. I might've even given her some ideas in the past." He swallowed.

"So, how long do you have?" Zot repeated.

"Five days. Four if you count from sun-up. I was supposed to set loose some

CHAPTER 18

creatures those people stole from Sachrya, but..." He trailed off, gesturing at the burning warehouse in the distance. Zot understood.

"I won't let anything happen to you," he said. There was a look in the man's eyes that Wane had never seen before. Usually, looking at Zot was like looking at one of the mannequins used in a cheap theater; now, for the first time, he felt like he was looking at a real person.

CHAPTER 19

After the trial, Brina and the others were ushered back into the magnificent white spire and up a winding marble staircase. Though their sleeping quarters were some of the most lavish lodgings Brina had ever seen, there was a hollowness to them. The coldness of hearths which hadn't heard a proper tale in centuries, was accompanied by the smell of decay built up over years of silent darkness.

Brina's chambers comprised a sitting room decorated with velvet curtains and furnished with a set of meltwood chairs arranged in front of the icy hearth. To the side of the sitting room, her bedchamber contained a giant four-poster bed the size of an average shack in Doorstep's Ditch. Eight people could have slept in it side by side. The wooden frame was carved with layered patterns of leaves, making it feel like the occupant was sleeping among the trees. The sheets were woven from glimmering silk. They slid through Brina's fingers like water.

Before Brina had a moment to catch her breath, multiple platters of food were brought up by a sallow-faced man whose bulging eyes and twig limbs made him look like an oversized insect.

Before Brina could thank him, he'd already scuttled back into the corridor, pulling the door shut behind him. Though their trial had ostensibly been a success, the Morassians were nervous around them, treating them the way one might treat a chained tiger. *Serves them right.*

Brina's meal consisted of smoked bass, dried and boiled swamp roots, and a mountain of caviar. Other local delicacies were served throughout the three main courses. After almost twenty-four hours of terror and physical exhaustion, Brina could have eaten sawdust if it had a sprinkling of salt on it.

A stack of dry clothes lay ready on the bed. They were far too ornate for Brina's tastes, however. If she had wanted to look like a foreign duchess out of one of De Malheure's sappy historical novels, she would have raided the man's closet a long time ago.

CHAPTER 19

Instead, she hung her sopping wet trousers and tunic on a chair to dry and tucked herself into the soft, dusty sheets of the four-poster bed.

Although they were being well taken care of, perhaps even too well considering the living conditions of the Morassians on the pontoons outside, Brina couldn't help but resent the reckless and pointless way Archdruidess Evana had put their lives on the line.

In minutes, they'd gone from intruders ready to be executed to long-lost friends of the people. It reeked of theater. The archdruidess knew what she was doing. There was calculation behind all of this somewhere, even though Brina couldn't see the end goal at the moment. All of that would have to wait until she had gotten a decent night's sleep.

As soon as the insect-like servant came to retrieve Brina's empty dishes, she slid a rusty deadbolt into place behind the door and stumbled over to the four-poster bed. She was asleep before she hit the sheets.

Brina's sleep was disturbed by images of nine pairs of yellow eyes watching her from the shadowy corners of her room. She swam through thick murk with heavy limbs, never making progress, while those nine shadows drew nearer.

When the creature lunged at her, all nine heads bore Cardinal De Leliard's twisted, greedy face. Though she had never seen the man in person, she imagined him to be greasy and bald, with multiple bulbous chins from gorging himself on the very best things the realm had to offer, while people starved in droves in front of his gates. She imagined beady, angry eyes burrowing through her skin and into her very soul.

Brina awoke to the first rays of sunlight sneaking in through a gap in the curtains. She grabbed her script pouch, hoping to get in some imprinting before breakfast, and descended the winding staircase. She exited the spire into the sleepy, drifting village. At this hour of the day, the pontoons were deserted.

A low veil of mist hung over the lake, and the gnarled ancient trees surrounding the clearing cast uneven shadows on the water's surface. It was like something out of a dream. Now that the air was no longer filled with the smells of cooking fires and gutted eels, an acrid undertone of sulfur made Brina wrinkle her nose. Even over the clear lake, the stench of the surrounding swamp was inescapable.

She made her way to the rope bridge that led to the dock. From there, she would have a perfect view of the surrounding nature. It would be as ideal a place as any in Sunken Spire for a focused imprinting session.

Inducing and sustaining the meditative state required for imprinting had never been Brina's strong suit. She was too easily distracted by the smallest noises or twitches of movement in the corner of her eyes—the fruits of years of hunting and being hunted. Nevertheless, she would have to grow used to imprinting in strange places among new people. Their journey had only just begun, and there would be no turning back until they had brokered an alliance that could keep Bior out of the empire's clutches.

As she neared her destination, cajoling voices rang out across the water. Brina's pulse spiked. Her feet moved into a solid stance, fingers inching toward her belt. Then she saw where the noise had come from.

On top of the bridge, a group of four children lay flat on their stomachs, leaning over the edge, arms outstretched into the rippling lake. The oldest of them couldn't have been much older than twelve. *Nice one, Springtide. Now even a handful of children are enough to make you jump out of your breeches.*

"You've got to wiggle your hand more, Lacea," the oldest boy told a girl of about six years old. "They need to think you're alive."

"But I am alive," the girl said, her blond eyebrows furrowed in indignation. She waved her free arm to illustrate the point.

"I know that," the boy said. "But fish are stupid, aren't they? If you stay still, they'll think you're just a branch, or something rotting."

"I'm not rotten." The girl jumped up, her pale freckled face screwed up. "It's no good, anyway. I'm too slow. They always get away."

The boy wore a self-satisfied grin. "It will get better when you're older. Melas here"—he jabbed his elbow into the ribs of the boy beside him—"didn't catch one until he had ten cycles under his belt. Now look at him; in a few years, he might even be as fast as me."

Behind him, the kid named Melas scowled at the older boy as he pulled a wriggling silver trout out of the water with a smooth snatch.

The girl shrugged, unimpressed, then wandered off down the bridge. When she noticed Brina, she froze. The girl looked stricken, like a deer faced with a pack of wolves.

"It's okay," Brina said, holding up her hands. "I was just going for a walk."

The girl looked up at her with suspicious eyes. "You're the magic lady from yesterday."

Brina shook her head, unable to keep from smiling.

"There's no such thing as magic," she said, surprising herself with her blunt honesty. "It's just a trick. Anyone could do it."

"Even me?" the girl asked, her eyes widening.

CHAPTER 19

Brina stiffened. She had spoken without thinking, not wanting the girl to think she was something she wasn't. On Metten, all the new recruits eyed her with awe, whispering behind her back and pointing as though she were a mythical character that had leaped off the parchment to join their struggle in the flesh. Brina had had more than enough of that.

"Could I?" the girl prodded.

Don't go around spreading false hope, Springtide, a voice deep inside warned her. *These people are one darkhelm scout away from annihilation.*

"Yes," Brina said, a defiant edge to her voice, angry at herself for her moment of cynicism. "Yes, you could. I will teach you how. My name is Brina, by the way, though 'magic lady' sounds nice too."

"Lacea," the girl responded.

Brina felt drawn to this girl in a way that she couldn't quite fathom. Maybe it was because she was just a few years younger than Brina had been when her father had been arrested. Maybe it was because they both, in their own ways, felt like outsiders.

Before the rational part of her mind could catch up with her, Brina got down on one knee and dropped her script pouch onto the pontoon. It made a hollow thud as the heavy stone tablets banged against the wood. She retrieved the script for *Veloce*, a pentagonal rune granting the user quick reflexes and enhanced speed.

She beckoned for Lacea to sit down beside her. "This is all there is to it," Brina said, holding out the tablet to the girl. "You just look at this shape and focus on it as though it were the most beautiful thing you had ever seen in your life."

"But how does it work?" Lacea asked.

"It's simple," Brina said. She kneeled down over the side of the rope bridge. She stuck her arm into the cool water and wriggled it back and forth like she'd seen the older kids do. When she spotted a silver shimmer below the surface, she burned *Veloce*.

Time slowed down. Her heartbeat pounded in her ears in slow pulses. She bent down and snatched the fish out of the water as though it had been floating along like a branch on a stream.

She held up the fish and presented it to the young girl. "Here, this is yours," she said. "You'll have to catch the next one yourself."

The girl gaped at the wriggling trout, open-mouthed. "That was amazing."

Brina shrugged. "Like I said, barely more than a trick. Here, try it."

She held up the script for Lacea to imprint on. She didn't expect anything to happen. Imprinting was a fickle technique, even for many older, practiced gazers. But at least the girl would have a fair shot at it.

Moments later, however, Lacea gasped. For the briefest moment, her eyes flared up in venom green.

The girl jumped up and down. "I'm doing it! I'm doing it!" As she cried out with joy, she lost focus. The sigil went out, leaving her eyes their original light blue. Her face fell.

"That was pretty good," Brina said. "It took me a lot longer when I started out."

Lacea smiled. "That was cool. I felt like a hero. Like you."

Brina laughed. "There's nothing heroic about it, or about me."

Lacea shook her head, unconvinced. She held up the script toward Brina. "Here," she said, "thank you for letting me see. One day, I'll find one of my own, and I'll be just like you."

Brina looked down at the girl. Though Brina guessed she couldn't be much older than six or seven, there was an intensity to her gaze that matched someone far older.

"You know what?" Brina said. "Keep it. Just promise me you'll practice for a handful of minutes every day."

The girl's eyes went wide with surprise. "Really?"

"Really. But hold on to it well. They're exceedingly rare."

"I will," Lacea said, "I will guard it with my life."

Brina chuckled, "No need to take it that far, kid, but your spirit's in the right place." She gave the girl an awkward pat on the head, then walked across the rope bridge to a lonely section of the docks, where she began imprinting.

As she placed the first script in front of her, a huge grin spread across her face. It was indecent, really. Especially given the fact that Saf would skin her alive once she figured out that Brina had given away one of only four *Veloce* scripts the entire order had in their possession. Brina didn't care. This one had belonged to Acheron, and she was sure he would have understood.

She remembered what her first bow had done for her when she was a lonely kid on the streets of Doorstep's Ditch. It had set her on a lifelong trajectory that even now determined her path. If she could do something like that for this little girl, it would all have been worth it. The whole point of the Order of the Prism was to make sigils accessible to all. Since the empire was closing in, this might just be as good as it got.

CHAPTER 20

hen Archdruidess Evana summoned them later that night, Brina was surprised to find the circular throne room decorated with the light of a thousand candles.

In the center of the room, an exquisite banquet table had been set, laden with piles of fish skewers, silver cups filled with cranberry wine, and other local delicacies.

The atmosphere was as close to a party as any serious political gathering could get without straying into indecency. Brina had never liked parties. Too many people around made it hard to watch your back. Besides, a feast was never just about feasting. Whether they were organized by gang leaders to keep their soldiers satisfied and numb, or by lofty druids in their forest spires, there was always an ulterior motive.

Evana's only other guests were the members of her private guard. They sat at the far ends of the table like book ends, staring straight ahead. Not a drop of stew touched their immaculate wooden plates.

Brina sat down beside her father, who had been granted the pleasure of sitting at the archdruidess's right-hand side. Abrasax, however, didn't seem to care much for the honor.

Up close, his skin looked pale and waxy. Nobody had seen him emerge from his room since the trial the day prior, and Brina wondered whether he'd eaten anything at all over the past few days. If he had, she hadn't seen him do it. His eyes had a glassy quality to them, like crystal balls gazing at murky visions of the future while missing the present unfolding in front of them.

Bron and Sneak, who sat to Brina's right, were having the time of their lives. Both of them had helped themselves to a mountain of food, and were comparing notes on which of the Morassian delicacies were the slimiest and the most disgusting. When Sneak tried to catapult a spoonful of mashed roots into Bron's ginger beard, Brina had to intervene.

"So," the archdruidess began, dabbing at her lips with a delicate white handkerchief, "your business with my people must be quite important, given that you were willing to risk your necks over it."

Willing? Brina ground her teeth.

The pale druidess gave Abrasax a pleasant smile, as though she herself hadn't been the one to have them tied to a stake and fed to a hydra.

"Right." Abrasax cleared his throat, shaking his head like a dog trying to get water out of its ears. "Right," he repeated. "There are important matters to discuss…"

"…regarding the empire's military campaign in the isles," Brina hissed in his ear. Now was not the time for him to drift off into another of his catatonic states. They had come all this way, having almost drowned on multiple occasions. There was no margin for error.

Abrasax fell silent, staring into his own reflection in the silver cup of cranberry wine he had been sipping on. That made at least four full cups he'd emptied since he sat down. Though he didn't seem overly drunk, watching the silver bottom of the cup glimmer in the candlelight put Brina on edge. Every word mattered.

When he spoke, Abrasax's voice was firmer, though a faint waft of sour cranberry stung Brina's nose as he opened his mouth.

"Our informants have discovered ironclad proof that the church is planning a large-scale assault on the nation of Bior. Their darkhelms could land as soon as spring. We must not allow this to happen." His voice grew more confident. "Bior's fall would be an unprecedented tactical disaster for all the free peoples still thriving on the many isles in the Sundered Sea."

The archdruidess's eyebrows raised. "Would it? I don't see it that way. These are difficult times, Master Springtide, for all of us. The empire has driven us from our coastal settlements like a herd of game. They may not yet be brazen enough to push further inland, but they are scheming, looking for ways to encroach upon what little territory we have left."

Abrasax nodded. "Which is precisely why we need to ensure they cannot establish control over Bior. The Skullbeards are the fiercest warriors from here to Hawqal, trained since birth to feel neither pain nor fear. They hold their lines past the point where many platoons of elite warriors would rout. They fight to the last spear if they are so ordered.

"If the entire Biori population is enslaved, how many of them do you think will be tempted, or forced, into joining darkhelm ranks?"

Evana's jaw worked as she considered this. She waved over a servant to refill her own golden cup.

CHAPTER 20

"Even if I were to agree with that assessment," she said, "that doesn't mean that I have warriors to spare. What if the information you have is wrong? What if it is a clever diversion, designed by the church to make us pool our defenses in the wrong place? We could be overrun within days. Our way of life would end."

"I know the Biori well," Evana went on, casting a sideways glance at Bron, who was in the middle of devouring two half ducks, one leg clutched in each hand like a drummer. "They have nothing in common with us. We, stewards of the forest, have protected and pruned this island's ecosystem for thousands of years. No foreign tyrant has taken that away from us yet. I do not intend to let this one succeed where his predecessors have failed."

Abrasax shrugged and beckoned for the servant to fill up a sixth cup of wine. A red blush had appeared on his hollow face. "Then you underestimate them. The Cardinal has amassed a great army over the last few years. He has been scheming since he was a mere adviser to Estav II. Everything De Leliard does is carefully planned. He will not overplay his hand as easily as some of his predecessors did."

"That may be so," Evana said, "but if my people's blood is to spill, I'll have it water our own trees. I will see our bones and sinew become one with the roots of the ancestral tree before I will have them burned in a mass grave on foreign soil."

Abrasax shuddered. His fingers grasped at his empty cup. He seemed uninterested in trying a new angle or pushing the talking points they had set out so meticulously on their journey here. Instead, he just waved his cup at a servant until it was full again.

Brina, unable to bear this pathetic display, leaned forward and took over. "If the rebellion destroys the church's legions on Bior, your lands would be all the safer for it. Bior could become an outpost for the new alliance, the beginning of a shield that could ward all the Sundered Isles from further incursion. How can you set that future aside?"

The archdruidess scoffed. "You might be a great warrior, Ms. Springtide, even an able sigilist. But that does not make you a politician."

"And what is that supposed to mean?" Brina asked, her fingers tightening on the edge of the table.

"It means that you are not considering the morale of my people. As long as they are here, they are fighting for their homes. They are fighting alongside their families, and if they should die, then they will die alongside their brothers and sisters.

"If I send away even a fraction of my able-bodied warriors to die elsewhere, spirits will be broken. Families will be torn apart, and as a result, our defenses will weaken. War is not about figures on a map, Ms. Springtide. It is about what my people are whispering about right now in the silence of their huts. As of yet, their courage is strong, and that is what I believe in."

"But how can you hope to withstand the Heilinist armies after we've allowed them to wipe out our mightiest ally?" Brina's voice rose. Bron's and Sneak's heads turned, alarmed.

"The Biori have been fending off the church for decades," Brina droned on. "Who else has that type of experience in warfare? Their soldiers possess iron muscles and steel wills. Their smithies create impenetrable armors and spears that soar like a diving falcon. If all that were to fall into the Cardinal's hands, what chance do any of us have?"

"I think," Evana said, her tone growing dangerous, "that I have made my position on this matter clear."

Brina thumped her fist onto the table. The impact echoed in the giant throne room. All around them, guards looked up, startled. *Damn me and my short temper.* She was making things worse. *Time to shut up, Springtide.* Unfortunately, her mouth had a will of its own.

"This kind of short-term thinking will get all of us killed." She didn't care that Evana's face looked like the sky before a storm. "In three years, all of us will pay taxes directly to the Cardinal. We will work the fields for a nib a week. We will have to buy our stolen grain back from them. We will be listening to their hideous songs in our inns. We will watch our blood spill in our own streets. Every last tree in this forest will be felled to fuel their machines.

"That is the future we are heading toward. Bior might be the first to fall, but it will not be the last. We cannot hope to win this war alone. You must know this."

"Hear, hear," Bron said. He slammed his cup down onto the table, causing a wave of red to spill over the edge. It spattered onto the immaculate white marble floor like blood from a slit throat.

The archdruidess locked eyes with Brina. An infuriating smile curled at the edges of her cherry-red lips. "So young," she said, shaking her head, "so very young and so very naïve."

She leaned closer and whispered so only Brina could hear. Behind her, Brina could see the Morassian guards shuffling on their feet. "This is not some hearthside tale spun by an old drunk. This is not a legend from a dusty tome. This is real life. I know there is no hope. I have known it for quite some

CHAPTER 20

time now. It was the final secret my predecessor, Caldessa, passed onto me the night her fever finally got the better of her. She warned me this day would come, told me of the choice I would have to make.

"But if my people are to be annihilated, I would have them spend one last carefree spring before the time comes. Let them die amongst flowers rather than blades. Such is the burden of my position."

Brina felt the floor shift underneath her feet. She understood. Evana planned on lying to her people until it was too late. The Morassians would sit here in the depths of the forest, oblivious to the war raging all around them.

Before Brina could open her mouth to do even more damage, Abrasax opened his eyes and stared at Brina. "She's right. What use is it to stand against an avalanche? All of us will be crushed; let the Morassians do what they will with their remaining days. And we shall do what we wish to do with our own."

He shook his head, downed another half cup, and let out a soft groan of desperation. "It's over," he said. "The rebellion is doomed. We're all doomed."

He got up and made to grab a bottle to fill his cup again. Brina jumped up, a hand closing around the arm holding the bottle.

"Is that necessary?" she whispered in his ear. "This is our duty. We were sent out to convince the other states to help before it's too late. And now you're rolling over?"

Abrasax shrugged, put down the bottle, and trudged up the winding white stairs, back to the bedchambers above. Brina stood dumbfounded. She looked over her shoulder to find Evana leaning back on her throne, a peculiar expression on her face. Brina couldn't tell whether it was amusement, shock, or something else entirely.

"Well," Sneak said through pursed lips, "that was awkward."

CHAPTER 21

hat in the Seven was that?" Brina asked. She leaned against the doorframe to Abrasax's bedchamber with one hand, while the other raked through her short black hair in frustration.

"How could you undermine me like that, after all the risks we took to get here? People are counting on us to get this done."

Abrasax shuddered, as though he were a man making his way to the gallows. His face was pale, and his forehead was dotted with beads of sweat. His wide eyes jumped from Brina to the door to the window behind him, like a cornered animal.

"It's no use," he said. "What can a few Morassians do against the full might of the empire? Well-armored darkhelm platoons are being shipped across the realm as we speak. And what do we have? A couple dozen farmers, ex-slaves with improvised weapons, and a handful of sparkgazers scrounging for scripts like pigs digging through mud."

"I can't believe this." Brina slammed the door shut behind her to block out any eavesdroppers. "You are the one who gave those peasants and ex-slaves hope. They pick up their improvised weapons because you have shown them that the empire is not some infallible machine. That the darkhelms, too, can suffer defeat. That even a cardinal is mortal."

"That was before," Abrasax replied, sitting down on his four-poster bed and burying his face in his hands. "I believed, foolishly and erroneously, that enough of us could make a difference. But now I see. To resist is to die, to face torture, and to have everything taken away. How different both of our lives could have been if I hadn't been hardheaded enough to have to learn that lesson the hard way."

Brina kept her distance. Watching her father, the one person whom she had believed to be fully dedicated to justice, buckle under the church's boot was like watching Doorstep's Ditch burn all over again.

It was the collapse of something that meant home to her. All those years,

CHAPTER 21

the only thing that had allowed Brina to bear the scorn, the stigma, and the insults that came with her last name had been the thought that her father had at least stood up for what he believed in, and for the people who couldn't do so for themselves. Now, he was telling her that all of that had meant nothing.

Brina shook her head. "You don't mean that. You're drunk."

Deep down, she already knew there was more to it than that.

Abrasax gave a watery smile. "Not drunk enough."

He took a deep breath, then continued. "Evana has a point. Why should she send what remains of her people to die in a foreign land in a futile attempt to delay the inevitable?

"Why spill all that blood when they could just wait here until the church comes to collect them? They could have one more good year. Maybe even two. That's more than most of us have left."

"What kind of existence is that?" Brina thumped a fist against the door frame. "To cower in the shadows? To allow everything you stand for to be burned to the ground while you watch from a distance? Is that freedom?"

"It is life," Abrasax replied. "I need you to see this, Sabrina. Only one thing will come to those who resist the church's progress. Death."

Brina shook her head in disgust. "I can't believe this is coming out of your mouth," she said. Her voice had grown cold and hard, like a blade between ribs. "I looked up to you."

Abrasax crumpled.

"Please. Leave with me. Let us have a few more months or years of the life that was taken from us."

Brina ground her knuckles into her temples, trying not to explode. She felt like she'd stumbled into a deep hole and fallen out in some parallel world where everything was wrong and backward. *Leave? Now?*

"Leave with me," Abrasax repeated, more insistently this time. "We can sneak off in the night. We have the skills and scripts to stay out of the church's hands for a while yet.

"Let us at least have those weeks, months, or years in peace. We can live off the land, just you and me. For the first time, we could be a family. The Seven know how much we have already sacrificed for the cause."

Brina swallowed. For the first time she could see what God's Maul had done to her father. Abrasax Springtide, the Viper, the Cardinal Slayer, was broken. And not even he himself realized just how deep those wounds went.

"We made a promise," Brina said. "We promised Saf that we would do whatever it took to keep Bior out of the church's hands. We stood up in front of all those recruits and told them we would ensure that their fight was one that could be won. I cannot abandon that promise. Not when so many lives hang in the balance. I will not stand for it."

Abrasax swallowed, straightened up, and leaned on the windowsill, looking out over the dark, star-strewn lake outside.

"Forget everything I said," he said. "I am being stupid. Forgive me."

Brina's anger deflated. She exited the room, feeling a strange mixture of disappointment and guilt. Her father had sensed her disapproval. He was hurt; that much was clear. And what if he was right? What if this was their only chance to be a family before the inevitable end?

Once, that had been all Brina wanted. But in pursuit of her father's freedom, she had made everything so much more complicated.

Brina closed the door to her bedchamber behind her and opened a dusty bottle of blueberry wine from a rack beside the four-poster bed. It looked old and expensive. *Perfect.*

She took a huge gulp, then another.

They had to stand strong; they had to fulfill their promises, no matter the cost. Once they left the maze of Morassia's swamps, she would keep an eye on Abrasax at all times. He was not to disappear. If word got out that the Viper himself had abandoned the ship, the rebellion was as good as dead.

CHAPTER 22

lack dirt gathered under Zot's fingernails as he scooped another handful of soil out of the shallow hole he'd dug with his bare hands. It couldn't be much deeper now.

"What are we looking for again?" Wane piped up beside him, throwing aside a rock.

"Silence. You'll know when we hit it." Zot gritted his teeth. Every fiber in his body told him this was wrong, yet he knew it needed to be done.

When his fingers scraped the wooden lid of the casket, his heart swelled in his throat. *Seven, forgive me for what I am about to do.*

He yanked the casket free and placed it on the ground beside him. It was smaller than he remembered. For years, the thought of that wooden box had kept him sane when the demons of his past threatened to consume him. From now on, he would have to face them head on.

"What's in there?" Wane's eyes went wide as he stared down at the chest.

"Your way out of this mess."

***

Zot watched his dirty hand close around the diamond-encrusted knocker of Dhune and Dhimple's banking house. Time and again, he had promised himself he would never do this. Yet here he was. Taking a deep breath, he knocked three times in rapid succession.

With every impact, the solid silver doors clanged like a church bell. This was, of course, a deliberate effect. It announced that someone with considerable riches and influential friends was entering this sanctum of greed. *So much for discretion.* Zot looked over his shoulder.

The door's echo undoubtedly served as a call to arms for every crook, bandit, and conman within a three-block radius. It signaled that chum had just been dumped into the water. Naturally, most of Dhune and Dhimple's clientele wouldn't be so foolish as to arrive at the bank's doorstep accompanied solely by a thirteen-year-old boy.

The doors glided inward without a sound. A tiny, frail man stood in the arched entryway. A monocle wobbled on his protruding cheekbones, and his wispy hair resembled cobwebs, as though he had been roused from his crypt by Zot's knocking.

He made a shallow bow, his back producing a series of crackling pops. Zot feared the man might never straighten up again.

"Greetings, gentlemen. My name is Sturgis. How may I be of service today?" The man croaked in a fancy Hawqallian accent he most certainly hadn't been born with.

"I wish to make a withdrawal," Zot said, ignoring Sturgis's disapproving eyes scanning his mud-stained clothing. Less than a year ago, a man like this would have stumbled over his own shoes in his eagerness to attend to Zot's every whim. Now, this walking relic looked down on him as though he were a vagrant. How times had changed.

"A withdrawal, you say?" The butler's tone dripped with skepticism. "I'm afraid Dhune and Dhimple's does not offer loans, sir. We are in the business of safeguarding the fortunes our esteemed clients entrust to us. If you are interested in a loan, might I suggest the pawnshop down by—"

"I know what your business is," Zot growled.

With a sigh, Zot pulled aside his cloak, revealing the wooden chest they had dug up that morning. Flecks of dirt fell onto the banking house's pristine marble steps. Even to Zot's own eyes, the rusty "D&D" logo on the chest seemed strange. It was an anachronism, a relic from a different timeline, crossed over into this one.

"I see," Sturgis said, bending closer to examine the tattered logo. His back straightened, and his face assumed a dignified expression. "Follow me, gentlemen."

As they stepped across the threshold, Zot heard Wane gasp beside him. Pink marble pillars rose on both sides of the rectangular hall. The vaulted ceiling was adorned with scenes of unimaginable riches: mountains of gold and lakes filled with sapphires shimmered beneath diamond clouds.

For generations, Dhune and Dhimple's had been the preferred vault for the wealthiest families and entrepreneurs in the Sundered Isles and much of Hawqal. As an independent city run by merchants, Merkede was exempt from the Hawqallian emperor's taxes and avoided the grasping clutches of

CHAPTER 22

the Heilinist empire.

Its isolated location made escape difficult for would-be thieves, while the absence of public building regulations and registrations allowed Dhune and Dhimple's labyrinthine hallways to remain a closely guarded secret. On top of that the bank possessed many security measures that could only be described as "overly thorough"—as a banker had put it when Zot opened his account many years ago.

Once, Zot would have shared Wane's excitement at the grandiosity and mystery of it all. But today, the banking house's entrance hall no longer symbolized the gateway to glory and riches in his mind. Today, the bank's silver doors led only to loss.

Sturgis shuffled over to a massive desk at the far end of the hall, the clickety-clack of his heels echoing like hammers striking an anvil. As they approached the desk, Zot was reminded just how unnecessarily grandiose everything at Dhune and Dhimple's was.

The desk resembled a preacher's pulpit more than anything else; it would have reached shoulder height for most men but towered over Zot. Its entire front was engraved with scenes of wealth so lifelike that one's eyes could become lost in them. Near the top, a small gilded placard read "Phillipus Grapevine, Master Banker."

Clearing his throat, a bald man in a magenta suit leaned forward over the desk, looking down on Zot as though he were a child in need of scolding. The banker's face held the same skepticism that Sturgis had displayed at the door. The butler gave an almost imperceptible nod to the banker, as if to say, "They're your problem now."

Without a word, Zot heaved the chest onto the desk. The banker lurched backward, mortified by the cloud of dirt that burst all over his workspace. However, when he noticed the chest was authentic, his professional demeanor recovered with astonishing speed.

"Key?" Grapevine asked, looking from the muddy chest to Zot. Though he wouldn't dare question the holder of an official vault chest, his arched eyebrows spoke volumes. Zot restrained himself from yanking the arrogant man down from his perch and slapping him until his bald head resembled a ripe grape.

"Key?" Grapevine repeated, more insistently this time. Zot could feel three sets of eyes boring into his skin. He couldn't keep them waiting much longer. His fingers curled into fists. This was going to hurt in more ways than one.

"Right," he said, "about that. Do either of you fine gentlemen have a letter opener I could borrow?" The banker scowled but reached into a drawer and withdrew an ornate letter opener with a gilded handle and a curved blade.

"You might want to look away if you're the type to get queasy." Zot removed his coat and pulled his tunic over his head. His index finger probed his skin for the familiar hard lump—a bump just below his clavicle, marked with a thick scar. Before either gentleman could protest, Zot placed the tip of the letter opener over the scar. In one determined motion, the blade sliced downward. Blood splattered onto the gleaming white floors and the mahogany desk in front of him. Fine droplets of crimson rained down like rubies tumbling from an hourglass.

Zot dug into the open wound with his fingers, ignoring the stinging that rippled across his upper body as he extracted a golden key. He slapped it down on the desk, maintaining eye contact with the banker the entire time. "There might be some caked-on dirt and blood, but it'll fit."

The banker gave the tiniest of nods. The doubt in his face was replaced with horror. Like Zot, the man was accustomed to a clean, perfumed world. One where blood spatter and mud were abstract concepts.

"Very well," the man muttered, picking up the bloodstained key with a white handkerchief. With a series of clicks and rattles, the lid opened to reveal two scrolls of parchment. The banker snatched up both documents and unrolled them on his desk, then placed five crystal bottles filled with brightly colored liquids beside them. Grapevine poured a small pool of each liquid onto the documents before sitting back, his eyes bulging with focus. Zot couldn't help but smile as the liquids were absorbed into the parchment, leaving no trace they had ever been there.

"Authentic," Grapevine said with a sigh. "You may follow Mr. Sturgis into the vaults." The banker kept one scroll, put it into a mahogany tube, and dropped it into a circular hole in the top of his desk. It disappeared with a sucking sound. He handed the other copy to Sturgis, who had gone almost as pale as the handkerchief he used to shield his nose from the metallic smell of Zot's blood.

"Very well, Mr....?"

"Zot," he replied, "Dimimzy Zot. And if you wouldn't mind, we're in a hurry."

"Of course, Mr. Zot," Sturgis replied. He marched toward a door behind Grapevine's desk. There were identical ones behind each of the other desks in the hall. Zot could feel two dozen bankers glaring at him as he marched past. He placed a hand on Wane's shoulder and steered the boy through the

CHAPTER 22

silver door after Sturgis. As it shut behind them, the temperature dropped, causing the hairs on Zot's arms to stand on end.

Ahead, a narrow corridor was lit at intervals with red jelly lanterns built into the ceiling. Sturgis moved forward in complete silence. After a few minutes, they arrived at a crossing where four identical paths branched off. Sturgis stood at the intersection for a moment, the rustle of his ragged breath lingered in the silence. Then he turned on his heel and marched down the eastward corridor to the right. A few steps in, he stooped and retrieved a jelly lantern from a niche in the wall.

Moments later, the small passage opened around them into a massive natural cavern. Pillars of stalagmites sprouted from the floor, similar to the marble pillars in the hallway above. Stalactites hung from the ceiling like a dragon's fangs. It resembled a landscape from another world.

"It's impressive, is it not?" Sturgis remarked. He raised his lantern, illuminating a few more feet of this alien environment. "They only grow an inch every five hundred years, did you know? Makes you think."

Sturgis led them toward a massive stone column in the center of the cave, where a doorway was hewn into the rock face.

"After you." Sturgis stepped aside, gesturing inside.

"There's nothing in here," Wane said as he and Zot pressed their backs against the walls of a narrow, circular space in the rock. It was about five feet in diameter. Zot's eyes narrowed as he watched Sturgis fiddle with something in the pocket of his coat.

"Get in here," Zot growled, feeling a sudden desire to keep the man within eyesight. A tightness formed in his chest as he remembered being tied to the floor in the old warehouse. His influence hadn't helped him then, and it wouldn't help him escape from this dark labyrinth. He was more vulnerable these days than he could remember ever being. Physically weak, empty pockets, and today, he was breaking the one vow he had left.

"Of course, Master Zot." Sturgis gave a faint smile as he stepped into the room with them. The man retrieved a long key and ran it through a crack in the rock beside the door. A door slid out of the crack with a grinding noise that grated on Zot's eardrums. Then the floor plummeted.

Wane yelled out.

"Not to worry, young man. It's only an elevator." The corners of Sturgis's mouth twitched, but he kept himself under control.

"An ele-what?"

"An elevator," Zot hissed. He, too, had felt that initial rush of panic in his guts. Though he knew that some of the most lavish palaces in Hawqal possessed elegant cranes for moving people up and down floors, he'd never in a million years expected one to fit into a narrow underground shaft like this one. His head spun as he tried to imagine where the bank had hidden the system of ropes and pulleys to power this contraption. What if they just kept falling? Who was even operating the elevator, and how would they know when to stop the cage?

Before Zot could decide whether he could overcome the humiliation of having to ask Sturgis how it worked, the cage came to a halt. The door opened into a yawning chasm. An icy draft brushed Zot's cheeks as he stepped out behind Sturgis. As soon as the door closed behind them, it felt like they were stranded on a foreign planet, a world alien and separate from the one they had left when they entered Dhune and Dhimple's.

CHAPTER 23

Over the following days, Brina tried to distract herself from the disastrous banquet in the audience hall by wandering around the village, bartering for all the supplies they would need for the journey back to the ship. With the help of the Morassians, she packed two thin canoes with sacks of dried roots, a crate of guava wine, four barrels of potable water, and more dried fish than she could stomach in a lifetime. It wasn't enough to keep the crew fed and comfortable, but it was all the besieged Morassians could spare.

The next leg of their mission would take them to the mining nation of Onderheem, located across the Sundered Isles. It would have been a lengthy journey even in better days, but with Mallion's Bay and the waters surrounding God's Maul prison teeming with the red-sailed vessels of the church, they would have to move with caution, which would slow them down.

The Heemian nation was built in and around a hollowed-out mountain that had been excavated for centuries. Alongside the Morassians, the Heemians were the last standing nation in the Sundered Isles with enough economic resources to maintain their independence, at least for the time being.

On the morning of their departure, a thick veil of mist hung above the lake, shrouding the sunken spire in a cloak of white. Silas, who had volunteered to guide them back to the outskirts of the forest, stood waiting for them on the rope bridge. On the wobbly dock behind him, the canoes Brina had filled with rations lay moored. Brina, Bron, and Silas took the leading boat, while Sneak and Abrasax followed in the rear.

As Sunken Spire receded into the mists, Brina let out a heavy sigh. She had hoped there would be some way to turn the situation around. But, after considering Evana's position from every angle, she realized there was nothing left to do to persuade her. Evana's mind had been made up. *May they never come to regret this decision.*

Brina thought of Lacea, whom she had given her *Veloce* script, and wondered how many months of childhood remained before the world would force her to grow up. How long would it be before fire and the clatter of steel on steel overtook the peaceful silence of the woods surrounding the mighty spire?

"It's a shame," she told Silas, who looked away when she addressed him. "Your people seem like capable warriors—inventive and silent as death itself. We could use people like you in our fight against the empire."

Silas's jaw worked, but he kept his mouth shut. Bron grumbled something about cowards, just loud enough for the Morassian scout to hear. If he had, he gave no outward sign of it.

Silas steered them to a distant corner of the lake, where a small but rapid stream meandered off into the woods.

They had been gliding down this frothing white water, covered with vines and overgrown bushes on either side, for half an hour when Silas cleared his throat and spoke. "I will not defy the will of the star amongst man. If Evana has weighed her decision, then I know it to be the right one."

He let out a sigh, his eyes focused on his oar as he used it to push the boat away from a cluster of jagged rocks. "Nothing gives me more joy than to hurt the darkhelms every chance I get. Those bastards wouldn't even have a peaceful moment to sit down to eat a piece of moldy bread if it were up to me.

"I have not forgotten the raids on our coastal settlements. I suppose I never will forget the smell of the fire and the sound of the screams as entire tribes were put to the blade. There has been no vengeance for our people."

Spots of red appeared on the Morassian's pale neck. Then he shook himself. "But my personal grievances are not to get in the way of what is right for our people. If it is my duty to remain here and help my people weather the storm from within our forest, so be it."

Brina nodded. She understood what he meant. All of them had made their vows and sworn loyalties. With the weight of impending war pressing down on all their shoulders, it was all anyone could do to stick with the promises they had made.

"I heard you gave my daughter something," Silas said. Brina eyed him, confused.

"She came home a few nights ago with a dozen fish in a bucket, mad with excitement." He gave her a hard look. "She says she can do magic now, that you taught her how."

Brina felt her cheeks flush. Although it had felt like the right thing to do, she suddenly second-guessed giving the girl what amounted to a weapon. A

CHAPTER 23

dozen disastrous scenarios raced through her mind. What if the girl pushed her little body too hard under the influence of the sigil's power? What if the darkhelms came and found her in possession of sparkgazing paraphernalia? Surely they wouldn't send a little girl to God's Maul. Maybe not, but she had parents. She had a whole tribe of people that could suffer.

"It's one of the scripts we use," she said, weighing her words. "It makes the user faster. I noticed she was having trouble catching fish, and I wanted to help her. Besides, given the state of the world, I thought it would help her protect herself."

Silas nodded.

"My apologies if I overstepped, I..."

"You did what?" Bron's bushy beard swayed back and forth as he shook his head. "You know, I like to joke about you flatlanders, but I'm starting to think you really are insane."

He laughed as Brina gave him a death glare, a high-pitched chortle of a laugh that only grew in volume once he got started.

"Saf... is going to... hang you... for this," he said between fits of giggles. "Giving away scripts to a soft-boned babe, unbelievable."

"Script. Singular," Brina corrected him. "Besides, it was mine to give. Acheron left his pouch to me when he died."

She swallowed. It had been weeks since she had spoken his name out loud. It seemed to linger in her mouth, a bitter numbness that threatened to suffocate her.

The hole Acheron had left would never be filled. At first, she had hoped the hurt would fade away with time, but she was slowly beginning to accept it as a fact of life.

He would've been able to talk sense into her father. He would have known what to do. Despite his less than stellar manners and his hair-trigger temper, he had guided her in a way no one ever had. He'd had answers for everything, even if he sometimes couldn't be bothered to share them.

"Those things are rare, aren't they?" Silas shuffled as he paddled the boat into a side branch of the river. "I heard someone mention them a very long time ago, but this is the first time I've seen one with my own eyes."

Brina shrugged. "They are rare, but they belong to all of us. Our ancestors created them for the benefit of all. The church has tried for centuries to keep them out of our hands. We shouldn't let them."

"Still," Silas said, "you have spares, don't you?"

"Not of the one I gave Lacea, no." Brina shrugged. "I've managed most of my life without scripts, and if I need to, I can do so again. It's no good keeping them all to myself, only to get killed while carrying my script pouch, is it?"

Bron chuckled. "Classic Springtide."

Brina gave him a punch on the shoulder, which shut him up.

"Keeping our scripts to ourselves is selfish. Even Saf herself said that our end goal should be to provide everyone with the same opportunity to learn to imprint."

Bron shrugged. "They are yours to do with whatever you want. If you want to give them to some kid in a swamp, who am I to stop you?"

Silas frowned, seemingly unsure of what to say. "I will make sure she keeps practicing with it. Once she is old enough, I'm sure she will be a great warrior."

Brina nodded. "I'm counting on it. We'll need her."

CHAPTER 24

A shiver crept down Zot's spine, and he regretted not going back to the inn to gather his spare clothes. *It would've been suicide*, he reminded himself. *Even if it was a setup, I was the last one to see those people alive.* This time, real constables might ask difficult questions.

As his eyes adjusted, Zot realized that the cavern they had stepped into wasn't dark. It glowed. Massive green pillars rose all around them, stalagmites coated in luminescent moss.

The effect was disorienting. Zot looked over his shoulder to see if the boy was still following, only to find him standing about twenty feet behind, gaping with an open mouth at a ceiling covered in green and red. It was like standing in a cathedral.

"Keep up," Zot grunted. "If we lose you in here, chances are you'll be stuck down here forever."

"There are worse places in the world."

The hairs on the back of Zot's neck prickled as a leathery flapping sound erupted from somewhere above. As they marched, it swelled. What started with just a single pair of wings now sounded like a storm, a building rustling as though of an approaching tornado.

Sturgis looked up, and Zot was unnerved to see that the old man appeared apprehensive. Sturgis produced a gilded instrument and put it to his lips. No sound came out. Instead, the flapping faded. Zot looked up but couldn't spot where the sound had originated.

"How did you do that?" he asked.

"Secret," Sturgis croaked. "Wouldn't do to tell outsiders."

"Fine," Zot said. "Keep your secrets."

"It's a wailer," Wane interrupted as he caught up with them. "Makes a high-pitched noise we can't hear, but it annoys most species of fleders to no end."

Sturgis's face shifted as though he had just been showered in pus. Zot grinned; the kid was on the money.

"A what?" Zot asked, relishing Sturgis's discomfort.

"A wailer," Wane replied. "It's what we used to get into the old headquarters underneath the brewery before everything burned down."

Zot's eyes widened as the puzzle pieces fell into place. He remembered sending his goons into the brewery to clear it out before he entered. He hadn't actually seen the creatures, but the sounds they had made made his skin crawl. It had taken three trained fighters to kill them. And however many of those damnable creatures had been in there, it sounded like this cave held at least a hundred times that number.

"Right," Zot said, swallowing a sudden excess of saliva. "Keep that thing close, banker. I'd hate to think what would happen to us if we lost it."

"Don't you worry about that, Master Zot," Sturgis said. "I know what I'm doing."

As the journey proceeded, a growing stain of unease bloomed inside Zot. It had less to do with the glowing eyes he kept spotting between clusters of pillars or the repeated flapping of wings overhead than with what he was about to do. Memories of the day he had opened his account at Dhune and Dhimple's haunted him.

How different life had been back then. There had still been a chance. A chance to make right what he had done, a chance to reunite his family. It had been on the very day she left, the day he had last seen his two beautiful boys. A bitterness filled him as he thought about that, followed by an immediate stab of guilt. It hadn't been her fault, not one bit.

She had warned him. He had been reckless. Constantly looking over their shoulders and making their family a target for every crook and bandit in the realm. It wasn't the life she'd envisioned for their children, but he hadn't gotten the message until it was too late.

For Zot, it had all been a matter of stacking the money high enough so that nobody could deny that this was the life he was born for. *She will see*, he'd thought. And so he had continued, even as she begged him to stick to safer avenues of business. He'd been convinced to the very depths of his soul that the wealth would open her eyes.

In the end, it hadn't even been his stubbornness that had made the bucket overflow. It had been his deceit. Even though he had made mistake after mistake, she hadn't left him, not until he'd started pretending he was going to work at the docks.

Every day at sunrise, he had gotten out of bed, put on a pair of boots, kissed her goodbye, and walked out the door. For months, she had thought

CHAPTER 24

that he was making something of himself, that he had learned the value in a hard day's work. In reality, he spent most of that time at the docks collecting shipment after shipment of cloud straight from the desert.

It had been the start of his empire. Zot felt like the king of the world. In his own little bubble, not even the Cardinal himself could tell him what to do. Until one day, she had come to surprise him at work, talked to his "foreman," and found out he had never worked for the imaginary company he'd made up.

Zot shook his head. This wasn't the time to dwell. He had decided that Wane's life was worth giving up on the dream he had fostered for a decade. Now he could either hold on to the impossible or watch another family fall apart.

Nobody could deny the obvious similarities between himself and Wane, even without a blood bond. The boy was clever, daring, and willing to do whatever it took to get the job done. He was everything Zot had wished his own boys would become as they grew.

Zot had spent years trying to track down his ex-wife and sons, only to realize that if she didn't want to be found, no amount of resources and investigators could bring her back to him.

"This might be a tight squeeze," Sturgis called from up ahead.

Zot looked up just in time to see the banker disappear into a gap between two huge pillars carved into the cave's wall. As the gap widened into a narrow tunnel, Zot shivered. The walls were covered in thick strands of luminescent cobwebs. Here and there, he could swear he could make out bundles of remains tucked into the deep corners of the tunnel, like arachnid mummies.

"You guys sure take security seriously." Zot chuckled to distract himself from his gnawing unease.

"Isn't that why you entrusted us with your belongings?"

Sturgis didn't seem bothered, which made Zot feel like a coward. A feeling he'd grown a distinct distaste for over the years.

"It was," Zot replied, sounding unlike himself. "Which is why I'm glad to see that your security measures are adequate."

Not even he could deny the slight tremor in his voice. Behind him, two small hands grasped his tunic. As Wane pressed himself closer to Zot, he caught the boy's eyes; they were terrified. *I have to be strong,* Zot thought to himself. *Show the boy how we act in situations that require courage.*

He tapped Wane on the shoulder and said, "Don't worry, kid. Sturgis knows what he's doing."

The kid gave a weak chuckle. "We're in good hands here, aren't we?"

"Yes, yes," Sturgis mumbled. "We're almost there. To your right here." Sturgis pocketed the gilded flute and used both hands to pull apart a thick sheet of cobwebs in the tunnel to his right, behind which another tunnel appeared.

"After you." Sturgis gestured for them to enter the tunnel.

Neither of them needed to be told twice. As soon as they entered the tunnel, Sturgis let go of the sheet of cobwebs behind him and walked backward, his hand in his pocket, eyes fixed wide on the hole behind them. The intensity of his glare did nothing to subdue Zot's nerves.

"Are we okay?"

"Oh, yes," Sturgis replied, "quite okay, I daresay. Doesn't mean one doesn't need to take precautions."

"Precautions. Right," Zot mumbled.

"Keep a lookout for the door labeled number seventy-three." As soon as Sturgis's words faded from the echoing tunnel, Zot noticed doors set into the side of the cavern, each labeled with gilded numbers. The numbering made little sense as far as Zot could tell: number seven followed number twenty-nine, which in turn followed number ninety-one. On and on it went, in a sequence that no mathematician could make sense of.

"Seventy-three," Wane called out, his voice loud in the silence. "Right here."

"Excellent," Sturgis shouted back from behind him, approaching and kneeling in front of the door. Though he didn't ask them to look away, his annoyance with both of his guests looking down at his fingers was showing. He cleared his throat. Reluctantly, Zot turned away, grabbing hold of Harrod Wane's shoulders to force him to do the same.

Seconds later, the door opened with a smooth rattle. Zot's heart leaped into his throat. A pile of gemstones glimmered back at him through the open door. At the time, this had been every shard he could spare. He'd put it into a savings vault in his name and in the name of his boys before he dove headfirst into his career as an organized crime leader.

Eighteen percent of all the shards he had gathered over years of hard work were in here. Afterward, he had accumulated a far greater sum, but all of that had been confiscated or destroyed by the scepter after their raid of Doorstep's Ditch last year.

This was what remained: fragments of a dream that his old life could one day be restored.

"Here," he said, extending a large sack to Harrod Wane. "Take every one of them. We will need most of it to buy back your safety from the druid."

CHAPTER 24

Wane took the sack, eyes wide as the chariots in the night sky.

"Is this yours?" Wane asked.

"I guess now it is," Zot replied.

"Why didn't we come here in the first place?" Harrod Wane asked, jingling the heavy sack of shards in front of his face. "This is like... three fortunes."

Zot gave the boy a sad smile. "I must have forgotten it was here."

"Forget? How could you forget? This is worth more than the house I grew up in."

"Fine," he said after a pause. "Maybe I didn't 'forget.'" He made quotation marks with his fingers. "Maybe I just wasn't ready to spend it."

Wane's eyes narrowed. "But why? After all the trouble we went through to get money, now it turns out you had more than enough even before we tried anything."

"It's not that simple," Zot replied.

"Seems simple enough to me," Wane said. He poked a finger into Zot's ribs. "So tell me, why?"

"This money," Zot began, his voice embarrassingly thick with emotion, "was a savings fund. I had been saving it for twenty years. That's why I didn't want to spend it." The kid wasn't quite buying this.

"What else could be this important? Either we win, or the scepter crushes us like bugs. You were already in a gibbet once. How much more motivation do you need to use your savings?"

"It was a savings fund for my children."

"What children?" Wane asked. "By now, you would have—"

"No. I. Wouldn't. Because I don't get to see my children anymore. My wife took them and disappeared into the desert."

Shock washed over Wane's face. "Did she take them from you?"

"It's a bit more complicated than that. I made mistakes. She thought she was doing what was necessary to protect them. I thought the same. Turns out, all I needed was a few years to realize she was right, and I was wrong."

"What do you mean?" Wane asked.

Zot was tiring of the boy's questions. Not because he didn't want to answer them, but because the answers hurt. It was all stuff he had known for a long time, but saying it out loud made it worse. "Think about it. What have you heard about me?"

When the kid looked confused, he added, "You know, rumors, stories..."

Wane squirmed in his seat, looking from Zot's face to the empty vault and back. Zot smiled.

"Take what you heard and make it three times worse. That's who I am, boy. Do you think a person like that should be anywhere near growing children?"

Wane opened his mouth, but Zot waved him off.

"I've had enough of this. How about we take a nice long bath of silence? Besides"—his fingers brushed through the bag of shards—"the druid is taking half of this, more if she decides that you running away constitutes an extra charge. So it's not like this changes much. All it does is buy us time."

"Well, I for one am glad to have the extra time," Wane said, rubbing his forearm as though trying to squeeze the poison out of his veins. "Now that we've got something to work with, we'll figure out a way to get enough to go back to Metten and help the others."

CHAPTER 25

rina sat with her back to a crate of smoked fish. It smelled like an open sewer on a hot day, but the comfort of having her sore back supported made it worth it. Besides, the acrid swamp gas bubbling all around them overpowered most of the fishy odor.

She lay back, watching dusk close in on the swamp like a tightening fist. She activated *Lux*, and the nighttime jungle came alive around her. A family of eight-armed arachian monkeys swung from vine to vine overhead, making clicking noises as they called back and forth to each other. Seagull-sized bats fluttered around bushes laden with berries on the far bank of the river.

A deep sense of peace overcame Brina. She was home, surrounded by the peace of the wild. This was where she had spent the better part of her life. Nature had provided her with food, goods to sell, and, most importantly, a place where no insults and threats were hurled her way simply for existing. For being a Springtide.

Brina's smile waned as she spotted a distant prick of light. The orange glare stung in her *Lux*-sensitive eyes, like she was staring into the sun. She let go of the sigil, her heart racing. Even at a distance, there was no mistaking that flickering quality—fire. A camp.

She tapped Silas on the shoulder, held her finger to her lips, then pointed. The light grew as they were carried toward it by the stream's gentle but irresistible pull.

"That's not one of ours," the Morassian whispered. His lips tightened into a line, his eyes dark.

"How can you be certain?" Brina asked.

"We're not stupid enough to make fire." A smirk appeared on his pointed face. "I mean, look at that glare. They might as well have blown a horn."

Brina grunted. The bruise on her ego from making that very mistake mere days ago hadn't quite healed yet. It had been the first time she'd ever allowed herself to be outsmarted in the wilds. And it had been the last time.

As the current carried their boat around a bend in the stream, a sandbank in the center of the river appeared up ahead. A circle of four red tents stood at its highest point, hidden by the surrounding clusters of reeds.

Around the campfire in the circle's center sat half a dozen men and women. Black and gilded armor glittered against the uneven firelight.

Even though their namesake helmets lay forgotten at their sides, there was no doubt as to their identity.

"Darkhelms," Bron muttered, reaching for his spear.

Brina's stomach clenched. If the darkhelms had spotted their ship moored in the lagoon near the shore, Samok and the others could be in serious trouble.

"We need to do something," Silas said. He jabbed his oar into the muddy riverbed to stop the boat. "They've progressed too deep into our lands already. It's a matter of days before they find Sunken Spire. And once that happens…" He trailed off, his mouth twitching as he stared at the armed figures lounging by the fire.

There was no need to say more. The image of dozens of withered corpses swaying near the tree line forced its way to the forefront of Brina's mind once again. This time, she imagined Lacea's body among them. Her forearms tensed as she heard the darkhelms up ahead break out in raucous laughter, undoubtedly entertaining themselves with tall tales of all the blood they'd spilled over the past months.

"Oh, it's like that, eh?" Bron rumbled, glaring at Silas. In her anger, Brina had almost forgotten he was there. The broad-shouldered warrior shook his head with an amused expression. "First, you tell us my people can rot in a mass grave. Own folk first and all that. Now you want our help?"

"Quiet," Brina whispered, alarmed as Bron's voice rose.

On the embankment ahead, the laughter died.

Now you've done it.

A moment of tense silence passed before another round of laughter echoed amongst the trees. Brina slumped with relief.

The Seven bless those idiots.

Silas's jaw worked. He stared at Bron as though he'd just been slapped. "You know full well that decision wasn't mine to make."

"But its consequences are mine to bear." Bron stared right back, his expression growing dangerous.

Silas let out a viper's hiss. "Don't worry. You can keep those soft hands nice and clean while I deal with this the Morassian way."

He withdrew a blowpipe from a pocket on the side of his woven reed

CHAPTER 25

armor and leaned forward to brace his elbow on the side of the boat.

Brina put a hand on the weapon. "You can't do it alone; there are too many of them. Besides, if you die, we might as well drown ourselves, because we won't find the way out without you."

Silas shrugged. "Nothing I can do about that. I have a duty to my people. If these leeches discover Sunken Spire's location, what remains of my people are as good as dead."

He was right, and they all knew it.

"We have to get rid of them." Brina locked eyes with Bron. "It's the only way."

"Why in the name of Boghrod's chopped-off big toes, would we do that?"

"How can we ask everyone to risk their lives by joining the rebellion if we're not willing to lead by example?" She gave Silas a sideways glance. "Everyone trying to get one over on the church deserves our help."

"Besides, look at those boats." She pointed out two sloops tied to a tree stump near the edge of the sandbank, both stocked to the brim with supplies. A rack of maces reflected starburst hues from the fire. "With any luck, we can spear two eels with one jab."

Bron sighed. "I keep telling you, Springtide, you're too good for this world, and once it notices, it will chew you up and spit you out."

Brina chuckled. "A sandworm tried that before. Didn't take."

CHAPTER 26

rina, Sneak, and Silas glided toward the darkhelms' camp in the lightest of the two boats they had taken from Sunken Spire. It had taken a while to stack their most precious supplies onto the second boat, which Bron and Abrasax were paddling down a side branch of the river. If all went according to plan, they would meet up later near a crossing where both branches of the rivers met again. If it didn't, the two of them were to board the ship and leave the island at once.

As they approached the slanted tents, Brina's shoulders tensed. A single windup quarrel in the dark could be fatal. However, it looked like the darkhelms hadn't bothered to put out a sentry. They were too wrapped up in a game of cards and too far from civilization to be worried about such mundane issues as intruders.

Brina studied their movements the way she had stalked prey when she'd been just another roamer on Hammerstroke. She took her time to identify every weakness and danger before they struck. The sluggish, slurred speech of the thin woman dealing the cards. The way the large man on the left kept swaying back and forth on the stump he sat on. These soldiers were drunk, distracted, and in unfamiliar territory. *Inattentive specimens are first to be culled from the herd.*

Though they had every advantage on their side, something gnawed at Brina. Nerves, perhaps. Or something she was missing. A niggling anxiety pricked at the back of her mind. She kept seeing tiny disturbances in the water out of the corner of her eye, but when she looked, there was nothing there. *Pull it together, Springtide. It's just the boat's bow breaking the surface.*

"I say we get them right now," Silas whispered. His silver sickle rested on the side of the boat while he oared them down the stream with his other hand. "We could charge them from the shadows before they know we're here." He dragged the point of the sickle across his own throat.

"No," Sneak said. "Why risk our necks when we can just strand them

CHAPTER 26

and let nature do the rest?" He pointed at the two boats moored up ahead. Both of them were stuffed with supplies the darkhelms had brought for their incursion. Two strands of rope tied around a fallen tree were all that kept them in place. They bobbed up and down as the current struggled fruitlessly to drag them away. "Just get us close, and we will do the rest."

Silas looked as though he'd been forced to drink a bucket of swamp water. There was unmistakable bloodlust in his eyes. Brina had seen that look many times over the past couple of months. Most often in mirrors.

Brina grabbed Silas's shoulder. It was knotted with tension. "It's for the better. By the time they notice they're stranded, we'll be long gone. The outcome will be the same. We both know how many things around here are waiting to finish our job for us."

Silas grumbled but put away his sickle. He guided them into the left branch of the stream, which passed nearest to the darkhelms' boats. Brina and Sneak burned *Leve* as they passed and leaped onto the moored boats. They landed with a light tap, which was drowned out by the ruckus of the soldiers' merrymaking.

Silas stuck his oar into the mud, keeping the boat stationary while they worked. Brina struggled to suppress a giggle as she crawled across the crates of supplies. *Dumbasses.*

She sawed at the thick mooring rope with her dagger, severing one strand after another. It was almost too easy. The darkhelms seemed to have forgotten that they weren't alone on the island.

Brina leaned forward to get a better angle on the last strands of the rope. Something exploded upward to her left. Murky water sprayed into Brina's face, blinding her. She screamed as enormous jaws closed around her forearm.

Brina burned *Forte* to keep the bones in her arm from being pulverized by the force of the bite. The alligator jerked its head, trying to pull her off the boat. Her free arm grabbed on to the other side of the boat to brace herself. Even aided by *Forte*, she was no match for the alligator's ancient strength.

Beside Brina, the second boat began drifting downstream. Sneak stood frozen as he watched Brina struggle with the beast, his eyes wide, mouth agape.

"Do something, you moron," Brina screamed. "Anything."

"What was that?" The darkhelms around the campfire jumped up. A bearded man with white scars contrasting on dark skin came lumbering down toward the edge of the sandbank. Behind him, others scrambled to grab their weapons out of the mud.

As Brina struggled to keep the alligator from taking her under, Sneak jumped from the drifting boat to dry land. In his haste to reach Brina, he landed a fortified kick on the bearded darkhelm's chest. The man toppled backward and fell into the water with a splash.

The alligator let go of Brina and whirled around, its tail thrashing up out of the water. A cloud of crimson formed where the darkhelm had vanished. The man's arms flailed up out of the water once, and then he was gone. Brina stared as the remaining bubbles popped on the surface and faded away. *That could have been me.*

A hand seized her shoulder. "Come on, Cap. Let's get out of here."

Sneak drew his knife across what remained of the mooring rope. Brina shuddered as the boat drifted across the bloody water.

"They're stealing the boats!" A second darkhelm was surprised when the alligator lunged at her from the water's edge. The woman brought her mace down on its skull. It bounced off as though it were a toy. The alligator's jaws closed on the woman's leg, pulling her to the ground. She turned onto her stomach, clutching at handfuls of mud but found no purchase. Her fingers closed around the branches of a small bush. The alligator rolled over. There was the audible snap of breaking bones, a guttural scream, and then the woman vanished below the surface.

A handful of darkhelms barreled toward the shoreline. They skidded to a halt as they saw the gore floating in the water.

"Get in, cowards," an officer near the back of the group shouted. "If we lose that boat, we're dead."

The darkhelms rushed forward, terror written on their faces. Rather than wading into the water, they tried to leap from the edge of the shore to the boat carrying Brina and Sneak away from the bank with increasing speed. One of them made it. His hands closed around the side of the boat, tilting it off balance.

"Peek-a-boo." Brina leaned over the side of the boat to smile at the darkhelm, then flared *Forte* and pounded her fists down on his fingers. He let go with a howl and went under.

A windup quarrel whizzed past Brina's ear. She flung herself flat onto her stomach, fingers searching for her dagger, which she'd dropped when the alligator attacked her. Sneak flung his own dagger into the dark. It rattled among the reeds, then splashed into the water.

He cursed. A second quarrel thumped into the boat's side, inches away from his head.

Brina found her dagger on the bottom of the boat between two folded

CHAPTER 26

tents. She rose to take aim. It was a one-in-a-million shot. The darkhelm archer stood all the way at the top of the sandbank. She'd need to use *Forte* to reach that far, but that meant she wouldn't be able to burn *Lux* in order to see in the dark. *Make it quick, Springtide; he's reloading.*

A tiny feather bloomed on the archer's neck. He reached for it with a trembling hand, then collapsed.

"Over here," Silas called, holding up his blowpipe. "Let's go. There are too many of them."

A second dart took out one of the darkhelms who was swimming towards them.

A few seconds later, they drifted around the bend, and all was quiet.

Eyeing the water, Brina waited until Silas drew level with them. Then they tied the torn mooring rope around the back of their boat to drag it behind them. There were hundreds of windup quarrels, rations for weeks, weapon oils, replacement springs for windup bows, and even a full spare bow. Freshwater casks lined the bottom of the boat.

"Looks like the final frost festival came early this year." Silas chuckled to himself. They met up with Bron and Abrasax further downstream.

"That was fantastic," Silas said. His eyes glowed with glee as he stared back at the campfire's light receding in the background. "We showed them who these swamps belong to."

"Speak for yourself," Sneak said, rolling his shoulder and wincing. "I think I sprained my shoulder throwing that dagger."

Brina laughed out loud. "Oh yes, you definitely got it worst." She patted him on the head with her mangled arm. Blood and transparent wound fluids dripped onto his forehead.

"Ew." He wiped at it, but only spread it around.

"You look like a novice spearman," Bron bellowed from the second boat, before bursting into uproarious laughter. "You might become a real warrior one day, little man."

"Get over here, and I'll show you who's a novice," Sneak muttered, but quietly enough so only Brina heard.

Brina shook her head, grinning. "Big babies, both of you."

"I don't see what's so funny, Cap," Sneak moaned. "Your arm looks like someone's smeared ground beef all over it."

"Just a scratch." Brina grinned at him. "Besides, I still have this to speed the healing along." She pulled at her pyramid's string and swung the script like a pendulum in front of Sneak. "If you do my laundry for a month, I might even let you borrow it."

"And touch your sweat-sodden socks?" He wrinkled his nose. "No thanks. I'll heal the painful way."

Their eyes met, and as they drifted off into the darkness, Brina couldn't help but laugh. Sneak struggled to keep a straight face for a moment, then caved and joined in. With the others staring at them as though they'd gone mad, they laughed until their throats were hoarse and their ribs hurt. Relief washed over Brina with every heave and giggle. It had been close, but they had made it.

Once more, the church had suffered a loss. And that was all it took to make Brina's day.

CHAPTER 27

"At least the view is nice," Brina said as they emerged from the tree line at long last. Her clothes clung to her skin, wet with sweat and bog water. She stank like a three-week-old corpse. Her mouth was dry, but they had made it. By the Seven, they had made it.

Below, the landscape opened onto the vast blue of the Sundered Sea. Craggy rocks littered the hillside. To their left, the hidden cove where they had moored the ship was accessible only through a steep, rocky path.

Even after they had spotted the mainsail, hanging limp from the mast, it took them well over an hour to make the treacherous descent to sea level. As they marched down the last stretch, Sneak sighed. "Man, all that effort only to return empty-handed. We're not even getting paid to do this."

"Don't forget, we still have to hike back up the hill to retrieve all those supplies we cached," Bron responded with a wicked grin. He wiped at a green stain on his trousers, nostrils twitching.

"We told the Morassians what they needed to know," Abrasax said. His shaggy black hair obscured his face, but his posture was rigid and proud. "Giving someone a choice and having them walk the path that is right for them does not constitute failure."

"Easy for you to say," Bron grumbled. "It's not your people's heads on the chopping block."

Abrasax kicked a rock down the path. It skidded down the steep embankments, then plunged into the blue water below. "I have some idea of what that might be like," he said, his voice artificially level.

"Then perhaps you ought to remember it." Bron's beard quivered.

"Look, it is a painful thing to see one's loved ones suffer through great peril." Abrasax sighed. "And, truth be told, having the Morassians in our pockets would've been an excellent bargaining chip when we reach Onderheem. Krocht is a cautious man, but he is also a proud man. Comparing him to the Morassians could have been an excellent strategy to convince him to come to our aid."

"No reason we can't still tell him they're joining the defense," Brina said, looking back over her shoulder as the others struggled to catch up. As a roamer, she'd spent more than her fair share on uneven, tricky paths out in the wilds. And though she would be glad to return to the comforts of her cabin aboard the ship, she did not find the march as tiring as the others had. *Just another day on the job.*

"That's a great idea," Sneak said, eyes gleaming. "He has no way to tell we're lying. By the time he's sent a messenger to the Morassians to confirm, he'll already have committed. It's the kind of move Zot would think of. And though that guy scares the life out of me, you know how I admire him."

"We will not cross the moral border into deceit," Abrasax snapped. "We will lay out our case, we will defend it tooth and nail, but we will not lie."

"We will do whatever is necessary," Bron said. His face looked like it was hewn from solid granite. He had taken the Morassians' refusal harder than anyone else. Given the generations-long trade between the Biori and the Morassians, Bron viewed their refusal to support them as nothing short of betrayal.

They marched the rest of the way in silence. When they arrived, Bron was first across the gangplank, and before anyone else reached the deck, he'd disappeared below deck into his cabin.

"So," Samok said, "I take it your expedition was no success."

"What gave it away?" Brina said with a grin. She liked the man. Though he was older than her, Samok had a cheerful, youthful attitude to life. He was the type of guy who didn't care whether he drank the finest wine with the fanciest of company or was sipping on a batch of life-threateningly poor kelp with the foulest and basest of scoundrels. He was simply happy to be there.

"There was the enraged bull stomping past me, for one," he replied with a wink. "What happened?"

Brina shook her head. "Where to begin? First, they tried to feed us to a hydra, and then, well…" She waved a hand toward the ladder where Bron had vanished. "You get the gist. Oh, right, almost forgot, we also ran into a platoon of darkhelms."

"So they *were* church soldiers," Samok said. His face fell. "We saw a group of them carry sloops uphill in the dead of night a few days ago; idiots carried torches and everything. That's why I thought they couldn't possibly be enemies. I mean, who waits for the cover of darkness and then ruins it by making themselves visible for miles?" He shook his head, then broke into

CHAPTER 27

a grin that showed off his white teeth. "Well, onward and upward, I say."

"How are things here?" Brina asked. "Any trouble while we were away?"

Samok thought about it for a while, then slapped his hand to his forehead. "Right, almost forgot. You have a visitor."

"A what?" It was Abrasax who spoke.

Brina looked over her shoulder to find him and Sneak standing right behind her. She took a few steps aside to gain some more personal space.

"She arrived yesterday morning. Waved at us from a distance and told me she was an acquaintance of yours." He nodded at Brina. "She said something about needing to speak to you. Seemed urgent."

"And you didn't think that strange?" Brina asked. Her eyes narrowed. "Nobody is supposed to know we're here."

Samok shrugged. "I locked her in a cabin below. Given every comfort, of course," he said, holding his palms outward. "Seemed like the safest of two options, you know. If it's someone you'd rather get rid of, we already have her cornered and ready on a platter for you. If she's someone you know and wish to speak to, this seemed safer than turning her away."

Unease grew in Brina's stomach, squishing organs and crushing blood vessels. *She's dead. You watched her fall.* Still, she couldn't help but picture that dreadful spiked helmet and the way she had crushed Versa's chest like they were a bug under her boot.

"What did she look like?" Brina asked, dreading the answer.

Samok scratched at one of his dreadlocks just behind his ear, looking uneasy. "Her hair was long and pale, the color of a beach. Her skin was as white as a Biori's. But strangest of all, her eyes were missing."

That was all Brina needed to hear to know what needed to be done.

***

"Sabrina, wait!" Abrasax thundered across the deck after her, but Brina, burning her final store of *Veloce*, was much faster.

"I'm going to kill her," she shouted. "Then I'm going to eat her, puke her out, and kill her again."

"Wait," Abrasax shouted again. "It might be dangerous. We need to think this through."

"We'll think about it after we feed her corpse to the sharks." Brina jumped down the hatch leading to the lower deck. She kicked open the first cabin door and found it to be empty. Then she turned around and repeated the process. Bron opened the third door to Brina's left, eyes blazing blue, spear clutched in his hands.

"What's going on?" he asked. "Are we under attack?"

"Somebody is," Brina shouted back. "I just need to find her."

Bron looked confused, but didn't drop his weapon. Brina tried the door opposite his cabin and found it locked. *Here we go.*

She could've waited for someone to bring a key. Could've tried to finesse the door open with a lock pick, but there was no time. She wasn't waiting for anyone else's opinion. This was going to happen. And it was going to happen now.

She flared *Forte*, braced herself against the opposite wall, and mule-kicked the door with both feet. The doorframe splintered.

A woman with foot-long sandy hair rolled sideways off the bed in surprise, then pushed herself up. Scar tissue crusted her eye sockets. She wore no armor, no helmet. For the first time, Brina could see the face of the woman who had killed Acheron.

The woman held out her hands in a gesture of submission, "Wait. Please. I come in peace."

"And you're leaving in pieces."

Brina charged forward, ready for a wave of cold at any moment. The last time she had faced the eyeless priestess, Brina had been weak, only an apprentice sparkgazer. This time, she was ready.

No frost came.

The woman sank to her knees, shielding her face with thin arms. Brina jumped up to do a running kick. Two arms gripped her from behind in a bear hug, pulling her back. Brina burned *Forte* and tried to break free, but it was like fighting a cage of reinforced steel. She thrashed, kicked, elbowed, but it was no use. Abrasax Springtide may have lost some of his former flair, but he was unmatched as a sparkgazer.

"Let me go," she screamed. The force of her struggling spun Abrasax around. Brina glimpsed Sneak, Bron, and Samok standing in the door to the small cabin, staring at her wide-eyed.

Shame contaminated her rage. They were looking at her as though she were some kind of wild animal on a rampage.

"It'll be all right," Abrasax said, his tone low and soothing. *Bastard's burning a psycho-sigil.*

"Don't you dare use that crap on me," Brina snarled. "Don't you dare try to subdue me."

CHAPTER 27

"I'm not burning anything," Abrasax said. "I'm just trying to help."

"Please listen," the eyeless priestess said, still cowering on the floor. "I gave my prayer book and my other possessions to your captain yesterday. I couldn't fight you if I wanted to."

"Lies," Brina said, eyeing the woman with more hatred than she had ever felt in her life. "We all know that stored power carries over for much longer than a measly few days."

"Do I look like the type of woman who has stored power in abundance? I almost died trying to make it here. Look at me." She raised her arms, showing thin bony limbs, the kind Brina had only ever seen on the worst of floaters back in Doorstep's Ditch. Her cheeks were caved in, her hair wispy.

"You killed him," Brina said. "You killed Acheron, and you're going to pay for it."

"Allow me to explain," the priestess said, desperation shining through in her tone. "If after that you still wish me to die, I shall not resist."

"It's a trick. It's always a trick with you people."

Abrasax, feeling a momentary lapse in Brina's struggling, loosened his grip. Brina didn't attack, not yet. If she was going to do this, she would do it right. She would savor every second.

"Let me talk to Miss..." Abrasax gave the eyeless priest a questioning look.

"Solana," the priestess replied.

Abrasax nodded, then turned to Brina. "Give me half an hour to talk to Miss Solana. I'm sure we can figure this out."

Brina tensed. Every fiber in her being resisted the idea of not obliterating this insect right now while she had the chance. Half an hour's delay might as well be a century.

"Come on, Cap, let's go have a drink." Sneak put an arm around Brina's shoulders, and she allowed herself to be led out of the cabin and into Samok's quarters down the hallway.

Behind them, she could hear Abrasax's frustratingly level voice.

"Samok, would you do me the favor of locking Miss Solana in a cabin with a functioning lock for a little while? Guard the door."

CHAPTER 28

rina was embarrassed to see just how badly her hands were shaking as she took a generous mug of kelp rum from Sneak. Their eyes met as she grabbed it from him. He averted his gaze. *I scared him. They think I'm unstable.* She took a large gulp from the mug, willing the rage that was consuming her insides to settle.

She took deep breaths in between mouthfuls. Before she knew it, the hollow thunk of an empty cup echoed against the captain's mahogany table. She held it up.

"Could anyone fill this?"

Someone took the cup from her hands; she didn't bother to look over her shoulder to see who it was. It didn't matter. The only thing that mattered was getting it full, and then empty again. Her whole body was aching with a mixture of fury and grief. It took everything in her power not to get back up and march down the corridor to finish what she started.

Someone put the cup on the table in front of her. Abrasax sat down beside her.

"Make that the last drink," he said. "This is too important. We need clear minds to think this through."

Brina gave him the kind of side-eye that would've made Acheron proud, then gulped down the rum in one long draught.

"So," Bron began as he closed the cabin's door behind him, "who is that, and why does she turn you into a wild woman?"

"She killed Acheron." Brina swirled the few remaining drops of rum around in her mug. "She's the one who threw him off that tower."

The metal skulls in Bron's beard tinkled as he shook his head. "Then why is she still alive? We've got her cornered. I say we go in there right now and send her after him."

Brina slammed her mug against the table. "That's what I've been saying. It would've been done already if someone"—she glared at Abrasax—"hadn't stopped me. The world would've been a better place for it."

Abrasax held up a hand.

"Please," he said, "let us think this through before we act."

"What's there to think about? She killed him. I saw it. Heil, you saw it."

"Let's put that aside for a moment," Abrasax said.

"Put it aside?" Brina's hand closed around the mug's handle. At the last second, she thought better of flinging it across the room. She needed to refill it.

She got up and rummaged through the glass liquor cabinet in search of the most expensive and strongest booze she could find. The rum Brina had smuggled on board before leaving on this trip would do the trick, but it was rough and hollow in flavor. Not the kind of stuff she needed in a situation like this.

At long last, she found a half-empty bottle of Hawqallian wine in the back. She held it to the light of the jelly lantern that hung above the table. About one-third was left. With a shrug, she put her filthy mug on top of the cabinet. *Might as well get rid of that. Don't need it.* She grabbed the bottle and sat back down.

"Let's line up the facts," Abrasax said, shooting Brina a disapproving glance. "She came here of her own free will, gave up her scripts, and didn't fight back when you attacked her. That has to mean something. It would be foolish to throw her overboard before we know what that is."

"It's obvious, isn't it?" Brina snapped. "She's here to spy for the Cardinal. She guarded you when you were in God's Maul. How could you think this is anything other than a poor attempt to infiltrate the rebellion?"

Abrasax's hands combed through his black beard. "Of course, that is the obvious scenario," he said, "but it would be such an obvious way to go about it that De Leliard must think little of us if he believed it would work."

"Maybe he knows not all of us have the guts to slaughter a wolf if it wanders into our village," Bron said, his fingers tapping against the tabletop.

"I don't see it," Sneak said. He glanced from one end of the table to the other as though he was afraid someone might flip it at any moment. "It's a big risk to take, especially with one of your elite soldiers. Why wouldn't he send darkhelms to pose as new recruits?"

"Because the eyeless are strong. Freakishly so," Brina said. "If we leave her alive for just one night, I guarantee you she'll break out of that cabin in no time, and she will murder us one by one in our sleep."

"Then why didn't she fight back just now?" Abrasax said. "If I hadn't stopped you, that fortified kick could've snapped her neck right then and there."

"She knew you would stop me," Brina took a long draught from the bottle of wine. "It's an act."

"Or maybe she didn't defend herself because she couldn't," Abrasax said. "Did you see the state of her? She looks like death. Her skin is covered in bruises and cuts. According to Samok, she didn't even have her helmet with her."

"All part of the ruse."

"A Heilinist never lets anyone see them without their helmet unless they're of equal rank. You think that De Leliard's elite would agree to walk amongst a group of heretics barefaced?" He let out a mirthless laugh. "Seems far more likely that this woman has run afoul of De Leliard and is now looking to join the opposing team."

"Let's say that's true," Sneak said. He seemed eager to steer the conversation away from violence. "What could we gain?"

"She knows all about the inner workings of the church. She's a sense surger, after all," Abrasax said. "Their power is immense. If she could teach us how to unlock that potential, we could become unstoppable."

"If she killed Acheron, all of that is moot," Bron undid the braid in his beard to better show off the countless metal skulls he had earned over the years. "Blood requires blood. It is the way of the world. If we allow her to murder one of our own, and then allow her into our midst, we welcome dishonor and bad luck into our lives."

"Thank you," Brina said. Her tongue was thick in her mouth, causing the words to come out as a slurred mess. Gravity's pull intensified, encouraging her to put her head down on the wooden tabletop. "At least one of you is making sense."

"We are not talking about slaughtering a pheasant here. We are talking about ending a human life in cold blood," Abrasax said. "Whether or not we want to admit it, those are the kinds of actions with consequences that are hard to foresee. Unless it is absolutely necessary, I would not commit such an act."

Brina's jaw worked. She took another swig from the bottle, which had become considerably lighter. Against her will, the image of the bloody darkhelm in that tower in Doorstep's Ditch, lying in her bed as a tsunami of blood washed over her, forced its way into her mind's eye.

"Fine," she grumbled through gritted teeth, "give her a weapon, then. Let's make it fair."

Bron scratched his chin through his thick beard.

"Abrasax has a point," he said. "I've killed many men, women, and beasts

CHAPTER 28

alike, but never one so thin and frail. Never in captivity. Maybe it would not be such a bad thing to make sure we make the right move."

Sneak nodded. "See, that's what I was saying."

"Cowards," Brina mumbled. Sneak turned red around the ears but didn't take back what he said.

"Then it is decided." Abrasax pushed himself up with both hands on the tabletop and said, "Allow me to be presumptuous for a moment, but I think I should be the one to speak with her."

Sneak and Bron cast sideways glances at Brina, then nodded in agreement. Brina made a dismissive gesture. "Do whatever you want. I don't care. As soon as you're done, I'm getting rid of her."

Brina peered into the bottle of wine, saw the bottom clear as day, and allowed her head to sag down onto the tabletop.

CHAPTER 29

"Thank you, Samok." Abrasax put a hand on the young man's shoulder and gave it a squeeze. "You did well here."

"I did?" the first mate said, casting a doubtful glance at the closed door of the captain's cabin.

"Oh yes. You made sure we had a choice, allowing cooler heads to prevail."

"Is Sabrina going to be okay?"

"It's a sensitive matter, but we'll figure it out."

Samok nodded. "I see. Be careful in there." He nodded at the door. "I overheard some of what you guys were saying. Sounds like she could be dangerous."

Abrasax couldn't help but smile at the young man's concern. "It's good to be careful," he said, "but I have ways of ensuring my safety. Don't worry about me."

Samok nodded and stepped aside. Abrasax took a deep breath as he heard the door lock behind him. The time to act had come. He needed to dig through the rubble of his own psyche to find a shred of the power that had once been there. If not for himself, then for Sabrina.

The sense surger jerked upright in bed. He'd caught her dozing. It seemed like a strange thing to him, to have such inner peace moments after having her life threatened. He hadn't had a solid night's sleep in years. First, it had been God's Maul, but even now, he felt like an animal. Hunted. Trapped.

"It is you," she said. "Cardinal Slayer."

"You know," Abrasax said, his tone light, "that has never been my favorite nickname."

"But it is what you are, is it not?"

Abrasax closed his eyes with a sigh. There was no denying it. It had been his hand holding the blade that had slain Estav the Second. He had insisted on it even though every one of his friends in the Signum had volunteered for the part. He had not wanted to stain their consciences, nor have them face

CHAPTER 29

the wrath that would fall on the one who had done the deed.

In a perverse twist of fate, that decision had caused him to be the last one alive out of all of them. In life, the things one does to protect those close to them have a peculiar way of backfiring in unforeseen ways. He shook himself. It wouldn't help to enter this dialogue with any distractions left in his mind.

"How about we use our proper names? Mine is Abrasax, but you knew that, of course." He gave the sense surger an expectant look.

"Solana," she whispered.

"Why did you risk it all in coming here?" Abrasax leaned forward, eyes narrow. Every twitch in the woman's face was crucial information.

"It's a long story," she said after a silence that spanned multiple deep breaths.

Though he could never let it show, Abrasax himself had much riding on this very question. The longer he thought about it, the more certain he became it was no longer within his power to kill.

Once, he would not have thought twice about ending a life if it fell within the bounds of the justifiable. If it served the cause. But ever since Sabrina had come and opened the gates that had barred him in the dark for so long, he realized just how precious life was, and what an arrogant act it was to take it away from someone else.

Not even if he were certain that someone would raise a blade against him would he be able to make the first move. *But what about Sabrina,* he thought. *What will you do to protect her?*

He hoped with all his being that the next words out of Solana's mouth would give him an excuse not to find out the answer to that question.

"Look at me," Solana said, her voice hoarse and thin with the kind of weakness that only followed months of hunger and thirst. Her skin was loose, and the joints of her limbs stuck out as she moved.

"I see," Abrasax said. "Unless I am much mistaken, you, like many before you, found out just how dispensable you were to the church you served so faithfully."

"What's that supposed to mean?" She snapped.

"I seem to have touched a nerve." Abrasax attempted his former casual, in-control demeanor but found he didn't have it in him. He sounded tense, like a man in a room with an assassin. "It means that I saw you tumble from the top of God's Maul's tallest tower straight into the roiling waters below. A fall that took the life of my dearest and oldest friend, one of the most talented sparkgazers that ever lived.

"It means that I see you here now, looking as though you haven't had a square meal since you cascaded into the ocean. That tells me you weren't received the way you should have been as a champion of your church. Which brings me to my deduction that the empire has forsaken you when you needed it most."

"You're wrong," Solana snapped. "It was the other way around."

A smile crept over Abrasax's face as he twirled the ends of his long mustache, taking his time to assess what she meant.

"If it is the truth you speak," he said, "you have made a very bold choice. Not one many before you have taken. There must be a reason." He didn't bother formulating the question. "I remember we spoke about this not too long ago, when you were so kind as to visit me in my cell. Do you remember?"

Solana's mouth worked, and Abrasax could hear her teeth grinding. "Not a day has gone by since that I haven't thought about it," she said. "Maybe the Cardinal was right, you know. It's dangerous to enter conversation with you. Dangerous in ways I could've never foreseen."

"Enough of this flattery." Abrasax smiled. "It won't help."

"I mean it," she said. "For years, every waking hour I had went straight to the church. I was devoted to it with heart, body, and soul. Not even when my mother fell ill, did I ever consider stepping aside from the trajectory that I was on.

"Even last year, after I was outcast and sent to the abbey at Everberg to lose my vision, I did not waver in my conviction that my commitment to the church was the noblest cause my life could serve. How is it that after a handful of minutes of conversation with you, I take a fall I should never have survived, and when I do—a clear sign that Heil was watching over me—I instead chose to run?

"As I lay there retching on a beach, I could not bear the thought of living under De Leliard for one more day. He had threatened me for so long, but to meet you was the drop that made the bucket overflow. Why is that?"

Abrasax sighed. Out of everything she could've asked him, this was a question he had not been prepared for. "It wasn't my intention to manipulate you, if that's what you're asking. I merely saw in you what I have seen in countless of your brothers and sisters: the strain of living under constant tyranny. And if you think what De Leliard did to you was bad, you should see what he does to those he considers less than servants."

The muscles in Solana's jaw clenched.

"He is not the Keeper," Solana said. "He is just the vessel. Do not think, heathen, that because I walked away from the Cardinal, that I walked away from Her." The muscles around Solana's eyes twitched, and Abrasax was certain that if the skin hadn't been seared shut, she would've cried.

"It wasn't Heil who lowered the trapdoor and forced my brothers and sisters to swing from the noose. It wasn't Heil who suppressed the outwalled for generations and swept across the Sundered Isles like a lash. That was the church. And I hope in time, you will see that distinction for what it is, especially as a sense surger.

"How did you justify it, going after those with talents much like your own? And how do you justify your choices today, in returning to us?"

"I came here for my sister," Solana said.

Abrasax's eyes narrowed. "Is she in Mallion's Depth?"

"I don't know," Solana said, "but I doubt it. Last I saw her, she was with your daughter. Sabrina Springtide is the only link I have between myself and my sister, who I thought lost for years. That is why I came here. When I fell from the tower, I thought it was all over, and when I woke up, it was like I had died, and all the regrets of the life I lived stood out all the clearer to me.

"I started thinking about what was important to me in this world. And I found that chasing an ever higher rank in the church was hollow. What matters to me is retracing the family I have lost."

Abrasax stared at her, trying to separate truth from lies in that scarred face. Even though he was terrified of the consequences a faulty judgment might have, he believed her. He just did. It was exactly how he'd felt after unexpectedly gaining a second lease on life.

Even now, the pointlessness of it all got to him. The ebb and flow of ideological regimes seemed like little more than the cycling of the seasons. Why fight that which is endless and irresistible? Why deny yourself the chance to be with those you love while you still have the chance?

"I'm not well," she said. "I need my prayer book to function. My wounds are many, and only the prayers can help me refill my strength."

"Don't worry," Abrasax said, "I am much aware of what your prayer book does." He took a deep breath, then said, "Fine. I will bring you your prayer book, and I will stay in the room as you recharge yourself."

"You have my thanks," Solana replied. "I knew you, of all people, would understand."

"But let me warn you," Abrasax said. "Just like you long to spend time with your sister, so do I long to spend time with the daughter I've had to miss for a decade. If I so much as suspect that you intend to harm her or anyone else on this ship, my response shall be severe and unyielding. Are we clear?"

Solana nodded. "Of course, and I hope to prove to you in time that I can be an asset rather than a liability."

CHAPTER 30

 ot kicked aside a loose rock as he strolled down the shopping district of Merkede. The scent of ginger still lingered in his nose, a painful reminder of the scene that had just taken place inside Sachrya's apothecary.

The pouch tucked away in the inside pocket of his coat was now unbearably light. Ever the negotiator, Sachrya had sensed her advantage and pushed it for all it was worth. If he hadn't been so infuriated, Zot might even have respected her for it.

One day, he thought, *one day that woman will pay for how she treated me.* But it wouldn't be today, and she had known that just as well as he had.

Zot ran his fingers through his long, unkempt beard. The worst part of it all was that he was growing accustomed to suffering losses. The anger and indignation weren't as sharp as they had been a few months ago. That was a bad sign. He was coming to accept his new place in the hierarchy, and that was the last thing he wanted to do.

"I can feel it," the boy croaked beside him. He was rubbing his forearms, staring at the veins that bulged from the skin. "It's like ice is coursing through my veins, extinguishing the flames of the venom. It hurts, but in a good way."

"Well," Zot grumbled, "let's hope that's how it's supposed to feel. I wouldn't put it past that woman to give you something else, forcing us to go back there and hand over every nib we have." He spat into the dust.

Deep down, he knew that wasn't true, and he shouldn't burden the boy with any more unnecessary anxiety. Sachrya was a shark, yes. Ruthless? Definitely. But dishonest? No. Zot had always made it a point never to associate with someone he couldn't trust. When you made a deal with a person like Sachrya, no matter how painful it might be, at least you could be sure you were getting what you bargained for.

As they reached Aurelian's Square, Wane made to turn right toward the dock district.

"Do you think we'll be able to secure passage on a ship to Hammerstroke?" the boy asked. "I imagine there are not too many crews going that way anymore. Not with everything that has been going on. Do you think we'll make it?"

Zot stopped in place.

Wane turned back, looking confused. "The docks are that way."

"We're not going that way."

Wane scowled. "We've got our money. It's not as much as we'd have liked, but it's something. Must be a few hundred shards left in there. That's more than we could have hoped for, given everything that went wrong. We could buy a few crates of dried fish, some sacks of grain. With any luck, we can feed the recruits for a few extra weeks. It's over for us here. Word will spread about what happened at the warehouse, and we still don't know who was after you."

"I have a plan," Zot said. He put a hand on the boy's shoulder and began steering him toward a narrow alley crammed between two buildings on the left side of the square. From a distance, it was only visible as a sliver of shadow in the marble facade of the hotels beside it. As soon as they entered Glisade Avenue, the sweltering heat turned to a mellow cool.

The rough, dusty cobbles of the square and surrounding streets smoothed out into a path made up of crystal-clear marble slabs. On either side of the pathway, gaudy storefronts screamed at them. Zot grinned as a curse of surprise escaped Wane.

"It's something, huh?" Before he knew it, his mind went bounding down memory lane. Glisade Avenue was home to some of the finest and most exotic boutiques in all of Merkede. Once upon a time, his idea of vacation had been to fill his pockets with as many gems as he could carry, and saunter down the alley for hours on end, snapping up every trinket, piece of clothing, and delicacy his eye fell upon. Today, he wanted to live that life one more time, even if only for a moment.

A group of older ladies, dressed in exquisite gowns that sparkled even in the shade, strutted toward them from the opposite direction. Zot could almost hear the crackling of their ancient skin as they turned up their noses at him. Zot grinned as he passed them; if only they knew who he was.

"Ladies." He tipped an imaginary hat.

"Where are we?" Wane asked, staring from a storefront that held rejuvenating powders and creams, to the opposite side of the street where a shimmering display held an array of mahogany chairs that looked more like thrones.

"This, my boy, is where dreams are born."

CHAPTER 30

"You mean where purses come to die?"

"Those two often go hand in hand," Zot said, a note of anger spiking his voice. "Besides, didn't I just tell you I had a plan?"

"We don't have time or money to be acting like something we're not. We've got a decent amount of shards left. Let's just buy some supplies and get off this cursed island. Nobody will fault us for not magically coming up with a fortune in a few months' time, you know."

Zot shook his head. "That would be unacceptable. Dimimzy Zot doesn't set out to fund an army, only to return with scraps."

"In case you haven't noticed, you're not who you were two years ago. Times have changed. For everyone."

Zot waved a hand, silencing the boy. "There's a lot you have left to learn, and I intend to teach it to you, beginning right here, right now." He held up both of his hands, reaching for the sign above a gilded storefront to his right. Sapphire lettering read: "Chrysanthemum's Fineries and Foibles."

In the window, slender mannequins with glossy faces stared back at him. Their rich garb glittered in the ruby glow of a strategically placed jelly lantern. The one nearest to Zot wore a doublet embroidered with so much gilded thread that his eyes watered just looking at it.

"Are you out of your mind?" Wane whispered. "We can't afford that."

"We can and we will," Zot said, undeterred by the boy's incredulous glare. Before Wane could raise more concerns, he grabbed him by the back of the neck and shoved him through Chrysanthemum's front door.

A crystalline door chime announced their arrival. It was a magical sound, one that was liable to transport one into a world of wonder and imagination. A cloud of sandalwood engulfed Zot. He closed his eyes and took a long breath. He was home. Finally home.

The door chime hadn't quite faded when a pear-shaped woman with ivory glasses came scurrying from a door on the far side of the store. Her black hair was tied in a tight bun on top of her head. Here and there, patches of gray were clawing their way up from her scalp. Before she'd come to a stop, she bowed low.

"How might I be of service today?" Low wheezes interspersed her words. When she straightened up and saw who had entered, her eyes narrowed.

"Good afternoon." Zot reached for her hand. He made to kiss it, but then thought better of it. His once well-oiled charm felt rusty, like a machine that had sat in a forgotten basement for too long.

"As you can see, my nephew and I ran into some trouble on our way to

Merkede. I hope you will forgive our shabby appearance." He lingered on the word "shabby." A spark of approval lit up Chrysanthemum's eyes. It had been the word she had been thinking of.

"We shall require two full outfits today, both of which should be fit for a banquet in the emperor's own halls."

"That is a tall order," her voice was smooth as silk and sharp as a razor. "It will not come cheap."

Zot smiled, withdrew the purse from his coat, and jangled it. "I think you'll find that we will be able to give you a satisfactory advance. As soon as my crew is finished unloading our trading goods, I shall cart them off to the palace, after which you will have more than your fair share."

"I don't do advances." Chrysanthemum pulled up her nose. "I shall need full payment before any of my pieces leave the store. A necessary precaution, as I'm sure you'll understand."

Zot made a display of wringing his hands and dabbing at a sweaty forehead. "Of course. A justified precaution for an establishment such as yours," he said. "However, as I mentioned, we ran into some trouble on our way here. Skullbeard mercenary ships are everywhere these days, and I only just managed to save my precious cargo from their filthy hands. In doing so, I lost most of my wardrobe on my other ship.

"You see," Zot said, "I have an appointment at the palace in two days. As you are well aware, no guard worth his bread and wine would let in someone looking as unkempt as myself. However, I've come all this way to do business with the emperor's nephew. He has been awaiting my arrival, my sources tell me. He would be most grateful to hear that it was you who assisted me in arriving at the palace in a presentable state.

"I could put in a good word for your store. Neheb is a voracious shopper. He is renowned for his fashionable attire throughout Hawqal. The parties he hosts here in Merkede are said to be some of the finest occasions anyone of a better standing could hope to attend. I'm sure you've heard of them."

He could see in the way Mme. Chrysanthemum's bottom lip quivered, that she *had* heard of the lavish parties thrown by Neheb. That Zot himself had never been invited to such an event, and that he had no business with the prince whatsoever, was irrelevant.

"Very well," Mme. Chrysanthemum said after a moment of silence. "Let's begin then, shall we? Does the gentleman know the direction he wants to take?"

Zot smiled. "Yes," he said, "the gentleman has an idea or two."

CHAPTER 31

Brina sat on the stairs leading to the *Chimera*'s quarterdeck, staring off into the distance. As they neared Onderheem, more and more redsails were apparent. Some days, an endless procession of ships moved across the horizon. It had been a long time since Brina had been this close to the Cardinal's fleet. The sight of the crimson sails whipping in the afternoon breeze made her stomach churn.

Aboard those ships, there must have been hundreds, if not thousands, of darkhelms moving to occupy territories in every corner of the Sundered Isles. The closer they got to Onderheem, the more uncertain their mission became. What if they found the Heemians already subjugated by the church? Would there even be any Heemians left by the time they arrived?

Images of the burning streets of Doorstep's Ditch were never far from Brina's mind. What little sleep she could get was plagued by screams and visions of destruction. Some days, even the smoke from a dying candle was enough to make her heart race.

"Could I bother you for a moment?" a soft voice asked from behind.

Brina looked over her shoulder and felt her stomach crawl into her throat. Her fingers clenched on the wooden step where she sat, nails digging into the wood.

It was her.

Brina stared up into that mutilated face, feeling as though she had been launched into a free fall. It was like having her nightmares turn to flesh right in front of her. She had been there, had commanded the burning and the killing. Only a few months later, Acheron had died saving Brina and her father from this monster's grasp.

"What do you want?"

"To talk to you," Solana said.

"I'm not interested." Brina turned her back on the woman, then remembered that Solana was blind and the gesture might not convey her message.

"You've shown me all I need to see. The only reason I haven't thrown you into the sea is because I promised my father. Don't push your luck."

Solana hesitated. Her breath rumbled in her chest as if she were breathing gravel.

"I just want to know where Luna is. Then I'll leave you alone."

Brina spat into the sea. "I don't know who that is."

"I think you do," Solana insisted. "You were with her in Doorstep's Ditch when…"

A fireball swelled in Brina's belly as she realized who Solana was talking about.

"You can say it," Brina said, "when you and your buddies murdered countless people and ensured that the rest of them would be homeless."

"Where is she?" Solana repeated. "You were with Luna that night we fought. You're the only lead I have."

"One, their name is Versa. Two, you're not going anywhere near them. I saw what you tried to do to them, and I'm not about to let you finish what you started."

Solana's mouth moved, contorting her scarred face into a grimace. The ocean spray caught in her empty eye sockets, causing the scar tissue to glisten in the sunlight. "You, of all people, should understand. These things aren't personal. I was acting under orders. At the time, I was… I didn't…"

"That's where you're wrong," Brina snapped. "It is personal. You did what you did. I saw it. I know what you are. Nothing you do can change that. You made your choice. You've shown your allegiance. Now go away. I was counting your friends in the distance."

She gestured at the redsails drifting across the horizon. Solana turned her back and began walking away. Then her feet hit the deck with a determined thud. She stopped.

"They blackmailed me. At first, I thought I was doing the right thing. I was doing what I was raised to believe was right. Serving the church and serving the Keeper were the same thing in my mind. I was taught that, just as Luna was taught that. Then, once I realized what the church truly was, it was too late. I was in too deep. You must understand what that feels like?"

Brina ignored her. Her fingers scratched at a loose flake of paint, reaching for something in the back of her mind. A memory of that dreadful night, one that would be forever engraved in her memory. Versa stepping between Brina and Solana, trying to keep Brina from wounding her. What was it Versa had called her?

CHAPTER 31

Sister.

"You've got to be kidding me," Brina whispered under her breath.

Standing before her was the reason her father had ended up in prison. The sister Versa had been so determined to protect that they had fed her father to the Cardinal. Brina laughed out loud. The irony was overwhelming. Versa had tried to protect their sister from the church and, in turn, their sister had become the church's weapon.

"Please," Solana said. There was an undignified, begging undertone in her voice. "You're the only one who knows. The only one who can give me the chance to make amends. She has to know that I wasn't in my right mind. I panicked. That the sister I thought dead for over ten years was alive, and standing up against everything I believed in, was unbearable to me.

"I didn't believe her. I didn't believe my own eyes, but the truth came to me. Afterward, in those quiet, dark hours when I had to face myself while sitting with your father at God's Maul. I know how wrong I was. And I need you to help me make amends for what I did. I need you to help me regain the only thing I have left in this world: family."

There it is, Brina thought. *The F-word.*

Few things could drive one to do crazy things like family. She found her eyes wandering to the ship's upper deck, where her father was talking to Samok.

"Fine," Brina said through gritted teeth.

This isn't about you, she reminded herself. Versa was willing to die to protect this piece of trash. After the burning of the Ditch, they had languished in the dark for weeks on end, grieving for this woman. *It's their choice. Not yours.*

"Fine," Brina repeated, "but I'm doing this for Versa, not for you. Understood?"

"You mean Luna?" Solana asked.

"Whoever Luna was doesn't exist anymore," Brina said. "Their name is Versa now, and for all I know, they want nothing to do with you." She sighed. "When we return, I will send them a message. I will let them know you want to get in touch, and it'll be their choice. Not yours, not mine, theirs."

Solana was silent for a moment, then nodded.

"Thank you," she said. "It means a lot to me you would be willing to set aside our differences."

Brina held up a hand to cut her off. "I'm not setting aside anything. If you died yesterday, it would still be too late. So know this: if you give me even a shadow of an excuse to send you to the beyond realm, you're done."

"I can repay you," Solana said. It was a testament to the confidence that came with her abilities that she hadn't even flinched as Brina threatened her. It annoyed Brina to find she respected this. Most people she pressured couldn't get away from her fast enough. Then there was this woman, who refused to budge.

Solana produced a small, leather-bound book comprising stone slabs from inside her robes.

"This is my prayer book," she said. "It is where my power comes from. Most of your kind—"

Brina raised an eyebrow.

"I mean, most fire-eyes cannot access the prayer book's power. It takes a sacrifice to activate the Keeper's power." She scratched at an empty eye socket. "Given your situation, I thought it might be worth a try. Who knows, maybe if I teach you how to pray, you can learn to use them too."

Brina stared at the small booklet. She wanted nothing more than to seize it and cast it into the ocean. The only thing stopping her was the realization that she couldn't pry anything from Solana's grasp, even if she tried. Not now that she had refueled her power. It was one thing to hate the woman, but Brina never underestimated an enemy.

"So that's why you're alive then," she said, eyes lingering on the book. "Why you're alive, and he is dead?"

Solana shook her head. "That had nothing to do with prayers. That was just sheer dumb luck. I don't know why I am still here. I couldn't explain it if I wanted to.

"I'm sorry your friend is dead, and I'm sorry we found ourselves on opposite sides of a war that shouldn't have been ours to begin with. But if you let me, I will try to teach you what I know. If we work it out, you might very well be the first person in history to master both disciplines. You can't tell me that wouldn't at least be worth something in the upcoming war? You could become more powerful than any of us."

Brina's mouth worked. Power. Of course. That's what it always came down to. Power. Who had it and who didn't.

"I've got plenty of power," Brina said. "Now get that thing out of my sight."

She walked away from Solana, finding Bron sitting against the mainmast, basking in the afternoon sun, his pale skin growing dangerously red. She nudged him in the ribs with the tip of her boot.

"Wake up, you lazy sack of bones. Let's go have a drink."

CHAPTER 32

e shouldn't be here," Wane said. The stench of decay hung heavily in the abandoned house. It was like wading through rancid soup. The second-floor carpet was sticky with black goo, and the sparse furniture was coated in dust and cobwebs.

"Shut up," Zot said with a dismissive flick of his wrist. He sat on a chair in front of the window, staring out at the street below. He'd been perched there like a hawk for hours now. "There's a thin line between brilliance and insanity, and I've gotten it down to a science over the years."

"I think we may have crossed that line when we cut through that lock on the front door," Wane said. A shiver crawled down his back as his eyes returned to the black stain on the floor.

Though he had never encountered the Hawqallian plague in Mallion's Depth, stories of it had reached his ears from an early age. It infected and consumed its victim within two days and nights. The corpse then turned into a beacon of disease, contaminating everything and everyone it touched until it was burned.

"Don't worry so much," Zot shook his head like a horse besieged by flies. "The plague evaporates after a week. After that, it's superstition keeping these houses empty. Besides, where else were we going to go?"

Wane bit his tongue to keep his thoughts from spilling out. Zot's maniacal behavior was getting old. It was as though sometime after his arrival in Merkede, he'd been bitten by something venomous and evil.

On their long journey from Mallion's Depth, they had agreed that speed was the priority. As soon as they got their hands on some shards, they would return with provisions that could feed the rebellion. After their first week in Merkede, Wane had sensed that things wouldn't go so smoothly.

Time after time, Zot had run into one of his old contacts, only to be dismissed or ignored. With every such occasion, Zot had drifted farther away from common sense. Now, it was getting to a point where Wane was questioning whether he was enabling dangerous behavior.

After their visit to Chrysanthemum's boutique, which had slashed their funds, Zot had undergone a metamorphosis that made him all but unrecognizable. He wore boots with heightened soles to disguise his short stature. His bald scalp was obscured with a realistic black wig, and he wore a billowing purple robe that could have made the Cardinal himself jealous. The Zot who had departed from Metten was being consumed by a brand-new version, hell-bent on regaining the respect and status he'd once had.

Back when he'd lived off snatched purses in the streets of Mallion's Depth, Wane had known a lad by the name of Hector "Scarbrow" Williams. Scarbrow had been a decent enough kid, but contrary to Wane, he hadn't been able to roll with the punches that inevitably came with thievery. One day, old Hector cut the purse off a Biori merchant's belt. When the man accused him, Hector's pride glued him to the spot. Instead of running, Hector had stood his ground, declaring to everyone who would listen that the merchant was a liar and a cheat.

Wane remembered shouting at the lad to let it go and to run, but Hector wouldn't—or maybe he couldn't. The uproar had drawn guards to the scene, and forty-eight hours later, Hector had been marched through Mallion's Gate into the mud-soaked streets of Doorstep's Ditch.

Zot found himself in this same mental loop right now. His pride kept him in Merkede. It'd been bruised by the cold shoulder he'd received from his former contacts, and then mortally wounded when he was kidnapped.

Then do something about it, Wane told himself. *Don't let him become another Hector.* But what could he do? Though small, Zot was still a grown man. He couldn't force the older man to go anywhere he didn't want to. Was staying by his side the same as supporting his behavior?

There was one thing keeping Wane tied to the man. The realization that abandoning Zot was tantamount to abandoning the rebellion. They were counting on them to return with weapons, rations, and money for bribes to keep their militia afloat. Without those supplies, they would run out of energy, and the church would crush them like grain under a millstone.

"Remind me again why we spent all that money on these ridiculous clothes?" Wane asked, more to shake off his own spiraling thoughts than because he expected a sane answer out of Zot. He tugged at his own dressing gown, which was a nauseating shade of lilac and covered in about as many frills as anyone would need in three lifetimes. It reeked of the sandalwood perfume that permeated Chrysanthemum's boutique. Wane didn't care for

CHAPTER 32

it. It smelled like the type of people he used to target. The type of people who would think him scum.

"Because," Zot said through gritted teeth, "we need to blend in. How many times have I told you not to question the plan? I've been doing this since before you were even thought of, boy. If anyone knows how to get a lot of money quickly, it's me.

"So here it is for the last time. We go in. We make an impression, win some money, but not too much. Then, when they're all nice and comfortable around us, we make sure that Prince Neheb notices us. When he does"—Zot snapped his fingers—"we are in. Easy as that."

"Into where?" Wane asked. He was having a hard time keeping his cool. It was one thing to be treated like a child, but he wouldn't be treated like a dumb child.

"We get ourselves invited to the palace for an audience with the prince. Where we will then trick him out of as much money as the two of us can carry. Is that clear?"

Wane buried his face in his hands. "How are you so confident? This entire plan is based on gambling away what little money we have left. You keep saying we'll win more, but you know what gambling is, don't you? For all you know, we could end up empty-handed, with an angry boutique owner reporting us over our outstanding debts. Didn't you say you saved that money in the vault for your children? Something about having held onto it for all of your criminal career, and never wanting to touch it? How could you gamble it away now?"

Zot jumped to his feet, turning his back on the window. "It's not gambling if I'm the one playing." It couldn't be clearer that he considered the conversation over.

There was a clang on the street below. Zot whirled around. "Get over here." He beckoned for Wane to come closer. "Have you been practicing that script I got you?"

Wane sighed, but nodded.

"Excellent. Focus. They'll speak the password any second now."

Wane peered over the edge of the windowsill, watching as a group of laughing sailors approached the abandoned-looking house on the opposite side of the street. The first of them, a tall, broad-shouldered man with a beard that approached two feet, wrapped his knuckles against it in an intricate pattern.

Wane closed his eyes and pictured the oval rune of *Auris*, the hearing sigil. At first, he thought it wouldn't work, but then the groan of hinges across the street screeched in his ears like a flock of fleders. He winced, but held on to the sigil for dear life. This was what they had been waiting for. If he failed, they might be stuck in this plague-ridden dump for hours.

"What do you want?" a gruff voice growled from behind the door on the opposite side of the street.

"I want to buy a pair of new, shiny, exquisite breeches," the man with the long beard said, "with my esteemed colleagues." He pointed over his shoulder at the men standing behind him.

"Very well," the man behind the door growled, "and what color should these breeches be?"

"Magenta," the man replied.

The door opened a crack, and the group disappeared. At once, the door swung shut again, and the street was dark once more.

"And?" Zot asked.

"They were talking about buying breeches," Wane said, "magenta breeches."

A sharp smile broke Zot's grim face. "We're in. You remember the fake name I gave you?"

CHAPTER 33

alking into Ran-Sabacc's gambling den was like stepping into a cloud. Sweet smoke reminiscent of Acheron hung thick in the air, making it impossible to see the full extent of the cellar. The chain of rooms with vaulted ceilings seemed to go on forever.

Tucked away in alcoves around the walls, dozens of tables stood, surrounded by the most diverse crowd Wane had ever seen. His eye was drawn to a bald Hawqallian woman with a sapphire snake around her neck. The beast must have been at least as thick as Wane's own neck.

He shuddered and looked away, only to find a group of sailors huddled around a game of cards, each of them in various states of undress. Their stinking clothes piled up in the middle of the table.

A large wooden wheel stood in one corner of the room, divided into colorful slices stamped with symbols. Zot looked in his element as he strutted across the basement in his high-top shoes.

"Is that your thing?" Wane asked, nodding at the wheel.

"Oh," Zot said with a faint smile, "we won't be playing anything as basic as the death-wheel tonight. The Prince of Hawqal is known for his more exciting tastes. If we wish to draw attention to ourselves, we'll have to find a more interesting game to play."

"Such as?"

Zot pointed at a red door near the far end of the basement. A small but broad-shouldered man sat on a chair beside it, eyeing the two of them as they approached. "Regulars only," he croaked, pointing at the symbol on the door.

Wane made to turn away, unwilling to anger a man who looked like he could squash a watermelon in one hand while strangling a wolf with the other.

Zot smiled. "One little game of scolopendra, that's all I want." He stood on tiptoe to whisper in the man's ear. "If I win, I'll give you ten percent of whatever was in the pot."

"And if you lose?"

"Then I was never here to begin with, and no one need be any the wiser." The man chewed his bottom lip, watery eyes trained on Zot.

"I assure you," Zot said, smiling, "once you see me play, I think we'll both agree that I should be considered a regular here."

He held up the pouch containing all their remaining money, and Wane felt his stomach drop.

"Give me one game," Zot said, "and you might make more money tonight than the rest of the week combined."

"Not the first one to promise me that." The guard let out a long sigh. "Suit yourself. Your funeral."

He opened the door, and Zot wedged himself through.

As Wane went to enter, the broad-shouldered man stuck out an arm. "The kid stays here. What we've got behind that door isn't suitable for someone his age."

Zot gave the man an icy stare. "My assistant has seen plenty. I'll need him to carry my winnings when I leave tonight. You leave what is suitable for his eyes up to me."

For a moment, it looked like the broad-shouldered man might stand his ground, but then he shrugged. "Whatever."

***

As Wane stepped through the door, a tornado of noise greeted him. The back of his head collided with the door, which had already been locked behind him.

"Come on, boy," Zot yelled from somewhere up ahead, his form already lost in the throng of dozens of people clustered together. "I want to get in on this round. If you make me miss inspection, the money we lose will come out of your pocket."

There was a musty, humid stench to the room, like jamming your nose into the rotting mulch on a jungle floor. The back of Wane's neck tingled. He could almost feel something crawling down his dress robe.

"Then why did you bring me here in the first place?" he snapped. "If you're going to treat me like dead weight, you could have left me out of this. Then we'd at least have the money you spent on this monstrosity"—he gesticulated at his own gaudy attire—"to give to Saf."

"I need you."

"Whatever for?" Wane asked, struggling to clear a path behind Zot.

CHAPTER 33

"For this."

A wave of jeers and roars rose from the surrounding crowd, and Zot raised his hands like a conductor standing in front of a choir. As he drew level with the man, Wane could see the subject of all that enthusiasm and frustration.

In the middle of the room stood a circular table with six people crowded around it. Glass walls lined the table's edges, and at fixed intervals, holes were cut in the glass, through which the contestants had stuck their arms up to the elbow. Inside the cage, a miniature jungle bloomed.

As Wane got closer, he noticed one of the six contestants wiggling in his seat. He tried to stand up, then toppled backward. Though plenty of people stood behind him to stop his fall, nobody did. There was a dull crunch as the man's head smacked into the stone floor.

Wane moved closer, trying to see if there was anything he could do to help the man. When he kneeled down beside the still figure, two of the guards pushed their way through the crowd. They each grabbed one of his arms and dragged him away into a chamber on the opposite side of the room.

"Was he...?" Wane turned to Zot, who shrugged.

"It's not always fatal. But I have seen plenty who were never the same afterward."

"After what?" Wane asked, eyeing the glass cage with apprehension.

The remaining five players had now also withdrawn their arms, and tiny metal sliding doors closed off the holes in the cage so that whatever was inside could not escape into the crowd.

"Some things are easier shown than explained," Zot replied. He stepped over to the table in the middle where the five remaining contestants sat back in their chairs, all of them seeming both relieved and thrilled.

"We've got a lively one today, then?" Zot asked the others. They all looked up at him. Silence fell like a hammer stroke. The surrounding crowd all turned to face Zot, who must have looked like something in between a lunatic and a rich lunatic to them.

"Maybe," one of them said. "What's it to you?"

A broad grin split Zot's face. It was an ugly thing, false in every way, and yet it seemed to disarm those around him. Zot wandered over to claim the empty seat at the table.

"I'm a bit of an expert at scolopendra," he said. "Mind if I join?"

"Don't matter to me if you sit there," a man with a braided black beard beside him replied, "but be warned, this table has seen plenty of rotation tonight."

"Excellent," Zot replied. "How many are in there?"

Wane's stomach dropped. *So that's what scolopendrae are used for.*

"Four," a woman on the opposite end of the table replied, brushing a hand through a mop of short curls. Her brown eyes glittered with pride. "They're quite deadly."

Zot nodded. "Drop in some bait, will you? As a new player at the table, it's my right to see what I'm getting into."

He beckoned for Wane to come closer. One woman at the table called for a guard. The guard lifted a circular lid in the center of the glass cage and dropped in a squirming mouse.

The mouse spun around in the center of the cage, kicking up sawdust and mulch. Its squeaks of terror were muffled by the glass as it darted from one side to the other, then back, realizing there was no way out.

Wane bent closer to the glass. Before he had even noticed it was there, it struck from atop a gnarled branch. It landed on top of the mouse, two long razor-sharp front legs dug deep into its prey's neck. Its long scaly body was crimson and black, well over half a foot long, and lined with long, sharp legs. Dozens of them.

Three more appeared from the underbrush in the cage. They began circling the one eating the mouse. Still sitting on top of its prey, the first scolopendra unleashed a series of furious clicks, curling its body around the mouse. The others charged, swiping at each other with innumerable legs. It was like watching a ball of yarn roll down a hill. A red mist spread across the cage as the mouse was torn apart. Wane let out a gasp.

He looked up at Zot, expecting to see at least some of his own shock mirrored in the man's face, but he was smiling, as though everything was going according to plan.

As soon as they had appeared, the scolopendrae vanished. They were impossible to see in their hideouts under the leaves and branches in the cage. The five players seated around the cage looked up at Zot.

"Well?" the broad-shouldered man who had won the previous round asked. "Lively enough for you?"

"They'll do."

Though Wane didn't understand the rules of the game yet, he'd seen enough to realize that what Zot was about to do was madness. Sticking your arm into that cage was like cramming it down a lion's throat.

It was one thing to face danger when you had no choice. But to get anywhere near those things proved just how far gone Zot was. It was nothing

CHAPTER 33

to admire. A smart man knew when to cut his losses and keep a hold of at least something that could help those who depended on him.

Instead, Zot was becoming maniacal. His sense of self-preservation had died under the weight of his bruised ego. There was a noise in his right ear. Wane's head whipped around to find Zot snapping his fingers at him.

Wane bit his tongue to avoid spitting at the man. Who in Heil's name did he think he was?

"Boy, come here."

It took every ounce of self-control Wane possessed to bend down beside Zot to hear what he had to say.

"If I get bit," Zot said, "don't take me back to the inn. Drag me to Sachrya. Her tinctures will give me the best chance of survival."

"What?" Wane asked. "We just spent half of our money trying to get away from that woman. Now you would have us go back there?"

"Look," Zot whispered, "I'm good at this. Very good. But should the impossible happen, you drop me on Sachrya's front step and you run. I'll be fine. Bites are only fatal about half the time. The venom gets weaker with every generation of scolopendra bred in captivity. I believe that's why they've got four in the cage now instead of one."

"Don't do this," Wane shook his head. "Why risk everything we've worked so hard for? Let's just leave this place and go home. There's no one forcing you to do this."

"We can't," Zot said. "There is no returning until we've gathered what is needed. I am not a man to make promises I can't deliver on."

"But you didn't know," Wane muttered. He was having trouble keeping his voice down. "You didn't know how difficult it would be, how far the empire's actions had undermined your influence. Saf will understand. She'll be happier to see you return empty-handed than to hear of your death through me."

"Would she?" Their eyes met. Wane hesitated. Saf was the type of woman who put it all on the line every single time and expected little less from those around her. Maybe Zot had a point. He rubbed his eyes with two knuckles, trying to regain some clarity amid the panic that was building in his head.

"Fine," he said. "If you get bit, I'll take you to the shamanka. What else?"

"Make sure she gives me water and a tincture to neutralize the venom. I should be fine after that."

"And if you're not?"

"That's a risk worth taking." Zot gave Wane a shove in the sternum to indicate that it was time to back off. Zot took a deep breath, and Wane watched his face shift.

His serious demeanor was gone, replaced by an arrogant, casual smile. Zot turned to the broad-shouldered man who had won the previous round. "Unless the rules have changed since my last time, it's up to you to place the first bet, is it not?"

"It is." The man grinned. "Let's go with twenty-five shards. Just to keep things light, seeing as how our friend didn't fare so well in the last round." He nodded his head toward the door where the unconscious man had been dragged off to. "Call it my way of welcoming you to the table."

Zot scoffed. "Twenty-five? You know you can do better than that. Make it a hundred."

"I thought it was up to me to place the first bet?" The man's chest swelled, cheeks flushing with anger.

"Maybe I misread you. I thought you were a big boy."

The other players at the table shifted, eyes darting from the broad-shouldered man to Zot and back.

"I'm here to make a little money, not lose a month's wage in a single round. Let's keep it reasonable," the short-haired woman with the blazing eyes said.

The man with broad shoulders drew a finger across his lips to indicate that she was speaking out of turn.

"Fine," he said, looking at Zot, "betting starts at a hundred shards."

He looked to his left, where a stocky woman with long black braids sat. She opened a leather pouch and began counting.

To her left, the woman who had spoken up to keep the bet lower shook her head. "You idiots have fun with this one. I'm not trying to end up in a shallow grave. I'm out." She stood up and walked away. The crowd parted to let her through.

The fourth player was already getting up. Shaking his head, he looked at the broad-shouldered man and said, "This. This is going to get you killed." He looked at the woman with the long braids. "Good luck with these two." Then he marched off.

Zot was the last one to place a bet. Wane looked at him and saw how relaxed his posture was. He leaned back in his chair as though he was sipping a mug of kelp and listening to an entertaining tale of events that had happened long ago and far away.

There was a detachment to him that both impressed and frightened Wane.

"In," Zot said. "Raised to one hundred and fifty shards." He grabbed the leather pouch containing the rest of their money and placed it on top of the

CHAPTER 33

glass cage, staring at the broad-shouldered man, the braided woman, and back.

The broad-shouldered man laughed. "You think you're going to screw me out of a hundred shards by playing a game of chicken? I'm not backing out. One fifty it is."

The woman with the braids grinned. "Well, this night is turning out a lot more exciting than I expected." She put her pouch on top of the glass cage.

Wane could feel a hollow sense of dread in his stomach. All of their money hung in the balance. Money Zot had been saving for his own children. He had cherished it so much that he had preferred to deal drugs and get himself kidnapped in the process to make money rather than touch it, but now that he had it in his pocket, he was willing to gamble it all away on one round of whatever this madness was.

"Don't," Wane whispered. "We need money for a charter back home. We'll be stranded."

Zot held up a finger to call for silence. He was immovable.

"So," the man who had dropped the mouse earlier said, "looks like we have quite the pot this round. Thorough inspections shall, of course, be administered."

He waved two fingers, and a man entered through a door in the back of the room with a cage. The cage held a long, furry creature, which resembled a snake with four tiny paws. It wasn't quite a weasel; it was much longer than that, but it was just as thin and wriggly.

The referee took the creature out of the cage, coiled it around his forearm, and walked around the table. The broad-shouldered man held out his hands, and the referee brought the weasel down to sniff them. When no reaction came, he nodded and checked the woman with the braids. She, too, seemed clean. Zot was last in line.

Nervous sweat broke over Wane's back. It would be just like Zot to think he could get away with cheating.

Had that been why he was so confident? Though he couldn't see his face, Wane prayed Zot was not about to land both of them in trouble. The weasel bent down, sniffing at Zot's hand.

"Clean," the referee pronounced. Wane let out a deep breath. His relief was supplanted by renewed anxiety.

Their money was staked on a fair game of chance. Zot had done nothing to tilt the odds in his favor. His confidence was based on the presumption that he would be lucky.

CHAPTER 34

Excitement, such as he hadn't known in months, surged through Zot's veins. He was back. Finally back. With a flourish, he swept the winnings of the previous round into his pouch and smiled at his competitors. *Tough luck, my friends,* he thought. *When Dimimzy Zot sits down at a table, victory is a foregone conclusion.*

He stood up, holding the bag of winnings, and jangled it at the crowd of onlookers, who cheered. He was on top of the world, and soon everybody would know. Zot turned around and looked at the broad-shouldered man he had challenged in the previous round.

"What do you say, big guy, double or nothing?" There was a groan somewhere behind him, and Zot knew the boy was about to complain again. He held up a preemptive hand. Whatever his grievance was, Zot didn't want to hear it.

He was in the zone, taking back what was rightfully his. One day, when the boy had a reputation of his own to maintain, he might understand. But not today. So there was no point in explaining or negotiating.

"Double or nothing?" he repeated, looking at the rest of the table. "Who's in?"

He jangled the pouch one more time, just to feel the weight of it. *Not bad for a day's work.*

Since he was the winner of the previous round, it was his right to place the starting bet. Generally, it was a stupid move to start too high because if nobody bought in, there would be no money to win.

That didn't matter to Zot. This was about sending a message. Winnings were merely a side effect. He set down his entire pouch as the starting bet. Two men got up, shaking their heads. One of them nodded at Zot. "I'm out. You have a good night, Mr...."

For a split -=second, Zot was tempted to give the man his real name. He caught himself at the last second. "Roosebeke," he said. "The name is

CHAPTER 34

Jacob Roosebeke."

The man gave a salute, then followed his partner out. That left three of them at the table: the broad-shouldered man, who now looked at Zot as though he were a wolf that had just devoured his firstborn son; the Hawqallian woman with long black braids; and Zot himself.

"I'm in," the woman said.

Zot breathed a sigh of relief. There would be a game. If everyone bowed out, he would have proved himself bolder than the others, but there wouldn't be a story.

Winning one game was a fluke. Anyone could get lucky once, but doubling down and winning again? That would cement his reputation here for good. You needed to be a special kind of lunatic to put it all on the line twice, and Jacob Roosebeke was just that kind of lunatic.

"In," the broad-shouldered man grumbled. "No raise."

"Excellent."

There was a renewed round of inspections. The referee circled the table with the sniffsel to detect malfeasance. This time, the man lingered on Zot, inspecting his hands and encouraging the sniffsel to take its time. The creature didn't alert to any suspicious scents. Zot couldn't refrain from giving the referee a taunting grin.

He didn't need to cheat. In fact, he wouldn't. Not even if he was certain he could get away with it.

Sure, if he wanted to draw Prince Neheb's attention, he'd need to impress those around him. But at its core, this was about showing himself that he was still the man who could take nothing and build everything out of it. That he was still fearless, and that he could still put everything on the line when it mattered most.

The referee opened the gates. A waft of acrid air burned Zot's nostrils. He placed his hand in the cage with slow, deliberate movements to avoid creating unnecessary tremors that the scolopendrae would pick up on.

On the other side of the cage, the Hawqallian woman's face turned into a slab of stone. Her hand darted forward into the cage with the graceful agility of a striking serpent. The broad-shouldered man took a deep breath. Some of the blood had drained from his face. It took a stern look from the referee to get him to extend his lower arm into the cage.

Zot chuckled, just loud enough for the man to hear.

"There we go," the referee announced. "We start the round off with three contestants. Who will remain? Place your bets now or regret it later."

He began making the rounds of the crowd, jangling a large sack full of shards and writing the wagers on his bare arms.

Zot closed his eyes, not bothering to see where the scolopendrae were relative to his hand. It didn't matter; he would not retract until he won or got bitten. It was a strangely relaxing feeling. He would either walk out of here a rich man or be carried out in a coma and be off no worse than he was a few days ago. The die had been cast; now it was up to fate to do the rest. Win-win.

That was the glorious thing about having nothing to lose, he realized. It made you all but invincible. You could do whatever you wanted. He lounged in his chair, enjoying the bliss that came with this newfound realization, when something sharp prodded the tip of his index finger.

His eyes shot open. One of the scolopendrae was prodding his finger, trying to determine what it was. It was an exploratory movement, one he had seen many times right before a strike.

Hot patches rose on his cheeks. Now that the time had come to commit, he realized he'd forgotten to account for one thing: fear. It was one thing to make a rational decision when you were dealing in hypotheticals. But once reality's sharp pincers began poking at your bare skin, that part of your brain shut down in favor of a much more visceral and ancient instinct to survive.

Withdrawing his hand meant losing all their remaining capital. They would be stranded on Merkede with no money to return to Hammerstroke. Once Madame Chrysanthemum notified the constabulary of their outstanding debt, they might end up worse than stranded.

Zot remained motionless as the scolopendra wriggled underneath his fingers, trying to wrap itself around his hand. He thought of his boys and their mother, tucked away in some far-off corner of Hawqal. If he died here, would they ever find out what happened to him? Would they care if they did?

You let go of that life. He had made peace with that when he'd emptied his vault, but now that it all might be over in one quick flash, he couldn't help but return to those buried feelings.

His hand crept back toward the edge of the cage. Something ancient and deeper than himself screamed at him to retract his hand, to survive at all costs. The scolopendra wrapped itself around his hand, taking its time to restrain its prey before the strike. Escape was impossible now. Beads of sweat rolled down Zot's forehead. Transparent venom rolled down the beast's front pincers. It seemed tiny and insignificant for a substance that would destroy him.

Now that it was too late to save himself, clarity washed over him. What in the Seven was he doing? He'd had so much money in his hand minutes

CHAPTER 34

earlier. They could've walked away, and nobody would have blamed him. The boy had been right. At this very moment, they could be sleeping in a comfortable cabin aboard a ship bound for Hammerstroke. Within weeks, they would have arrived in Metten with a decent chunk of cash. Perhaps not a heroic amount, but something. Instead, he was about to die because of his stupid pride.

There was a scream on the other side of the table. The broad-shouldered man jerked his hand back, staring at it wide-eyed. Two wounds on the palm of his hand oozed blood. For one moment, he looked around the crowded room, eyes lingering on Zot with disgusted fury. Then he sank back in his chair, foam frothing from his open mouth.

That's going to be me, Zot thought, looking at the creature curling itself around his hand. *That's going to be me in one second.*

His eyes found the woman sitting opposite him. She leaned back in her chair as though they were having a drink in the afternoon sun.

"One down," she said. "Why don't you get up before it becomes two? You're looking pale."

It was the smirk curling her lips that jolted Zot from his panic. Who did she think she was? Mocking him in front of all these people as if he were some pampered nobleman's offspring.

Let the venom come. Death with dignity was nothing compared to cowering like a schoolboy. His eyes met hers. She shifted in her seat, unsettled by what she saw in his face.

Zot acted with the determination of a charging shark. He twisted his hand, grabbing the scolopendra just behind its head. It fought, kicking and scratching with its needle-like legs. Zot pressed his thumb into the creature with all the strength he could muster. A droplet of venom dripped down onto the back of his hand. It burned like boiling oil. The scolopendra hissed. The crowd fell silent. It sounded like a cat being skinned alive.

Zot forced himself to keep his eyes on the Hawqallian woman. Her smirk had been replaced with an open-mouthed gape of horror. Zot squeezed until he felt a pop. The scolopendra went limp in his hands.

There were gasps from the onlookers, followed by a scream from the woman on the other side. She withdrew her hand and jumped up, blood seeping down her forearm from two puncture marks just above the wrist.

Dangerous area. Almost certainly fatal.

"Take it," she spat at Zot. Her pouch sailed through the air, and Zot caught it with his free hand. Two of her friends rushed forward to catch her as she toppled backward. For a few steps, she tried to stand on her own legs, but before the trio reached the door, the tips of her boots dragged along the floor.

Without realizing it, Zot punched his fists into the air. The dead scolopendra was still clutched in his fist. He swung the carcass around for all to see. A cacophony of noise erupted as the onlookers cheered and yelled.

"Grab the money. We're done here," he told Wane.

The boy swept three pouches up in his arms.

"The name is Jacob Roosebeke," Zot yelled out. "Remember it. We will stay at the Rosemary Hotel. I'll be waiting for any worthy challenger."

With that, he flung the dead scolopendra on top of the cage and strode out of the room, leaving silence in his wake.

CHAPTER 35

rina spent the rest of the week hiding in her cabin, accompanied by the last cask of rum aboard the *Chimera*. None of the other travelers dared to come knocking to take it away from her, so she sat and drank, watching through her tiny window as the horizon crept past.

Late one night, as she was finishing up her last mug of the day, she could've sworn she saw a huge shape cresting the horizon, illuminated by the last chariot before the world dipped into darkness.

She thought of Razorwing. The poor creature must be confused now that it was forced to live on Metten with only Saf and her recruits to keep him company. She'd abandoned him, plain and simple. And for what? They had achieved nothing, and it didn't seem like things would look up soon. She sighed and drained what was left in her mug.

It's for the better. The farther away from me you are, the safer.

That same sentiment applied to anyone aboard the ship. The name Springtide and the people attached to it were, now more than ever, target number one. When she'd still been in Doorstep's Ditch, she'd occasionally woken to find a crude sketch of her own face staring back at her from hundreds of pamphlets on every surface they would stick to. Over the months, the price on her head had increased.

Of course, those sympathetic to the rebellion tore all of them down within a day or two, but the fact remained that where once the Signum had been symbols of what happened to those who dared resist the empire, so now were Brina, Abrasax, and those who had helped the latter escape from God's Maul last year.

It just remained to be seen what that symbol would come to mean. There was one thing Brina knew for certain as she lay down on the musty straw pillow of her bunk. She wouldn't end up like the original Signum. She wouldn't be captured alive. Whatever happened, she would go down like Acheron, crashing into the earth before she'd ever allow herself to be dragged away in chains.

With that thought, the alcohol circulating in her blood dragged her down like an anchor, pulling her into a restless sleep.

***

There was a shout and a bang. Brina bolted upright in bed, a dagger clutched in her hand. It was light outside. The door to her cabin stood open. Sneak's face poked out through the gap.

"We're here."

The long journey hadn't done him much good. His already sharp face now looked gaunt and malnourished. There was a hollowness to his eyes.

"What?" Brina groaned, throwing her dagger onto the wooden floor with a thunk and turning over in bed. Her head felt like a millstone, and a dull throb behind her eyes told her everything she needed to know. Today was not her day. As the ship's water rations had dwindled to the bare minimum, her daily rum was leaving her dehydrated.

"We're here," Sneak repeated. "Onderheem is only half an hour away. Samok asked me to fetch you."

Brina sat up, pressing her palm to her eyeball to still the hammer blows in her head.

"Fine."

She struggled out of bed, realized that she hadn't undressed the night before, and clambered up the rocking wooden stairs to the main deck. Samok stood on the quarterdeck, directing his crew to take in sail as they neared the shore.

"I thought I'd never set foot on dry land again," Brina said, clapping the muscled captain on the back.

"Well," Samok said, "that's what I wanted to talk about. Look at this."

He held up a telescope and pointed at a distant cluster of buildings. Brina put the instrument to her eye and groaned. The harbor looked like someone had pitched a thousand crimson tents. *So that's where all those red sails were going.*

"The harbor is overrun," Samok said. His dark eyes narrowed to slits as he stared at the horizon. "The darkhelms have thrown up a blockade, and every ship that wants to get in is searched."

Abrasax stood leaning over the deck railing, staring off into the distance. His scraggly beard was growing at an alarming rate, and even though no one

CHAPTER 35

aboard the ship smelled fresh after a month at sea, Abrasax was eye-watering.

They couldn't walk into a king's hall looking like a bunch of runaway servants who had traipsed from pigsty to pigsty on their way. She would need to fix that man up, but first, there were more pressing matters.

"What do you think?" she asked Abrasax.

"Sailing in there would be like sailing into a leviathan's open mouth," Abrasax mumbled. "Every darkhelm in the empire has our description, and I'm afraid we make a rather recognizable pair." He pointed at Brina's scarred eye and at his own scraggly appearance, including the God's Maul brand seared into his skin. "If we walk in there, we'll make some darkhelm officer very happy."

Brina thumped a fist against the ship's deck railing, and the impact pulsed through to her temples, causing her headache to spike.

"What if you had a darkhelm officer with you?" a clear, thin voice said behind them.

Brina turned to find Solana leaning back, holding on to the stairs on her way up to the quarterdeck.

"Yes," Brina said, "and while we're casting wishes, I'd like a golden dragon who shits coins."

"What I mean is," Solana said, undeterred, "I was one of them. I spent the better part of two decades learning every detail of how our army functions, how our officers behave, and how to get our recruits to do what I wanted them to. All we need is a helmet. I could pass the rest of the crew off as mercenaries accompanying me on a secret mission ordered by the Cardinal. I've seen his seal too many times not to be able to make a believable forgery. Besides, when I tell soldiers to do something, I don't need to ask twice."

Brina let out a mirthless laugh. "Right. Sounds like a great idea. We'll just sail right in there, let you do the talking, while you know full well that delivering us to your master would make you rich beyond compare. There's no way that could backfire."

She wanted to spit at Solana's feet but redirected her motion at the last moment when she saw Abrasax's disapproving stare. The glob of slime went flying over the side of the deck, where it merged with the roiling water of the sea.

"I have explained to you once that I am in as much danger of being discovered as you are. If our last conversation didn't convince you that returning to De Leliard would be my death sentence, then nothing will." Solana turned around.

"What are the chances they'll insist on a search of the ship?" Abrasax said, causing Solana to halt on the stairs.

"All but zero," she said. "They'll search any ship not flying the Mallion's Depth flag, but I'd like to see them try to go against me. I can be persuasive when I need to be."

Abrasax nodded and turned toward Brina, who held up a finger.

"I don't want to hear it," she said.

"What are our alternatives, Samok?" Brina asked the captain, who looked stricken to be asked for an opinion.

"We've got Port Cordwain to the south of the island, and Little Cove a little further west. The latter is the smallest of the two ports, but our supplies are running low, and we would need a small miracle to find everything we need there for our journey back. Port Cordwain is our only alternative."

"Very well," Brina said, clapping the man on the shoulder. "We will set sail there, and if you'll excuse me, my head feels like a troupe of gorillas are doing a mating dance in it. I'm going to lie down. Wake me up when we get there."

***

By the time Brina woke from her afternoon crash, dusk had arrived. She stumbled onto the deck, where Sneak, Abrasax, Samok, and, to her great displeasure, Solana stood engaged in a heated discussion.

"But once they know we are there, it's over," Sneak said.

Brina stomped up the stairs to announce her presence. All turned to look at her, faces clouded with disapproval.

"Where were you?" Bron asked, ruffling a hand through his beard. "Didn't you see this?" He pointed a muscled arm at the harbor town of Port Cordwain. Here too, the harbor was blocked by a chain of red-sailed ships. Merchant vessels lay anchored outside, clustering into a growing pileup.

"I was…" Brina began, but then found she couldn't bother to justify herself. *I told them to wake me up. So who is really at fault here?*

She shrugged, then took a drag from the flagon of rum tucked away in her pocket.

"They're letting ships in one at a time," Sneak said. "Everyone gets boarded and searched before they're allowed to enter the harbor. That's why there's such a long wait. We've talked to some merchants. Some say they've been here for weeks. No way we're getting in."

"Then why bother?" Brina asked. "If there's so many merchants stuck out here, we could just buy our provisions from them. There's no reason we need to enter the town."

"That's the problem," Samok began, pulling a face. "The darkhelms have prohibited all of them from trading until their cargo has been searched and their documentation stamped. The scepter's got their own ships mixed into the group." He pointed out a few crimson sails between the sea of stranded sailors. "So far, they've confiscated cargo from three ships who were trying to trade on the water. If they see us approaching another ship, they'll do the same to us. And when they board the ship, it's only a matter of time before they figure out who we are."

Brina sighed.

She was growing frustrated with their mission. They kept running into one obstacle after the other. It was like navigating a maze with no exit.

"There is a way to get around their security measures," Abrasax began.

Brina knew at once what he meant. She looked from Abrasax to Solana, who had remained silent the whole time the others had been speaking.

"I told you," Brina said, "we're not putting ourselves at her mercy. It's suicide. The first chance she gets, she'll betray us."

Sneak cleared his throat. "Abrasax was just explaining Solana's plan to us, and we kind of agreed that it is our best play in this position."

Brina's headache spiked alongside her anger. "You're taking her side?" she asked. "You know what she did. Acheron died because of her."

Solana kept quiet, but Brina continued. "And now we're going to let her do the talking, surrounded by her old allies?"

"I know how you feel. And I respect it," Sneak said. "But we are running out of supplies, and in case you've forgotten, we've got two dozen crew members working day and night to make this journey happen. Their bodies don't run on saltwater alone, nor do ours." He looked at Brina's flask. She felt the urge to grab Sneak by the vest, but pushed it aside. She knew her temper had been short lately, with anger, grief, and desperation building inside her. Solana's presence only added to the pain.

Sneak placed a hand on Brina's shoulder and leaned in. "For once, I need you to trust me. We need this," he said, peering over his shoulder at the crew working on the deck. "Even at minimum consumption, our provisions will run out sometime next week. You can go hungry if that's what you want, but I won't let them starve after they've worked so hard and risked so much to get us here. I know I am not Saf, but I've listened to Solana. I've burned every psycho-sigil I know, and I don't believe she is trying to set us up."

"Sigils," Brina muttered. "Since when do we need sigils to sniff out a liar?

She's the Cardinal's puppet. What more do we need?"

Bron cleared his throat. "You are a great warrior, and I respect your instincts, but even the greatest warrior cannot survive without her brothers and sisters in the spear wall. Remember that."

Though she didn't like admitting it, Brina knew they were right. Without a crew to man and defend the ship, they were nothing.

"Fine. What's the plan?"

CHAPTER 36

As Brina reached for the door handle to Solana's cabin, her hand curled into a fist. Every cell in her body resisted what she was about to do. She had told the woman once that she wasn't interested in learning anything the church had developed. A mere week later, the serpent had pressured her into doing just that.

Do it for the crew. This wasn't about what she wanted, but about the agreement they had come to as a team.

She turned the handle and found Solana sitting behind her desk. Her fingertips traced an engraving in her prayer book repeatedly. She appeared stuck in a trance. A blue jelly lantern hung from the wall beside her.

"I thought blind people didn't need light," Brina said as a greeting.

"I like the heat." Solana's fingers met in the center of the engraving one last time, and she snapped the book shut.

"Jelly lanterns don't emit heat."

"It's a subtle feeling. One I wouldn't expect you to pick up on."

"What's that supposed to mean?" Brina said, her hand still clasping the door handle.

I knew this was a bad idea. I knew this was a bad idea. I knew this was a bad idea.

"It's not an insult. What I mean is that my senses have been elevated through my training as a monk of the blind order. For example, I could smell you before you came in by the scent of rum on your breath."

Though Solana's voice was neutral, Brina couldn't help but feel accused of something.

"Couldn't help it," Brina said. She grabbed a stool that stood in a corner of the cabin and sat down with her back against the door. "Just thinking about your face makes me need a drink."

"You are tense," Solana remarked. "Your heart is racing. Your muscles are tight as violin strings. Why?"

"You know why," Brina growled. "I told you I wanted nothing to do with this religious nonsense, and now you've found a way to force it on me."

Solana held up her hands. "I'm not forcing anything on anyone. Multiple times I have offered to steal the helmet myself. I can already access the prayer of dreams. If you wish, you could still change your mind and allow me to undertake the mission alone. There would be no need for you to learn the prayer."

A cynical smile sliced across Brina's face. *Always the veneer of righteousness.* Solana was trying to make Brina sound like the lunatic.

"You're not going anywhere. Sneak and I have it handled. At least I know he'll have my back when something goes wrong."

Solana took a deep breath, and Brina was glad to hear that she was getting a reaction out of the woman.

"I doubt it will be fruitful for us to repeat our earlier discussion," Solana said, her tone and expression remaining neutral. "If you've made your choice, then I suggest we begin our first lesson. It's uncertain whether it will even work, but I believe it's worth a try."

"Get on with it, then," Brina's finger tapped an uneven rhythm on the desktop.

"Before we get started, it's important to highlight the difference between accessing the prayers and the method "sparkgazers" use. Am I saying that correctly?"

"I've got one. Anyone could learn our method if they have a script, while your prayers are shrouded in secrecy and are used to control those who lack the same power," Brina said.

"A fair criticism," Solana said, unperturbed, "but they are also mechanically very different. In the absence of vision, we of the abbey develop a canvas behind our eyes, upon which we can project prayers we have internalized through touch."

She showed the prayer book to Brina. Tiny bumps and grooves littered the page, shaped in a complicated pattern. It was unlike any script Brina had ever seen. A script depicted the sigil as it was supposed to be held in one's mind's eye. This looked like a load of random nonsense.

"The difficult part," Solana said, "is transposing that which we feel here"— she raised her fingers and used her other hand to indicate her fingertips—"to here"—she pointed at the white scar tissue around her eye sockets. "At first, it took me many days before I could attune to a prayer, let alone harness its powers in any useful capacity. I hope you will be a quicker learner."

CHAPTER 36

Great, just what I needed. More pressure.

"Those who retain their vision cannot access the prayers in the proper manner. But I hope that given your partial blindness, you too will be able to summon the necessary canvas to project the prayers into being."

"I still don't see how that would help. It only hindered my imprintation when I learned to burn sigils. Why would I differ from any of the others on the ship? There are better sparkgazers than me aboard this vessel."

Solana shook her head. "You are different because you have sacrificed part of your vision for something greater."

"I sacrificed nothing. That's something you fanatics do behind those stone walls. Believe me, if I had a choice, I would still have both of these." She jabbed a finger at her good eye.

"But you did have a choice. Master Bron told me all about how you stayed behind to give the others a head start when we released our bargheist."

Those words made Brina realize just what she was doing. A year ago, it had been this woman's idea to lock Acheron up in a cage in the freezing cold, just to bait Brina into the open so that they could both be captured.

"Guess your plan had holes in it," Brina said, unable to suppress a smirk.

"Yes, it was quite a shock. But the essence of the story is that you stayed behind to save your friends, and you lost your eye because of it. That is part one of why I think you should be capable of bridging the gap.

"Part two is the fact that you share part of the canvas that we of the abbey use. In time, you could learn to separate it from what remains of your vision."

Brina still saw a million reasons it wouldn't work, and each of them was a fine excuse, as far as she was concerned.

"In any case," Solana said, "we have little time to be discussing the technicalities of the process. So I suggest we start our training. If Samok is correct, the ship's rations will last another week, two at the very most. Which means we are operating with haste."

"No need to remind me," Brina said with a sigh, resigned to the fact that no excuse would get her out of this one.

"So while we shall need to scale up our training more quickly than I would've liked, I think starting the first session with one of the easiest prayers is the safest bet. This right here is the prayer of heat. It draws on the natural heat of our blood."

"So it's like *Gnis*," Brina remarked.

Solana looked confused for a moment, then nodded. "Yes, there is likely an analogous script you sparkgazers use. I will have to trust you on the nomenclature."

Solana opened her prayer book to the very first page, revealing a much simpler pattern of grooves. "If you are familiar with the effect, I need not remind you that digging too deeply could cool your body to a dangerous degree."

Brina remembered the first time Acheron had taught her to imprint on the sigil, when she'd almost set grouchy Zelda's shop in Mallion's Depth on fire. An involuntary smile crossed her face, followed by the crushing knowledge that he was no longer here, and that she was sitting side-by-side with the woman who had killed him.

A small, traitorous part of herself mumbled it had technically been Acheron who had seized Solana and jumped off the tower, but that was a voice she wasn't ready to acknowledge yet and one she would ignore for the rest of her days. Sometimes, things needed to be black and white for wounds to heal.

"Very well," Brina muttered. She placed her hands on the prayer tablet, feeling her way across the many bumps and gouges on the surface.

"I fashioned this to aid your learning." Solana lifted a cloth eyepatch from her desk drawer and handed it to Brina. "Obscuring your vision should make it easier to project the shape on your mental canvas."

Brina accepted the thing with a grunt. There was little she wanted less than to put herself in a vulnerable position while she was with this woman. One wrench of her arms, and she could snap Brina's neck.

Then again, if she wanted to kill me, there is very little I could do about it.

She put on the eyepatch. The halved field of vision she had grown accustomed to dissolved.

"Focus." Solana's voice seemed far away. "Feel the pattern, then map it out across the canvas of your vision, like you would picture a familiar face."

Brina's fingers found the prayer tablet and recoiled. It was unnaturally soft.

"No matter," Solana said. "Feel for as long as necessary until you know where every bump in the tablet is. It needs to feel like second nature to you."

"Then shut up," Brina snapped, taking out her frustration on the easiest target. "I can't think with you nagging me."

There was a sigh, and Solana's encouragements stopped. Sitting in complete silence, Brina found her thoughts wandering. She thought of Versa in De Malheure's fortress and wondered what they would say if they knew Brina was in the company of their long-lost sister.

Would they be happy, angry, something in the middle? Their last encounter had nearly been fatal. Solana had smashed most of Versa's ribs. Had it not

CHAPTER 36

been for Acheron's expert care, the innkeeper wouldn't have made it. Brina could feel her hatred rising again. Solana's presence was like a nail burying itself in her skull.

"It's not working," Brina snarled. "I give up."

"You can't." Solana said. "We need to make progress today. Every hour counts."

They both knew what giving up meant. It would mean accepting that Solana would have to join the mission to steal a darkhelm officer's helmet from a red-sailed ship. That seemed the worse option by far, and so Brina tried once again to set aside her feelings.

She forced herself to take a deep breath, then returned to mapping out the pattern on the prayer tablet in her mind's eye. After what felt like an eternity of trying and failing, something clicked. For a brief moment, the dots interlinked into a cohesive shape, the way stars coalesce into constellations.

Then the moment passed, leaving her with a warm, tingling sensation in her fingertips

"Good," Solana said, "very good. There is our proof. You *can* do it."

Though there was genuine excitement in Solana's voice, Brina didn't share her enthusiasm.

"It faded," she said. "It's much harder than imprinting the regular way."

She thought about it and realized that this wasn't quite true. When she first began learning to imprint on the shapes, she'd been the same—constantly distracted, forgetting what even the most basic shapes looked like.

A handful of attempts later, Brina managed to light a small candle Solana had procured from the Samok's cabin. They both held a hand toward the tiny flame as it flickered in front of them.

"It works," Solana said, curling and uncurling pale fingers. "The Keeper must have looked into your heart and found you worthy."

"Nobody did any such thing," Brina snapped. "Acheron explained it to me. Heil tried to lock away our natural gifts. And we're just finding all kinds of ways to break the lock. As far as Heil is concerned, we weren't supposed to have an ounce of power while she rules."

Solana frowned. "You think this is all just a technical process? No different from learning how to wield a windup bow or swing a mace?"

"That's what it is," Brina said, smiling. She couldn't help but enjoy the look of confusion on Solana's face. "There is no god who takes an interest in anything we do. You realize that, right?

"The only thing Heil was interested in was making sure we could never rival the gods again. She put chains on us, and the scripts have unlocked them. That's all there is to it."

"So you have never found that when you were cornered, scared, or angry that you could find just a little extra power within? You're telling me that your anger, considerable as it is, has never fueled your use of the shapes?"

Brina drummed her fingers against the desktop, focused on the flame flickering in front of her.

"Of course it helps when you're angry," Brina scowled. "It makes you try harder."

"So it is fair to say our feelings do impact our ability to access the divine." Solana smiled. "Heil finds us in situations of great need, and she sees us through them."

Brina had had enough. "I'm tired," she said, jumping to her feet. "I'll come back tomorrow to try something more complicated."

Solana opened her mouth, as though there was more she'd wanted to say, but then said, "That seems like a wise idea. You've exerted yourself. I can feel it. There's a lot of tension in you. Your breaths are becoming shallower with each attempt."

Brina couldn't help but feel insulted, but her haste to leave this woman's presence helped her ignore the subtle jab. She closed the door behind herself without saying another word, then pulled a flask from her inside pocket and took a deep drink.

She imagined herself crawling inside the vessel of smooth, warm liquid and drowning there, never to be seen again. The mere idea of it was bliss. What she wouldn't give to just dissolve.

Over the following days, Brina spent a tormenting number of hours in Solana's cabin, tracing and retracing her fingertips across a handful of increasingly complex prayers, until they were ready to work on the prayer of dreams.

The shape that would, if Solana was to be believed, allow Brina to imprint a false memory in a darkhelm officer's mind. One where they lost their helmet. It was the only way to ensure that the theft wouldn't be suspected. The officer had to believe that the loss was their fault.

"This is the one?" Brina asked as her fingers rolled across the dream prayer for the very first time. "It's like the person carving this had a stroke halfway through the process. There's no rhyme or reason to it. No shape to be discerned."

"Oh, but you are wrong," Solana said. "It is there, as it was there with all the others. This one, I'm afraid to say, is a complex prayer as it involves

CHAPTER 36

twisting reality as the subject experiences it. I believe you fire eyes use similar techniques."

A twinge of guilt stirred in Brina's guts as she remembered how she'd used *Consol* on Versa last year to force them to tell her about their experience of God's Maul. Afterward, she'd used the same shape to pull information from a Heilinist spy, almost killing the poor fellow. After that, she'd never quite shaken her dislike of psycho-sigils.

It was bad enough to think about how she had bent people to her will, but planting false memories felt like a step beyond that. It somehow felt more wrong to her than slitting the bastard's throat.

At least cold steel was honest. There was a collision of strength, skill, and cunning, and at the end, one party was left standing while the other lay in the dust. That seemed fair. Natural even.

She'd witnessed the same thing happening among the various monstrosities that lived on Hammerstroke when she'd been a roamer, trapping and killing all sorts of creatures in exchange for payment.

But planting a false memory? That was violating someone from the inside out.

Still, she had to admit the plan was solid. If the darkhelms didn't realize a theft had taken place, there would be no cause for suspicion when Solana presented herself as an officer. As soon as anyone suspected that an officer's helmet had been stolen, suspicion would fester among those blockading the city.

"All right," Solana said as Brina struggled for half an hour without even coming close to assembling the shape. "We will start from the beginning again. As you map out the shape across your mental canvas, you gain entry to the other person's consciousness. You will have their full attention, and every word you say will be recorded in their memory as events that occurred. Do you understand?"

Brina nodded, even though she didn't.

"So when you break into the officer's quarters on a nearby ship, you will search their room, find out what their flaw is, be it alcohol, sex, or cloud, and you will paint a memory in which they lost their helmet in a way that they wouldn't want to confess to. Are we clear on that point?"

Brina grunted her approval.

"Excellent, then let's start from the top."

As the week progressed, Brina faced an ever-growing mental block when it came to the prayer of dreams. So much so that during their last practice session, she had walked out of the room, overwhelmed with the weight of the responsibility on her shoulders, resistance against Solana's teaching, and the sheer complexity of the shape itself.

At the start of the session, she'd managed to compose the shape in her mind's eye but had failed to implant a memory in Samok, who served as a practice target.

"I feel weird," the man groaned afterward as he and Brina stood side-by-side on the deck. "As though something wormed its way into my brain and moved things around. I can't remember what I did today or the day before."

"Yeah, I didn't do a very good job of it," Brina admitted. "Any chance you remember anything about slugs?" Samok closed his eyes, as though digging deep into his memory.

"Nope," he said, "no slugs."

Brina sighed. "That settles it. I can't do it."

"You'll figure it out," Solana said. "Don't give up."

Brina's jaw worked. She would either have to admit that she couldn't do it and accept Solana's help on the mission, or state confidently that she had things under control and that they didn't need backup.

Brina left the cabin, lugging a millstone in her guts. She wasn't ready, and time was running out. The last of the rations had already been distributed among the crew, and what little fresh water remained was turning stale, a sickly layer of green algae coating the cask.

"How did it go?" a hopeful voice asked behind her. Brina turned to find Abrasax standing in his cabin doorway, a peculiar smile on his face.

"I'm proud of you," he said. "I know this has been difficult. To do something you resist with your entire being for the good of the crew requires a big person. Honestly, I didn't think you had it in you, not after so many years alone."

"It went well," Brina lied, knowing that speaking the truth would require reopening the dialogue about the possibility of sending Solana in her stead. That wasn't an option. As soon as they let that woman out of their sight, anything could happen. It needed to be prevented at all costs.

"I think I'm ready. With some luck, I could do it in another night or two."

Abrasax let out a deep sigh. "I spoke to Samok earlier tonight. He thinks it needs to happen tonight. Calculating for the waiting time other ships have taken to enter the harbor, it might take a few days for us to even reach the blockade. Navigating between all those merchant ships will be tough, and we'll need favorable winds to avoid collisions." Brina's eyes filled with frustration. "I need you to be honest with me, Sabrina. Can you handle it? There's

CHAPTER 36

no shame in admitting that this task is beyond you. It's a lot to ask, after all."

"I can do it," Brina said through gritted teeth. "I'd like some more practice, but I'm ready. If it needs to be tonight, so be it." Abrasax's smile deepened. He nodded.

"Excellent," he said. "Soon we'll be sitting at a dinner table once again laden with all the good things the Sundered Isles have to offer."

Brina nodded. "I will see it done."

CHAPTER 37

Brina scaled the *St. Lawrence* using a grappling hook attached to a section of rope. Although Samok had maneuvered the *Chimera* to be near the cluster of ships that lay anchored in front of Cordwain's blocked port, Brina still had to swim over a hundred yards through open water to reach the red-sailed galleon.

As she climbed, droplets of saltwater rained into the sea below. Her clothes clung to her skin, weighing her down like sheets of molten steel. She let out a breath of relief when she reached a window near the top of the ship. After a quick glance inside, she threw herself headlong into a storage area filled with barrels and jute sacks stuffed with moldering ship's biscuits.

Hiding behind a barrel, Brina touched on *Gnis*—just enough to dry her clothes without setting them alight. The sound of water dripping on the wooden boards would give away her position at once. Stealth was of the essence. A cloud of steam rose as her clothes dried. When she felt warm, she shuffled to the opposite side of the storage room and exited into a narrow corridor with doors on both sides. Brina burned *Auris* and the snoring of sailors became a drone in her ears. Excellent. She had reached the crew's quarters. Now she needed to find where the officers slept. Brina crept down the hallway, listening at each door.

"What do you think you're doing?" Brina's heart stopped as she kneeled down beside one of the closed doors, hearing stumbling on the other side.

"I'm doing what's right, Cornelius," a second voice replied. "I don't care how high they promote you. As long as I'm captain of this ship, what I say goes. Have you looked at these people? They're starving. The Heemians on the shore are near death from exhaustion. They look worse every day."

"What concern is that of ours?" Cornelius's voice rose. "We're here to keep the peace."

"To keep the peace, but not to torture those who have committed no greater sin than to be born under a different set of beliefs than us."

CHAPTER 37

"They're heathens, Captain." The last word was filled with contempt. "Their very existence is a mockery to the Keeper. We've given them every chance to convert."

"And many have," the captain replied. "Many more will, but to convince them to do so, we need to set a better example than this. Tomorrow we're handing out our rations, and I won't hear another word against it." Brina flung herself aside just in time as Cornelius stomped out of the captain's quarters and up the stairs to the main deck. The man was so furious, he didn't even notice Brina lurking in the shadows behind him.

It was now or never. By the sounds of it, the captain wouldn't be going to sleep soon, and Brina needed his helmet. If the prayer of dreams worked on someone who was sleeping, it would work on someone who was knocked out just as well. Sneaking through the open door, Brina saw a man in his late forties sitting at a small desk topped with open ledgers, an inkwell, and a quill. Tufts of graying hair protruded from his wrinkled scalp.

Brina closed the door as quietly as she could. Careful to muffle her footsteps, she crept behind the captain, ready to hit him in the temple for a knockout blow. "Back already, Cornelius?" the captain asked as he turned around. Brina cocked back her hand, braced for the blow, but then found she couldn't. There was something in his terrified eyes that gave her pause.

"Your eye," the captain said. "I know who you are." Usually, when these words came from a Heilinist, they carried an undertone of accusation and disgust. From the captain's mouth, they carried only the weight of sadness.

"Of course," he said, glancing at Brina's ruined eye. "Sabrina Springtide. You're just about the last person I expected to meet tonight. Why don't you have a seat?"

Brina let out an involuntary, faltering laugh. *Do it,* she told herself. *Knock him out. He could scream at any moment.* Brina might make it out alive, but not unseen. The success of tonight's mission hinged on secrecy. Instead of hitting the man, Brina heard her own mouth open.

"Why?"

"It's only polite to offer a guest a seat, is it not?" the captain asked. "Besides, if you're going to assassinate me, I'm afraid there's little I can do about it. I'd rather go out with one last stimulating conversation than have it all end in such a brutish fashion as a fistfight."

"I didn't come here to kill you," Brina stammered. Something about the man's gray eyes made her feel as though she needed to make excuses for herself, as though she needed to explain why she was standing there in the dead of night, looming over him with her fist cocked back. She hadn't let go of *Forte*, and now that she had realized this, she struggled to hold the shape. It flickered in and out of her vision, as though it too was embarrassed.

"Indeed?" The captain gestured once again to a second chair that stood against the far wall. "Then why are you here?"

"I am here because people who don't deserve it are suffering."

"We agree on that," the captain said. He ran his hands through his graying hair. "Though I presume there are many things on which our opinions differ, we at least have that in common." Seizing the opportunity, Brina changed tactics. She switched into *Consol*, looking at her shoes to disguise the glare in her eye.

"All I want is for the people on that island over there"—she pointed out the window—"to have decent lives, to have food on their plates and wine in their glasses. That is not an unreasonable thing to ask." Brina could hear the effects of the sigil in her own words. Her brash voice had turned soft and was all the more dangerous for it, the way water seeps through rock more easily than a blade.

"It's not that simple," the captain said. "If I were to have it my way, everyone in the Sundered Isles would have such basics. But we are at war, Miss Springtide, and though we are at opposite ends of it, both of us will feel its weight in time."

"And what if I told you," Brina said, leveraging *Consol* more openly now, "that in the here and now, you could ensure that fewer people will suffer?"

The captain let out a sad chuckle. "I can't deny that I have been looking for ways to make it so. But what would it cost me? All my life, I have known my place in the hierarchy. I have worked hard and done everything right so I could be in the position I am in now. I cannot and will not throw that away by collaborating with the state's enemy number one."

"And who decided that I am the state's enemy number one?" Brina asked. "Last time I checked, my only crime was wanting to have a father in my life. Can you name one other thing that a reasonable man could hold against me?"

The captain swallowed. "I understand, of course, from a human point of view. But your father isn't just any father, is he? He's the Cardinal Slayer. He earned that moniker for good reason, and in breaking him out, you are complicit in the crimes that he committed and will commit now that he roams free once more."

"And what of a daughter's love?" A quick glance at the captain's bedside table revealed a sketch of the man beside a woman, cradling an infant between

CHAPTER 37

them. This was it, the angle she'd been looking for.

The captain remained silent.

"Look," Brina continued, using *Consol* like a bard playing a lute, "the only thing I require is for you to go to sleep and forget that I was ever here. I need only take a few supplies of yours, and I can promise you this: I can ensure you will not remember what we discussed tomorrow. I will have become nothing but a memory of a dream. If you can do that, much suffering can be avoided. I will not have to harm you, and I, in return, shall not have your blood on my conscience."

The captain laughed and held out his arm. "Here," he said, offering her his wrist, "my heart is beating like a galloping horse. How could I go to sleep at a moment such as this?" Brina reached for the man's arm, feeling his pulse. Then, as naturally as slipping into a pair of well-worn shoes, she recited the prayer of dreams.

"Because it is so late," she said, her voice turning into a drone, a soothing noise that could wheedle its way through any skull and straight into that part of the brain which controls conscious thought. "It's late and you've worked hard. You fell asleep at once after Cornelius left."

She grabbed the captain by the arm and guided him to his bunk on the opposite end of the chamber. "Arguing with Cornelius drained you. Your sleep was fraught with strange dreams." The captain allowed himself to be guided, and by the time his back hit the straw mattress, his eyes fell shut. Brina reached over to the writing desk and picked up the man's officer's helmet, tucking it underneath her arm. Now for the finishing touch.

"You woke up later that night, seasick, worrying about what Cornelius might do tomorrow. In your struggle for fresh air, you stumbled up to the main deck. You leaned over the side of the ship, and the latches of your helmet, which you had not properly fastened upon awakening, let go. You watched in horror as your helmet sank to the depths. You'll wake up tomorrow feeling embarrassed and unwilling to depart your chambers. Cornelius is the only one of sufficient rank to see your face. You will have him fetch your spare helmet, and you will make him promise never to speak of the matter to anyone. To do so would be tantamount to mutiny."

The captain stirred in his sleep. Satisfied that she had done a thorough job, Brina spun around on her heel. She marched back into the storage room, crawled out through the window, and swam back to the *Chimera*. As she braved the icy waves, helmet clutched in one hand, her heart sank. She was no better than Solana. Tonight, she had become a sense surger.

CHAPTER 38

ane sat staring out of a third-floor window in the fabled Rosemary Hotel. The hotel bordered Glissade Avenue, where Chrysanthemum's boutique lay. In fact, there was a tiny window on the side of their room, through which one could stare straight down into the glamorous shopping street.

After his big win, Zot had insisted on upgrading their lodgings to something he called "more appropriate for people of our stature." Wane called it a waste of money.

Zot refused to tell him how much a night at the Rosemary cost, but the room's gilded faucets, marble walls, and vaulted ceilings left little to the imagination. Never had Wane slept so poorly in a bed so comfortable. Living with Zot had become like being trapped with a rabid animal that fancied itself at the top of the food chain.

Wane's fingers tapped out a restless rhythm on the windowsill as he watched waves of shoppers and travelers roll across the square below. For the second night in a row, Zot was nowhere to be seen. He'd left on a secretive errand, insisting it was important enough to leave Wane alone in this gilded cage.

In the distance, Wane could see the white sandstone palace atop the hill. Its many windows glimmered with blue jelly light in the approaching dark. Though Merkede was led by an elected council consisting of merchants and career politicians, the Hawqallian imperial family had been allowed to construct this monstrous fortress overlooking the city, under the condition that aside from housing the imperial family whenever they deigned to visit Merkede, it would also provide rooms for the Merkedian parliament to convene.

As always with merchants, economic considerations had won out over the obvious symbolic weight of allowing the Hawqallians to build the largest and strongest fortifications on the entire island. Whenever the parliament convened, they were, in essence, guests on their own soil.

CHAPTER 38

That was the end goal, Wane realized as he tried to count the square towers on the palace's outer wall. Zot had gotten it into his head that he would get both of them into the palace to meet Prince Neheb, and that somehow, he could convert that opportunity into a fortune.

His luck at the scolopendra table had only fortified his belief that he could pull off everything he put his mind to. Zot's confidence was at such a high that Wane wondered whether he even remembered why they were doing all of this.

Just as Wane decided to take a stroll up the hill to get a closer look at the palace, there was a knock at the door. Wane froze. The old him would have rushed to open the door, welcoming any diversion from the monotony, but now that he'd seen the dark side of the city, he found his hand lingering in front of the bolt.

There was a second knock, followed by the slow voice of Mr. Pennyworth, the hotel's concierge.

"Hello, Master Roosebeke. Are you in there?"

Wane shivered. The concierge, a slender man who looked much like a skeleton wearing a suit of human skin, was nice enough in his own way, but there was a rigidity to both his posture and his way of dealing with the guests that Wane found off-putting. The idea of engaging him in one-on-one conversation without Zot there to act as a shield did little to spur Wane to action.

There was a third knock.

"A messenger has arrived for Mr. Roosebeke," the concierge called. "She claims it is urgent."

There was a great deal of scuffling outside, after which Pennyworth added, "She is quite adamant about delivering the message tonight. Says it cannot wait."

"I know you're in there, young master. In fact, your uncle himself asked me to keep an eye on you to make sure you were doing well. The least you could do in exchange is open this accursed door so we can end this foolishness."

Then, in a whisper, Pennyworth told the unseen guest, "See, I told you, he's just a boy."

With a slight knot in his stomach, Wane swung open the door. Pennyworth's hollow face glared down at Wane, but before he could speak, he was shoved aside by a woman so tall that she almost had to bend double to fit into the corridor. Her long neck and narrow skull left little question as to her Hawqallian heritage. Except that these features were much more pronounced in the messenger than they had been in any Hawqallian Wane had met before.

"Young Roosebeke," the woman intoned in a sonorous, not unkind voice, "I have a message to deliver to your master. I'm afraid it is urgent, hence my insistence on your accepting it in person. I hope you can understand that the imperial family does not like to deal with middlemen."

She cast a scathing glance at the concierge, who shrugged and walked away, his footsteps echoing on the wooden steps as he returned to the hotel's lobby.

"That's fine," Wane said, trying and failing to contain his nerves as the woman towered over him. She handed him a scroll of parchment stamped with a wax seal shaped like a map of Hawqal, which he took with trembling hands.

He waited for the woman to leave, but she didn't. Instead, she stood there, watching him the way a hawk regards a hare.

"Am I supposed to open it?" Wane asked. "Right now?"

"It would be favorable."

Wane felt his pulse quicken. He couldn't remember if the woman had blinked at any point during their interaction. He didn't think she had.

"I should wait for my uncle," he tried, already moving backward to shut the door. She moved forward to block it.

"I'm afraid I shall need an answer straight away. You are his assistant, no?"

Wane remembered the cover story. "Oh. Yes, I suppose so."

"Then I assume you know your master's schedule?"

Wane sighed and broke the red wax seal on the parchment. Inside was a note written in a flourishing cursive.

Dearest Jacob Roosebeke,

I, Prince Ashur Neheb Ka, invite you to a luxurious promenade through my gardens tomorrow evening at nine. I have arranged a game that will challenge your skills and indulge our mutual love of exhilaration. Arrive at the palace in your finest attire, prepared for a night you won't forget. Do not be late.

Yours in indulgence,

Ashur Neheb Ka
Prince to the imperial throne

Wane sighed. Once he saw this, Zot was going to become insufferable. He just knew it.

CHAPTER 38

"So," the messenger snapped, "will your master attend?"
"Yes," Wane said with a sigh, "he will."

CHAPTER 39

"It's like home," Brina muttered, "and I hated home."

The dreary streets of Cordwain were paved with soot-stained flagstones, wide enough to allow carriages laden with unrefined ore to pass each other side by side. On both sides of the town's central street stood identical multistory houses, narrow and crooked like a row of rotten teeth. Their tarred roofs glittered with recent rainfall.

A blanket of smog blocked the sun, as though dusk had fallen the moment Brina stepped off the *Chimera*'s gangplank. She pulled her makeshift dust mask over her nose, looking over her shoulder. They may have made it into Cordwain, but Solana could still hand them over to the empire. All it would take was a wrong word aimed into the right ear.

The priestess had guided them into the harbor, forging documents so precisely that not even the dour harbor master had been able to take issue with them. Perhaps her desire to meet Versa was greater than the temptation to garner a mountain of gemstones. Regardless, they wouldn't have gotten this far had it not been for Solana. It was a bitter pill to swallow.

Behind Brina, following at a distance, were Sneak, Bron, and Abrasax. They'd all agreed that wandering the streets as a group would draw attention. Instead, they marched at different paces, attempting to blend in with the bustle of Heemian laborers pushing wheelbarrows or pulling at stubborn oxen.

Meanwhile, Samok and the rest of the ship's crew were stocking the ship with biscuits, dried fish, barrels of drinking water, and, per Brina's secret instruction, a nice stash of booze to tuck away under her bed. The mere thought of that lifted Brina's mood. Then she looked around the town, and her optimism faltered.

The town was one giant factory. All around, hammers beat out a fervent rhythm against hardening steel. Now that she took a closer look, Brina realized the houses bordering the street had all either been turned into workshops or abandoned. On impulse, she turned into an alley, leaving behind

CHAPTER 39

the bustle of the town's main street. When she reached a narrow, unpaved street, her stomach dropped. Houses stood empty, doors hanging ajar from their hinges. Windows were shattered or boarded up left and right. A furtive glance inside the nearest house revealed smashed furniture and a hearth cluttered with cobwebs. Brina's heart stopped when a hand fell on her shoulder. It was Abrasax.

"Look, Heemians," he said, pointing out a group of brawny men and women pulling at a heavy cart piled with lumps of coal. "Things must've gotten bad if Krocht is allowing his people to be treated like this on his own island."

"It's not his island anymore," Bron growled from beneath his drawn hood. "I've seen this happen in the Bay of Bones. The darkhelms arrive at your doorstep with an army just large enough to make you afraid of how many lives all-out war would cost. Then, when people are frightened—" His fist clenched. "They take what doesn't belong to them and force the people who dug it up and cultivated it with their own hands to carry it onto their ships."

Sneak looked tense, his eyes darting from Bron to the men and women pulling the carriage under the watchful gaze of the group of darkhelms clustered on the street corner up ahead.

"We need to do something about this," Bron growled. "These people are being treated like animals."

"We are doing something," Abrasax reminded him. "We want to ensure what happened in the Bay of Bones won't befall the rest of your people. Remember?"

Bron stared at him in disgust. "Sitting in pretty little halls. Talking to highborn folk about things they know nothing about. That's what we're doing. Do you think this king, whatever his name is, cares?" Bron jabbed a finger at the Heemians pulling the cart in the distance. "Do you think he loses even a second of sleep over how hard the darkhelms work his people? As long as his table remains laden with meat and drink, and his chests remain full of silver and gold, do you believe he will march down here himself to put a stop to this?"

"We have to try," Abrasax replied, "and keep your voice down."

"They're listening," Brina added. She pointed at a group of darkhelms on the main street who'd stopped at the mouth of the alley.

Burning *Auris*, she could hear one of them saying, "What are those layabouts up to?"

"We'll have to let this one go," she whispered before dashing into another side street. Once they were out of sight of the darkhelms, she put an arm around Bron's shoulder. "I understand your anger. I feel it too, but we're not helping anyone by getting ourselves caught."

"Fine," he said, "I'll try it your way one more time, but if this turns into another Morassia, I'm cracking some skulls."

"And I'll happily join you." Brina winked. "For now, let's try diplomacy first. Who knows, maybe things will be different here."

As they made their way to the town's northern gate, Abrasax held out an arm to stop them.

"Damn it all," he said, jabbing his thumb at a cluster of darkhelms at the gate's base. A single-file line of Heemians passed through at a snail's pace. "They've set up a checkpoint. Probably trying to prevent the workers from stealing product or equipment."

Brina squinted and saw one of the darkhelms handling what looked like a length of silver rope. The rope crawled over a worker's shoulder, slipped into his pocket, then poked its head out again. The darkhelm picked it up, gesturing for the man to pass the gate.

"They're using tinheads," Brina frowned, making a mental list of all the metal items they had on them.

"Using what?" Sneak asked.

"Tinheads," Brina repeated. "Serpents that feed on metal. They prefer copper and iron, but they'll take silver if they can get it. If you keep them hungry enough, you can even get them to eat most alloys."

As they stood there, observing the checkpoint and looking for a weakness to exploit, the tinhead struck. It jerked itself out of the handler's grasp in its eagerness. When two darkhelms dragged it away, a glimmering sliver of refined steel was trapped in the serpent's mouth.

Though the scene was too far off to make out what any of the parties were saying, the darkhelms went to work like a well-rehearsed theater troupe. Two of them stripped the worker down to his undergarments and tossed his clothes onto a heap of confiscated items beside the gate. A third darkhelm swept the man's legs from under him. There was a sharp crack as a heavy boot shattered the man's shin. Brina watched as the three darkhelms took turns stomping on the man, looking up at the line of Heemians between kicks as if to dare them to say something. When they'd had enough, they returned to their posts and began checking the next batch of workers, leaving their victim in the mud.

The injured man rolled onto his belly and began crawling. His broken leg dragged through the mud, the foot twisted at a sickening angle. Soot and

CHAPTER 39

blood mixed on his face to form a mask of agony.

"Wait. Stop!" Abrasax yelled out, but Brina was already running.

As she emerged from the alley, a few of the workers' heads turned toward her. The darkhelms, busy patting down workers exiting the town, seemed not to care. When she reached the man, he raised his arms in front of his face.

"No," he whimpered. "I told you it was a mistake. I wasn't stealing. It won't happen again."

"I'm not with them," Brina said. She grabbed his arms and began pulling him back toward the alley where the others stood. As soon as she was confident they were out of sight, she kneeled and lifted the pyramid-script from around her neck by its chain. It had saved her life once, and ever since, she'd kept it within reach at all times.

"Listen to me," she said, placing a hand on the back of the man's head and tilting his neck upward so he could see. "You need to focus on this as intensely as you can. I understand it's painful and you're feeling weak, but I need you to do this. Trust me, you'll be fine." As she spoke, she burned *Consol* to soothe the man's nerves. Worry flickered across his face when he saw the light in her eyes, but when she placed the script before him, he obeyed. His brown eyes widened as he stared at the pyramid.

"Good," Brina whispered. "Hold it for as long as you can."

The blood oozing from the man's shattered leg slowed from a spurt to a trickle and then stopped altogether. The bone righted itself before Brina's eyes. It was a horrifying display. Like watching a tree branch snap in reverse.

"My leg," the man exclaimed. "It's—"

"Don't talk," Brina interrupted. "I know it feels better. Just hold your focus for as long as you can. You'll thank yourself later."

The man let out a gasp. His whole body shuddered and went still. As the shape escaped him, he passed out. Brina tucked away the pyramid with a smooth movement, letting it disappear down the front of her shirt.

"That was very heroic and everything," Sneak muttered, "but how do we know he won't rat us out? Once he goes around telling people what he saw, someone is bound to put one and one together."

"I won't tell a soul," a hushed voice rumbled. Brina looked down to find the man blinking. "I don't know what it is you just did to me, but I will be forever grateful." He pushed himself up into a seated position and touched his lower leg. It was severely bruised, and the wounds where the bone had penetrated his skin would take weeks to heal, but the bone itself had straightened out just enough so the man wouldn't remain crippled for life.

"I didn't do anything to you," Brina said. "You did that."

"What? How?"

"It's a long story. One I don't have time for right now."

"I thought that was the end of my walking days." The man shook his head as tears welled in his eyes.

Brina shook her head. "Not today."

"But wait." As though it had only just dawned on him, the man said, "You're not Heemian."

Brina shook her head.

"Then what are you doing here? This place is a nightmare. Did they force you to come here? To work?"

"We're on our way to the Shimmering City," Brina said, ignoring the anxious hisses from Sneak and Abrasax behind her. "We want to have a talk with your king. Does he know how his people are being treated?"

The man shrugged. "Hard to say what he knows. Krocht hasn't left the mountain in fifty years, and it doesn't look like he's about to start. It's no paradise out here." He let out a weak chuckle. "The name's Jeremiah, by the way. Most call me Miah, though."

"Any idea on how we could get out of Cordwain?" Brina asked him. "Are all gates guarded like this one?"

Jeremiah nodded. "I'm not supposed to tell outsiders, but..." He gestured at his bleeding forehead and his precariously mended leg. "If you can support me, I think I can hobble the rest of the way there to show you. There's a secret tunnel some of us use when we need to get something special in and out of the city without the foilfaces knowing."

"You should have used it today. Would have saved you a beating," Bron grumbled.

The man smiled. "Like I said, I wasn't stealing. It was an accident. I forgot I had that piece of steel in my pocket. But that's the thing—the foilfaces don't care. They just want an excuse to make an example out of us. In their minds, for the rest of this week, everyone who saw what happened to me will triple-check their pockets before leaving, and that's a win to them."

They followed Miah to an abandoned house in a desolate neighborhood of the city.

"In here," he said. He reached underneath the windowsill, withdrew a crooked brass key, and unlocked the front door.

As Brina entered the living room, mold and dust crept their way into her nostrils. Half a dozen heavy chairs stood arranged in a semi-circle around

CHAPTER 39

a hearth that hadn't seen flame in months. The cast iron stove beside it was topped with a stack of grimy pots and pans. The only section of the room that was suspiciously devoid of dust were the floorboards between the front door and a moth-eaten jute rug that lay in front of the hearth.

"Let me guess," Brina said. "There's a trapdoor underneath that rug?"

Miah chuckled. "Good to know our safe house is as transparent as a firejelly."

Brina grinned as she entered the basement. It reminded her of the order's old headquarters underneath the brewery in Doorstep's Ditch. Stuffed chairs stood around a circular table, which was cluttered with playing cards and empty glasses.

"It's behind those barrels," Miah said, gesturing toward a pile of barrels leaning against the far wall. As Bron and Sneak shifted the pile, a narrow earthen passage appeared. Brina couldn't help but smile.

"Where there's a will, there's a way, or so they say. Did you dig this all by yourself?" she asked.

"There's a bunch of us," Jeremiah said.

"Who's 'us'?" Abrasax asked.

Miah gave a faint smile. "Let's just say that not all of us are happy being treated as slaves on our own island, being worked to death, breathing in that disgusting smog that never seems to dissipate. So wherever we can, we make life just a little more difficult for the foilfaces."

"That's answer enough." Abrasax nodded. There was a strange look on his face, as though he were a merchant weighing one end of a scale against another.

"Excellent," Brina said, grinning. "Every enemy of the church is a friend of ours."

"Likewise." Miah dropped into one of the chairs with a groan. "I will get them back for this." He prodded at his leg and winced. "But not today. Nor tomorrow, I'm afraid.

"If you need to reach the Shimmering City, I might be able to help. My sister, Marret, knows of a secret way into the mountain. Tell her what happened here, and she'll make sure you get where you need to go."

"That could change everything. I doubt the darkhelms will let us in through the front gate." Brina gave a grateful nod as Jeremiah sketched out the route they would need to take to find Marret on a piece of parchment.

"Come on, let's go," Bron yelled, already disappearing out of sight into the tunnel. "We have a lot of ground to cover before nightfall. I don't fancy being stuck halfway up the mountain in the dark."

"What are you going to do?" Brina asked Miah.

"I'm gonna hang around here for a bit," he said. "It won't be long before someone hears what happened. This is the first place they'll come looking for me. Don't worry," he said, seeing Brina's expression. "Before nightfall, I will be among friends, drinking moss liquor until I can't feel my leg anymore."

"How about you get a head start?" Brina said.

She reached into her inside pocket, and with a small pang of regret, filled an empty glass with kelp rum from her own flask. Her stash was supposed to tide her over until they'd made their way to the Heemian capital, but Miah needed it more. He grabbed the glass with both hands.

"Thanks," he mumbled. "I won't forget this."

CHAPTER 40

Dusk settled over the island as they made their way up the rocky slopes of Mount Heem. Aside from a small strip of land encircling the mountain, most of the island was made up of steep, craggy terrain, interspersed with swaths of dense forest wherever the soil allowed.

The result was a grueling march that seized the lungs and refused to let go. The sun had traded places with the two chariots in the night sky when Brina spotted it.

She stopped dead in her tracks, raising a hand to alert the others. The silky rustle of boots dragging through dead leaves ceased.

"It's right over there," Brina whispered, pointing at a clearing in the forest up ahead.

A circle of mossy buildings surrounded a larger-than-life statue of a short, stout man. Atop his imperious visage stood a crown almost as tall as the man himself, encrusted with real rubies and sapphires, which made the statue glimmer in the pale light of night.

The forest had reclaimed much of what had once been a fortified town. Vines had wedged themselves into the gaps between the heavy limestone blocks, eating away at the mortar until the buildings were held in a tight embrace of branches and leaves. Swaths of lavender blossomed between abandoned houses, perfuming the brisk night air.

"Took us long enough." Bron marched past Brina. He forged onward through the undergrowth with the grace of a spooked ox.

Brina threw out an arm to stop him. "Wait, I think there's someone…"

Too late. He barreled onward through a ruined archway in the crumbling town wall. By the time Brina caught up to him, Bron stood at the foot of the ancient statue, staring at the deserted town square.

"Great." Brina threw up her arms in frustration. "You scared them off. They're gone."

"No, they're not," Abrasax muttered. His eyes glowed with the orange hue of *Auris*. He tapped Brina's shoulder and pointed at an overgrown house on the opposite end of the square. Rotting boards covered its empty windows like bandages on festering wounds. Darkness oozed from the open doorframe.

Brina scurried around the side of the house, burning *Leve* to keep her steps light. There were no windows on the other side. She smiled. *Friend or foe, at least they're trapped.* She crept back around and positioned herself beside the open doorway. A musty stench spilled out.

"Come out. We're not with the church." Brina touched *Forte* in case of a hostile response. No answer came. Bron and Sneak moved to Brina's side, eyes searching the boarded-up windows for movement.

"Let's run in and get them," Bron tapped the end of his spear against his arm bracer. "They're hiding like rats. I say we grab them by their furry little tails."

Brina shook her head. "Not yet."

"Miah sent us," she tried again. The distant croak of a bullfrog was the only reply. Brina looked over her shoulder at Abrasax, who stood behind the statue, eyes still bright with *Auris*.

"Definitely in there," he said. "They are arguing."

Brina crouched and unslung her windup bow. With a few backward steps, she had a decent angle on the front door. Any moment now, they would either come out or fire the first shot. Either was fine. She was prepared.

"You have ten more seconds before we come in," Brina called out.

Sneak looked back at her in alarm. Bron grinned, baring yellowed teeth.

"No need," a level voice said. "Lower your weapons. We are coming out."

"Nice try," Brina chuckled. "You come out with your hands up. We'll decide when it's safe to lower our weapons."

There was an exasperated sigh from within.

"Fine, but keep that itchy finger off the trigger. I'm happy with what holes I've already got."

The woman who strutted out into the moonlight was younger than Brina by a handful of years. Long strands of white hair ran down to her waist. With every step she took, her heavy suit of iron plate clattered in the silence. How anyone could walk with such cold metal weighing them down was a miracle to Brina.

"So you met Miah?" the woman asked, looking around the clearing. "Where is he?"

"In Cordwain."

CHAPTER 40

"You better not be lying to me. I know my little brother. He's got a little too much nerve for his own good." She looked over her shoulder at the dark doorway and added, "Something in short supply these days."

"The darkhelms got him pretty good, but we patched him up before we left."

"The what?" The woman smirked.

"Darkhelms," Brina repeated.

"Is that what you banished call the foilfaces?"

"How do you know we're outwalled?" Brina asked, taken aback.

"Something about your attitude." The woman shrugged. "Also, you're with *him*."

Her head tilted toward Abrasax, who stood at the edge of the clearing, eyes trained on the windows and door of the house where the other strangers were hiding.

"Forgive me," Abrasax said without looking away, "but I don't believe we've met."

"We haven't, but pamphlets with your face, and something resembling you lot"— she pointed at the others—"have been sprouting from every surface in Cordwain for the past few months. The name's Marret," she added as an afterthought, "but I'm sure Miah's blabbed about that as well."

"How many of you are left in there?" Brina pointed at the door behind Marret. She would not let her change the subject until every threat was out in the open.

"Just a handful of cowards." Marret looked over her shoulder at shadows moving around in the house's dark hallway. "See, I told you it was them."

A group of armored Heemians emerged from the doorway. Each of them seemed paler than the last. Their skin took on an almost pinkish hue. Not even Bron's lighter complexion came anywhere close. Their hair was unnaturally light, like spiderwebs covered in hoarfrost. They looked as though they'd spent months floating in a tub of water until all color had leached out of their being.

Their eyes were a pale green, and although they weren't short of stature, their hunched-over postures diminished their height. Their cheekbones stuck out as though they had rocks stuffed underneath their skin.

When the first man spoke, it was like watching a skeleton come to life. "So it is true. The Viper slithers through the empire's grass once more."

"That nickname never grew on me, I'm afraid." Abrasax's gaze seemed to pierce right through the man, as though he were looking at a wisp of smoke. "Abrasax will do."

The man let out a subdued chuckle.

"Why have you come here?" Marret asked, positioning herself at the group's head. "The entrance to the Shimmering City is at the summit of Mount Heem."

"You know as well as we do that route is being watched, which is why Miah informed us of this alternative."

"Miah doesn't speak for all of us," the white-haired man grumbled.

"And those who cower behind my back shouldn't speak at all, Hrid," Marret snapped, eyes bright with fury.

Hrid's jaw worked, eyes cast on his own shoes. "Fine. Whatever you say, milady."

Brina laughed out loud at Hrid's expression, then laughed even harder when the man glared at her but didn't dare open his mouth.

"Milady, eh?" Brina smirked. "Are we in the presence of nobility?"

"No," Marret replied, a blush like two ripe apples appearing on her face. "I mean, technically, yes. My father is the borough lord of House Source Searcher, but he and I walk different paths in life. My blood has nothing to do with the work we are doing out here.

"That said, Hrid has a point. No matter what Miah may have told you, he is not in a position to decide who gains entrance to the mountain.

"As of yet, we have walked a very tricky tightrope between our loyalty to the king and our distaste for our new overlords. Introducing you to the mix would be like combining alchemical elements at random. Exciting, but foolish."

"Look, *lady*," Bron began. Brina stifled a groan, knowing from the Biori's tone where this was going. "Your brother was almost bludgeoned to death because of a sliver of steel he'd forgotten in his pocket. Wretched thing was this big." He stuck out a pinky finger. "Now, I don't know about you cave crawlers, but where I come from, that warrants a response.

"Tell me, if we were to go up to the main gate into the mountain, what would we find there? More of your countrymen, sweating in the open sun, carrying sack after sack of your hard-won ore?"

Marret took a step forward and leaned in so close that her nose almost touched Bron's. He didn't back down.

"We know things are bad. Better than you or any other outsider. But the king is fighting hard to keep the enemy out of our capital. The gate to the mountain remains in our hands. No foilface has set foot across the threshold into the Shimmering City. For now, we must consider that a victory." Marret began pacing back and forth, gauntleted hands rubbing together.

CHAPTER 40

"Many of us want to see things differently. We do not abide by the king's decree that all resources are to be handed over to the Heilinists, but we focus our efforts on what matters now, which is feeding our own. We have no interest in upsetting what little balance is left." Hrid and Marret's other companions nodded as she spoke. "As it stands, King Krocht's tenuous understanding with the Cardinal of the White City is the only thing keeping us from direct subjugation."

"And what makes you think the Cardinal is planning on leaving things that way?" Bron's mouth curled into a mirthless smile. "You know what he is doing."

Marret's face contorted as though she'd swallowed something bitter. "We realize the precariousness of our position. The church is bleeding us dry, making sure our resolve as a people is withered to the bone without so much as a single blade being drawn. When they escalate to a full-on invasion, we need to be ready. And make no mistake, there are those of us, Miah included, who are working hard to ensure that we can put up a worthy defense when that day comes.

"The king may not be able to do so in an official capacity for fear of the Cardinal's spies, but we, his people, have been working behind the scenes. Don't you worry about that." Marret spat on the ground, hands trembling with anger. "But we cannot allow you to enter the mountain and upset what little peace we have left. Not before we are ready to drive this scourge off the mountain once and for all."

Brina nodded. It made sense. She, too, had made sacrifices to keep a dire situation from growing worse. But Marret, good as her intentions might be, did not yet have the full picture of just how dangerous things had become. Their strategy of waiting out an assault meant that when the time came, they would face overwhelming numbers.

She looked over her shoulder at Abrasax and saw the same dilemma etched on his face. They shared a look, realizing they were caught between making this woman see just how important it was for them to speak to the king and revealing information that might be tortured out of her later.

"We need to speak to the king," Brina said, resisting the urge to add a touch of *Consol* to her voice. She hadn't enjoyed messing with the darkhelm captain's dreams, and he had been an enemy she would have happily stabbed in a full-on confrontation. This woman, however—an ally to their cause in every sense of the word—Brina couldn't and wouldn't coerce her.

"There is crucial military information that we need to share with the king. There is less time than you think." Brina pointed backward, where a tiny sliver of the ocean was visible above the treetops. "If only you could see the fleets that the Cardinal has amassed in Mallion's Depth. How redsails swarm the Sundered Sea like a flock of ravenous gulls snatching up every piece of carrion they can find. If you have your people's best interests at heart, you will help us."

"All we ask is a chance to see the king," Abrasax added. "The rest we will handle from there. Your name need not be attached to any of this. As far as King Krocht and those around him are concerned, we found our own way in, and we have conveniently forgotten where it lies."

"Things have grown that dire, have they?" Marret frowned. There was no disbelief in her voice, no skepticism. Only sadness. "I feared it might be so. I feared it last year when our port cities were stripped of their independence, and then when we saw the foilfaces marching up to the mountain's gates for the first time. We knew then that times were about to grow harsh. But we had no idea just how far the Heilinists would go."

She sighed, looking up at the darkening sky where the first pinpricks of stars were appearing. "So be it. Hrid, give the signal."

"But, milady, these are outsiders. Wanted rebels. When the scepter finds out—"

"If the foilfaces find out and they betray their own pacts, then we shall know we stand atop a battlefield. If those times must come, let them come now, rather than months down the line when all of us will be skin over overworked bones."

Hrid swallowed, then limped past Brina to the base of the statue, where he used a wooden beam to drum a solemn rhythm against the marble dais.

"There," Hrid said. "It won't be long before they open the passage."

"Please," he said, staring straight at Abrasax, ignoring Marret's warning glare, "when you meet with the king, remember how many lives he holds in his hands. Do not agitate him into wasting those lives needlessly."

"I have felt the weight of a life lost in pursuit of freedom more times than I care to admit," Abrasax said. "Your people's wellbeing is front and center in my mind."

"I hope it is," Hrid replied, a slight tremor in his voice. "I hope it is."

CHAPTER 41

"ormally, I wouldn't come out here alone, but I've got a feeling you know how to handle yourself," Marret said, looking over her shoulder at Brina, who smirked.

"I do okay." The light of Marret's torch in her *Lux*-sensitive eyes was like staring into the sun. She raised a hand to shield her face, grimacing.

All around them, a network of labyrinthine caves and tunnels stretched out into darkness. Under Marret's guidance, they strode past countless side passages, squeezed through narrow gaps in the rock and crawled over boulders blocking the path.

Brina caught up to Marret as she was assessing which way to go at a four-way crossing. The others' dragging footsteps echoed behind them. Each of them was likely wondering the same thing Brina was: If they lost Marret, they would never find their way out of this abyss again.

"This next section is a bit of a squeeze," Marret said. She got to one knee and shoved her torch into a horizontal crevice near the cave floor. It angled downward, making it impossible to see how deep it ran. "Toward the end, you might have to breathe out to fit. Remember to stay calm and keep moving."

Brina stared as the Heemian got down flat on her belly and disappeared into solid stone like a burrowing mole. Moments later, all that remained of the woman was the low scrape of her metal armor against the stone walls. She made it look so effortless that Brina had no choice but to follow suit.

Using her shoulders to pull herself forward, she kept her eyes focused on Marret's boots, a handful of feet ahead of her. All she had to do was follow Marret's lead, and she'd be fine. It was an unusual luxury to know that there were people in front of and behind her. As a roamer, she'd had to squeeze herself into tight spaces alone.

Not everyone shared this optimistic outlook, however.

"No," Bron exclaimed at the crevice's opening, his voice booming in the cavern. "Absolutely not. It's unnatural. Not to mention dirty."

The arguing voices were muffled by the rock as Brina emerged into a vast circular chamber. Ore deposits shimmered in the ceiling and walls like metallic cobwebs. The chamber was so vast that not even *Lux* could help her see the other side. Marret paced back and forth in front of the crevice, her torch held high above her head. Her eyes were wide and alert.

"What are you worried about?" Brina looked around more closely herself, unsettled by the unease in Marret's posture.

"Used to be there was little to worry about this close to the surface, besides the occasional deep spider brood, but these halls have been abandoned for many years." She pointed with the torch, illuminating rectangular mine shafts laid out systematically along the edge of the chamber. Leftover iron ore crumbs glittered in waste piles that littered the central chamber like miniature mountain ranges.

"These days, it's hard to tell what we might find here. New shafts have been opened and closed more quickly over the last century. The borough leaders are encouraged to only excavate those areas of the mountain with the richest veins of ore, leaving a system of half-finished shafts running through the mountain like a series of rabbit holes. Some connect to a wider network; others run into dead ends.

"It used to be standard procedure to backfill closed shafts, but that costs time and labor—both of which they would rather spend digging up more ore. All kinds of vermin from the depths have made use of those abandoned passages to inch closer to the inhabited sections of the mountain."

"So all of this ore will just be left here?" Brina gestured at the glittering veins above them.

Marret nodded.

"Since the foilfaces arrived, a process that had been gradually speeding up already has reached its tipping point. Not only do we need to dig up enough to keep the Shimmering City and all of Heem afloat, but now our mines have to feed a parasite as well." Marret kicked at a nearby waste pile. A spray of pebbles scattered everywhere. They clattered in the dark like rain on the hood of a cloak. "Shafts are opened one week and closed again the next. Safety regulations have vanished in favor of speed."

Brina's jaw worked. All this talk of underground monstrosities was raising the hair on the back of her neck. Memories of her disastrous trip into the elder mine on Hammerstroke clawed at her nerves.

She hadn't been this far underground since then. *Get it together, Springtide. This is not the time or place to dwell on that.* A twinge of panic stirred in her

CHAPTER 41

gut. *You don't know the way out.* She imagined a hundred beady eyes watching her from the shadows. Every boulder or jagged outcropping took on a new life. *You don't know the way out.*

Something stirred behind her. Brina's heart spiked. She dropped into an instinctive crouch before processing what had happened. It was Abrasax, crawling out of the crevice flat on his belly.

"Have I been scaring you with my campfire tales?" There was mockery in Marret's voice, as though she were addressing a startled child.

"I've got a bad conscience," Brina grumbled. To hide her embarrassment, she rounded on Abrasax. "What took you so long?"

"It's Bron." Abrasax's *Lux*-infused eyes blinked. "He... erm, had trouble convincing himself to follow you."

"Where is he?" Brina helped Abrasax to his feet. There was no one in the passage behind him.

"Sneak should help him through any moment now."

Sure enough, moments later, Bron's bearded face appeared in the constriction. He grinned, attempted to wave at Brina, then got his elbow stuck. Instead of reversing his movement to get it unstuck, the Biori stared at the trapped limb with the same grin pasted across his face. His eyes were dull and unfocused.

"What's wrong with him?" Marret kneeled beside Brina, looking confused.

"I had to *persuade* him to enter the constriction," Abrasax muttered. "It had been a while. I'm afraid I might have overdone it."

"No way." Brina laughed. The sound echoed through the chamber like boulders cascading down a mountainside. "Look at the poor guy; you might have cooked his brain."

Bron joined in with her laughter, cackling as he crawled onward. When Brina helped him up out of the passage, she had to restrain him from turning right back around for another run through the constriction.

"You're okay," Abrasax said, voice drenched with *Consol*. "You made it. You can come back now."

The glazed expression on Bron's face evaporated like water on a hot stone. He glared at Abrasax, cheeks flushing with fury.

"You used me like a stringed puppet. You coerced me, like I was some kind of darkhelmed twit."

"My apologies," Abrasax said.

"That was..." Bron fumed, spittle flying. "That was..."

"Necessary," Sneak said as he crawled out of the passage and dusted himself off.

"Well, yes." Bron's chest deflated. "Maybe it was. But still. It's not proper. A warrior's courage is sacred. To circumvent it like this is an insult to the Allmother herself."

"The crevice is right here." Sneak tapped his boot against the entrance. "You could always make one more trip on your own courage if you think that would please the Allmother?"

Bron looked at it, and the blood left his face.

"Once meted out, an insult cannot be taken back," he said. "Such is the state of things."

"Now he's a philosopher." Brina shook her head in amusement. "Let's push on before he starts reciting metaphysical treatises."

***

They spent the rest of the first day trudging through a tangle of both natural and man-made passages. To conserve their depleting stores of *Lux*, Sneak borrowed a torch from Marret, which they passed around in turns. Brina felt exposed without the sigil, painfully aware that they were visible, while the things that lived in the dark had a thick veil of black to skulk in.

Every so often, they would rest while Marret examined their surroundings, looking for symbols in the rock that marked subsections of routes. There was no logical pattern to be discerned, and Marret refused to explain what she was looking for. They transferred from one route to the next, never following the same path for more than a few hours at a time.

Brina had been resisting the temptation to add a little *Forte* to her aching legs for what felt like a handful of hours when Marret led them through a narrow natural cavern that ended in a man-made staircase. Steep, almost knee-high, steps ascended out of view of the torchlight.

"Here we are," Marret said, out of breath. "The Steps of Osel. At the top of the stairs, we can make camp."

"Then what are we waiting for?" Bron pushed past Brina and charged up the steps. His short Biori stature forced him to hop rather than step onto the next steps. Sneak followed, muttering something about smoked ham.

Behind Brina, Abrasax snorted.

"What are you smiling about?" she asked.

"Oh, just thinking about something I read once." With that mysterious quip, he gestured for the others to climb so that he could take up the rear.

CHAPTER 41

They found Sneak half an hour later, lying flat on his back against the tall steps. He was clutching a stitch in his side, wheezing.

"We're going in circles," he puffed, raising his torch to illuminate dozens of additional steps reaching for the heavens.

"That's absurd," Brina snapped, pacing her own burning lungs through a series of deep breaths. "We're in a one-way passage."

"Then explain how we're still in this accursed staircase," Sneak said, between huge gulps of air. "It makes no sense. We must have walked up thousands of steps. I lost sight of Bron ages ago."

"So you have. We're about one quarter of the way up, by my estimate." It wasn't Marret who spoke, but Abrasax. There was a rare twinkle in his eye.

"You're joking," Sneak said. It was a statement, not a question.

"Afraid not. The Steps of Osel are eleven thousand six hundred and seventy-four steps long. So far, I've counted about three thousand."

"Why?" Sneak gave Marret a hurt look, as though the very existence of these stairs was an insult to his entire bloodline.

"It's an ancient passage, hewn centuries ago, to connect the higher galleries to the underlying cave system we just exited. The longest single flight of stairs in the known world," Abrasax explained, smiling. "Even at my age, I'm constantly amazed at what we as a species come up with."

"There's no way I'm making it to the top without puking out my guts." Sneak shook his head.

"If you do, make sure to swallow them again," Brina said with a smile. She stepped over the groaning man and resumed the ascent. "You'll need them."

CHAPTER 42

"Here we are," Marret said. "Hora's Hall." She held out both arms as if to embrace the vast cavern in its entirety.

They stood in a long, narrow hall. Massive pillars rose on both sides of the chamber, sprouting from the stone floor and blending seamlessly into the jagged ceiling. For a moment, Brina had the ludicrous sensation of standing inside a heart, watching those giant stone veins pumping around the lifeblood of the mountain.

In the center of the hall stood a life-sized statue of a stout woman with long, braided hair. Her face was regal, with eyes that seemed even now to stare straight at Brina. Despite this, there was a warmth to her features that could almost make one forget she was carved from stone.

The silence was interrupted by a creaking sound that made the hair on the back of Brina's neck stand up. Her mouth fell open in horror as a huge marble wing stretched out from the statue's back, followed by a second one. *It's alive. The damn statue is alive.*

Tick.

Tick.

Tick.

Slowly, with the sound of stone tapping against stone, a second head appeared over the statue's shoulder. Its features were brutish, with giant eyes set above a leering mouth. It was only when the enormous wings closed around the statue in a protective embrace that Brina realized what she was looking at.

"Gargoyle," she whispered to the others, taking a step back. "We have to turn back."

Her voice was calm, but her heartbeat was not to be deceived. Blood pounded in her ears as she tried to think back to what she'd read about them in *Carralnar's Cracking Compendium of Critters*. Nothing came. She vaguely remembered a single page entry about them, but was pretty sure Carralnar had written them off as ancient concoctions of the imagination. She didn't

CHAPTER 42

even bother reaching for her windup. Against a stone beast of this size, no weapon short of a siege catapult would suffice.

Marret let out a hoot of excitement, as though she'd spotted a breaching whale. The sound echoed through the hall like a trumpet. Brina cringed as the gargoyle's head snapped around to peer straight at them.

Holding out her arms, Brina began herding the others backward toward the Steps of Osel. Marret, however, remained where she was, a peculiar smile plastered across her face. There was a twinkle in her eye, part joy, part sadness.

"Cuama en vrethen," she called out to the creature, holding out her arms, "ewiga liothe heyligan Hora."

The gargoyle's expression changed. Its mouth closed, hiding its dagger-like teeth.

Marret bowed, gesturing for Brina and the others to do the same. Brina hated exposing her neck in the face of danger, but something about Marret's calm and confident demeanor made Brina trust her.

The gargoyle looked at them for a moment, then laid its head on the statue's shoulder and froze there.

"Amazing," Marret said, wiping a tear from the corner of her eye. "It came back. It really came back."

Marret led them to the left side of the hallway, into a gallery behind the row of pillars. Windows fogged with dust alternated with heavy steel doors. Somewhere in the middle of the gallery, a round fortification wall protruded from the rock. Marret slammed her shoulder into a rusty iron door, which scraped against the stone floor as it opened. As soon as they were inside, Marret shoved three deadbolts in place. They had clearly been installed recently, their gleaming surfaces not yet coated in decades of oxidation.

"Grab what you need; just put it back where you found it." Marret pointed out a pile of moldy mattresses.

"What was that thing?" Sneak pulled a face as he unfurled his mattress on the floor and a cloud of dust wafted in his face.

"A gargoyle," Brina said, casting a nervous glance through the barred window. The thing was still out there, clinging to the statue as though it were part of it. "They're statues that have absorbed so much suffering from their surroundings that they come to life, bent on purging the evil from their being by passing the pain on to others."

"Wrong." Everyone turned toward Marret, who fixed Brina with a wide grin. "Alright, fine, maybe you're not far off the mark. Romanus *is* a gargoyle, and, like others of his kind, he was born from suffering. However, don't let anyone under the mountain hear you call him evil."

"Looked pretty evil to me," Bron said, lying on his back with his eyes closed. "Bastard's lucky I don't have a decent smith's hammer with me." He slapped his palm against the floor to indicate striking an anvil.

"Fool," Marret's voice shot up in volume. "When Lady Hora's betrothed, Lady Eleanor Fontis, was killed in a mining collapse, she had a block of marble from that very shaft brought up here.

"During the day, she continued to lead her people as though nothing had changed, but every night she could be heard in her workshop, chipping away at that vast block. For years, she poured her grief and longing into her work, giving a tangible shape to her sorrow. It is said that the night she finished one of the greatest masterpieces in Heemian sculpting, she fell asleep in her workshop. When she woke up, Romanus had awakened.

"From that day on, Romanus went everywhere with her. When she gave speeches, she stood atop his shoulders. When she led expeditions into the depths to prospect rich veins of ore, Romanus listened to the stone, guiding her. So it went on for almost thirty years until the weight of years and loneliness claimed Hora. Romanus was beside himself.

"The eminent historian Breydel, who lived nearby at the time, wrote of how Romanus could be seen aimlessly wandering the caverns and shafts of the mines, listening to the rock. Weeks passed and people lost sight of Romanus. It's hard to say how long he was gone. The only thing known for certain is that one day, the people of Hora's Hall woke up to find the statue of Lady Hora placed in the center of the hall, with Romanus sleeping at its feet. He lay there as civilization passed him by. As mines dried up, the population of Hora's Hall dwindled, and knowledge of Romanus's true nature faded. Those who remained here mistook him for part of the statue. After Hora's Hall was closed off to keep creatures of the deep from infesting it, he vanished.

"Until tonight, I wasn't even sure I believed the tales. But there he is"—she pointed out the window—"still waiting for Lady Hora to awaken beside him, the way he awoke beside her all those centuries ago."

Marret wiped her eyes with her sleeve. "So yes, Brina Springtide, Romanus was born from suffering, but he is filled with the worst kind of pain, that which can only be inflicted by love. That's why he hasn't fizzled out the way other gargoyles do. Hate, bitterness, and greed fade with time, but the wound left behind by loved ones lost never scabs."

Brina clenched her jaw. She wanted to say something sarcastic, something that could dissolve the knot forming in her throat, but all that came to mind

CHAPTER 42

was the image of Acheron falling into the dark. Silence fell in the guard tower. All eyes were fixed on the window, where Romanus clung to the stone image of his mistress.

That night, Brina lay awake for hours, waiting for the others to go to sleep. When her father's ragged breathing slowed, she dug into her pack to retrieve a bottle of moss liquor she'd stolen from Hrid at the outpost on the mountainside. Sliding back the deadbolts with a thief's silent finesse, she stepped outside and sat back against the wall.

She raised her bottle to the gargoyle in a silent toast, then drank.

CHAPTER 43

The earth shook.

It was as though the cavern had come alive around them and was now coughing to eject them from its mighty lungs. Brina staggered to her feet, reaching for the bars in front of the guardhouse's windows. The world lurched, and she slammed into the ground.

As she touched the icy stone, some of the fog in her head cleared. She felt as though someone was digging into her temples with a tablespoon. Behind her, the door to the guardhouse stood wide open. *Damn it, Springtide.*

She wasn't mad because she'd drank until she passed out—that had been the goal—but leaving the door open was an unforgivable mistake. With every passing week, her focus slipped further. She kicked the empty liquor bottle and watched it shatter against a pillar.

Relief washed over her as Abrasax and the others poured out through the front door. At least her mistakes hadn't been punished this time. She made a mental note to keep herself in check. Getting sloppy wasn't a luxury she could afford.

"Oh, praise the Seven," Abrasax yelled over the churning of stone on stone. "You're already out. I didn't see you get up."

"We need to head for the sealed gate," Marret said. She was fiddling with the leather straps of her gauntlet, her helmet pinned underneath one arm. "It's just a tremor. If we stay calm and keep our eyes open, there's nothing to worry about."

Brina grimaced as a torso-sized block dislodged from the ceiling and exploded on the floor. The sound made her headache spike. She fought the urge to throw up; it would lead to questions. She could sleep it off later.

"Let's go." Marret broke into a run toward the far end of the gallery. Brina took up the rear, jaws clenched. Every footfall made her stomach lurch as though she were somersaulting.

Marret led them into a new tunnel that circumvented the enormous steel

CHAPTER 43

doors that sealed off Hora's Hall from the rest of the cave system. Brina put a hand on the ceiling and felt rhythmic vibrations course through the rock. It was a miracle that the mountain hadn't swallowed them whole yet.

At the end of the passage, Marret halted.

"Now for the tricky part," she said. She pointed her torch into the dark chamber beyond. "There's a shock shelter on the opposite side of this chamber. We'll be safe there."

"But..." Sneak supplied with a sigh.

"To get there, we'll need to cross a bridge over Reinaudt's Chasm. We'll be exposed to falling debris, and should the bridge collapse while we're on it—"

"We'll fall right into an early grave." Bron sighed.

Marret nodded. "To be safe, only one of us should be on the bridge at a time. I'll go first to check for damage. Once I'm across, I'll wave my torch over my head to show you where to go. When I do, start running and don't look back until you reach the shelter."

Brina groaned. Her stomach rebelled at the very idea of sprinting. She shifted her weight from one foot to the other to keep her heavy legs from numbing.

Marret closed her eyes, placed both palms against the rock, and spoke in the same arcane tongue she'd used the night before.

"Sielan bergan, biskirm unsa." With the last word still on her lips, she charged onward into the cavern. As the torch vanished in the distance, Brina realized she had been relying on it for light. She attempted *Lux*. A gray outline of the chamber beyond appeared in her vision, then faded. *What the...*

She tried again, focusing on the shape as it appeared in her mind's eye. As she held on, the pounding in her head swelled and she was forced to relinquish the shape again. *Uh-oh.*

"Oi." Bron thumped her on the shoulder. "We're the last two. Who's next?"

Brina blinked, feeling around in the dark. Sneak and Abrasax were gone. The mountain shook, Brina's knees buckled, and she was forced to grab onto Bron's shoulder for support. In the cavern, blocks of stone showered the floor. She had to tell him what was wrong. If he ran, and she couldn't maintain *Lux*, she'd be left alone in the dark.

"Were you just feeling the air like a blind woman?" The amused edge to Bron's voice was a nail hammered into Brina's ear.

"I was just distracted. You go ahead, I'll catch up."

With the sound of stomping boots, Bron disappeared. Brina gave him a few seconds head start. *Come on, pull yourself together.* She took one last deep breath, then ran for it. She seized *Lux* and spotted Bron a few dozen yards ahead of her, dashing between boulders. In the distance, the flame of Marret's torch provided a general direction to aim for.

"Damn it!" There was one second of frustration as *Lux* winked out, then Brina's foot caught behind a rock, and she went flying. Rolling head over heels, she slammed into a boulder. Her elbow collided with the stone, and she yelled out, part pain, part anger. When she opened her eyes, she was alone in the dark.

The mountain roared. It was unlike anything Brina had ever heard. No amount of force pushed through a set of vocal cords ought to produce a growl like that. The earth trembled, the vibrations rattling Brina's bones. *This must be what it sounds like inside a hydra.*

Brina vomited. The noise and tremors squeezed her guts, forcing the sour contents of her stomach onto the cave floor. She rolled over and pushed herself to her hands and knees, heaving. On all sides, boulders cascaded down from the ceiling, their impacts blending with the bestial roar. In the distance, Marret's torch went out.

A deep sense of shame washed over Brina. All she had to do was run across a bridge. Years of experience surviving in the wilds, hunting the foulest creatures that roamed the earth. Thousands of hours spent exhausting herself to get stronger, more agile, smarter. All of it wiped out by a stolen bottle of booze.

A rock crashed down a few yards to Brina's left. Shards of stone sprayed everywhere, shredding Brina's forearms and face. She didn't even flinch. It was no use.

"There you are." Bron pulled Brina to her feet with a rough jerk. "Why didn't you get back up?"

"I can't see."

"What do you mean, you can't see? You're a sparkgazer."

"I seem to have misplaced my stores," Brina said through gritted teeth, attempting not to throw up again.

"That makes no sense."

"I've got a monstrous hangover, you moron," Brina screamed over the sound of the world ending around them.

Bron laughed like a maniac, then picked her up and threw her over his shoulder. Whatever was left in Brina's stomach took this as its cue to vacate the premises.

"Put me down!" She wanted to struggle, but in her miserable state, all she

CHAPTER 43

could do was flop helplessly, which only made the nausea worse.

"Can't do it," Bron grunted as he charged through the cave. "The traditional punishment for a Biori warrior who has sunk too deep into her mug on duty is to be carried everywhere she needs to go by her compatriots. There is no greater shame." He chortled again. "Besides, you don't want to know what the punishment for leaving a fallen sister behind is."

A whoosh of icy air told Brina they were on the bridge. Moments later, Bron used her as a door knocker to bash against the door of the shelter. The torchlight inside was blinding.

"Don't ask." Brina shook her head at the worried expressions on Abrasax's and Sneak's faces.

Marret sat in a corner. She looked even paler than usual, and there was a noticeable shiver in her hands. "We have to go," she breathed, "now."

"I thought you said it was just a tremor?" Sneak went from dozing on one of the handful of cots in the shelter to sitting bolt upright.

"I was wrong."

"What are you talking about?" Bron asked, offering an arm for Marret to lean on as the woman grew weak in the knees.

"The dourhand," Abrasax whispered. "That's what it's called, isn't it?"

Marret nodded, unable to speak.

"It's a creature of legend, also known as a chasm eater," Abrasax explained. "An elemental being of monstrous proportions that has been said to sleep under this mountain for millennia, waking up when the world has stepped out of balance, to restore equilibrium."

"Equilibrium?" Brina yelled over another fit of roaring grinding noises. "This is what equilibrium looks like?"

Abrasax shook his head. "Like I said, it's a myth. Whatever is causing these tremors is the real-life version of whatever inspired the ancient Heemians to create the myth of the dourhand. Its arrival is said to be announced by a thousand drums, causing the earth to rumble. Sound familiar?"

Brina shook her head in disbelief. "So you're saying this thing has been dormant for millennia, and it chose now to wake up?"

"This is no coincidence," Marret said, holding on to Brina's shoulder as she regained her footing. "The dourhand senses what is going on. It senses the change in our people's behavior. Our lack of respect for the mountain and the resources it provides. And it's come here to set things right," she concluded, her voice hollow.

"We need to make our way to the Shimmering City. At once. It is paramount that the king hears of this. We'll wait out the worst of the quake, then we run."

CHAPTER 44

ane didn't know whether to laugh or cry as he watched Zot saunter across the inner courtyard of the Hawqallian palace atop Seer Hill in Merkede. Swagger didn't even begin to cover it. When he'd heard that his plan to draw the attention of the Hawqallian emperor's nephew, Prince Neheb, had worked, his self-esteem had shot straight past arrogance into megalomania.

Zot felt like he was on top of the world. Wane felt like he was watching someone tumble down a cliff in slow motion.

"Hey, keep up, boy," Zot yelled from up ahead. "This isn't the place to be loitering."

He pointed upward at half a dozen guards stationed atop the outer walls of the fortress. They wore minimal leather armor, which left plenty of room to expose rippling muscles.

Quickening his pace, Wane drew level with Zot. A clinking noise drew his attention.

"When did you get that?" he asked, pointing at an ugly necklace of polished rubies draped across Zot's neck. Each of the gemstones was the size of a grape. They shone so brightly in the afternoon sun that Wane had a hard time looking at them. "That must've cost..."

"Never you mind how much it cost," Zot snapped. "I have to look the part, don't I?" He gestured at his attire, which he'd had "improved" by Madame Chrysanthemum.

Patterns of gilded thread ran across his robes, making him look like a walking sheet of gold. Upon closer inspection, both of his wrists were adorned with identical bracelets matching his necklace.

Wane felt his stomach drop; every shard that had gone into all that jewelry was one less shard the rebellion would have to work with. Just like every day they wasted gallivanting around palaces crossed off one day of the shortening time before Cardinal De Leliard could complete his conquest of the Sundered Isles.

"That money was for equipment and rations," Wane said through clenched teeth.

"Look around," Zot said, waving his arms. He spun around like a dancer, gesturing at the towering sandstone pillars of the inner gallery and the ceiling, which had been painted in such a way that anyone walking below it felt like they were staring up at a clear sunny sky, no matter the weather.

Zot flashed his hands toward two marble statues that stood back-to-back in the center of the courtyard, hewn in the likeness of the emperor and empress. Ten times larger than life, they looked so heavy that no force in the realm could move them from where they stood. Wane couldn't suppress a shudder at the sight. They would stand there for a thousand years after humanity had crawled into oblivion.

"See," Zot said, a self-satisfied smile curling his lips. "I can't come in here looking like some beggar."

"Then why am I still wearing the same clothes?" Wane asked.

The point wasn't that he desired fancier attire for himself. Quite the opposite. He wanted to point out that for all his excuses, Zot had bought these things not with their mission in mind, but to satisfy his own vanity.

Zot's face reddened, and the muscles in his jaw tensed. "You're just the assistant, aren't you? I mean, I'm the master."

Wane gave him the sort of look Madame Arturia had taught him to fear back at the orphanage. The type of look that told a boy he was one more word away from a leather belt being unbuckled. It seemed to work on Zot, too.

"You know," he whispered, "that's the cover story, remember?" He shot Wane an unconvincing wink and quickened his pace, so that he wouldn't have to look him in the eye.

Wane shook his head. He'd liked the man much better when their pockets had been empty. Without money, connections, or a reputation to call upon, Zot had shown wisdom, kindness, and, or at least it seemed to Wane, he'd had the cause at heart. Zot was no longer the man who had emptied his own vault to save Wane from suffering a gruesome end through the workings of Sachrya's poison.

That thought stirred guilt in Wane. Perhaps he was being too harsh. Even though he had no faith in the plan, he couldn't deny that so far everything had gone as Zot had predicted.

Maybe that's why he used to be a criminal genius. The thought cheered Wane up. He found himself much more able to enjoy the absurd wonder of

CHAPTER 44

the place where he found himself. If one year ago, someone had told him that today he would be walking through an imperial palace, marveling at Prince Neheb's fishpond, which was the size of a small lake, or that he'd be taking in the sweet perfume of blooming agapanthus flowers in early spring, he would've thought it preposterous.

Yet here they were, passing guard detail after guard detail without being stopped, carrying an invitation from none other than a member of the imperial family of a land he had only heard spoken of in tales.

They met Prince Neheb in the palace's central garden. Most of the space was taken up by a series of sand cherry hedgerows that interconnected into a labyrinth. Though the garden was enveloped by buildings on all four sides, the labyrinth felt boundless, as though anything imaginable could fit within those purple walls.

Neheb sat at the labyrinth's entrance, reclining on a marble bench topped with heavy pillows. A broad smile graced his face. Two women leaned against him, one on either side, whispering things in his ears that seemed to bring the prince great satisfaction.

"My Prince." Zot bowed.

He sounded much more confident than Wane felt. The mere sight of Neheb, dressed in long purple robes embroidered with silver thread and lined with sapphires, made his mouth go dry.

Though seated, the prince was at least eight feet tall, his elongated Hawqallian neck stretching a full foot, atop which sat a bald head. His enormous black eyes seemed to gaze straight through everything they rested upon.

"Welcome, my esteemed friends." Neheb's voice was a sonorous drone. "I have looked forward to making your acquaintance."

Zot seemed at ease, meeting Neheb's gaze with equal measures respect and confidence. He looked like a man who had just walked into his regular bar after a hard day's work.

The prince arose from his bench, dismissing the two women with the tiniest twitch of a hand. They vanished so quickly and elegantly that they might as well have evaporated.

"The infamous Master Roosebeke," Neheb said, extending two fists stacked atop each other in the Hawqallian gesture of greeting. Zot stacked his own fists and pressed them against the prince's as he spoke. "You, Prince Neheb, need no introduction. Your name is known and respected from Hawqal to the far reaches of Bior."

"You are too kind," the prince replied. "Please call me Ashur. Neheb is my mother's name."

"Duly noted."

"Please," the prince said, beckoning for Zot and Wane to follow him, "let us enter my maze of amazement." He chuckled at his own wit as he guided them into the constricting passages of the labyrinth.

It only took a handful of turns for Wane to realize he would never again find the exit on his own. He tried desperately to memorize the sequence of turns they took, but it was pointless. It was impossible to tell one hedgerow from another, and the prince's brisk pace ensured that within minutes, Wane felt like he had entered an alternate world.

"My maze wasn't in the original design plans," Neheb remarked, waving a hand at their surroundings. "But a little over a decade ago, when I first started visiting the city, I felt the palace could use some more private places, you know?" He looked at Zot over his shoulder. "A place where a one is free to do whatever they must, safe from the prying eyes of servants and uninvited guests."

"I agree. I have that very problem more and more frequently these days. It is hard to find good help whose eyes and ears can filter out those things we would rather they didn't pick up."

"Exactly." The prince nodded. "When I heard about your exploits, I thought, now there is a man who understands the point of living. Someone who might understand my way of life. My vision, as it were."

Zot smiled. Wane was annoyed to realize that he was no longer just sucking up to the prince to get what he wanted out of him, but that he was genuinely enjoying Neheb's praise. Zot thought he was a man on equal footing with the prince, and with every lie that came out of his mouth, his words sounded more and more truthful, as though he believed them himself.

They entered a circular clearing, which held a gazebo with windows obscured by wickerwork patterns from which thick plumes of white mist escaped.

Wane was immediately reminded of Acheron as a stinging sweet smell penetrated his nostrils. He could tell that Zot, like him, realized that vast quantities of cloud were being burned inside. The prince strode around the gazebo without comment, taking a corridor to the right of it. Moments later they passed a second closed-off gazebo, from which sounds emanated that made Wane's cheeks burn scarlet. He glanced from Zot to Neheb, but neither of them seemed to notice. In fact, they marched straight past the gazebo as though it weren't even there.

CHAPTER 44

It took them the better part of fifteen minutes to reach the center of the maze, where an oval pitch stood, covered in sand and surrounded by marble tribunes four rows high. It resembled a theater hall Madame Arturia had once taken Wane and the other kids to in Mallion's Depth.

"Here we are," the prince said, extending his arms and turning in a full circle. "My most prized possession, my sanctuary, if you will. Now," he said, "unless I'm very much mistaken, Mr. Roosebeke, you enjoy the more challenging aspects of gambling. You like to take it just that one step further, in search of the perfect thrill. Am I right?"

Zot smiled, but before he could answer, the prince went on. "So I have taken the liberty of preparing for us today a rare treat. The type of entertainment usually reserved for my close family circle. After I heard about your marvelous hand-to-hand struggle with the skull of Penrod, the most venomous of scolopendrae, I knew you were a man that I could share this with."

He clapped his hands twice, and a dozen men and women, dressed in a variety of spectacular sets of armor, marched from the gate on the far end of the arena. Their oiled bodies gleamed in the sunlight, each strand of muscle standing out like the ropes above a puppet's head.

As they stood before Zot and Neheb, they bowed in unison.

"My friend," the prince said, beaming, "these men and women have trained day and night, summer and winter, to provide a few lucky ones with the ultimate thrill."

Wane took a step backward, watching the sharpened blades and maces hanging at the warriors' sides as he realized what was about to happen. Back at Madame Arturia's home, there had been only a handful of books, one of which was an ancient history of Hawqal, which held a chapter detailing this exact practice.

Flamma. Combat to the death for sport. It was supposed to have been outlawed centuries ago. Most of today's royalty and Hawqallians considered it barbaric. But here, in the safe embrace of his own labyrinth, Prince Ashur Neheb had resurrected the sport for himself.

CHAPTER 45

hould it be this easy for us to just walk in here?" Sneak's voice rang out as Abrasax, Brina, and Bron climbed a set of marble stairs into the entrance hall to King Krocht's luminescent marble palace. Abrasax frowned. Under normal circumstances, security should have been tighter than it was, but given the natural disaster that had just rocked the mountain, this might be a momentary breakdown of protocol under duress.

When Marret had led them into the Shimmering City, they had walked straight into chaos. The quake had caused vast blocks of stone to rain down onto houses and people alike. The wounded and homeless numbered hundreds. Roofs had collapsed, rubble blocked off entire streets, and everywhere people were searching for missing loved ones. The guards at the gate had been so busy fending off a mob of panicked civilians screaming for help that it was all too easy for the group of sparkgazers to jump the fence into the royal garden.

"Let's consider it a lucky break," Abrasax said. "If I remember correctly, the audience hall should be to our left. There might be more guards at the door, but..." He trailed off as he noticed the entrance to the audience hall was just as poorly guarded as the rest of the castle. *Seven have mercy, he thought. If we were empire assassins, it would be over already.*

He made a mental note to address the inadequate security measures as soon as he had a chance to speak with Krocht in private. It would do little good to gain his support, only for him to be killed a month later. The Cardinal would try to replace him sooner rather than later, and although none of the borough leaders would accept an outsider as a sudden replacement, bribing one of them to assume the throne would be a plausible course of action. The top job would be temptation enough for most to consider it.

Abrasax approached the double wooden doors, entered first, and directed the others to sit beside him in the back row of the audience hall.

CHAPTER 45

Designed like a theater, the hall was a half-circle, with a stage on the ground floor where Krocht reclined on a grand golden throne, surrounded by his advisors. The borough leaders and their delegates occupied bench rows that ascended to where Abrasax and the others sat.

In the past, one's assigned seat correlated to one's social status. The borough leaders were the only ones allowed in the front row, while their deputies sat just behind them. Abrasax's lip curled into a grimace as he surveyed the room.

A stifling mix of perfumes wafted from the assembled nobles. The odor was so thick that Abrasax was surprised there wasn't a visible pink mist hanging over the scene.

As was the case everywhere, Heemians prized most those things they could not access at home. Thus, wisps of rose perfume filled the room, accompanied by moldy lavender and even a touch of kelp. The open sea, like the open air, provided many delicacies for Heemians, most of whom never left the mountain in their entire lives.

The notion that just outside their homes lay vast pools of water teeming with an unimaginable wealth of plant and animal life was both thrilling and frightening to the average Heemian. Even common fish were considered a delicacy among those who could afford them, while lower-born individuals would not dare touch the strange, slimy creatures, even if presented with one.

Each of the five borough leaders wore their traditional heavy armor, made of silver with a gold trim that represented their house and their personal deeds. For example, House Source Searcher, of which Marret was a daughter, featured flowing patterns all the way down the shoulder pads of their breastplates. These lines appeared as though molten gold had been poured onto the armor. In contrast, House Hardbrick preferred a trim of hard, ninety-degree angles that formed a brickwork structure around their chest.

Each house also wore a cloak symbolizing their distinct lineage. In the midst of it all sat King Krocht, wearing full golden armor and a cape adorned with five patterns, one for each house. Though Abrasax remembered him as a broad, muscular man, it was difficult to see him that way as he sat upon his throne with red velvet steps.

Atop his head stood a tall crown that had been part of Heemian royal tradition for as far back as written histories went. It was a roughly wrought piece, one that would not have met contemporary standards, but its simplicity and the wear of centuries lent it a unique dignity. The crown was almost a foot tall and made of white silver. Five spikes pointed toward the ceiling, each engraved with the patterns of the five boroughs, as if the collective wisdom of the houses was trickling down into the king's thoughts.

Sneak gasped at the magnificence of it all. Abrasax considered reminding the young man how impolite unprompted noises were among the Heemians, especially when in the presence of their betters, but then thought better of it. *Let them have their fun. It is my vanity that has brought them halfway around the world.*

His attention was drawn away from his somber thoughts by a burst of anger from below. The leader of House Forgefire, whom Abrasax thought he recognized as a son of Bruno "The Sledge" Hammer, was gesticulating toward the king.

"I have been warning of this for months now," the man yelled. His long black mustache quivered with rage. "For months, we have felt the tremors and have pleaded with you to exempt us from the need to dig deeper and further into our oldest shafts. You have denied us time and again, favoring the needs of the Heilinists over the safety of our own people.

"Now, it is proven. It was as I feared. A chasm eater has awoken in the depths, and it is making its way to our cities, where it will devour all it comes across."

"What do you know of the matter?" A small gray-haired man with a long beard, whom Abrasax remembered as Nick Longfinger of House Delving, interjected. Longfinger had always struck Abrasax as a difficult man. The one time they had spoken one-on-one had been at a banquet years ago. All night, Longfinger had attempted to treat Abrasax as a servant because he lacked Heemian blood. When that didn't take, the man had screamed until he went purple in the face.

It seemed Longfinger's quarrelsomeness hadn't left him over the years. "No chasm eater has been seen or heard from in these parts for centuries. For all we know, the very idea of the dourhand is made up. The ancients were looking for a way to explain the regular tremors that are part and parcel of living beneath the earth. The mountain has a life of its own, and now and then it snores. That is all there is to it."

Bruno Hammer's son opened his mouth, red splotches visible on his neck and face, but the king held up a hand, and the shuffling and muttering in the room stopped at once.

The king stood up from his throne, using two gnarled hands to press himself upright. The clinking of his armor was a bell ringing to demand silence. "Please, my kindred, let us keep things civil. Let us observe at least basic dignity, even in these trying times."

CHAPTER 45

Both men bowed their heads. Though delivered in a mild voice and with a smile on his face, he had just told them in front of everyone that their conduct was boorish and better suited to banter among mine workers than those who dwelled in marble halls.

"I shall send a team of investigators to your boroughs tonight, and by morning they will begin a thorough investigation into the source of this quake and the possibility that more might follow," the king said. "Meanwhile, I want to express that there is no need to jump to conclusions." He gave a nod toward Longfinger. "Chasm eaters haven't plagued these parts for as long as monarchs have sat on this throne. It would be an odd coincidence for them to appear now, when our nerves have already been strained by the presence of strangers in our lands."

"But that is precisely why," the younger man said, unable to help himself. "We have been digging deeper and deeper, leaving good veins of ore untapped just because they wouldn't yield as much as the church is demanding from us as quickly as they demand it.

"These are people who have never set foot in a mine. They are making us waste valuable resources while not allowing us the proper time to backfill abandoned shafts. My people have been worked to the bone, and some have fallen prey to cave spider infestations in the deeper shafts. Am I alone in this?" He looked at the four other borough leaders, all of whom refused to meet his gaze. "We have been consuming our mother mountain at an alarming rate, and now this happens. That is no coincidence. It is a sign. A sign that we have been going too far and risking too much. The mountain demands we slow down. I implore you to listen to its call."

The king remained silent for a moment, then sat back on his throne. "Young Hammer, I appreciate your vigor, your passion, and your concern for the people who are your responsibility. These are all qualities that will make you an outstanding leader, but we must wait until a formal investigation is concluded before we can take further action.

"As for the Heilinists' presence in our lands, I can only say this: I have been working hard and corresponding with Cardinal De Leliard himself in Mallion's Depth. The Cardinal has assured me that his presence here is merely a matter of necessity on their part.

"They have always been our business partners, and while I agree that the pressure they are exerting on us is taking its toll, I need not remind you of the gravity of the consequences we could face if we were to ruin our relations with such a powerful force."

"My liege," a third borough leader said, a woman whom Abrasax did not recognize, "I think the time is right for us to question what the Heilinists seek to do with all this iron and steel we have been providing them with. Though I can only calculate the weight of what has left my borough, if all of us have been delivering equal amounts, the Heilinists now have enough metal in their possession to equip thousands of soldiers with full plate. I cannot help but wonder why they would need such overwhelming quantities now, when we have been dealing with them voluntarily and on our own terms for years. Why force themselves upon us now? There is a bigger plan at play here, and I'm afraid that if we do not see it in time, graver perils may yet await us."

"These concerns have troubled me of late." The king nodded. "We are walking a tightrope above an abyss, and I have felt the rope wobble beneath my feet many times. I thank you for your earnest contribution, and I assure you that these matters are being looked into. That is all I can say at the moment."

He then looked around the room, to see if anyone else was going to offer a rebuttal, when his eyes fell on Abrasax. For the briefest moment, Abrasax could swear there was a twinkle of recognition in the king's eyes. His gaze lingered.

"Please, for today, let us adjourn this wagging of tongues and see to immediate business. I am sure that each of you has urgent matters to attend to in your own boroughs, given the devastation that today's quake has left in its wake. I encourage you all to rise now and attend to them, and we shall convene here next week."

Everyone in the room understood at once that the king had declared the discussion closed. Though there was some muttering as they left the room, no one dared oppose this turn of events. The king had played for time, and they all knew it.

CHAPTER 46

"You can't do this," Wane whispered.

"Shut up, boy," Zot bit back at him.

"He's going to have them kill each other," Wane insisted, looking into Zot's furious eyes.

Zot waved a hand, trying to shut him up. It was too late. The prince had heard.

"Is there something you wish to address, servant?" Neheb asked, his eyes locked on Wane. It surprised Wane that he didn't melt on the spot. He could feel two beams of heat on his skin where the prince's eyes found him.

"No, no," Zot said, "everything is fine. Don't mind him. He has a hard time figuring out his place sometimes, that's all." He shot Wane a glance over his shoulder that could have dropped birds from the sky.

"My apologies, Mr. Roosebeke," the prince said, "but when I address someone in my palace, I expect *them* to answer me. No intermediary will do, I'm afraid." Though he smiled and his voice was cheerful, his eyes were glacial.

Zot shot Wane a warning look, but he didn't care. He wouldn't stand here and watch someone die.

"You can't force these people to kill each other," he said, looking Prince Neheb in the face. "It's not right. There's a limit to what you can ask of a servant, and I think you've reached it."

Neheb smiled. "Oh," he said, chuckling with relief. "I thought there was something you didn't like about my arena." He looked around the sandy pitch surrounded by white marble arches with the expression of a parent peering into a newborn's crib. "Don't worry, these warriors are being paid well to train and fight. They know what they signed up for. Don't you?" His voice exploded in volume. Neheb whipped around, facing his warriors.

"Yes, my prince," they barked as one.

"You see," Neheb said, "there's no coercion here. There is a simple payment for service and delivery of said service. Each of these men and women have my full assurance that should they perish in the line of duty, their families will be taken care of long after they are gone. In fact, many of them will have better lives than they ever would have without my intervention. Your conscience can rest easy."

No, it can't, Wane thought, but he didn't dare argue the issue any further. Zot was staring daggers at him over the prince's shoulder, and he had the distinct sense that he'd pushed his luck to the breaking point. This man could make Wane disappear with a word. Zot just might let him.

"Please let me demonstrate my warriors' true devotion to their art. Six, come."

A woman with muscular arms and a stocky build stepped forward. She carried a small circular shield and a long spear made of bronze with a fierce tip and a barbed hook. A dagger was strapped to a holster near her waist.

Neheb strode toward her. Something clattered in his hand as he withdrew it from his pocket. A mahogany box lay in the palm of his hand, inside of which rolled around a twenty-sided die. Wane could see golden letters inscribed on each of its sides. Neheb held out the die, and the warrior took it.

The prince held out the box toward the warrior.

"If you roll an odd number, you are to drive your dagger through your heart at once. Is that understood?"

"Yes, my prince."

Without hesitation, the woman cast the die into the wooden box, which the prince covered with his hand so the warrior couldn't see the outcome.

He then beckoned for Wane to join him. With a feeling like trudging through quicksand, Wane walked up to Neheb.

"Young master," the prince said, grinning. "Would you do me the honor of reading out the number that Six has rolled?"

He's making me pronounce her sentence, Wane realized, his hands trembling at his sides.

"Please," Neheb said. "You are a guest in my house. Surely, you could acquiesce to such a minor request?" There was no choice, and Wane knew it. The prince had maneuvered him into a corner. With shaking hands, Wane lifted the lid and looked at the die. Eleven.

Odd. Death.

He thought of lying, then saw the prince's eyes staring down into the box right beside him. The corners of Neheb's mouth curled into a grin. There was nothing Wane could do.

"Eleven," Wane croaked, looking the warrior in the eyes, trying somehow to convey an apology for this whole scenario, which had gotten so horrifically

CHAPTER 46

out of hand.

It had been Wane's discomfort and his need to speak up that had gotten this woman killed. As soon as he'd spoken, the warrior's hand darted to the dagger on her belt. Metal flashed in the sun. She extended her arms and pulled them back, the tip of the blade aimed between her breasts.

At the very last second, Neheb's hands fell on the warrior's wrists. He gave her a fierce tug, pulling her off balance and halting the dagger just before it struck flesh. The warrior gave him a questioning look but didn't speak.

"Thank you, Six. That will be quite enough for today." He gestured, and the woman stepped back into line. Her face was a slab of ice.

The prince looked down at Wane and burst out laughing.

"Pardon my exuberance," he said, holding a hand in front of his mouth. "But your expression is quite amusing."

Wane swallowed, too shaken to speak. Seconds before, he'd been sure that he'd gotten someone killed. He walked away, taking a seat on one of the marble benches. As soon as he sat down, the rush of relief nearly made him pass out.

"So, Master Roosebeke," the prince said, "as my guest, it is up to you to choose your fighter first." He draped an arm around Zot's shoulders. Wane was disgusted to see a self-satisfied smile creeping onto the small man's face at being addressed so familiarly by Neheb. If the sickening display of power and manipulation that had just occurred in front of them had somehow registered with Zot, he hid it well.

He's among his equals now, Wane thought with disgust. *This is what he is at heart. He and the prince are the same, ready to exploit every grain of power handed to them.*

CHAPTER 47

Abrasax's nerves soared as King Krocht's hall emptied. He looked down at the ancient king, who sat immobile on his throne, as though he were a marble relic. Even from this distance, Abrasax got the impression that the king's eyes were focused on him. The end of the borough leaders' audience had been sudden and unceremonious, skipping the usual reading of the names and titles of those present.

Abrasax couldn't help but fear that his own sudden appearance in the king's midst was the source of this abrupt change in the king's mood. For the thousandth time in recent months, he wondered why he, of all people, had been so dull-witted as to allow himself to be roped into this. Every time he showed his face somewhere, he risked letting not only himself but Brina and the others fall into the empire's clutches.

He tried to remind himself of the look of disgust on Brina's face as he had fallen apart during their meeting with the Morassian archdruidess. It was a look that would be imprinted on his retinas for as long as he lived. The absolute certainty that his daughter, his only child, had seen the weakness in him. A weakness that he had denied was there for all these years.

If they were to die right now, the image his daughter would be left with of him was that of a cowering weakling—a shadow of a mythical figure whose notoriety far exceeded his real cunning and daring.

He mustn't let that happen again. No matter the risk. Things had to go differently here. Not for the good of Bior, or even for the freedom of the Sundered Isles. This was about being a better example than his own father had been to him. *If only you could see me now, you sour bastard.*

When the king summoned him, Abrasax rose from his seat and marched down the polished wooden steps toward the first row of benches nearer to the king's throne.

"Abrasax Springtide," Krocht boomed, extending his arms as though to sweep him into an affectionate hug. "It is a pleasure to welcome you into my

CHAPTER 47

halls once more. I shall ensure you and your guests will be as comfortable as my own flesh and blood."

He beckoned for them to sit down in the first row of seats, the one reserved for borough leaders. Up close, Abrasax couldn't help but wonder if he had imagined the haggard look that had plagued the king's face moments prior.

From a distance, the king had seemed old and weary. Now, however, a jovial man sat in front of him. Krocht bared yellowed teeth in a grin, cheeks rounded by food and splotched by drink. Even now, the king held a goblet of what the Heemians called coaldrank. It was black as pitch and strong enough to make kelp rum taste like seawater.

"I must say," Abrasax said with a bow, "I had expected a somewhat cooler welcome, given my undesirable standing with the Heilinists."

The king made a gesture as if to swat away a fly. "I am glad to see the rumors confirmed for once. When the news broke of your escape from imprisonment, I thought my advisors had been fed poor information. Now that I see you sitting here with my own eyes, I can't help but be amazed. You, my good fellow, have managed what no one else has done before you."

"I had help." Abrasax nodded toward Brina, Sneak, and Bron, who slouched on the bench beside him, gaping at the surrounding hall. A half-circle of marble knights, double life-sized, surrounded the throne, positioned so that they appeared to be watching over the king.

Their faces were those of the king's predecessors, who the Heemians believed would guard the throne even in death. Myth foretold that should anyone unworthy of the position try to ascend the golden throne, the statues would step down from their platforms to remove the traitor.

Mirrors were built into the domed ceiling, aimed at the golden throne, causing dozens of small light beams to fall on the platform before the king's feet, as though light itself were bending the knee to the Heemian royal line.

"You are not displeased that I have placed you in a tough situation by appearing here before you?" Abrasax asked. He was determined to keep ahold of the conversation this time. Every argument Krocht could make, he would defang by getting ahead of it. Once, he had been a diplomatic force to be reckoned with. He would be so again if he wanted to win Brina's respect, and by extension, his own.

"The enemy of my enemy is my friend. Or so they say." Krocht smiled. "If said enemy proves to be an old friend of my people, then who am I to be displeased at your visit? Yet, I take it you did not travel so far to sample the refined cuisine of my house."

"Indeed, I did not. I appear before you with grave tidings. As one of your borough leaders noted just now during your council, the Heilinists have been hoarding resources with the tenacity of a dragon. They are like a leech, engorged with the blood of those they prey upon. Compatriots of mine discovered a monstrous foundry on one of the empire's slave colonies, fueled by the labor of captives and the ore from your very mines. This single foundry churned out crates upon crates of weaponry and armor every week. All of it was shipped back to Mallion's Depth, where an army has been amassed, the size of which we have not yet seen in our lifetime."

The king's face creased like a book with a broken spine. "I am not blind. Not yet. The threat of which you speak is one that has kept me awake for a long time now. Cardinal De Leliard is a demanding man. His political maneuvering has grown bolder with every passing year. Not so long ago, he and I could sit across a table in this very palace to negotiate balanced trading agreements. He has grown greedy. Our conversations have turned into letters. Only his god knows what plans ferment in the depths of that man's mind. We can only hope that things can return to the way they were."

Abrasax couldn't help but smile. Krocht was a politician's politician through and through. In one breath, he would speak of De Leliard as an oppressor, implying that he was a madman, devoid of reason and humanity. Just as fluidly, he admitted he had invited this man into his halls for years and had provided him with the refined steel and ore that were now being taken from the Heemians through threats and force.

Abrasax would not confront him with this yet, however. Like most politicians, Krocht required a sensitive touch. His ego, which had been sizable enough when he was a young man, was likely to have grown over the years, as it often did with kings and queens among the Heemians. Gemstones and absolute power corrupt even the pious and the righteous.

"It pains me to tell you this, my king, but we have received credible intelligence that the scepter is planning an all-out war against the Isle of Bior. Their troops are to land as soon as winter thaws into spring. The Sundered Sea is littered with their crimson sails, and just as they have done here, so have the Heilinist forces increased their grip on all neighboring countries they once treated as equals. You have had long-standing relations with the Biori, have you not?"

The king nodded. "I have welcomed half a dozen headmothers in my halls over the years. Should the current headmother have cared to pay my people a visit these last few years, I would have treated her with the same hospitality

CHAPTER 47

that I have shown all of her predecessors." Krocht scoffed. His pale fingers clawed at the armrests of his throne. "If what you are saying is true, then we are in grave peril indeed. While as a nation, Bior has long proved itself an ally to us, the Biori as individuals are elite warriors. I fear that the emptier their stomachs grow, the more tempted they will be to join Cardinal De Leliard's forces."

The obvious conclusion, Abrasax thought with a faint smile.

"Indeed. Your mind is as sharp as it ever was, my king. You have foreseen why we cannot allow the Biori to be subjugated. It would be the first event to set off a chain reaction which would lead to all the free peoples in the Sundered Isles falling under the scepter's sway."

"But he... he wouldn't," the king spluttered, his face growing red. "Surely, those who have treated with De Leliard will have the terms of said treaties honored, will they not? I have spent this last year in constant correspondence with Mallion's Depth. The Cardinal has become more demanding, it is true, but so far he has honored our agreement that his soldiers are not to cross the mountain's threshold. He has kept his word."

"Tell me," Brina called out from Abrasax's left. He looked over his shoulder and saw her holding an empty carafe of wine. "How long has it been since you have left the mountain and seen the cities on your coast with your own eyes?"

Abrasax winced. Brina's tone lacked the reverence a man like Krocht required. The king's face remained polite, but something shifted in those beady eyes.

"It has been longer than I care to admit," Krocht said, "but I have my reasons. The situation in the Shimmering City and its boroughs has grown tense these last few years. I would be a fool to abandon the city for even a single day. Today's disaster proved the need for my presence."

"Then let me describe it for you," Brina said, her voice growing in volume. It bounced off the curved walls like a rabid fleder. Abrasax shook his head, but she paid him no mind. "When we arrived at Cordwain, the port was blocked by a row of red-sailed ships. It took a great deal of effort to circumvent this blockade, which levies its own taxes on everything that enters and exits the island.

"When we set foot on land, we saw your people treated no better than the slaves the Cardinal keeps on his colonies in the North. The darkhelms, or the Enlightened Watch as you are likely to know them, work these people like cattle under threat of violence."

The king's face tensed. Abrasax's stomach lurched. The king had been unaware of this until it had been thrown in his face like a venomous spider. If there was one thing noble Heemians hated, it was being talked down to by someone of lesser status. Brina had just made him look like a fool in his own hall by informing him of the hardships of his own people. Krocht had been unaware, either through willful blindness or deceit by his officers outside the mountain. Both scenarios were embarrassing. The king's knuckles whitened as he gripped the armrests of his throne with both hands.

"Is what she says true?" His eyes flickered from Brina to Abrasax to Bron to Sneak. When no one responded, his voice lashed out like thunder. "Answer me!"

Krocht stood up from his throne, doubling in height. He towered over them. "Are my people being treated like slaves on my land?"

Sneak opened his mouth, but Abrasax coughed to shut him up. Whatever the pimply faced man was about to say wouldn't improve the king's mood.

"While my daughter's wording may be blunt"—he cast her a stern look—"I am afraid that she speaks the truth. I saw it with my own eyes, and I am sure many of your people working under the daylight could confirm what is happening if you were to bring them before you. Who manages your operations on the outside?" Abrasax was entering dangerous territory. Implying that one of the king's advisors was deliberately keeping this information from him was a risky move, but it would allow Krocht to shift responsibility for this shortcoming away from himself.

Comprehension dawned on the king's face. "Daylight affairs have fallen under Farradar Gilt's responsibilities for almost a decade. Though I used to visit the outside lands now and then in years past, my aged heart cannot abide the heat and burn of the sun's scorching rays. Once a month, Gilt returns to the city to give me an update on the goings-on outside the mountain."

Abrasax nodded, stopping himself from drawing the logical conclusion from this. He saw in the king's face that the man had been shaken to the core by the revelation of this betrayal. "I shall have a team of my own choosing investigate this." His voice was flat, as though he was trying to stop himself from screaming. "As for the situation in Bior, why travel all this way to inform me?"

"Because we are assembling an army of the willing to stand with the Biori against this incursion. The Heilinists think they have all of us in a stranglehold, and that Bior will stand alone. We must ensure that proves to be a devastating miscalculation. If we can avert the hammer blow in Bior, we can stop the chain reaction I mentioned before it begins. Instead of allowing the Heilinists to steamroll us one by one, we could turn the momentum of

CHAPTER 47

war in their direction and punish them for how spread out their troops are.

"Imagine a free Onderheem, where you once again choose how much to produce, who to sell to, and at what price. This could be possible in the matter of two or three campaign seasons. That's why I am here."

Krocht's face grew pale. The wrinkles in his face deepened. The haggard old man Abrasax had seen upon first entering the hall had returned. "Enslavement, war... What dark times. What treacherous caverns to navigate."

"I wish it was not so."

Krocht's lip trembled as the full reality of all he'd just heard set in. "Very well," he said. "If our brothers and sisters are under siege, we shall answer the call. I will send aid. Though it will require me to clean up the mess on my own shores first, I shall act, rather than be acted upon.

"I shall have to get the borough leaders on board, however. If you should agree, I would have you join me and them at a banquet tomorrow night. I would have you explain from your own mouth what you have seen and the intelligence you have received. It is crucial that we win them over."

Abrasax licked the bottom of his lip. It made sense politically. Having the support of the borough leaders would improve the numbers mustered manifold, but it would come at great risk. "How sure are you that we can trust them?"

Krocht's face hardened. "If any of them had not been as trustworthy as they seemed, the city would have fallen by now. The gates would've been opened, and I would've been assassinated and replaced. So, while they do not always agree with my way of doing business, I do not suspect any of them capable of treason. Any information that is safe with me is safe with them."

"Then we shall be present at your banquet tomorrow night and do what we can to convince them."

The king nodded and let out a deep sigh. "I will arrange lodgings for you here in the palace. For the rest of today and tomorrow, you are free to go wherever you want. You are more than welcome to take a tour of our mines if you wish. They are most impressive, and visiting them is an offer I can only extend once in a lifetime. But if you came all this way to trust us with your secrets, I imagine ours are equally safe with you."

With that, the king raised his hand, and Abrasax, realizing he'd been dismissed, stood up and exited the hall.

CHAPTER 48

Zot stood in front of the twelve armored fighters that Prince Neheb had summoned. He strode past the line, inspecting their physiques and equipment, much like a general might before a battle. Each of them was a superb warrior in their own right. There was no doubt about that, but Zot needed the best.

He smirked, turning away from Neheb to hide his growing excitement. Unbeknownst to him, the prince had challenged Zot to the one thing in which he couldn't lose. Over the years, Zot had overseen and hand-picked every single one of the bruisers and enforcers in his expansive criminal organization. If there was one thing he had familiarized himself with more closely than anyone, it was spotting the eye of a killer.

He searched for a distinct look, impossible to put into words, yet as recognizable to Zot as his own mother's face. It exuded the confidence that came with having killed before and knowing that one could do it again if necessary. It was the calculated stare that often hung about individuals who had grown up surrounded by violence and had turned it into an art. Above all, it was something that no amount of training could teach. A person either had that innate desire to go for the jugular, or they didn't.

Eight had it. Zot stopped in front of the woman, looking her up and down. She was muscled, but not so much so that it would hinder her speed. She was tall. Her arms hung almost to her knees, giving her exceptional reach. This would pair well with the longsword she had strapped to a leather belt at her side.

Her short rectangular wooden shield was light. It wouldn't stand up to many strikes from, let's say, the hammer carried by Five or the heavy club Eleven wore, but the shield's reduced weight would mean that Eight would only have to absorb a blow in the worst of scenarios.

Zot stood back, eyeing the line, trying to think ahead of what he would choose in the prince's position. Although the prince had tried to pass off

CHAPTER 48

getting to pick first as an honor and a privilege, Zot knew better. The prince wanted him to pick first so that he could choose the perfect counter to whatever Zot chose. It was clever, not the sort of thing a regular gambler would pick up on, but something that Zot himself might have done back in the day.

Again, he felt a smile tugging at the corners of his lips. For all the stories told about him, Neheb was walking into his own defeat without even realizing it. Zot took his time walking up and down the line again and again, just to give the prince the illusion that he'd been caught off guard and was considering things of which he knew little.

As soon as he chose Eight, Neheb would opt for Three, a woman with a long trident and net. The net had balls of lead sewn into it, so it could be cast from a distance to ensnare an opponent. Reach wouldn't matter if your arms were tangled in netting. That was what Neheb would count on.

The trouble was that the trident would be no match for Eight's longsword. The vigor in Eight's eyes told Zot that she wasn't the type to let herself be caught in a net. With any luck, she would have the good sense to wait until the net was cast so she could dodge it. After that, it would be trident versus longsword, which should be no match at all.

"Eight," he called out. "I choose number eight."

The woman stepped forward, staring straight ahead. She didn't meet his gaze, nor did her face betray any sign of fear at being chosen for a one-on-one fight to the death. Whoever had trained these warriors had done their job well.

Zot glanced over his shoulder to find Wane sitting on the lowest marble bench. His legs dangled over the side, feet kicking up clouds of loose sand. There was a dark look on his face. *That one'll be a handful later.* Zot sighed. Wane was a good kid, but he didn't realize what it took to seize power.

His youth, coupled with foolish idealism, made him unable to see the obvious. Zot winked at him, but the boy turned his head away, refusing to meet his gaze. Zot shrugged. He would understand later.

That was the thing about children. They didn't realize just what it took to make it in the world once a man had to fend for himself. They viewed the world in rosy hues, because they were provided for wherever they went.

Besides, it was all an act, wasn't it? The real Zot would never have gambled with a person's life for entertainment—or at least not anymore—but this was what he had to do to ensure that enough money would come their way.

Surely the kid had to understand that? And if he didn't, Zot thought with a smirk, that just meant that he was playing his role well.

"Eight?" Neheb asked, a twinkle in his eye. "An excellent choice, my friend, exquisite. I see you are a man of taste. In that case, I shall go with number..."

Three, Zot thought moments before the prince's voice rang out.

"Three."

Three stepped forward. The balls of lead in her net clinked together as she moved. The other warriors, realizing they were dismissed, marched off the pitch in single file, leaving one of their own to die without so much as a backward glance. These were not friends, nor brothers in arms. They were there to do a job and to receive the compensation that the prince provided in exchange.

Neheb placed a hand on Zot's shoulder. "Let us take a seat in my lounge so we can watch the spectacle with the highest standards of comfort."

He steered Zot toward a raised marble platform shaded by a tent of purple cloth. A handful of chaises longues topped with white pillows were arranged in a semi-circle.

A porcelain carafe and two glasses stood ready on a spindly glass table. Glimmering drops of condensation formed on the outside of Zot's glass as the prince filled it with deep red Hawqallian wine.

Wane was left behind below on the pitch, sitting in the first row of benches. The prince had forgotten all about him, and although Zot hadn't, given the boy's mood, it seemed safer to keep him as far away from the prince as possible.

As they sipped their wine, both warriors on the pitch took their positions opposite each other in the center of the arena. Their postures were slack, almost relaxed, as they waited for a signal to be given.

"Do you partake?" the prince asked, producing an ivory pipe carved with tiny skulls along the stem from a mahogany box.

Zot didn't need to ask what it was. The sickly-sweet smell washed over him even as he glanced at the tiny crumbs of white that had been packed into the bowl at the end of the pipe.

In the past, he had sampled his product, of course. When working with a new supplier or producer, he'd had to make sure that the cloud he was distributing was still top-notch. However, he had never done so with gusto and had always resented the risk he took every time he allowed cloud to fill his mind. He didn't like how it made him feel. Perhaps that was because of what he had seen the substance do to those he had sold it to over the years.

All he could think about when he saw those crystalline nuggets were the sunken eyes of floaters as they sat up to their waists in muck in dirty alleys,

CHAPTER 48

drifting off in their own minds to places that didn't exist, keeping the company of people who only half existed.

"Occasionally," Zot heard himself say, "under the right circumstances."

He cursed inwardly. He could have declined, but if he did so now, he'd essentially be saying Neheb's hospitality didn't constitute "the right circumstances."

The prince lit the pipe and took a long pull. At once, Zot could smell that it was a high-purity Hawqallian product, straight from the dunes of Dhu-Ho'c. Though he'd had many good batches over the years, he couldn't remember the last time he had smelled it this pure.

Be careful, he warned himself. *This will blast your mind back to the pre-Sundering.*

He accepted the pipe from Neheb and made a show of the tiniest puff he dared risk. Then it hit him. A wave of warmth, like sinking into room-temperature jelly. Everything around him grew blurry around the edges, like a painting suffering water damage. Before he knew it, he inhaled. The worries that had piled up inside him over the past few months evaporated like droplets of dew in the rising sun.

"It's good," his own voice sounded distant. Neheb shrugged. Zot noticed that the prince's eyes had grown red.

"Everything I have is good," Neheb said. "My wine, my warriors, my lovers. All the best Hawqal has to offer."

"Must be nice."

"It's okay," Neheb agreed. "Doesn't mean there are no downsides to being who I am." There was a gloomy undertone to his voice. He went for a second tug of the pipe.

"I couldn't imagine that Your Royalty has want of anything," Zot said, finding his oily tone once more. "Surely, your aunt would..."

"There it is," Neheb said. "You put your finger right on the sore spot. My aunt. Wherever I go, it's impossible to get away from that woman. The name Ka sticks to me like wax to a beekeeper. No matter how far I go, or what I try, I shall remain the emperor's nephew. Son of the high priest. Prince to the largest empire in the cosmos.

"Compared to the scale upon which we operate, the petty squabbles of the tiny kingdoms in the Sundered Isles are like the batting of a fly's wings in a vast dining hall. Though the Heilinists have been trying to unify this region for centuries now, their machinations are little more than a footnote in our histories.

"And that is what I have to deal with every day," Neheb said. He sounded whiny even to Zot's cloud-addled ears. "I don't command people," he rattled. "I'm *allowed* to command people. There's a difference. Do you understand?"

"I think I do." Zot found it hard to care about the man's woes, and it wasn't the cloud's fault. "But, my prince, it can't be all bad?"

"No." Neheb shrugged, taking another pull from the pipe. "I suppose it isn't. Let's distract ourselves from these unpleasant thoughts, shall we?"

He waved his hand, and the warriors on the pitch dropped into a fighting stance. Mere seconds passed before the first strike was swung. It was Eight, Zot's warrior.

She struck out with her longsword at Three's wrists, likely hoping to wrest the net from her grasp. Three saw this coming and stepped back just in time. The blade passed inches from her exposed arm.

Three's trident shot out like an arrow. Eight allowed the trident to pass just over her shoulder, then lunged, aiming a jab at Three's abdomen. With a last-minute twist of her torso, Three avoided taking the blow head-on. Instead, the blade glanced off the side of her armor, where it drew a slice in the hard leather. A trickle of blood escaped through the gash.

A wave of excitement washed over Zot. With all the wine and talk of the prince's woes, he'd almost forgotten what was on the line. If Zot's warrior lost, he'd have less than nothing. He'd bet more shards than he possessed, and he had nothing of value to barter with.

He needn't worry about that yet, he reminded himself as he watched the way Eight dodged strike after strike with effortless grace.

Soon, they'd have more money than they could've ever dreamed of when they set out from Metten. Enough for the rebellion to feed three armies. There might even be some left over for himself. He desperately needed a wardrobe expansion.

As he'd predicted, Three's stocky build and reduced range made her no match for Eight's long arms. It wasn't long before a desperate attempt to cast the net caused it to go flying across the pitch, nowhere near its target. Eight bent down, keeping her sword aimed upward to deflect incoming blows, and threw the net far behind her, out of reach.

Excellent. Without realizing it, Zot reached for the pipe and took another deep tug of cloud. He was winning, just like he'd predicted. Soon the prince would make all his dreams come true.

Three's slow trident was no match for the sword and shield combo that Eight wielded. Eight took a slow and methodical approach, which Zot liked.

CHAPTER 48

He had seen it in her eyes before the battle, and now he was seeing it realized. This woman was, at heart, a killer. Even in the heat of combat, she was calm and calculating, allowing a panicked Three to exhaust herself with strike after strike, which Eight deflected with her shield as easily as if they were twigs swaying in the breeze.

Sand scattered as both warriors circled each other, locked in vicious combat, each knowing that one of them would soon leave this plane of existence.

Three lunged with the trident, this time leaving an accidental opening. Zot saw the opportunity at once, and so did Eight. The longsword flicked upward. With a clang, Three's trident split in half, leaving her holding a splintered wooden shaft. It was over. All that remained was for Eight to claim a foregone victory.

Zot looked at the prince, wondering how he felt about watching his shards spiral down the drain. However, Neheb wasn't even paying attention to the battle. Instead, he reclined in his chair, gazing at the sky with a bored expression. His fingers fiddled with his pipe, but he made no effort to refill it with one of the many pre-cut blocks of cloud from the mahogany box, nor did he light what remained inside.

"Do you see that?" Zot asked, nudging the prince's ribs. He didn't want any possible confusion about whether his victory had been fair and well-deserved. "I think we're about to reach an early conclusion."

The prince pushed himself up in his chair, holding a hand to his brow to shield his eyes from the late afternoon sun. "Looks like it," he said, the way a man might comment on incoming rain.

Eight aimed for a low swipe, while Three jumped to the side at the last possible second. The sunlight blinded her, and she didn't see the second, crippling blow coming. There was a dull squelch as Eight's sword sliced through Three's leg just below the knee. Three let out an excruciating scream and fell to the pitch, blood spurting from her leg as tendons and muscles were severed. Blood pooled out into the sand, creating a brownish stain.

Eight approached, and Three held up the splintered wooden shaft. The adrenaline of battle now turned to panic. Neither of them looked at the prince for confirmation that the fight was still on. They knew what had been ordered: a fight to the death was a fight to the death.

Eight took her time, staying just out of reach of Three's broken shaft, trying to find a clean window in which to end it. Zot grumbled, his mind clouded with frustration as the battle dragged on. "Oh, for the Seven's sake," he yelled out at Eight, "just finish her already."

For a moment, the woman's eyes flicked upward to where he sat. She was surprised by the shout, or mistook his voice for a command ordered by the prince. Three lashed out, launching herself upward with her one good leg. She drove the splintered shaft of the trident into Eight's neck just below the chin, where it didn't stop. It flashed upward, sinking deep into Eight's brain. The woman gave a jerk and tumbled to the ground, where she shook as the wooden stake rested in her nervous system.

Zot let out a scream. "No! No, that's impossible. It's not fair, it's not…"

The prince chuckled. "Oh, it looks like you were right. The battle has reached an early conclusion." He smiled, then waved a hand for Three to leave the pitch. The woman dragged herself off to the distant gate, one of her legs still spurting blood and refusing to carry her weight. It seemed unlikely she would ever walk again. Meanwhile, Eight's corpse leaked like a punctured wineskin, turning the sand below her into mud.

Neheb pushed himself up on his reclining seat and clapped his hands together a few times. "Excellent display," he called out. "Great work, everyone." He gestured toward the empty pitch, which held nothing but Eight's motionless body and Harrod Wane's wide, staring eyes in the first row. Zot had lost everything. It was over.

Maintain composure, Zot told himself. *This is just a setback. It's not the end.* With a casual flick, he retrieved the pouch of shards from his pocket and placed it on the table between him and the prince. "You'll find the agreed-upon amount inside," he said. "That was a good battle." He tried to sound satisfied instead of devastated. With any luck, he and Wane would have already left the palace before the prince's servants tallied up the money in the pouch. He could chalk it up to a mistake if caught.

The prince shrugged, casting the pouch to the ground beside his chair. "It was okay, not the best one I've had this week."

CHAPTER 49

If Brina had disliked her lodgings in the slanted tower of Morassia's archdruidess, she outright hated the room Krocht had assigned her. It wasn't because of the gleaming marble floors, which were heated by a system of hot air traveling through hollow walls and floors, nor did it have to do with the colorful mosaics adorning the walls. She even ought to have loved the well-stocked cabinet of Heemian spirits that stood beside her bed.

What bothered her was the window. Specifically, what she saw through it as she stood in one of the most luxurious chambers she had ever seen. The palace, raised high above the city, had a clear view of the carnage that persisted below. All throughout the night, screams and the clinking of hammers and pickaxes against unyielding rubble were audible outside.

People slept in the streets, covered with nothing but the clothing they had worn at the time of the earthquake. Others, refusing to give up the search for lost loved ones, dug through the debris with bare hands. The sheer contrast between their situation and Brina's surroundings made the hair on the back of her neck stand up. What kind of leader could watch his people suffer and keep the front gates to his palace locked?

Once the luminescent fungus on the cave's ceiling faded, emulating the onset of dusk, she tried to exit her chamber to go out into the streets. Her hands ached for something to do. Every time she closed her eyes, she relived the scenes of destruction they had witnessed on their way into the city. There hadn't been time to do anything about it. And even if there had been, she would have been too hungover, anyway.

Her pile of scripts lay on the bedside table, looming over her like a judge. *"You're supposed to protect people,"* they whispered to her. *"That's the responsibility you took on when you accepted sigils into your life."*

When she flung herself out of bed and stepped out into the marble hallway, a group of guards waved her back into her room. They were polite but firm. There was no leaving the palace at night, for fear that the king's most esteemed guests might come to harm. They were to be accompanied by the king's security at all times.

The fear in their eyes as they blocked Brina's path when she attempted to stride past them sucked all the fight out of her. She felt like a glass golem. Terrifying to others, but fragile. The sigils were meant to be shared by all. Their power was too heavy to carry alone. She went back into her bedchamber and pulled the covers over her head.

By the time the luminescent fungus awoke, dawn under the mountain, Brina's eyes were dry with exhaustion. Her stomach grumbled, though she didn't think she could hold down so much as a crust of bread.

She leaped out of bed and opened the door. The hallway was deserted. Stumbling through a labyrinth of white corridors lined with statues, mosaics, and tapestries, she eventually found her way to a dining hall that could have seated an army. Bron and Sneak sat in the middle of a long table, surrounded by a mountain range of dirty dishes. A three-foot-long roasted salamander lay in a golden dish between them.

"By the crooked Seven," Sneak called. "You look like a herd of pronghorn used you as a doormat."

"Couldn't sleep." Brina sat down, reaching for a ceramic jug, which, to her disappointment, was filled with water instead of wine.

She waved over one of the king's servants and asked the woman to bring her a carafe of the wine she'd had yesterday. Though the woman's eyes betrayed judgment, she nodded without a word. Minutes later, Brina was gulping wine straight out of the jug. Guilt was like a newborn nest of rats. Best to drown it before you got attached.

"Doesn't this bother you?" she asked Bron, who was chowing down on a scaly salamander leg. "We're eating like nobles while people out there have just lost everything."

"Not like we can do anything about it." Bron shrugged.

"Besides," Sneak chimed in, "we're here to prevent those people from falling into slavery. I think we've earned a decent breakfast."

"If you say so." Brina's fingers drummed against the tabletop. "Where is…?"

"The Viper?" A mischievous grin appeared on Sneak's face. "He's somewhere on the upper floors. Said he had business to attend to."

As though the mention of his name had summoned him, the door to the dining hall opened, and Abrasax strode in, accompanied by a stocky woman whose impeccable uniform stretched tight over her belly. Her short hair was

CHAPTER 49

straight, her jaw set.

"This is Mistress Witdrager," Abrasax said. Though his tone was polite, there was an iciness to his expression. When Brina met his eyes, she saw a warning in them.

The woman stepped forward at once. "You," she called to one of the servants bustling in and out of the room to bring other nobles their breakfast. "Clear this mess up at once."

"Pardon me," Sneak mumbled through a mouthful of roast salamander, "but we haven't finished yet."

"We have a tight schedule to adhere to," Witdrager said. "I assure you there will be time and food aplenty later."

"I don't like her." Bron scowled as the woman whirled around on her heel and strode toward the dining hall door.

***

They waddled through the city like ducklings trailing Mistress Witdrager. As they traversed the broad cobbled streets, Witdrager guided them from one monument to the next. They beheld the statue of Queen Solaria in the square before Krocht's palace, then there was the temple devoted to the spirit of the mountain near the city's outskirts, and the historic city center, where architectural styles from centuries past contrasted with each other like colors in a tapestry. When they passed the prison, a red brick facade with heavy iron bars securing countless tiny windows, Witdrager remained silent.

"Is there a point to all this?" Brina asked. The lengthy walk and the incessant chatter about things she cared little for had eroded her patience.

"Why yes," Mistress Witdrager responded, her smile so tight it could have been a grimace. "We're on our way to get you cleaned up for the banquet this evening."

"What do you mean, 'cleaned up'?"

A blush spread across Witdrager's face. "It's a tradition among the Heemians to present oneself in fine condition when meeting the holders of important offices. Given your long journey, I couldn't help but notice you were—"

"We stink," Bron interjected. "The woman's right. We haven't had a proper bath since we left Metten. We must smell like we bathed in swamp water, dried in the sun, and then crawled through a pile of mud to get here."

Mistress Witdrager nodded, opening her mouth to speak. She closed it again when she caught Brina's expression.

"So, where are we going?" Brina rolled her eyes.

"First, Miss Springtide." She whispered the last word, casting a suspicious glance over her shoulder. "We're visiting the bathhouses. I've planned an afternoon of pampering and delights for you."

Sneak and Bron high-fived, whooping. "Now that's what I'm talking about!" Sneak exclaimed. "Eating, drinking, and soaking in a nice tub of hot water."

Brina groaned. "Is that mandatory?"

"It is encouraged," Mistress Witdrager responded.

Abrasax leaned forward and whispered in Brina's ear, "That's Heemian for 'yes, it's mandatory.'"

"That's what I was afraid of."

***

Stepping into the bathhouse was like diving into a cloud of perfume. The moment Brina crossed the marble threshold, she was enveloped in wafts of pine resin, oak, and the crisp undertone of blueberries. After the past months, it felt like waking up to a bucket of icy water splashed in her face.

The vaulted ceiling of the bathhouse's entrance hall was adorned with a mosaic depicting people engaged in various leisurely activities, none of which seemed appealing to Brina. Having grown up amidst the grime of Doorstep Ditch, the thought that such a vast amount of space and resources could be dedicated to the simple act of washing oneself seemed absurd, wasteful, and frivolous.

They were divided at the entrance to the baths. Mistress Witdrager gestured for Brina to enter a small dressing room before closing the door behind her. Inside, a servant waited, holding up a loincloth for Brina. As the servant moved to help Brina undress, she stepped back, bumping into the wooden door. The Heemian woman gave her a puzzled look. "You don't want help?"

"That's right," Brina said. "Now get out of here. I need privacy." Despite the withering look Brina gave her, the woman protested, gesturing toward the door at the other end of the room.

"It is my duty to ensure that our guests are comfortable and—"

"I don't need any help, I'm fine," Brina cut her off. The woman shrugged before exiting the room through the door on the opposite end.

Brina undressed herself and pulled the loincloth around her waist. Her clothes were stiff with filth, and it was only now that she was in a place that

CHAPTER 49

smelled of all things lovely, that she realized the contrast. The sweat, blood, and mud that had soaked into her clothes over the previous months seemed unbearably pungent.

When she exited the dressing room, her arms clasped in front of her chest in embarrassment, she found herself surrounded by three women, including the one she had just shooed out of the room. Each held a bucket of steaming water and bars of soap smelling of pine resin. They gestured for Brina to lie down on a wooden bench in the center of the room.

Brina contemplated fleeing, but the kind expressions on the women's faces made her reconsider. Offending those who worked hard to provide her with a service was poor form, even if the service was dumb and unnecessary. *Maybe this isn't so bad,* she thought. *They deserve a chance.*

Brina lay down and allowed herself to be scrubbed from head to toe. One woman took charge of her hair, rubbing an oily substance into Brina's locks, which dissolved some of the crust that had formed on her scalp. Another woman lifted Brina's arm to wash her armpits and winced as a waft of body odor hit her. Brina's cheeks burned with embarrassment. How had she allowed things to get this far? Hygiene had dropped to the bottom of her list of concerns. To these women, she must smell like a wild animal.

When one of them attempted to lift the loincloth, Brina grabbed the woman's wrist so forcefully that she let out a high-pitched yelp.

"Sorry," Brina said, "but I think I'll handle that myself. Thank you very much."

Though she seemed insulted, the woman nodded, and the three of them exited the room with a bow, leaving Brina with a bucket of soapy water to finish the job. She couldn't recall the last time she'd felt this uncomfortable.

***

When Brina stepped out of the washing room, she let out an involuntary gasp. Beyond the small room lay a vast circular room with a vaulted ceiling. Half a dozen pools were scattered throughout the area, some steaming, others with cubes of ice drifting on the surface. In the center of it all, a huge pillar was carved to resemble an ivy stalk winding its way to the ceiling. Smaller statues stood beside the baths, spouting water from open mouths and outstretched limbs. The air was filled with the vapors of hot water and a cacophony of perfumes that knocked Brina backward. One of the women who had washed her stood waiting for her beside the nearest pool, beckoning.

"Okay, Miss Highwater," she said, "as you are foreign to these lands, I imagine you have not yet had the pleasure of making acquaintance with our bathing traditions. This bath right here contains warm water, which is an excellent start to your journey. Next, we encourage you to proceed from one bath to the next in a clockwise order. Each successive bath will be warmer until you reach water straight from the hot spring itself. Once you've relaxed and allowed your muscles to soak up the heat, the next in line will be the ice bath, where the sudden cold will harden your body the way a smith quenches hot steel."

Brina nodded, not wanting to offend the woman a third time, and slipped into the pool, loincloth and all. The woman beside the bath looked as though she didn't know whether to laugh or cry. In the end, she shrugged and walked away. Brina stood there in the chin-deep water, contemplating her next move. To the best of her recollection, she had never attempted to relax just for the sake of it. It seemed like a profound waste of time to wait here for her skin to get wrinkly while outside the city lay in ruins. In an afternoon of hard work, she could have helped many people; instead she'd have to wait here until time ran out on their forced leisure. She looked around at the others in the bath, and was horrified to find...

"Marret? What are you doing here?" Brina swam over to the Heemian woman, one hand clutching at her loincloth, the other skimming the surface to propel her forward. Marret tried to look away at first, but when Brina approached, realized she had no choice but to acknowledge that she'd been seen.

"Oh, hi, Sabrina," Marret said. Red splotches appeared on her neck and face.

"Looks like being a borough lord's daughter has its advantages, after all," Brina remarked with a sly grin.

Marret tossed back her hair. "Fine," she said, "I enjoy a nice cleansing bath from time to time. It may be months before I'm in the city again. I figured I'd make the most of it. How was your audience with the king?"

Brina sighed, leaning back against the side of the pool, her head resting on the smooth stone tiles. "He's invited us to a banquet with all the borough leaders," she said. "It's supposed to be a real fancy occasion."

Marret let out a low whistle. "All the borough leaders in one place at a moment other than an official council meeting? That'll be a sight to behold."

"What do you mean?" Brina asked.

"Well, it's just that they rarely do anything that doesn't directly benefit them. If there's no money to be made or power to be gained, they seldom leave their mansions on the fringes of town. If Krocht has dragged them to a banquet on such short notice, he must believe things have gotten dire."

"Perhaps." Brina's legs kicked in the hot water. "Anyway, we will need to convince the borough leaders of that as well. That's why they're airing me out like a laundered blanket."

Marret giggled. "Well, to be honest, you could use it."

"Yeah, yeah," Brina acknowledged. "They're not done with me yet, I'm afraid. From what I gather, we're all supposed to be fitted for appropriate attire later."

"Ooh, fun." Marret winked at Brina's scowl. "Those banquets are torture. It's like playing a game with a library's worth of rules. I was fourteen before my father allowed me to meet the other noble families in the city. For as long as I can remember, we've had an etiquette master at home who taught us how to behave, what to say, and when. I don't envy you."

Brina scowled. "I'm an outsider. I doubt anyone will expect me to know all the rules. Besides, I'm here on business, not to waste time exchanging niceties with crusty old fools."

Marret sighed. "You won't get far with that attitude. They expect everyone they interact with to be as dull as they are."

Brina's jaw clenched. She was already annoyed, and the banquet was still hours away. In an effort to relax her tense shoulders, she moved underneath a stream of hot water that spouted from an amphora held by a marble cherub.

"Fine." Marret grimaced as though she were chewing a lemon. "I'll come with you."

"You would do that?" Brina asked, taken aback. "I thought you hated hanging out with those dust collectors?"

"I do, but I can see in your eyes that you're one backhanded compliment away from smashing someone's face into a bowl of olm caviar." Marret splashed water on her own face, shaking her head as though she already regretted the offer.

Brina grinned. "Great. It's a date."

CHAPTER 50

If Brina hadn't seen the rubble in the streets and heard the anguished sobs of Heemians carrying loved ones to untimely graves on her way back to the palace, there would have been no way to know that the kingdom of Onderheem was in a state of mourning. The king's dining hall was decorated with gold and black streamers. Marble sculptures lined the walls, and clusters of round tables were placed beneath the vaulted ceiling. On a stage at the far end of the room, a group of drummers played pulsating rhythms.

On the opposite side of the hall, upon a wooden stage, stood the king's table. A long line of Heemian nobles awaited their turns to kiss the king's ring. Krocht gave each of them a benign smile and a pat on the head before they were ushered away by servants so the next sycophant could take their place.

Brina pulled at the collar of her rippling blue dress. It chafed against her collarbones, and the perfumes from the bathhouse had caused the skin on her back to break out in painful red splotches. Though there was food aplenty, Brina was so preoccupied with the countless rules of eating etiquette that much of the joy was sucked out of the richly laden table in front of her. For example, one was never supposed to look at the food longer than it took to scoop some of it onto one's plate. Staring at a dish prepared by one's host implied a lack of trust. Cutlery was to be held between thumb and ring finger, while the other hand was used to hold the plate itself. Setting down the plate on the table before finishing dinner was considered improper.

"That's Tiberius Crookhammer," Marret whispered to Brina and Abrasax, pointing out a tall, elderly gentleman whose bushy white hair and beard made him look like a living snowman. His white skin was splotched with liver spots. "He's one of the old guard. Hasn't visited the surface since he rose to power thirty years ago.

"I'd be surprised if he knows that Cardinal Estav no longer holds the scepter in Mallion's Depth. Even if he does, I doubt he cares. He knows his time

CHAPTER 50

is up and just wants to spend his last years in as much comfort as he can get. I predict he will dismiss your request for aid as warmongering. Resisting the church is a threat to his luxurious retirement. He had both a daughter and a son at one point, but both have moved to the surface. Neither has visited the city in fifteen years."

"Must be because he's such a joy to be around," Brina mumbled, finishing the remainder of her pile of mashed cave roots with a huge spoonful. Marret shrugged.

"Most of the borough houses have skeletons in their closets. They didn't come into power by being docile and agreeable citizens. Now, that one"—she pointed out a woman with thick blond braids framing rosy cheeks—"her, you can reason with. Eleanora of House Longstride is unique in the Council of the Boroughs. She was appointed after the death of her aunt Halkia, who died childless. Though she hasn't received formal training in the art of politics and nobility, many say that this has granted her a perspective closer to that of the common miner than that of the nobility. If you could get her on your side, you might at the same time gain the support of the working people in the city."

"That's great," Brina said, "but who pays the army?"

Marret frowned, nipping at her goblet of wine. "The miners are the army, Sabrina. In times of peace, they work in the mines from artificial dawn to artificial dusk. In times of war, they don the armor passed down to them by their predecessors. Each adult Heemian shares this duty, but that doesn't mean everyone does so gladly. We haven't seen a conscription in a hundred years, not since House Onraad tried to usurp the throne. The fighting of brother against sister turned ugly. No one here has any illusions about the so-called 'glory' of battle. Everyone's ancestors fought in the Onraad Crisis, but I have never heard a living Heemian speak of it. A full conscription would terrify the citizenry. Unless you have someone like Eleanora on your side. She will be a crucial pawn in convincing those who will need to fight the actual battles that they are worth fighting."

"What about him?" Brina said, pointing to a table on the other side of the room where Abrasax sat deep in conversation with a man with an almost foot-long black mustache.

"Lord Hammer. Much depends on his mood of the day. While his father was considered a great man and leader, he himself has seemed more preoccupied with proving himself as different from his father as possible, rather than making sure that his people are well cared for. He is known as a contrarian."

Brina reached for the carafe of wine, found it empty, and raised it to a servant clad in silver robes to refill it.

As the woman bent down, filling the small carafe from an enormous amphora, Brina said, "When we arrived, he seemed rather insistent on reminding the king of his responsibility to his citizens. He was the one who wanted the king to do something about the chasm eater." Marret shuddered at the mention of the tremor.

"Well, that's the thing. That's the type of issue he likes to involve himself with. Nobody wants to believe a chasm eater has returned to these parts after centuries of silence, so he's convinced that there is one. No one wants to entertain the possibility that the current quota for ore production is squeezing the miners dry, so he makes it his pet project to change things. Even a broken clock is right twice a day, after all."

"So what you're saying," Brina said with a grin, "is that as long as I convince him that sending military aid to the Biori is an unpopular choice among his peers, he'll be all for it?"

Marret laughed. "You know, for all your outward hatred for the profession, a politician might lurk inside you after all."

Brina made a disgusted sound, then took a gulp of her wine and pretended to rinse her mouth. "There, I have been cleansed."

Marret smiled, causing the lines around her eyes to crinkle. "If only it were so easy," she said. "Anyway, I think you should take your chance now."

She pointed over at Eleanora, the miner who sat battling an entire carafe of wine by herself.

"Get to her now, before she gets swamped with opportunists looking to further their own interests. These events are an ideal moment for networking. If you want to get some time with her, I'd go for it."

"Good idea." Brina pushed back her chair and stood up, waiting for Marret to follow. Marret, however, remained seated. "Aren't you coming?"

Marret scowled. "I couldn't. You are an esteemed guest here, and as an outsider, a bit of a rare commodity. I fell out of grace when I departed from the city. It would be improper for me to throw myself into the mix."

"That's nonsense," Brina said. "With all due respect to your home and traditions, let us break the cycle of stuffiness for once. Even if just for tonight. After all, you said she was a miner's daughter. Surely if one of the borough leaders would be open to change, it would be her."

Marret shook her head. "It's not worth the risk. You're here on important business. I will not endanger what you are trying to do just to protest

CHAPTER 50

antiquated customs."

Brina stood her ground, ready to argue, but Marret put a hand on her forearm, looked her in the eye, and said, "It's fine. Go, before it's too late. I'm sure we'll have time to catch up later."

Brina sighed, then raised her glass to the woman in a sarcastic toast and stomped off, ready to put on her social mask.

"Excuse me, ma'am," Brina tried. Eleanora looked up from her mug of wine and cocked a heavy blond eyebrow.

"What do you want?"

A grin broke on Brina's face. Now that was a breath of fresh air. None of the faint politeness and oily flattery she had grown accustomed to in the company of leaders and royals, but a straight-to-the-point question.

"If you must know," Brina said, taking a seat beside the borough leader, "the free world, or what passes for it these days, is in trouble. We're in danger. And by 'we,' I mean you."

"That so?" Eleanora asked, tapping her mug against the satin-covered table. "And how is that?"

"Let me answer you with a question," Brina said, feeling more in her element with every passing moment. She filled her own mug from Eleanora's carafe and took the lack of a rebuke as permission to carry on. "How have your workers been feeling?" Brina asked. "Are they nice and relaxed, maintaining production quotas easily?"

Eleanora barked a laugh. "Speaking of hitting the nail on the head," she grunted. "We've been stretched thin. Too thin."

"Ever wonder why that is?"

"I know why that is," Eleanora countered. "It's because the king would rather we work ourselves to death than die at the bloody end of foreign maces. I can't say I don't understand his point. Our defenses are, for lack of a better word, laughable. We're not warlike people. We produce the tools for war, yes. But that is where it ends. We leave the fighting to other, less civilized people." Her eyes flickered toward Bron and Sneak, who were sitting red-faced and slumped at one of the tables near the edge of the hall.

"What will you do when those less civilized, warlike people are battering down the doors into the mountain? What will you do when Cardinal De Leliard decides that squeezing your people like an overripe orange no longer suffices?" Brina took a deep gulp of the wine and nearly spat it out. Whatever Eleanora was drinking, it was not the same as what the servers were carrying around. This wine was strong and sour, with a bitter undertone that numbed

Brina's tongue.

"Believe me," Eleanora replied, "that very thought has kept me awake for months now. All of us borough leaders know what is coming. I believe the king does, too. But it seems unavoidable. We can't train an army because our people are too busy. We can't build up a stockpile of arms because we're exporting our resources to buy our freedom for a little while longer. It's a vicious cycle, one in which we are at the losing end."

"And what if I told you that there was a way out?"

"I would think you were a fool or a liar. Perhaps both."

"The church is planning a full-scale invasion of Bior next spring." Brina watched this information rattle around in Eleanora's head. She saw the thinly veiled shock arise.

"Which means," Brina continued, seizing the advantage now that she had the woman's full attention, "that they will not invade the mountain simultaneously. They don't have the numbers for it, and they will need to keep reserves should the assault on Bior turn sour. We are here to ensure that it does. An alliance has been formed," Brina said, "a group of brave men and women, who are training day and night to stop the invasion in its tracks. The only problem is that there are too few of us. We need the other free peoples of the Sundered Isles to pitch in. All of us need to pull on the same rope if we wish to topple Cardinal De Leliard from his throne."

"So you would suggest war?" Eleanora asked. "A direct attack on the Heilinist army?"

"Not an attack," Brina said, "a defense. We have the advantage of knowing where they will strike. This means that we have a unique chance to be one step ahead of the Cardinal. Because if Bior falls..."

Brina nodded toward Bron, who was laughing and shaking a drunk Sneak so hard that he toppled backward off his seat. The golden skulls in his beard twinkled like stars.

"The Biori are strong. Expert warriors. The church has already forced you and your skilled miners into their service. What makes you think they won't coerce the Biori to enlist in their armies? Instead of a legion of foreign soldiers, you might face a horde of mercenaries against which your citizens will stand no chance."

"Why are you telling me this?" Eleanora said. Shock, fear, and anger fought for control of her face.

"Because I know you have influence over the miners. You know what it's like to put in a day of hard labor for someone else's benefit. I know what

CHAPTER 50

that's like. Every single one of the warriors in our alliance knows what that is like. Together, we could be a formidable force."

"It's not up to me to decide," Eleanora said. "Even if I agree that such a strategy might benefit all of us, it is the king who declares war. Not me."

"The king already told us he will put this matter to a vote. Which is why we are here. I need to know that when the time comes, I can count on your vote to assemble a militia of all five boroughs. I need to know that if the vote goes our way, you will stand behind the cause. It is now or never. Cardinal De Leliard seeks to consume all of us one by one, and once he has bitten off the head, the rest of the body will follow."

"That's a lot to ask from someone you've never met before. You would have me commit political suicide based on your word." Eleanora swirled the last of her wine around her cup.

It made sense, Brina thought. The downside of living under a mountain for generations was that the outside world must seem more like an abstract concept than an urgent reality.

"This will save lives. A generation's freedom and all those to follow hang in the balance. Your people's strategy of hiding in the dark has served you well until now. But out there, a man has risen from the bottom of the Heilinist church all the way to the top, and he will not stop until everything from Bior to Hawqal is under his dominion. He sees no value in trade agreements and diplomatic treaties, not when he knows he has the power to seize it all."

"And how is it you know so much about all this?" Eleanora asked.

"Because my father, that man sitting over there"—she pointed toward Abrasax who seemed to be locked in a heated debate with borough lord Hammer—"has put it all on the line once before to free the people of Hammerstroke from the church's yoke. That man right there is Abrasax, the Viper, Springtide. The man who assassinated Cardinal Estav the Second with his own two hands," Brina said. "That is how I know."

Eleanora went silent. Her hands drummed against the tabletop. "So it is true, then. The story about a man risen from the slums with a chip on his shoulder, who walked into the very heart of the Heilinist palace and destroyed their supreme leader?"

Brina nodded. "He led the way. He showed we don't just have to sit here and take their bullying. The Cardinal had all of his friends hanged. My father was supposed to be hanged last year. We couldn't allow that. His escape from God's Maul proved the empire isn't some invulnerable, ethereal specter looming over all of us. It is flesh and blood. It can be wounded, but it can also strike, and when it does, the blow lands hard."

Brina looked up to see where the pitcher of wine had gone when a chill crept from the top of her neck down to the bottom of her spine. Armed figures had appeared in the room, standing against the draped walls and leaning against a marble statue. Though members of the guard had marched in and out of the room at will throughout the evening, something about these soldiers was different.

At first, Brina couldn't put her finger on what it was. It irked something in the back of her mind. Then, with a gasp, she realized. These men and women had tanned faces. They had seen the sun.

Brina looked from the guards to Eleanora, then leaned in. She grabbed the woman's shoulders. "Who are they?"

"I almost forgot." Eleanora's eyes widened. "The king informed us ahead of time that an arrest would take place tonight, that a handful of rebels sought by the church had infiltrated our society. However, he withheld the reason for your presence from us. If what you have said is true, and I believe it is, I wouldn't have you fall into the church's hands."

Brina made to get up, but Eleanora grabbed her by the side of the robe and pulled her back down into her seat.

"No," she whispered, "they will not strike here. Not where everyone is watching. I would bet what remains of my left hand"—she raised a calloused hand with two missing fingers—"that they will wait until you leave, and then on the other side of those doors." She pointed at the magnificent double doors that stood at the end of the hallway. "They will seize you and drag you off, where you can't make any statements or resist publicly."

Brina spat onto the table. "Damn you, Krocht, you slimy, weaselly…"

CHAPTER 51

ait," Eleanora said, gripping Brina's forearm.

Blood pounded in Brina's ears, drowning out the noises of silverware on oaken tables, wine traveling down gullets, and laughter at unfunny jests told by mirthless old men.

"There might be a way out," the borough leader said. "Look over your shoulder, but don't make it too obvious."

Brina shifted in her seat, so she could see what Eleanora was nodding at.

"That door left of Krocht's table is the servant's entrance. They haven't blocked it off. The king has likely instructed them not to hinder his servants while so many of his nobles are feasting. If you can alert your compatriots, I'd wager you could make a dash for it and disappear into the kitchens before they could stop you. There's a wine cellar with a loading hatch that leads outside.

"The foilfaces will face a dilemma. They'll either have to make a scene at the banquet, and in doing so upset the king, or they can leave it to the guards positioned on the outside of the palace to catch you. What I suggest you do is head into the cellar and try to act like a servant unloading supplies. With any luck, you'll disappear in the bustle.

"Then, there is one place in the whole of the Shimmering City where you will be safe. Once they realize you have given them the slip, they will turn the entire city upside down. Except for one place that nobody knows is still there."

Brina swallowed. This was a lot of information to take in. And every step of Eleanora's plan, though recounted as casually as a move in a game of galleons, had the potential to fail catastrophically.

"When they took you into the city, did they show you the current prison building?"

Brina nodded. As they had made their way through the city to reach the baths, Madame Witdrager had pointed out various structures of which the Heemians were proud. The prison hadn't been one of those, but its huge brickwork facade and the heavy bars on all windows had been hard to miss.

"Right," Eleanora continued, smiling and drinking from her goblet, so as not to tip off the guards waiting at the edge of the room. "The current prison comprises two levels—one on the main floor and one in the basement. However, the ancient dungeons lie right beneath it. They were in use during the reign of King Krocht's great-grandfather. Given their less than civilized methods, they were a great blemish on the king's image. A little over a decade ago, he asked me to make those lower levels disappear.

"Pleased as I was to receive a job from the king, I did so. But, in my haste to make it quick, I chose the easiest solution, which was to seal off the passage leading into the ancient prison. The entrance is in what is now known as cell C-13. It is on the basement level. There is a grate on the west side of the building that leads there.

"You will notice that one wall of that cell is newer than the others. That is where the entrance to the lower levels lies. If you can sneak in there and grant yourself access to the lower levels, I bet you can hide out until the foilfaces give up."

Brina's eyes widened. It was just about the wildest plan she'd ever heard.

"Just so we're clear," she said. "You suggest I sneak into prison to avoid being imprisoned?"

Eleanora shrugged. "It's the only place I can think of where I'm sure they won't find you. But let that be as it may. There's still a lot of ground to cover between here and the outside of the palace. Whatever you do, try at all costs to avoid direct confrontation. Though I don't doubt your prowess in battle, the foilfaces will have come prepared. They know who you are, and if you've eluded them before, they'd rather die than give you the satisfaction of pulling that off again."

Brina sighed, filled her goblet with wine, downed it in one, then stomped over to Bron and Sneak to alert them to the danger.

"We know," Bron grumbled as Brina plopped down on the chair beside the pair. They were surrounded by piles of empty goblets and bowls. A haggard-looking servant was running laps between the kitchen door and their table, carrying off piles of dirty plates.

"What do we do?" Sneak asked, his eyes flitting around the room like the hands of a clock.

"First, we've got to disentangle my father from that guy's clutches." She pointed at the ancient borough leader Abrasax was in conversation with. "The borough leaders know. They were told we were going to get arrested,

CHAPTER 51

and all they're doing is playing for time until they snatch us up."

"Parasites," Bron grumbled. "This is the type of deceitful cowardice that would have them part ways with their heads where I'm from."

"Hang on," Sneak intervened, "and you know all that how?"

Brina looked over at Eleanora, then said, "It's a long story. I'll go grab my father. Meanwhile, get ready to make a dash for that door right there." She pointed at the open kitchen door through which the same servant was now striding with empty hands, ready to pick up a fresh round of plates from their table. "Just follow that guy when he goes back. We all have to make a run for it at the same time."

"Then where do we go?"

"Later," Brina said, waving an impatient hand. As she strode toward Abrasax's table, she saw him get up and walk in a straight line toward the nearest darkhelm.

No, Brina thought, *don't.* She sped up, hoping to catch up with him before it was too late. But he was too far ahead. People kept stepping in her path as they chattered away, eating and drinking. Servants wove in and out of the crowd, carrying platters of food. It was like a maze.

"Father," she called out, hoping against hope that he would hear. If he did, he didn't heed her call. Instead, he walked up to the darkhelms, who clustered around him. Brina saw the steely glimmer of manacles as they clasped his wrists.

"What did you do?" She looked from her father, who looked back at her and beckoned with his head for her to join him, to Bron and Sneak, who stood ready to run for it near the servants' entrance. Both of them looked aghast at what Abrasax had done.

"Trust me," Abrasax mouthed. Or maybe Brina had just seen in the movement of his lips what she wanted to hear. How could he have given up so quickly?

I should've known, Brina thought, remembering the conversation they'd had after the disastrous audience with the Morassian archdruidess. *He doesn't have it in him anymore. God's Maul broke him.* And yet, when she looked into his eyes as the darkhelms surrounded him, there was something different there. His cheeks were no longer hollow, his eyes no longer glassy. There was a fire there, and a sharpness that Brina remembered only from her childhood.

Brina hesitated. To go with her father meant that Bron and Sneak would have no other option but to do the same. They didn't know the way. Brina hadn't explained it to them. If she was wrong about this, she wouldn't only doom herself but them, too.

"Trust me," Abrasax mouthed again, clearer this time. One darkhelm beside him elbowed him in the stomach, knocking the wind out of him. Abrasax bent forward, coughing and spluttering. That alone was enough to make Brina decide.

She marched right up to the darkhelm who punched her father and slapped him in the face. The others went to grab her, but she turned her gaze to the woman reaching for her arm.

"Touch me, and you are in for the fight of your life. We will come with you, but enough with the brutalities. If it comes to it, I may not be able to take all of you, but I can take you, and I'll drag you down with me. Understood?"

The woman let go of Brina's arm as though it burned red hot.

"It's fine," she muttered to her cohorts. "We'll guide them outside."

As they were marched out of the dining hall, a deathly silence fell. All eyes followed them. Some looked horrified, others gleeful. King Krocht, seated behind his decorated table, looked away when Brina tried to catch his gaze. He couldn't look any of them in the eye. Behind her, a dozen darkhelms flanked Bron and Sneak.

I trusted you, Father. Please don't make me regret it.

CHAPTER 52

n the other side of the dining hall door, another dozen darkhelms awaited them. They crowded around the four sparkgazers like vultures.

"Wow," Brina said to one of the nearest darkhelms, "fun for the whole family, eh?"

The man withdrew his hand to strike her, but the officer with the golden helmet hissed at him, shaking her head. They had the advantage of numbers, but they were scared. Brina grinned, resisting the temptation to provoke the man further.

She tried to catch Abrasax's gaze, hoping to gain some clue about what his plan was, but the darkhelms kept him isolated at the front of the group, and he just marched along, head bowed.

There was a scuffle behind her, and Brina could hear Bron growl. "Touch me again, and I will eat you."

The situation grew more tense with every step. As they passed a hallway where four corridors converged, Brina thought of running. If each of them sprinted in a different direction, at least one of them ought to make it. She stopped dead in the crossing like an anxious mule.

"Where are you taking us?" she asked, playing for time, hoping for some sign from Abrasax.

"Back where you belong," the officer replied. "You knew that."

If the situation had been any less dire, Brina might have appreciated the officer's bluntness. But as it stood, it was all she could do not to lunge at the woman.

"Oh yes," she snapped back, "just stick everyone who disagrees with the party line in the dark. That strategy sure worked out for Estav. What makes you think it will work any better for you?"

"Enough!" the officer barked. "You can either come quietly, or I will have you muffled."

Brina laughed. "I'd like to see you try." She'd love nothing more than to headbutt the woman, but, remembering Abrasax's words, she allowed herself to be herded into the corridor to the left, which led to the palace's main entrance. The darkhelms were going to parade them through the whole town on the way out—an example for the people of Onderheem, showing what happens to those who oppose the Cardinal's demands.

As they entered the main hall, which was lined with statues of former Heemian royals, a marble staircase neared in front of them. Forty shiny steps down, surrounded by five-feet-high banisters, carved like long serpents.

They were halfway down the stairs when it happened.

Abrasax stretched out his arms with an almost imperceptible burst of speed. Both darkhelms beside him dropped, red stains blooming on their uniforms. As the ones in front and behind him turned to attack, Abrasax bent over backward, grabbed a darkhelm who stood behind him and flung her down the stairs, bowling over the one in front of him. Both bodies went flying down the stairs in a tangle of limbs and screams.

To Brina's left, a flash of silver caught her eye. A flasher. The darkhelm officer held it up, aiming for Abrasax's face. Brina flared *Forte* and kicked the officer's knee. It folded backward with a crunch. As the woman sank to the ground, Brina snatched the flasher out of her hand.

"Duck," Abrasax shouted.

Brina flung herself to the ground. Half a dozen wet thuds resounded overhead as darkhelms toppled over the banisters and fell to the ground where they stood. The white marble staircase turned into a canvas for an impressionist artist who only used scarlet paint. Abrasax's sigilist stars had buried themselves almost fully in their targets' flesh.

Though Brina carried a handful of them herself, she had never seen anyone throw them so rapidly and accurately. Before she knew it, the four sparkgazers had a circle of space around them on the staircase, with more than a dozen remaining darkhelms near the top and bottom of the staircase. They didn't dare close in. Instead, they formed a wall of armor and shields.

"Up," Abrasax shouted.

He stormed up the stairs, his eyes shimmering blue. He leaped straight into the upper shield wall, moving like a tornado of steel and fists. Brina followed, withdrew a dagger from her ankle holster, and flung it into an approaching darkhelm's throat. The man reached for his neck, then tumbled forward down the stairs. He rolled down a few steps, where he lay still.

Bron bent down to pick up the man's mace, roaring with fury as he stormed

CHAPTER 52

up the staircase. The handful of darkhelms who were left standing on the first-floor landing took a few steps backward. It was no use. Sneak leaped onto the stair banister, vaulted over them and stabbed two of them in the back. As the others staggered sideways, Abrasax struck out with a spinning kick that hit the first one in the head and sent him flying into his companions. The trio toppled down the stairs in a clatter of armor.

"To the king's quarters!" Abrasax shouted as he stormed down the hallway. "He's got a balcony overlooking the square. From there, we can launch ourselves onto one of the neighboring buildings. They can't follow us across the rooftops."

They ascended another flight of stairs leading to the second floor, one floor above the guest rooms where they had been housed the days before. The hallways were deserted. Both the royal family and all the servants were still present at the banquet below.

Brina imagined them all eating and drinking, satisfied that they had delivered four of the most wanted people in the Sundered Isles to Cardinal De Leliard. Krocht thought he would be rewarded beyond all others.

Bloody fool, Brina thought with a jolt of anger.

Two black granite gargoyles flanked the arched doors leading to the king's quarters. Normally, these would be guarded, but since the king wasn't present at the moment, a series of heavy locks bolted to the outside were thought to be enough to stop anyone from entering. They would have been right, had it not been for Sneak.

"Move aside." He kneeled down before the three golden locks, examining each one. From his inside pocket he unrolled a leather satchel containing a series of metal instruments. His eyes flared with *Auris* as he prodded and poked at the locks. After a handful of seconds, the first lock opened with a shuddering click. "These are some fine locks," Sneak said. "The cylinders are so smooth and precise, they're like little puzzles."

"Then puzzle on, stickman," Bron growled. His foot tapped against the marble floor. "They're right behind us."

"Your wish is my command, milord," Sneak said in a mock posh voice as the second lock opened. As soon as he'd begun working on the third lock, Sneak groaned.

"Uh oh." He sat back, staring at the lock with wide eyes. He held up his right hand, which contained one half of a broken lock pick. The other half was stuck in the lock. Sneak leaned back, pulling on the broken section, but it wouldn't budge.

"Stand back." Bron took a few steps backward, eyeing the door as though it had insulted his entire bloodline. "I'll deal with this."

"This is Heemian steel," Abrasax began, "You can't—"

Clang.

The door swung open as the lock broke.

"What were you saying, old man?" Bron bared yellowed teeth in a wide grin.

CHAPTER 53

Brina charged through the open door and almost bumped headlong into King Krocht's sizable belly. Behind him stood two dozen heavily armored Heemian guards. These were no darkhelms. The faces beneath their visors were pale from generations spent toiling in the dark under the mountain. Their short, narrow statures were well-adapted to stone cracks and narrow passages. Like the miners, their arms were corded with muscle.

"You..." Brina made to grab the king, but Abrasax stuck out an arm and held her back.

"Why?" he asked, stepping toward Krocht. The spark Brina had seen in his eyes earlier smoldered. "You fool. You have doomed us all. Not least of which yourself. Are you really that shortsighted that you would exchange your people's only chance at freedom for a measly few months of pseudo-peace?"

"You know nothing about what I have done for my people's freedom," the king spat. "I wish it didn't have to be this way, Springtide, I really do, but I pondered my options, and this was the only way. The appearance of a chasm eater means that my production will falter for weeks, maybe months. We were already falling behind our quota. I had to find a way to supplement my tribute to the church. And there you were. The mountain had handed me what I needed on a silver platter."

"So you have bought a handful of months at the expense of your people's future," Abrasax said. His voice was cold and hard. For the first time, he sounded like the living legend people made him out to be. "Once Bior falls, its warriors will be at your gates. Not that De Leliard needs them." He smirked. "These days King Krocht opens his gates readily enough to the enemies of his realm. He even lets them enjoy the comforts of his palace."

Krocht's face contorted. "I didn't tell them about your plan to save Bior. That had nothing to do with our deal. I still want De Leliard's invasion to fail. I still hope for a successful rebellion, but it will have to be one without you."

"How is any rebellion to succeed in a world full of cowards like you?" Abrasax said. "You have brought shame upon your bloodline and the very halls in which you dwell. You will be remembered as a pawn, nothing more."

"And you will not be remembered at all." Krocht's chest rose and fell like a smith's bellows.

"We shall see. Now let us pass, or suffer the consequences."

"Pass?" Krocht looked around incredulously. "Pass? God's Maul must have chewed up your brain far worse than I thought. I have two dozen of the mountain's strongest warriors behind me. Their armor is too thick for any of your tricks, and I expect the foilfaces will be here any moment to assist us. So no, you will stay right there. Too much depends on your delivery. I'm sorry. You're a decent man, but also a valuable one. A poor combination in these times."

Brina's hand closed around the flasher in her pocket, the tip of her thumb brushing the button on its side.

"I will ask you one more time," Abrasax said, his voice level. He turned his gaze toward the armored men and women standing behind Krocht. "I do not want to harm you, but I assure you I will if you do not get out of my way."

Armor rattled as the soldiers shuffled uneasily on their feet. Sighs mixed with clearing throats, but they didn't move. Denying a direct order from their king would bring consequences far more grievous than wounds sustained in battle. All of them understood that. Abrasax smiled sadly.

"So be it."

Brina could see the muscles in his back tense. She aimed the flasher straight ahead and pressed the button.

The room disappeared in a haze of white. Metal clanked against the marble floor as Krocht's troops sank to their knees, hands covering burning eyes. As though this had been the war cry they had been waiting for, the four sparkgazers charged forward. They leaped over the blinded and flailing soldiers, then jumped straight through the stained-glass windows and out onto the balcony in a hail of shattered glass.

"Flat roof to the left!" Abrasax cried. He leaped up onto the marble banister and catapulted himself through the air in a fortified jump. Brina followed. All four of them sailed through the air in a graceful arc, like a flock of birds. They landed on the flat stone roof of a two-story apothecary.

Commotion in the streets below told Brina that they were being pursued on foot by the darkhelms that had guarded the palace's perimeter. Because they'd expected prisoners to be walked out of the front door, they were un-

CHAPTER 53

prepared for what was taking place high above their heads. Windup bolts swished past as Brina broke into a run, leaping from roof to roof. After the initial volley of bolts, no more followed.

Soon, the clatter of armor and the cries of "step aside in the name of the Cardinal" faded to background noise. The flat roofs of the squat Heemian buildings made it almost too easy to cover ground quickly. Brina felt like an eagle flying over a dense forest. The solid stone beneath her feet couldn't have been more different from the mossy tiles of Doorstep's Ditch and the patches of rotten straw Brina had so often dreaded during her nighttime raids.

"Make for the northwest corner of the city, just before the mining district," Brina yelled.

"What?" Sneak shouted from behind her, opposite the gates. "That would take us deeper into the mountain."

"Exactly. I know just where to go."

Sneak's further complaints were lost to the rush of wind in Brina's ears. As the prison loomed in the distance, at least twice as high as any of the citizens' houses surrounding it, Brina held up a hand. The four of them stood on the edge of the street across from the prison, which was surrounded by a ring of wide-open cobbled square.

"Are you sure about this?" Abrasax asked. He was the only one of them not panting with exertion after their sprint across the city.

Brina nodded. "We don't have to go into the main building. There's a grate near the west side, which leads into the basement. From there, it'll be a short distance to a safe place where we can lie low until all of this blows over."

They slipped down from the rooftop, feet slamming painfully into the uneven cobbles. They floated across the square like ghosts in the night, hugging the prison's outer wall. Brina prayed to the Seven and anyone who would listen that Eleanora's word was solid. She scoured the ground, searching for the rusty grate the woman had described.

"Come on," she muttered under her breath. "Don't set me up, don't set me up."

She imagined Eleanora laughing with the darkhelms about how stupid Brina had been to run straight into their trap, but there was no point in second-guessing things now. In for a nib, in for a shard.

She spotted the rusty grate and knelt down. Before she pulled on it, Brina took a deep breath. Together with Abrasax, a brief flash of *Forte* was enough to rip the grate loose.

"I'll go first," Brina said. "If something goes wrong, leave me."

She slipped through the narrow hole, falling for what felt like an eternity before her feet slammed into an earthen floor. She burned *Lux*, and a dusty, cobweb-filled room came into view. Ancient furniture stained with mold stood gathered at one side of the room. Rats squeaked away as she stepped back to allow the others in.

"It's okay, I think." The others followed. Brina traced the walls, looking closely for the place where the centuries-old brick-and-mortar changed into the newer masonry Eleanora had described. If they broke down the wrong wall, they might as well tie themselves up with a pretty pink bow and deliver themselves to the Cardinal's Palace.

"What is this place?" Sneak asked, kicking at the skeletonized remains of a rat.

"We're underneath the prison," Brina said. There was a collective hiss from the others.

"It's not as stupid as it sounds," she said. "At the banquet, Eleanora warned me they were coming for us and told me Krocht put her in charge of sealing off the ancient dungeons from the current prison."

"Meaning?" Sneak asked, his eyebrows threatening to rise to the top of his head.

"Meaning that it's all still down here. It was supposed to be filled in with rubble so that no one could ever access it again. Except she didn't. Somewhere behind these walls is the old entrance. Once we find it, we break through a thin wall and disappear into a part of the city no one knows still exists."

"Eleanora knows," Sneak said. "These are the people who betrayed us fifteen minutes ago. All of them were in on it. And now we're backed into a corner on the advice of one of them."

"Do you have a better plan?" Brina said, taking a step toward Sneak. "If you do, I'd love to hear it. If you don't, I suggest we figure out which wall to tear down."

"This is madness," Bron growled, dragging his boots on the floor, drawing scuffs in the dust. "All we're doing is digging ourselves deeper into the same hole. We have no food, no water. What good does it do to hide amongst the rats?"

Brina felt her temper rising, mostly because both of them had a point. They were rabbits trying to outmaneuver an eagle, and they all knew it. Nevertheless, they had gotten this far. They had gone all-in on Eleanora's advice, and all that remained was to see where it led them. Brina opened her mouth, trying to think of a more encouraging way to phrase this, but

CHAPTER 53

Abrasax's hand shot into the air to silence her. His eyes burned with *Auris*.

"They're coming," he whispered.

Brina tapped into *Auris* herself. Forced to relinquish *Lux*, she was immediately engulfed in darkness. Thrumming boots echoed in the distance, like the strokes of an approaching war drum. It sounded like there were at least half a dozen of them—not insurmountable numbers, but even a single darkhelm could blow a horn to sound the alarm.

"There's no one here," a man growled overhead. "You're seeing double again from all that confiscated wine you've been drinking."

"I told you, Captain," another man replied, his voice resembling a stable hand who'd been kicked in the head one too many times. "They came this way."

"That so?" the captain snapped. "And what'd they do? March themselves into prison, hands outstretched for the chains?"

A handful of other soldiers burst out laughing.

"Yeah," a third, sycophantic voice mocked. "Great thinking, Karolus. The first place any fugitive goes is straight toward the nearest prison."

"Wouldn't complain," yet another darkhelm growled.

"You guys always do this," Karolus murmured. "You never believe me."

"I'll believe you as soon as something reasonable comes out of that mouth of yours. Until then, you can chew rocks," the captain said.

"They are here. I saw it. I know they must be around somewhere."

"The mines are being checked, Captain," the sycophant interjected. "Lieutenant Ontbering sent three squads into the shafts. There's no hiding down there. The miners work day and night. There's no getting past them unseen, and if a little money doesn't grease those palms, we've got other ways to make them talk."

"You guys do whatever you want," Karolus said. "I'm looking around. I know what I saw."

Come on, you moron, Brina thought, *let it go.*

"Might as well take a rest while we're at it," the captain growled. There was a clatter of metal against cobbles as most of the darkhelms sat down.

Meanwhile, Karolus wandered in circles, the thump of his boots drawing closer and closer. If he discovered the dislodged grate, there'd be no way out.

"You better find that entrance right now," Sneak whispered, gripping Brina's shoulder.

"Then help me," Brina whispered back, pushing him up against the wall.

Releasing *Auris*, Brina switched back into *Lux*. She scoured the wall systematically, tapping her bare knuckles against each section as hard as she dared. The darkhelm drew closer. The footsteps stopped, and Brina's heartbeat dropped right alongside them. They were trapped.

"Got it," Sneak whispered from the dark.

"Great," Bron replied. "Now all we've got to do is find a completely silent way to demolish a wall."

Brina stifled a groan. He was right. She'd been so caught up in finding the hollow wall that she hadn't considered the racket battering down a stone wall would make. Brina joined Sneak, put her ear against the wall, and sure enough, there it was. The hollow thunk that, minutes ago, would have solved all their problems. Now, it was only a reminder of just how close they had come to escaping.

Bron crept toward the grate, the mace he'd picked up resting against his shoulder. Brina waved her arms and shook her head. She retrieved her one remaining dagger from behind her belt, pressed the blade's edge into the mortar-filled gap between two bricks, and began sawing back and forth.

That was one of my best pieces, she thought, almost sentimental as she watched the razor-sharp edge fray and bend beyond repair. Soon, mortar piled up on the floor. Abrasax, picking up on what Brina was doing, joined her, as did Sneak, while Bron held his position beside the grate, watching the gap overhead with a hungry expression. With three daggers and the flare of *Forte*, they dug away at the mortar surrounding one brick. It wasn't enough to dislodge it, but they were close.

Then, the sound of heavy breathing made the hair on the back of Brina's neck stand up. All four of them looked up in horror to see a griffin-shaped helmet appear behind the rusty grate. The darkhelm closed his hands around it and tugged at it fruitlessly. Brina stopped sawing at the mortar at once.

"I told you empty wineskins. This grate has been loosened."

"What do you mean, loosened?" the captain called, clearly annoyed.

"Look," Karolus said. "The bars used to be embedded with a layer of mortar, but they've been torn free."

He put his foot down on the grate, making it shift under his full body weight.

"So?" the other darkhelms said.

"What if they're in there?" There was a sigh like a gust of wind.

"That thing's as heavy as an ox; nobody moved it. The mortar just crumbled away over the centuries, that's all. Try it, try to lift it."

"I can't," the Karolus said. "That's why I called you over."

"But if you can't move it, what makes you think a fugitive on the run could

CHAPTER 53

move and replace it?"

"They are different, aren't they?" Karolus said. "Unnatural and all that. I bet to them, this thing's no more than a blade of grass."

"And why would they be hiding in the prison's basement?"

"Because it's the last place we'd go looking."

"You know, Karolus," the captain replied, "that is the first sensible thing you've said all night. That *is* the last place I'm going to look for them. My back is bad enough as it is. You think I want to spend the next week walking crooked because you wanted to lift a two-hundred-pound chunk of steel?"

"We were to comb through the city as thoroughly as outwalled scum digging for each other's lice. Those were the orders. If you do not help me move this thing, I will report it to my mother."

This struck a nerve. Among a string of curses, more darkhelms approached.

"Dammit," Sneak muttered, panic raising his voice an octave.

"Okay," Brina said, her voice raw in her throat. "We've tried silence. Time to go for speed."

She burned *Forte* and kicked at the loose brick. It came loose with a crashing thunk.

"They're there, they're in there," Karolus shouted excitedly. "Move this thing now. We've got them."

Hands closed around the grate.

Bron, abandoning his post by the grate, yelled, "Stand back, stand back, coming in hot," his eyes flashed blue with such a fierce burst of *Forte* that the dingy basement was briefly lit up. Then he crashed into the wall, his steel greaves screeching against stone.

Multiple bricks around the hole came loose, falling inward. Bron hammered away at the gap with the stolen mace, widening it. "In!" he shouted. "Let's go!"

Brina dove through the opening. Abrasax followed, and as Brina got to her feet on the other side, she could hear the screeching of iron as the darkhelms moved the grate.

"Come on," Brina held out a hand toward Bron, who took it and pulled himself through the hole. For a moment, she thought about trying to hold off the darkhelms as they tried to enter the narrow hole in the wall, then she realized it wouldn't be any use. Already, the low rumble of horns resounded on the surface, a sure sign that every darkhelm in the city would soon be on their heels.

"Run," she shouted.

A sharp stench like vinegar washed over her as they stormed down a narrow passage with uneven steps carved into natural rock. Bron was the only one who didn't need to stoop forward to accommodate the passage's ever-decreasing height. Brina's hand brushed the rocky side of the tunnel, and she jerked it back in disgust as something slimy touched her hand.

After what felt like an eternity, the passage widened into a long rectangular chamber. Along the sides of it, rusty cell doors stood ajar. In the middle of the room stood half a dozen stone posts, heavy iron rings and manacles still attached to them. The surrounding floor was stained black.

Sneak screamed and tumbled to the ground. Brina scooped him up, then realized with horror that what he'd tripped over had been the outstretched legs of a human skeleton, bony wrists still clamped down in spiked manacles. "Seven Almighty," Sneak croaked, "they just left them down here."

Brina cast a sideways glance at the cell doors that were still closed, a sinking feeling in her stomach.

"Come on, keep running."

Abrasax and Bron were ahead of them, disappearing down a second corridor leading to a deeper level of the prison. There were shouts behind them, followed by the clatter of armor. The darkhelms had made it into the passage. They were trapped. The only way to go was deeper into the hole they were digging for themselves. They passed another cellblock, similar to the first, and the vinegary stench in Brina's nostrils swelled to a burning sensation.

She retched as the vile stench filled her lungs while they ran. Beyond the second cellblock, she could see Bron and Abrasax. Had it not been for Abrasax's outstretched arms, they would have sprinted straight past him.

"Careful," he gasped, and the terror in his voice made goosebumps run up Brina's neck.

Then she looked down.

CHAPTER 54

hey stood in a vast circular cave, the center of which was a black chasm. Not even *Lux* could help Brina see the bottom. Winding, uneven steps were carved into the cave's outer wall. In places, they narrowed to little more than a foot wide. Any slip would be fatal.

Countless cell doors lined the walls. On some of them, the wood had rotted away, leaving only strips of rusted steel, beyond which contorted skeletons lay abandoned.

"What is that covering those bodies?" Sneak pointed out an open cell a little way down the stairs. His voice trembled. Brina swallowed.

They were cobwebs, but not the wispy kind that had covered the entrance above. These were thick and viscous. Strings as thick as fingers ensnared human skeletons, forcing them into twisted positions. The remains, instead of having decomposed, looked mummified. They reminded of leather water-skins after they had been sucked dry.

"I think I know why the lower quarters needed to be sealed up," Brina muttered. "What in the Seven did they set free down here?" She looked up and found the ceiling of the cave covered in the same ropes of white. The longer she stood there, the deeper the stench of dried and rotted flesh crept its way into her pores.

"You're asking us?" Bron snarled from up ahead. "I thought you were the heildamned roamer."

"I've cleaned up infestations of all kinds of arachnids, but I've seen nothing like this." She wasn't even ashamed of the trembling in her voice. If there had ever been a time to lose her nerve, it was now. She didn't even want to think about how large something would need to get to spit ropes instead of webs.

Maybe it's dead, she thought. *It ate all the prisoners, then died when it ran out of food.*

"Please let it have died," she muttered aloud. As she descended the stairs, deeper into the chasm, her eyes kept flickering between her feet, inching down the narrow steps, and the shadows above.

It was the type of dark that could swallow a person whole. There was no time to think about what might lurk in those shadows. They had to get as far away from their pursuers as possible. There was a cry behind them. At the top of the spiraling stairs, a torch appeared. The darkhelms had reached the cave. Though only a few of them bore torches, there seemed to be dozens of them. Brina's hand strayed to the flasher she'd stolen at the palace. If the darkhelms had thought to bring one, they might have a spare on hand.

"In here," Abrasax shouted to their left. Brina peered over the side of the stairs and saw an ancient cage lift on a rusty chain. It was like the ones used to maintain the stoneward at Mallion's Depth. The cage was stained with rust. Remnants of a wooden floor had rotted, leaving only the metal bars for support. A system of pulleys anchored to the cavern wall had once been used to control it, but now it looked as though a single sneeze could blow it to pieces.

Abrasax hopped into the cage, causing the mechanism to groan. "Heemian engineering," he grinned, patting one of the cage's rusty bars. "Lasts forever."

"That won't hold all our weight," Sneak said. "It won't even hold one of us. And if that chain breaks…"

"Must you always burden others with your cowardice?" Bron snarled in a rare moment of lost composure. Brina knew the Biori well enough to realize he was scared. That, more than anything else she'd seen tonight, rattled her. They were in deep trouble.

"I'll go first," Abrasax said. "When I reach the bottom, I'll call for you to raise the lift. The darkhelms have a ways to go before they catch up. There should be time for all of you."

"And if there isn't," Bron said, thumping his fist into the cave's wall, "I'll gladly make a stand that will make the Allmother proud."

There was no time for Brina to protest. When running out of time, chivalry is as likely to be a death sentence as a blessing. Besides, if Abrasax died in the elevator, the rest of them were as good as dead. There was no outrunning the sheer numbers of darkhelms pouring in through the cave's entrance.

Abrasax pulled the lever inside the lift. A rusty clamp on the chain opened, and the lift began a rapid descent. As she watched her father disappear into the darkness, a sick feeling crept up on Brina. The chain rattled and echoed in the cave, bouncing off the walls. The reverberations made it sound ominous, like hundreds of legs tapping against stone.

On the opposite wall, the torchlights descended in a spiral pattern toward

CHAPTER 54

them. There was a heavy clank, followed by Abrasax's shout.

"I'm at the bottom. You'll have to pull the lift back up by hand."

Minutes later, Brina nudged Sneak into the cage and watched it descend once more. This time, Brina was sure of what she heard. Something else was moving in the darkness above. All the commotion in the cave had awoken something.

Bron had heard it too.

"You have no idea what it is?" he asked.

Brina shook her head. "Whatever it is, let's hope it likes the taste of darkhelms better than it does us." She listened, desperate for the sound of metal on stone that would announce Sneak had reached the bottom. The sooner all of them had their feet on solid ground, the better.

Then a rock the size of a human eyeball slammed into Brina's collarbone. As she massaged the bruised spot, a hail of pebbles rained down on them.

"Made it," Sneak called from below. Brina and Bron joined forces in hoisting the lift back up to the top, their muscles fueled as much by growing anxiety as the *Forte* sigil they were both burning.

"You get in there. I'll keep a lookout here," Brina said when the cage came into view. Bron looked like he wanted to argue, but Brina shoved him into the cage and pulled the lever for him. "I'm the roamer, remember? I may not know what this thing is, but I've seen enough filth in my time to learn to improvise when necessary."

When she was alone, Brina burned *Auris*, trying to separate the noise from the essence of what she needed to hear. There was the clinking of the chain, the clatter of approaching darkhelms, but there was something else. Layered underneath it all were the frenzied stabs of hundreds of legs against stone. Whatever they were, they were swarming. As Brina pulled on the chain to raise the lift for the last time, a strand of rope fell across her shoulder. It was hot, burning the skin underneath her robe. She tried to shrug it off, but it was stuck.

A white, slimy substance dripped down her shoulder. With a panicked tug, she jerked most of it off. It landed on the floor with a sickening plop. Then she saw what it had come from. A three-foot-long hairy body was perched on the wall behind her. The creature's shadowy outline was visible in the gloom only through a quick burst of *Lux*. There were dozens of legs covered in thick fur. Two long claws protruded on either side of a mass of a hundred gleaming eyes. The creature's tail was bent over in an arch, a long stinger hanging right above Brina, ready to strike.

Brina's throat went dry as she realized the creature was an ammitarach. Part myth, part theory, the ammitarach was thought to be the long-lost ancestor to most arachnid species that roamed the foul places of the world today. It was said to have been bred by the gods themselves as weapons to be unleashed on human cities during the first clashes of the Sundering. Until now, Brina had considered the descriptions of them that littered old bestiaries to be the work of frightened old men who'd encountered a deep spider and had let their imagination get the best of them. Even in their terror-fueled writings, they had not done the monstrosity justice.

She darted aside as the dagger-sized stinger swooped toward her neck. The ammitarach hissed, repositioning itself on the wall with terrifying speed, poised for a second strike. Brina dodged again. She reached for a dagger, then realized she had left her last one, blunted and useless, in the passage above after trying to loosen bricks with it. She was unarmed. Emboldened by Brina's lack of retaliation, the beast skittered down the wall, landing on the narrow stone stairs before her. It lurched forward, grabbing with both of its claws.

Brina leaped back, surprised by how sluggish her movements felt without the aid of sigils to fuel her. She needed to burn *Lux* to see in the cavern's dark, preventing her from switching to others. She had no weapons and no sigils. Worst of all, ammitarach were said to be venomous. On Hammerstroke, scorpions the size of Brina's hand carried enough venom to kill an adult pronghorn within minutes. She didn't even want to consider what a sting from this giant could do to a body as lean as hers had become over the past months.

The lift cage was stuck halfway between the ground and the platform on which she stood. She didn't dare look down to see how far away it was for fear of being caught by one of the ammitarach's lunges. She backed up to the edge of the lift platform. The beast followed, trying to corner her against the edge. From up close, Brina could see a circular mouth opening lined with dozens of tiny barbs. Milky green liquid seeped from its stinger, dripping onto the floor below. The stench of vinegar made Brina gag.

A sliver of rock fell onto her neck, and she looked up just in time to see a second ammitarach on the wall right above her strike with its long tail. Brina dodged the swooping stinger, and in a reflex that terrified even herself, grabbed the lunging tail with both hands and yanked. The creature's hooked legs came loose from the wall. Right before it fell on top of her, Brina jerked forward with all her might and flung it over the edge of the stairs. It vanished with a hissing screech that could slice marble.

CHAPTER 54

The one in front of her used her momentary lapse of attention as a window of opportunity. Its stinger sank deep into the meat of her left calf. Brina screamed, stomping down hard with her other foot. The ammitarach's tail snapped, the loose sections curling and uncurling like a broken snake. The stinger itself was still lodged in her calf.

The ammitarach lurched backward, deterred by the wound it had sustained. A warm glow rushed through Brina's lower leg. *No, no, no, no, no.* She cursed herself for allowing her natural reflexes to become slow and rusty. She'd become so reliant on the fuel provided by sigils that her natural fitness had decayed. Here, forced to stick to *Lux*, that had become her undoing.

She remembered a conversation she'd had ages ago with Acheron as they hiked up to Barrow's Perch, even before she had learned how to tap into the power of the shapes. Acheron had warned her that all sparkgazers eventually became addicted to sigils, unable to resist using them at every turn. Back then, it had seemed ridiculous to Brina not to use the sigils' advantage whenever the opportunity presented itself. She'd wanted nothing more than to harness that unnatural strength. Now, in this critical moment, she realized she had fallen into the very trap Acheron had tried to warn her about. She had allowed herself to become slow and weak, no longer relying on her instincts to keep her safe, but on artificial enhancements. She had just paid the ultimate price.

A reckless rage overcame her. It was already too late. She'd been stung. Nothing mattered anymore. She charged the ammitarach, leaped up, and ground the heel of her boots right into its many glittering eyes. There was a squishy crack as the eyes tore and leaked. The ammitarach curled into a defensive ball. Brina stomped on it again, and again, and again. The creature's tail twisted in agony, but it didn't have the force remaining to strike. Disgusted, her boots covered in slimy guts, Brina kicked it off the ledge. Its broken body tumbled into the abyss, spraying black ichor everywhere.

How soon would the venom set in? How much time remained before the darkness would come? Over the years, she'd gotten herself stung and bitten by countless venomous creatures. She knew of antidotes that worked against most common venoms, but against a venom so ancient and potent, she could only guess.

In a desperate move, she ripped the sleeve from her sapphire tunic, kneeled down, and tied it around her leg just below the knee. She relinquished *Lux* to flare *Forte*, allowing herself to tie the thing as tight as it would go. All blood flow from the affected limb needed to be cut off. If she could contain the venom to her lower leg, perhaps that would keep the worst at bay for a little while longer. As she let go of *Forte* and switched back to *Lux*, her stomach dropped.

On the right side, the cavern's wall was littered with dozens of the long, hairy creatures, surrounding her from all sides. Brina looked over the edge of the platform and thought she could just make out the top of the lift cage in the distance. An idea came, and she acted before she could think it through. She reached for the lift's chain, clung tight, then jumped over the side. Under the force of her full weight, the lift came rushing up the other side of the chain.

At the last second, Brina jumped, covering three feet of distance over the black chasm before her hands closed around the cage. The thing swayed and creaked as she hung from the metal bars, fiddling to get the door open. She climbed inside, closed the door, and pulled the lever as far down as it would go. Overhead, she heard the excited squeaks of dozens of ammitarach following her down. Wounded prey was not to be abandoned.

The cage slammed into the bottom of the cavern. Brina's envenomed leg buckled under the impact.

"What happened?" Abrasax's voice.

"Ammitarach. Huge. Got stung," Brina gasped for air between words. The burning in her leg turned to gnawing. She looked down and groaned. The skin near the sting was bubbling. The wound grew from a pinprick to a full-on hole as the venom ate away at her flesh. She screamed, not caring if the noise rang out all the way through the cavern. Let the darkhelms hear. Let the ammitarach hear. They were all doomed.

CHAPTER 55

hat is this place?" Brina asked, forcing herself to keep her thoughts away from the agony in her lower leg. "Is there a way out?"

"We don't know," Sneak said. "There are more cells down here. And we found..." He trailed off, eyes widening as they found Brina's leg.

"Keep talking," Brina snapped.

"We found some unpleasant tools." Sneak swallowed. Brina's eyes were drawn to the stone dais in the center of the room, upon which was arranged a gruesome collection of torture devices.

There were multiple heavy chairs built into the floor so they couldn't move. Chains hung from their armrests and legs. There was a wooden rack, rotting and bloodstained. Metal implements lay scattered on the tables surrounding it. Near the side of the dais stood a handful of stone sarcophagi with holes drilled in the top.

"This place rivals God's Maul." There was a tremor in Abrasax's voice. "They use those same sarcophagi." Brina realized it was the first time she had heard him speak about what had happened to him within the prison's walls. Even Versa, who had been disfigured beyond all recognition, hadn't been able to utter a word about that forsaken place.

"They keep you in there for hours, days, at a time," Abrasax went on. He sounded hollow, like breath rustling in a vast well. "They have you put your arms behind your head. You can't move. It's too tight. After a few minutes, everything hurts. You can't breathe because your chest is squeezed in an unnatural position. You fight, but that only makes it worse.

"Then they just leave you there." Abrasax's jaws clenched and unclenched. "I can imagine what it must have been like to be trapped down here in those cells, watching through those bars and seeing everything those barbarians did to your fellow inmates. The smells and sounds of it alone would be torture enough to break most. I see why Krocht wanted this whole place filled in with rubble. Makes it easier to forget it ever existed."

Abrasax was drawn from his mutterings when a swelling cloud of high-pitched hissing approached overhead. The ammitarach had reached the bottom of the pit. There were hundreds of them climbing down the walls, sprinting toward them. Every inch of stone was covered.

Abrasax put an arm under Brina's shoulder. With his support, she hobbled away from the lift cage. Bron and Sneak ran across the wall, searching for a way out. As the swarm approached, they were forced back to the dais in the center of the room. All four of them watched in horror as the cavern's floor flooded with chittering beasts.

Abrasax reached into one sarcophagus and put the mummified remains that lay inside on the ground beside it. Man, woman, or child—it was impossible to tell. The only unmistakable feature was the poor soul's face, etched into a grimace of agony. Rags of clothing still clung to the mummy.

"I'm sorry about this," Abrasax mumbled. For a moment, Brina was confused why her father was apologizing to a corpse. Then Abrasax's eyes lit up with *Gnis*, and the mummy erupted into flame, providing a halo of light. It was a clever move, one Brina would never have thought of. By creating an alternate light source, the four of them could relinquish *Lux*, allowing them to fight with their full capabilities.

The ammitarach crowded around the dais. One of them leaped up, landing right in front of them. Bron stepped in with his mace and squished its eyes with a furious blow. With a roar, the Biori kicked the twitching corpse back down, where it fell among dozens more trying to reach them. Sneak grabbed a metal pipe from among the torture implements and swung at the ammitarach, who were crawling over the edge of the platform.

Abrasax lowered Brina to the floor, where she sat against a sarcophagus. When he rose, his eyes were blazing with *Forte*. He snatched up two knives, one in each hand, and swung at three ammitarach crawling toward them. They were split clean in half, spilling black ichor everywhere like a toppled inkwell. Their upper halves crawled forward, every twitch of their carcasses bent on destroying their prey.

"There's too many," Sneak called. Brina's head snapped back just in time to see one of the ammitarach crawling up Sneak's back. He swung at it. The creature let go, skidding across the stone floor, before turning around, poised for a second strike. Bron's mace crushed the creature's skull. After a second blow, it stopped moving.

"A little exercise will do those twig-arms good," Bron said with a laugh.

CHAPTER 55

"You have grown weak and whiny."

Brina pulled herself up, trying to ignore the raging burn in her leg. She reached for a series of rusty scalpels and flung them into the mass of approaching ammitarach. Everything pointy or blunt enough to do damage went flying into the dark. Some of them hit home, others clattered to the ground in the distance.

Every time the darkness shifted, more scorpions approached from the dark crevices of the cave. Mounds of dead critters were forming near the edge of the dais, creating access ramps for their fellows to crawl over. The stench of vinegar was overwhelming. A sudden convulsion rocked Brina's entire body. Despite her best efforts in tying off the wound, part of the venom had leaked into her system and was wreaking havoc.

One of the ammitarach leaped at Bron, who blocked the attack at the very last moment with the handle of his mace. It went flying into the darkness. Bron let out a roar. "You think I need steel to pummel you into the ground?" He hammered a furious hail of fist blows down on foe after foe as they tried to surround him. Even though he fought like a lion, he was forced backward.

All of them were inching back from the edge of the dais toward the center, where the stone sarcophagi stood. Brina was running out of torture devices to fling at their approaching enemy. She looked at Abrasax, hoping against hope that there was some trick, some sigil nobody had ever heard of, that he could pull out of his sleeve at the very last moment to save them from the ravenous swarm of scorpions. But the look of increasing horror on his face told her that her hopes were in vain.

"The sarcophagi," he said, his voice trembling. "We'll have to get in there. Their stingers won't fit through the air holes. They won't be able to reach us." Then, more to himself than to anyone else, he said, "It's the only way to avoid certain death."

Taking his cue, the others ran for the series of cramped sarcophagi and, using *Forte*, lifted the heavy lids just far enough for them to squeeze through.

Abrasax scooped up Brina, lowered her into the nearest coffin, and put the lid on. The last thing Brina saw before the darkness closed in was the face of a ghost. Her father seemed to age with every heartbeat.

"We'll make it," he yelled. "We will make it."

Then, with the grind of stone on stone, darkness enveloped Brina. Her hands were kept at her side in the cramped space. She tried to reach for the pyramid that clung to her chest, but even though she could feel the lump of metal pressed against her skin, she couldn't bend her arms far enough to reach for it. She tried to grab at the string with her teeth—anything to get that last sliver of hope to combat the circulating venom.

Then, even as she tried to reach the string by some means, she realized she would need *Lux* to see in the darkness, and that she wouldn't be able to burn the pyramid, even if she somehow reached it. She lay down in the darkness, and allowed, for the first time in a very long time, tears to trickle down her cheeks.

CHAPTER 56

Anxiety hung in the air. Solana could feel it in the thrumming of footsteps marching up and down the docks. She could hear it in whispers carried on the wind. The troops on the island were on high alert. Something was pulling at their nerves. She walked up to the quarterdeck, where she found the ship's captain, Samok, sitting on the wooden stairs by himself. The long pauses between his breaths, followed by forceful exhales, suggested that he, too, had realized something was wrong.

"What do you see?" she asked. "Out there."

Samok shuffled nervously. Solana was reminded, with a stab of annoyance, that she wasn't trusted here. As far as these people were concerned, she was with the enemy.

Solana ground her teeth. It was laughable. If she wanted to betray them, she would've had many opportunities, especially in the last two days, when the watch had been within shouting distance at all times. Solana knew, as her "hosts" did not, that she was just as unwelcome in Mallion's Depth now as they were.

"Something's going on," Solana urged. "If the Springtides are in trouble, I need to know, so we can help them before it's too late."

Samok sighed.

"The darkhelms are patrolling more often," he said. "They're clustering together in larger groups than usual this morning. Ships they've already searched are being boarded again. Others are going door to door and digging through people's houses."

"They are looking for someone." Solana spoke the unfinished conclusion. Samok clicked his tongue in agreement.

The implication of what this meant hung between them. It would be a marvelous coincidence, bordering on the unbelievable, to think that days after both Springtides had left trying to gain an audience with the king under the mountain, that an uproar amongst the watch could concern anything else.

"Can you see what's going on up on the mountain?" Solana asked. It was a frustrating limitation of her senses that, while she could pick up tiny details at close range, she was useless at a distance. It was as though, when she had made the ultimate sacrifice, her world had shrunk while, at the same time, it had been blown wide open.

"No," Samok said. "The gates were visible earlier this morning. Heavy fog has settled over the island. The mountain is shrouded."

Solana stood. Her hand brushed along the ship's banister, feeling for the place where the gangplank was attached.

"Wait," Samok called after her. "Where are you going?"

"Up to the mountain," Solana said. "If something has happened, we should find out how bad it is and what we can do."

"You're not supposed to leave the ship." There was a hint of a command in his voice. He sounded like a subordinate officer asserting his would-be authority in the absence of the true masters of the campaign.

"Yes," Solana said, her patient tone becoming strained, "but that was assuming things would go as planned. If your friends have gotten into trouble, we need to know when the time has come for us to jump into action. Or do you think they would appreciate it if we left them to rot?"

Samok hesitated. "I should go."

"You couldn't," Solana said.

"Why is that?" Samok took a few steps closer, his boots landing hard on the deck. Shuffling on the other side of the ship betrayed the presence of a few of the crew watching the conflict unfold.

Solana tapped a finger against the heavy helmet resting on her head. "Because I can blend in, remember?"

"Fine," Samok grumbled. "But if you're not back by nightfall—"

"Then what?" Solana sighed. "You can't abandon the Springtides. You can't leave harbor without me to pose as an officer of the watch, and you can't leave the ship without dozens of eyes on you. If I'm not back by nightfall, that means I'm doing all I can to make sure that we leave this island with the same number aboard the ship we came with."

"I hate how right you are," Samok said. With that, he turned to his crew and began shouting for them to resume work on the rigging they had been replacing.

CHAPTER 57

A millstone weighed on Abrasax's chest. His body heaved as he struggled for breath. He writhed against the rough surface of the stone sarcophagus, but his efforts only tore his skin and drew blood.

He tried, as he had on countless occasions before, to reset his mind. *Return to the quiet. Silence is all around us. Retreat to the depths of the mind, where all are free and unencumbered.* He squeezed his eyes shut—a mere gesture in the dark—the desperation of a man praying for one more layer of denial to place between himself and the reality of what he was facing. Just as he thought he had found that place of inner peace, panic resurfaced.

He felt himself thrashing against the sides of the sarcophagus. His whole body contorted in agonizing convulsions. Oozing wounds reopened, old bruises flared. He screamed, seeking relief from the claustrophobia. For what seemed like an eternity, he raged against his stone prison, his blood mingling with the caked-on grime of centuries.

Then the lid slid backward. An all-too familiar face appeared on the other side.

"No," he groaned, voice reduced to a whisper. "Not you. Not again."

"Oh, but it *is* me, Cardinal Slayer," De Leliard whispered. His bulging cheeks spread apart as stubby teeth revealed themselves in a delighted grin. "We're going to have a little chat."

"You're not real. I'm free. I escaped!" Abrasax screamed in the man's face. Even as the sound came out of his own mouth, it grew distant, an echo in the canyon of his mind.

With a gasp, he found himself back in the present. He was still in the sarcophagus, but the hissing and skittering of hundreds of ammitarach told him exactly where he was. Through the breathing hole above his face, he could see a stinger descending again and again until it broke off on the sarcophagus's stone lid. He blinked.

Two pairs of gruff, gauntleted hands jerked him upward, forcing him to look the Cardinal in the eye. His naked body was chafed, bleeding, and covered in scabs and wounds from the days and weeks before.

"Looks like you've been giving my proposal quite a bit of thought," De Leliard said. He sat down on the bloodstained wooden rack to which Hammer Stoneblade had been tied only half an hour prior. Abrasax had been forced to listen as his friend and co-conspirator underwent unimaginable torment.

The others were dragged back to their cells after their interrogations. Not Abrasax. He was to listen to every single one. To hear the inquisitors asking the same questions over and over again, followed by bloodcurdling screams, when the members of the Signum refused to answer.

At first, he tried to communicate with them, shouting that they could tell the inquisitors anything they wanted to hear, just as long as it made the torture stop. The inquisitors soon caught on and put a cork in his breathing hole whenever they brought in their victims. It was enough to keep Abrasax's frantic shouts from sounding like anything more than unintelligible mumbling from the outside, but not enough to keep Abrasax from hearing the agony inflicted on his kin.

"My officers tell me that none of your cohorts have been willing to speak so far. I have to say, I admire a man who knows how to keep the troops in line. I, of all people, know how challenging that can be." De Leliard sucked at his teeth. "It is a burden to lead. All those decisions one has to make. The uncertainty of how well our orders will be executed. Having to weigh the benefits versus the costs."

De Leliard smiled. He withdrew a leather flask from his purple robes and took a long draft, smacking his lips. A rivulet of red wine escaped the corner of his mouth, making him look like one of the blood drinkers that lived in the dark corners of the world. "Which brings me to the reason for my visit today."

There it was—the endgame. The reason Abrasax had spent the last two weeks squashed into a coffin. His friends hadn't been tortured for what they knew. De Leliard already knew all there was to know. An inside source had tipped him off about the attempt on Estav's life, after all.

No, Abrasax realized. His friends weren't being tortured for information, but so Abrasax would understand that their fate rested in his hands—that he was the only one who could stop their pain.

"While I must admit, your cleaning up of that slobbering fool, Estav, was convenient to me. There are still some murmurings in my Enlightened

CHAPTER 57

Council about the possibility of unrest." De Leliard waved a hand over his shoulder. "They are concerned that my ascension to power might lead to some uncomfortable questions amongst the rabble outside of the wall. They fear you have swept up the populace with your heretical lies about the place of the holy church as the center of the universe.

"So here is what you are going to do. You have a choice to make." De Leliard raised a single finger. "Either you remain here, tucked away in your little suitcase, while I have my inquisitors disassemble your friends. Make no mistake, these people know what they are doing. Your cronies will live and scream until their beating hearts are the last organ to be ripped from their chests. It will be a long and arduous journey for all involved.

"Or"—De Leliard raised a second finger—"there is a far preferable option. You travel with me to Mallion's Depth tonight. You shall be kept under guard in the most luxurious quarters the palace offers; you shall eat and drink everything you have want for; and you shall testify in front of the grand jury of the Enlightened Council that your band of bandits were an isolated group, with no wider agenda.

"I do not care about how many other buffoons like you are out there. I will hunt them down myself. All I need is for the following words to fall out of your mouth at the right time: 'I acted alone. All of my people have been apprehended. I now, after serious consideration, see the error of my ways, and have repented for my sins, and will, along with my cohorts, turn to the one and only god, Heil, the Almighty Keeper.'

"You will give them a convincing demonstration of your aptitude in prayer. Afterward, you shall be escorted to the scaffold in the Enclave of what you savages call Doorstep's Ditch, where, for all the outwalled to hear, you will denounce your acts, you will praise Heilinism, and you will say that your actions were a mistake."

De Leliard accepted another cup of wine from a blood-soaked inquisitor, the sour stench of his breath mixing with the metallic blood. "That's not so hard, is it? In exchange for this small favor, your friends shall no longer be interrogated by my very thorough officers right here." He pointed at the two burly men with black masks. "They will remain in their cells until their execution. You, as a living symbol of the reformative power of Heil's glory, will remain in Mallion's Depth. Where you can live out your days in whatever material comfort you desire. You shall become a token of the rebirth that is possible under my regime.

"You will be a captive, make no mistake," De Leliard said with a chuckle, "but you will live for as long as you are useful to me. Now, Cardinal Slayer, which will it be?" De Leliard reached behind him and held up a bloody scalpel that had been used on Stoneblade. In the other hand, he raised his cup. He mimed the balancing of scales. "Blood or wine? Your choice."

Abrasax's mouth worked. It was lined with sores, and his voice was hoarse. He tried to speak and instead burst into a series of retching coughs.

"For Heil's sake," De Leliard snapped at his inquisitors, "give the man something to drink."

One of them rummaged in a wooden cupboard that stood in a corner, and returned with a glass bottle, which he forced between Abrasax's lips. At first, not knowing what was inside, Abrasax refused to drink. Then the executioner used his other hand to squeeze his nose shut. "Drink or drown," the executioner growled.

Abrasax took a large gulp. It was some of the strongest rum he'd ever tasted, setting fire to the open wounds inside his mouth and burning all the way down. Still, the executioner wouldn't lower the bottle.

"Again."

Abrasax obeyed. After four or five mouthfuls of the burning substance, the grip on his nose was released, and the bottle torn away. Abrasax gasped for air. Some of the liquid trickled down his chin and fell on his naked chest, running down to his bare legs. The screams of his friends, his family, resounded in his ears as he tried to think, tried to weigh the impact of both options. He couldn't save their lives, but he could save them a lot of pain before their ends.

He knew De Leliard would make good on his threats. Abrasax would spend as long in the cramped sarcophagus as needed to force him to agree. All the while, his friends would suffer. Resistance was pointless. All he had to do was say what De Leliard wanted to hear, yet Abrasax found he couldn't.

Standing up in front of the people of Doorstep's Ditch and the Enlightened Council to endorse this beast of a man would be a betrayal of all the Signum had strived for over the past decade. Every slave they had freed, every casualty avenged, every oath sworn would be forsaken.

He thought of the life he could have. Should he accept De Leliard's offer? He imagined himself in a warm bath, scrubbing off the layer of caked-on blood, urine, and excrement that clung to him. Every night, he'd be able to drink himself into a stupor to forget. The rum he'd been forced to drink on his empty stomach hit him hard. He felt woozy, almost giddy with the momentary relief. The pain in his body seemed like a thing of the past. Would it

CHAPTER 57

be so bad? A distant part of himself said, so much suffering could be avoided.

He closed his eyes for a moment. Then, with a deep breath, he looked De Leliard in the eyes, lay back down in the sarcophagus, and said, "Close the damn lid."

***

Abrasax's screams intermingled with the high-pitched chittering of the ammitarach swarming the sarcophagus. With a jolt, he snapped back to reality. The skin on his elbows and knees was raw, hot blood oozing where the stone had scraped away his skin. He burned *Consol* to calm himself. "It's not real. It's not real. You're away from that place. You're never going back."

With slow, deep breaths, he forced himself to stop fighting against the confines of the sarcophagus. As the fog of his panic lifted, he noticed a strange quiet falling over the circular cavern. The clicking of legs and stingers receded, and through the tiny hole above them, only darkness was visible. Eager to get out of the confined space, he shifted into a crouch and lifted the heavy stone lid just enough to slide it aside a foot or so. He stuck his head out, looked around, and relief swept over him.

"They're gone," he called out. "They gave up." With the scraping of stone against stone, both Bron and Sneak reappeared. Abrasax had to help Brina escape her coffin. She looked pale and on the verge of collapse. She tried to take a step and toppled backward. Abrasax seized her to keep her from falling. It was like holding on to a bundle of sticks. Her muscles were tense and unbending, but there was no life in her.

"Fine," she muttered. "I'm fine."

"Well," Sneak chuckled somewhere behind them, "they gave up. I thought we'd be in there for hours."

"Let's hope they filled their bellies with darkhelms," Bron responded. He began digging around the rusty torturers' tools for anything that was still usable as a weapon. Brina twitched in Abrasax's arms, drool dripping from the side of her mouth.

Her eyes snapped open. "They didn't give up," she said. Blinking, she grabbed on to Abrasax's forearms and squeezed. "They're yielding priority."

"What do you mean, yielding priority?" Abrasax asked. A seed of disconcertion sprouted in his chest. He'd never seen that look of terror on her face.

"It's a common behavior with group hunters. Wampyr do it, cave spiders do it—you get the picture. They're free to grab what they want until the queen asserts her priority."

"You're saying there's…" The cavern shook. The lids of the sarcophagi rattled; metal implements clinked against their tables. There was another tremor, then another. Chunks of stone rained down from the ceiling, each one a lethal projectile.

Then it came into view. The first of its legs, like a pillar supporting the temples in Mallion's Depth, stood ten feet tall. The bottom seemed hard, like a steel spearpoint pricking into the side of the wall. It crept downward. Sneak let out a panicked scream, and for once, Bron didn't mock his fear. Atop the creature's long legs, a scaly body was perched. Its upper body was translucent, with sections of chitinous carapace covered in slime. The hair on the back of Abrasax's neck stood up. How could something so large stand on the wall? It was as though gravity had forgotten this monstrosity.

The first of its four pairs of legs hit the cavern floor, and Abrasax saw that what he had taken for white carapace were bones integrated into the gelatinous mass of its body. Four slimy tentacles reached out toward them, in which floated hundreds of bones—some undeniably human. A hole opened in the center of the beast's chest, revealing a maw of sharp ivory teeth.

Abrasax's first instinct was to help Brina get back into the sarcophagus, to put any layer of protection between her and the beast. But she stopped him, pushing her good leg against the sarcophagus. "No," she croaked, "that thing will smash right through. We have no choice but to fight it."

"Fight it?" Sneak howled. "What do you want us to do? Challenge it to a battle of wits? We've got no weapons." He waved the iron bar he picked up from the torturer's table and managed a weak smile. "We're done for, aren't we?"

Abrasax's jaw tightened. Death didn't scare him. Over the past few months, he had suspected that facing death would be his best option for finding relief. He had done his part. Even after his unlikely second chance at freedom, he had done what he could to aid the rebellion. He had set an example and suffered for it. He deserved rest. What stopped him from walking to face his doom with his head held high was Brina, who was clinging to his arm for support. Black liquid oozed from her wounded leg, and her skin had taken on a sickly gray tinge.

She hadn't chosen this life. Everything she had gone through since his arrest had been his fault. He had led her down this path, with no regard for how it would affect her. He had been too busy thinking of himself as a hero to realize that he had fallen short of his responsibilities as a father. That

CHAPTER 57

needed to change.

"Can you stand?" he asked Brina. She nodded hesitantly and let go of him.

Abrasax held out his arms to prevent the others from following as he advanced. He needed to do this alone. As he neared the beast, he seized *Sonorus*, allowing the cavern to descend into darkness as he relinquished *Lux*. He could feel his voice swelling in his throat as the sigil ignited behind his eyes.

"Stay back, demon spawn!" His voice became a hurricane in the echoing cave. Its vibrations rattled his bones. His heart quivered in his chest.

A fire burst into life behind him. Abrasax glanced over his shoulder to see Sneak blush with guilt as another mummified corpse caught fire. The ammitarach queen let out a screech. Its front legs kicked at the air as Abrasax advanced on it. It needed to fear him. It would fear him.

"Crawl back into the shadows where you belong." He let out the deepest roar he could muster. It worked. With each step he took, the creature retreated further. It had expected easy prey, but now there was noise and flame. All Abrasax needed was for the creature to decide the darkhelms higher in the cavern were a more appealing meal.

Growling and snarling, Abrasax closed in on the creature's front legs. It was trapped between him and the wall; soon it would have no choice but to scuttle back into the darkness.

The ammitarach pounced. With an unexpected burst of speed, the creature lunged forward, swiping at Abrasax with its four tentacle-like arms. A surge of *Veloce* carried Abrasax sideways just in time to evade the attack. The tiled floor where he had stood shattered, spraying shards of stone everywhere. Abrasax cursed. He'd overplayed his hand.

The creature, realizing he posed no real threat, surged forward. It struck again and again, forcing Abrasax into an awkward dance. Somewhere in the distance, Sabrina screamed. A quick glance over his shoulder told Abrasax he couldn't retreat without luring the ammitarach queen toward the others. The only option was to push forward.

Burning *Veloce*, he shot toward the beast like an arrow loosed from a bow. At the last moment, he switched into *Gnis* and grazed the creature's front legs with his burning hands. The hair on them ignited, traveling up the black legs at speed, lighting up the cavern. The stench of burning hair was unbearable.

The creature thrashed, its tentacles flailing. One crashed down onto the dais, right beside where Brina and the others stood. It missed them by mere feet, demolishing half of the platform. There was the distant clank of stone tumbling down a deep hole.

"A passage!" Sneak yelled. "Underneath the rubble. Look."

"Go!" Abrasax touched *Sonorus* once more. "I'll keep her busy. It's me she wants."

He darted underneath the creature. It spun, trying to get him into view. In his euphoria, Abrasax almost missed the massive stinger at the end of the ammitarach queen's rectangular body. It stabbed at his neck. In a split-second reflex, he hurled himself to the ground. The stinger plunged at him again and again, forcing him to roll back and forth. He remembered to burn *Veloce* just in time to launch himself from under the beast and away from its stampeding legs.

Brina called for him to follow as she disappeared down the hole in the dais where Sneak had spotted the passage. Abrasax didn't need telling twice. With a burst of speed, he shot across the cavern and plunged into the dark tunnel below.

CHAPTER 58

Brina took deep, slow breaths. She'd forced the sleeve of her tunic between her teeth to keep from screaming. Even whilst flaring *Forte* as brightly as the shape would go, the pain in her lower leg felt like a colony of ants was burrowing its way into her living flesh.

Shrouded in darkness, all she knew for certain was that only ten feet above her, the ammitarach queen was still rampaging. The beast's stinger thumped down again and again on the rubble above, booming like thunder in the silent tunnel.

"What are those?" Sneak's disgusted voice squeaked somewhere to Brina's left.

Her curiosity got the better of her, and Brina switched into *Lux*. The pain threatened to overwhelm her. She sat in the middle of a hallway just wide enough for one horse-drawn carriage to ride through. On both sides, the long hallway trailed off into shadow. All along the passage, Brina could see what was giving Sneak the shivers.

Dozens of statues loomed over them. Each of them mutilated in its own gory way. Closest to them was a humpbacked man, with eyes bulging out of his skull. His mouth was open in a scream of agony, showing a missing tongue. Brina spat onto the ground in disgust, then returned her attention to *Forte* to keep the pain at bay.

"Left side is a dead end." Abrasax's voice rang out from a distance. "It's an old guards' room, but aside from a handful of rusty battle-axes, there was nothing left behind of any use. Food and water have, of course, long expired since these quarters were used."

"But where does it lead?" Bron asked. "The guards who rested there must have come from somewhere."

"It goes to the old prison above," Abrasax said with a hint of a chuckle.

None of them needed reminding of why returning there wasn't an option.

"Excellent," Bron rumbled. "That leaves us with only one choice, which means we have plenty of time for doing and no need for further blathering."

"Now that you mention blathering," Brina said through gritted teeth. "I've got some more of it to do, I'm afraid." She held back a scream as another excruciating stab made her back arch against the hard stone wall. "I'm not going anywhere like this."

In her time as a roamer, she'd been bitten and stung by an entire bestiary's worth of vile creatures. She'd survived this far, but it was this experience that told her she wouldn't be getting off easily with a sting like this. Though she couldn't see it, the hole in her leg felt like it was still growing. Even while she was holding onto *Forte* like a castaway to a raft. She didn't have enough light to try what effect the pyramid might have. Even if she could let go of *Forte* for more than a few seconds, she'd have to burn *Lux* to see anything, rendering the pyramid useless yet again. It was a vicious cycle, which would turn into a downward spiral soon.

Though one of her sleeves was bound below her knee, it wouldn't contain the venom forever. She'd done a good job of keeping it localized. If not, the pain would have spread further than it had. But she could feel it making its way around her system. It would escape her lower leg and then... What then?

The way you were supposed to treat the bite depended on the type of toxin injected. There were over a dozen varieties that she knew about, and many more she didn't. There was a clank as Abrasax sat down. The battle-axes he'd looted from the guard chamber scattered on the ground beside him.

Please don't make it come to that, please don't make it come to that.

It was a way out. Amputating her lower leg might prevent the remaining venom from spreading and eating her body alive.

But the pain, she thought.

Even if they saved her from the venom, and she could use the pyramid to close the wound before she bled out in this dirty hallway, she would be forever maimed. Her fingers found and traced the wrinkles of hard scar tissue where her left eye had once been. She had survived that injury, but it had taken adjusting, relearning all that had been natural to her. No matter what, her encounter with the bargheist had left her with an enduring reminder that her body was just as fragile as everyone else's.

For every corpse she'd seen rotting in the streets of Doorstep's Ditch, she had found easy ways to distance herself from a similar fate. She knew how to fight. She knew which fights to avoid. If she found an emaciated child, she rationalized that away, thinking she was more than capable of hunting for food.

Every year, during the scarlet nocturne, while waiting for her father to

CHAPTER 58

hang, she had seen his associates brought to their ends by the hangman's noose. Even then, when it had hit close to home, she had created distance with the thought that she would never be stupid enough to go against an empire of such overwhelming force. Over the past year, she had placed herself in the path of all those dangers. And once the bargheist had ripped out her eye, she had realized that all of those corpses had been just like her moments before they met their end. They too had found reasons why it wouldn't be them, why it always, magically, seemed to be somebody else. Now it had happened again. This time, with far more grievous consequences.

Yes, it was the rational thing to do. Find something that burned to create light. Ask Bron to swing the axe, sit through the immediate shock of the pain, and then close the wound with the pyramid before she passed out.

That would be quite a tale to tell. She'd get free kelp for life at any inn she ever stepped foot in with her wooden peg leg. A tiny smirk tugged at her lips.

It was the badass way of dealing with the situation. And the only way to ensure that the venom wouldn't spread to her heart, lungs, or brain, leaving her dead, or worse, rendered a shell of her former self by the venom.

A roamer she had known long ago, Batavian, had fallen into a nest of bog centipedes during one of his contracts. The swarm all but covered his entire body in stings. It had been the contract giver, annoyed with Batavian's lack of progress, who had gone looking for him. He and a friend had dragged Batavian out of the bog and back to civilization. The roamer floated between life and death for months, and when he awoke, he was worse than a child: His eyes had gone wild and crossed, and though he tried, his lips, mouth, and brain could no longer work together to form a coherent sentence.

Would I be willing to risk a faith like that in order to keep my leg?

If only she'd had the courage, it could have been done already. But she dug deep and found that she didn't have it in her. She couldn't take going through that process again: feeling helpless for weeks or months on end. Being reset to square zero, so each minor act became another obstacle. She couldn't face that.

"Did you find any torches?" Brina asked.

"Why?" Abrasax asked. "We can see fine in the dark."

"Correction, you can. If I let go of *Forte*, I'm going to scream so loud that all those ammitarachs are going to come running back, and you know how they get."

She chuckled, wiggling her wounded leg.

"Get something that burns, will you?" She could hear three pairs of footsteps receding back toward the guards' quarters, and moments later, there was a whooshing sound as the wooden handle of a mop erupted into flames. It illuminated the hallway in an orange glow, just bright enough to see by.

With trembling fingers, Brina reached down into her shirt and produced the pyramid.

Be strong, be strong, be strong.

She relinquished *Forte*, and a white-hot pain washed over her entire body like lava.

Be strong, be strong, be strong.

Her eyes grew bleary with tears, but she blinked them away, insisting on focusing on the object in front of her. Her eyes reflected crimson in the gleaming metal of the pyramid. Not daring to look away, she asked Abrasax if it was working.

"It's working," he said. "The wound is closing. Hold on, you're doing great, Sabrina. It's almost closed."

She held out as long as she could. When she was forced to let go, she was looking at a thin layer of transparent new skin. The hole in her leg had been filled in.

"Can you stand on it?"

"Only one way to find out." She pushed off the wall, and before her foot touched the ground, she knew something was wrong. Her full weight leaned on both feet. With a shriek, she toppled forward. A quick reflex on Bron's part kept her from falling headlong into the opposite side of the passage.

With a splattering sound, all the new flesh that had filled in the wound came flowing out in a gush of yellow pus. A renewed stream of black liquid mixed with blood seeped across her skin. She swallowed and looked at the rusty battle-axes propped against the statue of the humpbacked man with his limbs contorted in all the wrong angles. He seemed to leer down at her, as though wanting to watch the horror unfold up close.

Brina turned her gaze away. *Do it*, she thought. *Get it over with. If this is what the venom does to new flesh, think about what it will do to your heart and brain.*

Brina opened her mouth to tell the others the plan, then burst out into sobs. She couldn't do it. She didn't have it in her. Even Brina Springtide had limits to her courage. Limits she was being forced to confront more and more often as this terrible failure of a mission dragged on.

Without a word, she reached down and untied the sleeve from her lower knee. She looked up at her father, who reached out to stop her. He was too late.

CHAPTER 58

"Let whatever happens happen," she said. "I'm sorry." Then, with the whoosh of a waterfall cascading onto hard rock, the darkness engulfed her, and she was gone.

CHAPTER 59

If there was one thing Solana had learned over the years, it was that members of the church respected the helmet, regardless of who was underneath it. Things were no different now than when she'd been a legitimate Reynziel of the church. Salutes followed her as she passed, and she gave silent nods in return.

She couldn't outright ask them what they were looking for—it would be suspicious for an officer not to know—so instead, she hoped to pick up information between the lines by making the rounds and listening to the watchers' whispers. With the prayer of hearing attuned, even the faintest murmur became as clear as a shout.

"Now they've got officers patrolling our routes," one woman complained after she thought Solana had passed beyond earshot. "... always think they're so much smarter than us." Her partner grunted in response.

After a barrage of similar complaints and moping with little concrete information to show for it, Solana switched tactics. She walked straight up to a group of six watchers clustered on a street corner, murmuring among themselves.

"Any progress?" she asked.

"No," one of them replied, "we've searched every ship and dwelling as ordered, but nothing seems out of the usual."

"That's unfortunate," Solana said, her voice harsh. She opened up the prayer of intimidation as she spoke, hearing a collective shudder in the group's breath.

"Maybe the squads on the hill had more luck," a woman suggested. "I'm sure we'll find them soon."

"They can't leave the island," another added, "not with all the ports blockaded."

"I hope for all our sakes you're right. Keep looking."

They trudged away, their boots squelching in the muck, leaving Solana to

CHAPTER 59

ponder the implications of what they'd said. The watch hadn't figured out where the Springtides were—that was good—but the fact that every patrol had been placed on such high alert worried her.

Usually, simple foot soldiers would be kept in the dark for as long as possible regarding sensitive issues, a precaution designed not to risk information traveling to informants for the other side. Here, however, it seemed the Watch was so determined to get what they wanted, safety measures had gone by the wayside. She needed to find a way up onto the mountain and see for herself what was happening on the outskirts of the Shimmering City.

Though her body had strengthened over the past few weeks, aided by rest and three passable meals a day, the ship's cramped quarters had left her muscles weak and decayed. The arduous climb up the mountain proved more difficult than expected. Even with the prayer of fortitude thrumming in her ears like a mantra, she couldn't quite suppress the feeling that she could pass out at any moment. When at last she crested the top of the last hill and emerged from the tree line, what greeted her was far from what she'd hoped for.

***

Abrasax carried his only child in his arms as they marched through the endless corridor. The statues of the maimed and tortured never ceased. There must have been dozens of them. Each spaced twenty feet apart from the next, far enough that when one image cleared from your head, another, more macabre one was forced into it.

Abrasax knew where they were even before the tiny light appeared at the end of the tunnel. They were in a place called the Walkway of the Dead—he had read about it during his time with the first Signum. In his attempts to unify the people of the Sundered Isles, he had taken to studying their history, looking for any common threads that might unite the free peoples against Heilinist expansion.

The Walkway of the Dead, described in a tome from 11 KR, was said to be used on the morning before every full moon. Those who had been condemned to death in the intervening weeks were kept in prison until it was time. Then, along with the Heemian monarch, they would march toward the end of the hallway. Below them, a crowd of Heemians, entertained with free food and drink, stood waiting in front of the large metal gates to the city. The ceremony was conducted at night under the light of the moon. Back then, many Heemians believed the sun to be an evil influence. The condemned marched through this very hallway, forced to look at statues of those that had gone before. Then they reached the balcony.

"What the...?" Sneak called from ahead. They had almost passed the threshold of the dark corridor door into daylight when the rattling murmur of a crowd stopped him dead in his tracks. Sneak peered out of the end of the tunnel and withdrew his head again.

"The hallway ends in a balcony above the main gate?" Abrasax supplied.

"You knew?" Sneak asked, his brow furrowing. "Why didn't you say anything?"

"Would we have had another choice if I had told you in advance?" Abrasax asked.

"Well, no, but." Sneak shook his head, muttering something about common decency and saving people the shock.

So there it was: The tome had been accurate. They had arrived at a balcony carved out of the very mountain itself. In the middle, a chunk was missing from the balustrade. According to history, the condemned was to walk the final yards alone.

If they did without hesitation and without crying out, the punishment for their sins in the afterlife would be lightened by the spirit of the mountain. If, on the other hand, the Royal Guard had to force them into the vertical drop or they began to plead and beg, their punishment was to be a hundredfold worse.

A description Abrasax had read suggested that most of the condemned, at this final stage of a long and torturous road, were so battered and bruised they welcomed the prospect of death.

"By the tip of my spear," Bron said, sneaking a peek for himself. "There must be two hundred soldiers out there. It looks like a small army is marching on the mountain."

Abrasax smiled. He'd expected as much. With a sigh, he sank down against the wall, lowering Brina's slim body with him.

He put his hand on her burning forehead and burned *Pruine* to mitigate the fever that had her in its grip. Her forehead grew cool, but as soon as he lifted his hands, Brina's face flushed red again.

"What do we do now?" Bron asked, probing Abrasax with the tip of his boot as though he were an ox refusing to draw a cart.

Abrasax sighed. "Now we wait."

CHAPTER 59

***

Hundreds of soldiers were stationed in front of the tall metal gates. Their restless murmurs bounced off the mountain, creating an unpleasant vibration in Solana's ears. Her echolocation made her dizzy as dozens of shadowy bodies surrounded her. She had grown disused to crowds of this size, and after the physical exertion of the afternoon, she felt like throwing up. That was out of the question. Her helmet was all that stood between her and being discovered for what she was—a deserter.

Solana wandered among the gathered watchers with cool determination, attuned to the prayer of hearing. She strained her ears, sifting through shards of conversation like a theologian through ancient texts, digging for a fragment of meaning or sign of where to go next.

"Been standing here all day. I'm getting cold. Classic Pieterszoon. Makes a man stand in the whipping wind for hours on end without clear orders. I tell you, one of these days…"

"Any plans tonight? I squeezed a few bottles of good rum from one of those merchants from Merkede yesterday. Want to join me in making them lighter?"

Someone nearby slurped water from a canteen. Solana winced—it was like putting your ear underneath a roaring waterfall. She resisted the urge to slap the canteen out of the woman's hands and instead moved to a more quiet area. Then she heard it.

"There's too many of them; no chance we're getting down unseen."

She looked up. The voice, unmistakably belonging to the elder Springtide, had come from a place far up the mountain. Judging from the hazy profile her echolocation provided her with, they were above the tall archway that contained the metal gates leading to the Shimmering City. Her heart stopped—if they were out in the open, it was over: she'd come here for nothing. But nobody around her responded; it seemed like she was the only one who had heard.

"Guess we'll have to wait them out," a boulder of a voice grunted near the elder Springtide. "I'm not looking forward to this."

Solana breathed a sigh of relief. At least two out of four remained. There was a chance that the others were close as well. But how to help them get down? With the Enlightened Watch stationed outside the mountain and a handful of legions inside combing through the city, there'd be nowhere for them to go.

Leave them, a small, greedy voice whispered in the back of her head. She could still walk away, decide that this undertaking had been a failure, and try to find Luna herself.

Then she realized how foolish that was. The younger Springtide was the only one who could lead her to her sister. If Solana turned away now, she would be starting over without leads. It would be folly.

Luna was somewhere out there, and the younger Springtide was the most direct route. Solana had to try. She owed Luna that much.

Before her rational side took over once more, Solana pushed and shoved her way through the crowd toward a tall shape that had been erected right next to the gate. Judging by its pointed shape and the vehement flapping of canvas in the wind, it was an officer's tent, larger than average.

Of course, Solana thought, no hour can pass without absolute luxury. The proper hierarchy of authority must be observed. She marched into the tent and got a blurred image of four shapes shifting in their chairs. They were sitting around a circular table and had clearly not been expecting a fifth party to their conversation. A woman whose voice she recognized as Pisan Jacoba, under whom Solana had served when she was a mere recruit manning the Stoneward of Mallion's Depth, blustered, "What is the meaning of this intrusion? We have not summoned you, Captain."

Ah yes, the helmet. Pisan, as everyone was trained to do in the Heilinist forces, had looked at the helm atop Solana's head, determined that she was of lower status than herself, and struck a disdainful tone.

"Continue," Solana said. She used the renewed vibrations of sound in the room to search for a fifth stool and found one in the pavilion's corner to her left; she reached for it and sat down, ignoring the indignant gasps of two or three of the table's occupants.

"I am no mere captain," Solana spat, putting so much anger in her voice while she attuned to the prayer of persuasion that Pisan Jacoba would doubt herself. "I am a monk of the Blind Order, operating in this region under the direct orders of Cardinal De Leliard himself. You will address me with the respect my office commands."

As she focused on the prayer of persuasion, she could hear the weight in her own words. They were like mercury, heavy and smooth. "Your petty officers notified me you had a situation here. I figured, since I kept hearing that no progress had been made in the matter, that I might be of assistance. But I suppose that a bunch of what passes for officers of the watch these days know better than I, who have been endowed with the gifts of Heil herself."

CHAPTER 59

A long silence fell, marked by awkward shuffling and tapping of feet against the floor.

Finally, a man she recognized as Coen Pieterszoon, who had long governed the worker colony at Snake Island, spoke up. Even among his fellow clergymen, Pieterszoon was considered cruel. Some had even gone so far in the past as to suggest his demeanor toward infidels was in direct opposition to the tenets of the Keeper.

"I don't believe you," he said. "You're just trying to sneak in here, Captain, to seize glory for yourself. After which you will parade down to Mallion's Depth and deliver the fugitives to the Cardinal, hoping to gain his favor. We all know how the game is played. Get to the back of the line."

Though his voice was harsh, Solana recognized an undertone of anxiety. Even as he spoke, his pulse quickened. He was considering what to do if Solana refused his command.

"If you are so certain I am not who I say I am"—Solana stretched out her hand, elbow resting on the velvet tablecloth—"I'm sure you won't mind giving me your hand. I will prove to you I possess powers of which you have great need. I rather think the Cardinal would be disappointed to find his officers unwilling to accept help in a matter so important as the Springtide fugitives."

She dropped the name, knowing full well regular watchers wouldn't be informed of whom they were looking for. It would add to her credibility and unnerve the elder officers, most of whom likely hadn't been challenged in their authority in a decade. To ensure that Pieterszoon couldn't deny her challenge, she added, "I know who you are, Coen. And I know your reputation. They say you are a rash and disagreeable man. Are they right?"

Another silence fell.

"You dare..." Coen Pieterszoon muttered. He placed his hand on Solana's. She let go of the prayer of persuasion, attuning to the prayer of heat. As she grasped its elegant rhythm, Pieterszoon's fingers squirmed.

"A cheap trick," he said. "Everyone could make their skin feel warm for a moment." In a blast of genuine anger, Solana recited the prayer, pouring her will into it. There was a cry of pain, and Pieterszoon jerked back his hand, whimpering.

"Amazing," one of the other officers whispered. "You can see the imprint of her fingers on his skin."

Solana reached out with her other hand, pressed her fingertip to a carafe of water which stood in the middle of the table, and attuned to the prayer of frost. The water crackled as it froze. She knew by the amazed gasps of her audience that she had their full attention. "Now here is what you are going to do."

***

Hours of clinking armor and stamping feet below had faded into the background for Abrasax. His attention was on Brina, who convulsed as she succumbed to the venomous sting of the ammitarach. He wished he had stopped her before she untied the sleeve around her lower leg.

He had been too late. Part of him had thought to suggest amputating the kid's lower leg, but he hadn't been able to bring himself to it. After all he had seen over the years, enough blood soaked his memory. Besides, not even the Viper of Barangia wished to see his own daughter maimed before his eyes.

As they sat there, things started looking worse with every passing hour. They were trapped without food or drink for as long as the darkhelms laid siege to the mountain. With no way to gauge how long that would be, all three of them were becoming impatient. Bron paced back and forth at the tail end of the hallway, dragging a rusty battle-axe along with him across the floor, hoping to sharpen it against the dusty stone floor. The sound of it was maddening. When he turned and opened his mouth, presumably to suggest for the fiftieth time that they fight their way out, Abrasax shook his head.

He had made it clear that under no circumstances would he risk Brina's life. Someone would have to carry her at all times, and, in the chaos of battle, it would be all too easy for her to suffer a devastating blow. Abrasax would not allow it. He'd rather Brina die here in this hallway in his arms than under the darkhelms' violence. They had taken much from him during his life, but they wouldn't take his daughter—not even if that meant the venom was to have her.

"Maybe they'll conclude that horrible scorpion thing ate us and leave." Sneak scratched at the fuzz on his chin.

Abrasax smiled at the young man's naivety. If there was one thing he had learned about the church over the years, it was that principle always preceded practicality. No matter how many of their soldiers would need to be tossed into the meat grinder, they wouldn't give up on a pursuit they deemed righteous.

If any of those darkhelms following them had lived long enough to report where they had gone, the Cardinal would rather send an army down there to wage war on the dreadful ammitarach than risk the infidels running free

CHAPTER 59

for a day longer. Just as he was about to explain how the darkhelms would camp out there forever, a horn was blown.

Moments later, the rhythmic pumps of boots hitting the ground in unison followed. There was the creak and rattle of the enormous gates being opened from the inside, and the Heilinists began their march. All three of them peered over the edge of the balcony as two hundred darkhelms streamed into the city to the beat of a single marching drum.

The clatter of the drum echoed off the mountainside and droned on until it grew faint as the army disappeared into the mountain. Just when Abrasax was about to breathe a sigh of relief, he spotted a lone figure sporting a griffin-shaped helmet over reinforced black robes. He recognized those robes. The figure gave an almost imperceptible shake of the head, and then, a few minutes later when the monstrous gates rattled shut, waved up at them.

"Isn't that the helmet we stole?" Sneak remarked.

"Yes," Abrasax said, beaming. "Yes, it is."

CHAPTER 60

As they were about to sneak their way back into the harbor town of Cordwain, Abrasax looked back up at the mountain's peak, peering at the trees, where he imagined a horde of angry darkhelms would emerge at any time. So far, however, the coast had remained clear. For once, it looked like fate might be on their side. Abrasax had pulled off the most precise and gentle fortified jump of his life. If the situation hadn't been so dire, he may have been proud of it.

With Brina in his arms, he'd leaped down from the mountainside, as so many of the condemned had done before him, only to land at Solana's feet. As he landed, he had absorbed the shock with his own legs, trying with all his might to keep the impact on Brina's already delicate body to a minimum. After that, they had run like chased hares.

Solana explained to them what she had done, and Abrasax couldn't help but be amazed at the ease with which a darkhelm's uniform could confuse the senses of otherwise rational people.

They hastened back along the low passage Jeremiah had shown them, emerging into the safe house, where they had been welcomed by an alarmed Jeremiah who was still healing from the beating he'd received at the hands of the darkhelms.

After describing their predicament, he went outside to ensure that the coast was clear, then helped them sneak back into the town.

When they reached the harbor, Solana leading the group, a battalion of darkhelms had barricaded the street.

"Halt!" one of them yelled, brandishing a glittering halberd, while his comrades carried spears. "The harbor is under a strict lockdown. No one goes in or out without General Pieterszoon's formal verbal or written permission."

"I am here under direct orders from the general," Solana snarled at the man. The rage in her voice was overpowering, such that Abrasax recoiled. Then he identified the traces of her psycho-sigil at work. He could sense it in the unnecessary yet augmented anxiety the woman's voice provoked within him, separate from the danger in which they found themselves. The darkhelms blocking the street could feel it, too. They shifted from foot to foot, throwing surreptitious glances at each other.

"These workers are to unload ships full of potential contraband right now. Every second wasted will be on your head."

"What happened to her?" The halberd-wielding man asked, a poorly disguised squeak in his voice. He nodded at Brina, who lay in Abrasax's arms.

"She didn't listen to me," Solana replied. The sense surger had touched the sigil again, and its sheer power amazed Abrasax. She was good—but then again, she had almost beaten Acheron, the spider of Rothmoor.

The dark image of that night, and Acheron's body tangled with Solana's bouncing off the lower regions of God's Maul's walls, had haunted Abrasax ever since. But not as much as the knowledge that his last remaining friend had spent his last decade of freedom cowering in the dark, consumed by guilt that hadn't been his to bear. If only the fool had gotten as far away as possible from Hammerstroke, Mallion's Depth, and the church.

A knot formed in his stomach as he remembered an evening long ago, just after he met Acheron when—under the influence of cloud and drink—he'd recounted the horrors of his youth, and the abuse he had suffered throughout his life. He had been one-of-a-kind, that man. And now Abrasax was allowing the woman who had cost him his life to lead him through the barricade, under the darkhelms' watchful eyes, onto the docks. Before Abrasax could shake off the growing weight of his own thoughts, they had slipped back aboard the *Chimera*, where a terrified Samok rushed over to greet them.

"I can't believe that worked," Sneak exclaimed after they crossed the gangplank. "How stupid are these churchgoing, moronic sons and daughters of..." He fell silent as he stared back at the quay.

"I wish you hadn't said that, stickman," Bron said, shaking his head. Abrasax turned to find a legion's worth of darkhelms pushing aside their colleagues blockading the street, headed by a man in an eagle-shaped helmet and a purple velvet cloak.

"By the Keeper," Solana groaned, "it's Pieterszoon himself. We're found out."

"What do you mean 'found out'?" Samok asked, his wide eyes shifting from Abrasax to Solana and back. "What do we do?"

"We run," Solana said. "Now."

Without hesitation, Samok leaped into action. Not bothering to loosen the knot, he seized the knife hanging from his belt and cut the mooring lines to the ship. At once, the rest of the crew sprang into action, lowering the sails and cutting the other lines tying them to the dock. The gangplank splashed into the water.

"Stop them!" Pieterszoon cried, gesticulating at the ship. But before any of his soldiers could reach them, the ship had drifted far enough from the quay to make any leap suicidal. Samok's crew drew their weapons, but Solana shook her head.

"No use—we have to go through the blockade," she said, pointing ahead to where the mouth of the harbor was blocked by the chain of red-sailed galleys that had proved troublesome upon entering the city.

"What do you mean, go through?" Abrasax asked. "That's a solid wall."

"Yes, and when that solid wall receives orders to send out sloops to board us, we are done for," Solana replied. Abrasax felt anxiety squeeze him as her words sunk in.

"Don't use those cheap tricks on me," he snarled at Solana. The influence of her psycho-sigil ebbed away at once.

"Sorry. Habit," she said.

Abrasax raised his eyebrows.

"Come on!" Solana urged. "I know how they operate. They'll block the quay, send word to the blockade, and before we know it, dozens of sloops with boarding hooks will surround us. They'll fetch dozens of windups and pepper us with bolts until they can force us away from the edges of the deck so we can't cut their lines, then they'll board."

"How do you know all that?" Samok asked as he sprinted up to the quarterdeck to take his position behind the wheel.

"Because I helped design a lot of those procedures. Now move!" Solana rushed after Samok, directing him on where to steer the ship. Abrasax made use of the few moments they had left to lay Brina's body down in her cabin. She was murmuring and twitching in her venom-induced stupor, and a pang of guilt washed over Abrasax as he stood with the door to her cabin in his hands, ready to close it. Would she still be alive when he returned to check on her later?

He took a deep breath and closed the door, making his way back up to the main deck. There was nothing he could do for her except ensure that the ship made it through the blockade and out of the harbor. The rest was a fight between her and the seven saints.

Instead of using the rope ladder, Abrasax burned *Forte*, switched into *Leve*

CHAPTER 60

and jumped from the lower deck onto the main deck in a wide arc. For the first time in a long time, he felt the old exhilaration that preceded battle.

The sight of darkhelms at the docks, jumping into sloops to chase them, didn't scare him. It fueled him.

"Get down." Sneak's voice rang out from somewhere to his left. All of them hit the deck as a volley of windup quarrels sailed overhead. They slammed into the wooden railing, masts, and deck with a series of thwacks. Holes appeared in the mainsail, but none of the crew were hit.

Samok's commands floated like salt spray on the wind. The ship spun as the wind caught in the sails. It took forever. The same sluggish movement that Abrasax had once exploited to corner Heilinist slave ships, was now working to his own disadvantage.

He cursed and ran at one of the crew, who was reloading his windup to shoot back at the darkhelms who were exposed in the sloops.

"Give me that," he said. He tore the bow from the man's hands and whirled around. Aided by a blast of *Forte*, loading the weapon took only a fraction of the time a normal man would need. He cranked the string back, took a quarrel out of the quiver that lay on the floor near the deck's railing, and took aim. He burned *Claritas*.

Every scratch and dent on the darkhelms' armor appeared in his view as he took aim at the nearest boat. Through the slits in the helmet, he could see a pair of stark blue eyes. They looked terrified. They were right to be. Abrasax pulled the trigger. The quarrel shot off with a burst of speed, sailing straight through the narrow eye slits and penetrating his target's brain.

The darkhelm slumped against the side of the boat, dead. Abrasax reloaded and aimed at another darkhelm, exploiting the gap between helmet and plate and burying a quarrel deep in the soldier's neck.

"Ramming!" Samok's voice echoed from above. Abrasax turned just in time to see the ship's bow headed straight for the blockade ahead.

"Hold on!" the captain screamed again. Abrasax wanted to yell that this was madness and for Samok to turn the wheel around. Instead, he just whooped—a loud, cathartic sound, like a pack of wolves howling together under the moon. How he had missed this. He made a fortified jump up to the quarterdeck, where he had a better angle to aim his windup.

"What's the plan?" he asked Solana, who stood ready beside Samok. The captain's eyes were fixed, his face drawn as both of his hands clasped the ship's steering wheel. They had picked up a decent amount of speed on a fortuitous side wind and were headed straight for the gap between two of the ships forming the blockade. The first ship's stern was tied to the next one's bows with a single strand of rope to keep them together.

"We're hitting that weak point right there," Solana shouted. "It doesn't sound like they're aware of what's happening just yet. Be my eyes, will you?"

"What am I looking for?" Abrasax replied. He peered down the sight of the windup, finger itching on the trigger.

"What is the crew doing?"

"Standing at the side of the main deck, looking at us as though they've just seen a ghost." Abrasax smirked.

"Do you see the captain?"

"Yes. She's surrounded by her troops, looking stupefied. She doesn't know what to do."

"Take her out," Solana said with grim determination.

"My pleasure."

Abrasax took aim; the woman wasn't even wearing her full set of armor. It was almost too easy. If it hadn't been for her golden helmet, she would have been indistinguishable from the other soldiers.

Abrasax shot her in the heart. Just as the rest of the crew turned to help their fallen leader, the *Chimera* crashed into them. Samok groaned as the sound of splintering wood exploded up ahead. Fragments of wood sprayed everywhere. Samok tapped his hand against the steering wheel. "Forgive me, girl."

Snap!

The row binding the two ships together shot loose like a catapult. On both of the ships, crews sprinted away from the collision point in terror. There was a scrape of wood against wood on both sides of Abrasax as the ship squeezed through.

Then they were sailing out into the open sea.

"Where to?" Samok shouted. Then he turned toward one of the crew members. "Martin, check the lower decks for leaks."

***

"We may have shocked them," Solana said, "but they'll reorganize. Pieterszoon would rather die than let us get away with this. In fact, if we get away, his death is guaranteed."

"Captain," Martin shouted, head poking out from the trapdoor leading to the lower decks. "We're taking on water."

CHAPTER 60

Samok cursed. "Plug it. Use everything we have."

"Head for the Mist strait," Abrasax said.

Both Solana and Samok turned to face him.

"That's suicide," Samok said. "Ships only pass through there if they've run out of supplies and their only alternative is death."

"The chance of running aground on one of those reefs is very great," Abrasax agreed with a smile.

Samok looked at him as though he'd gone insane. "And you're okay with that?"

"Look at it this way: to pass through the Mist Strait, one needs a supernatural ability to navigate those reefs. It can't be done through vision. You could have two dozen sailors on each side of the deck, and they still wouldn't be able to spot all hazards. If we sail in there, our pursuers won't stand a chance."

"Fine," Samok replied. "But if we sink, I doubt I'm going to care much about what happens to the darkhelms after us."

"We won't," Abrasax said with a smile. "I know that the only people known to traverse the treacherous waters around the Abbey of Everberg are the monks of the blind order. They have a special affinity for detecting reefs underneath the surface." His eyes lingered on Solana.

"I... can't. I never learned how. When I arrived, I did so by sloop, and when I left, it was the same thing. It is said that my brothers and sisters of the order can navigate those waters. But during my training, I never left the abbey—not once did we discuss how our abilities are supposed to aid us in such an undertaking."

"You'll figure out a way," Abrasax said, turning to Samok and putting a hand on the man's shoulder. "Trust me: Sail for the Mist Strait. Keep that jagged basalt spire over there to your right, and we should make it just in time for nightfall."

"Nightfall?" Samok asked, letting go of the wheel to gesticulate with both hands. "That's even worse—you know why they call it the Mist Strait, right? Nightfall," he muttered. "That's..."

"Irrelevant," Abrasax finished. "Because you will have a scout unencumbered by such basic problems as the need to see."

Solana shook her head. "I can't. There has to be another way."

"Fine," Abrasax said. "If we traverse the open sea, how long do either of you think we can outrun those ships?"

"What ships?" Samok asked.

"Those ships," Abrasax pointed to the back of the quarterdeck, where in the distance the blockade barricading the harbor of Cordwain was dissolving. Sails were being lowered; crews were scurrying about like ants. "We've got a head start, but we're taking on water, and their ships are built for speed."

"Curse of the Keeper," Solana whispered to herself. "He's right. We can either try the Mist Strait or prepare for a naval battle, which won't be much of a battle at all."

Samok looked dumbstruck. "There's two of you lunatics now?"

"Just do it, son," Abrasax said. "Besides, an old acquaintance of mine lives in those parts. I'd like to pay him a visit while we're in the vicinity."

"This is no time for happy reunions," Samok balked.

"Oh, trust me, there won't be anything happy about it." Abrasax smiled as a memory blossomed in front of his eyes.

CHAPTER 61

When the prince's messenger arrived, Zot struggled to suppress the urge to kiss her on the spot.

For a week, he'd been stalling the hotel's concierge, insisting day after day that his shipment of trading goods would arrive at any moment and that he would pay double for the past week's lodging. The man was bound to see through the ruse soon, and once they were evicted from their room, Prince Neheb wouldn't know where to find them.

No matter. Let's not dwell on what could have gone wrong.

Everything had worked out, and that was what counted. How dare the boy question him? Zot had been dealing with people like Prince Ashur Neheb Ka his entire life. What did Wane know about gambling and taking an appropriate amount of risk when the situation demanded it?

Zot held the letter to his nose, relishing the faint scent of sandalwood perfume that clung to the parchment. He unrolled the scroll and scanned it as quickly as his eyes permitted. When he spotted the word "scolopendra," he hooted.

"See," he exclaimed, waving the scroll in the boy's face. "Neheb wants to face me in a game of scolopendra next weekend."

Wane, who hadn't moved from his post by the window for what seemed like days, looked at him with utter disgust.

"You're not considering going back there?" It was a rhetorical question. They both knew the answer.

"What do you think this has all been for?" Zot asked. "The whole point was to work our way into the palace. It's the one place in this accursed city where there's more money than we could ever spend. Now that we're in, you want me to abandon the prince?"

"Yes," Wane said, "that's exactly what I want you to do. Have you forgotten what happened last time? We're broke."

Zot shrugged. True, losing all the funds they had amassed had been a minor setback, but that had been a fluke, nothing more. Neheb hadn't mentioned the discrepancy between the amount of shards Zot had handed him and the amount they'd bet, meaning he hadn't bothered to have a servant count his money. That's how rich he was.

Zot had done everything right. He had chosen the superior warrior and predicted the outcome of the battle. The only thing he could not have foreseen was that his chosen warrior would possess the attention span of a fly.

Foolish woman, he thought. *If only she had taken care to finish the job when it was as good as done.* They could have been halfway back to Metten by now.

Eight's carelessness had almost ruined Zot's entire plan. *Almost,* he reassured himself.

"He wants to play a game of scolopendra," Zot told the boy. "You know what that means."

Wane gave him that look teenagers wear when they think they know better.

"It means we can't lose," Zot continued. "You saw what happened last time. If need be, I'll…" He made a gesture as though squeezing an invisible creature to death. "Just like last time."

He smiled, recalling that evening. Now there was a story he would share in inns for decades to come—just like he would tell anyone who would listen about how he swindled the Prince of Hawqal out of ten thousand clean shards.

"You're not gambling with money anymore," Wane said, springing up and approaching Zot. "You realize that, right?"

Zot raised his eyebrows.

"You're gambling with our lives. What do you think Prince Neheb will do when he finds out you can't cover the amount you owe him? Do you think he'll just slap you on the wrist and send us on our merry way? This is a man who keeps a stable of people at the ready, whom he can force to slaughter each other for his amusement. Does that seem like the type of man who would let us walk out the door owing him hundreds of shards? If he has us executed on the spot, it still wouldn't come close to the horror someone like that could inflict on us."

Zot shook his head. "He wouldn't."

"And how do you know that?" Wane asked, his eyes boring into Zot, who found he wasn't quite ready to meet the boy's gaze.

"Because he's my friend," Zot said. He couldn't help but smile as he said it. The Prince of Hawqal, the great Ashur Neheb Ka, was his friend and gambling buddy. Over the past week, Zot had been devising a strategy to

CHAPTER 61

reveal his true identity to the prince at a later point. There was no reason their relationship should end just because he was returning to Metten.

"Last time we entered that palace," Wane grumbled, "a woman died, and another was maimed. How does that not gnaw at you? By the Seven, it gnaws at me, and there wasn't anything I could've done to stop you and that wretched prince from making those warriors kill each other. It's haunted me every day since. When I close my eyes, I can still see that woman bleeding out on the sand, for no reason other than the prince's sport. A man who was too high to even notice the outcome of the battle until it was over. And now you're saying we're going to go back there, pretending to have money we don't have, and everything will be fine?"

Zot smirked. This was the thing about children; while they understood some things, they needed someone to show them the way of the world. It wasn't all just theory and high-minded, moralistic musings. Sometimes a man had to be pragmatic.

"And if we returned to Metten with no money to support the rebellion's army?" Zot asked, raising his eyebrows. "How many lives will be lost then?"

Wane stood up so abruptly that the mahogany chair he was sitting on slid backward and toppled onto the hardwood floor with a bang. "Don't pretend like you care about what happens to the rebellion. This is about you and your ego," he said. "In case you've forgotten, you're not who you were. At least, that's what I wanted to believe. But now..." The boy shook his head, then waved a dismissive hand and returned to staring out of the window. "Maybe you and the prince *are* friends, two peas in a rotten pod."

Zot couldn't help but grin as the words "prince" and "friend" lined up in the same sentence once more. He was clawing his way back to the top. It would pay off in the end, he was certain of that, and if the boy couldn't see it, that was his problem.

"I'm going," Zot said, "and I'm going to win us that money, and we'll sail back to Metten to be hailed as heroes. You can choose, boy," he added, his voice growing hard. "When they tell our story in decades to come, who will you be? The teenage brat throwing a tantrum and hindering me every step of the way, or the brave hero who put it all on the line alongside me, to ensure that our army would be as well-equipped as it could be?"

The boy's mouth jerked, but no words came out.

"If that's how you see it," he said, "then you're already lost. I'm not going anywhere. In fact, I'm not staying in this godforsaken hotel. The gold foil and marble have rotted your brain. And if I stay here for one more day, it'll do the same to mine."

With that, he stood up and walked out. Zot didn't stop him. The boy would come to his senses when he saw the pile of money that Zot was about to win in the scolopendra game against the prince. He would swallow every one of those harsh words, and he would see that there was still something he could learn from a man like Zot, a one-of-a-kind man, who did what it took to get things done. He leaned closer to the window and watched the boy's silhouette disappear into the bustling alley below. As he watched the tiny figure recede, he held the parchment scroll to his nostrils once more and inhaled the scent of sandalwood—the smell of victory.

CHAPTER 62

Zot entered the prince's palace the way a sailor enters an inn after two months at sea. He grinned as the guards searched him for weapons, then turned around, waiting for the boy to be searched as well.

At the very last minute, Wane had changed his mind, choosing to accompany Zot after all. Though he claimed he was there to prevent Zot from crossing another line, Zot knew the truth.

He knows we're about to win big, and nobody can resist the glow of victory.

The kid wanted to bask in the shine and fill his own pockets with the mountain of gem dust they were about to collect. The same messenger who had delivered the parchment scroll at the hotel escorted them from the outer gate, through a series of sandstone hallways, to a long dining hall, where a lengthy table had been set for three.

At the far end of the rectangular table, which could have served as a schooner's upper deck, sat Prince Ashur Neheb.

He beamed at Zot, raising both arms in greeting. "Welcome, Master Roosebeke. Here we are at last. I have been looking forward to our game all week.

"Wish that we could skip dinner and get straight to it, but my advisers tell me that the scolopendra's venom does less damage on a full stomach. So, I have had some of our finest dishes prepared."

He gestured at the table, which held a collection of glazed ceramic dishes standing on thick slabs of heated stone. The smell of roasted venison wafted from the table in overpowering waves.

"Can I at least see the creature before we get to dinner?" Zot asked. "It helps me get in the mood, so to speak. I want to see the little bastard before it kills me." He let out a booming laugh that disguised the growing jitter in his gut.

Scolopendra venom was fickle. Surviving a bite was often a scarier thought than death. While some got away with scarring and nerve damage in some irrelevant extremity, others had been left paralyzed, unable to speak or move for as long as their unfortunate shell remained on this plane. Zot had instructed Wane to end his suffering should this come to pass, but he didn't think the boy had it in him.

The thought of confronting his mortality for the second time in a month ought to have made him more nervous than he was. In the deeper crevices of his mind, he realized he was getting far too comfortable playing with fire, but that kind of self-reflection would have to wait.

It's sink or swim, and I've always been at ease in the water.

"Very well." Neheb rose. "Follow me."

He led Zot and Wane to a small chamber adjacent to the dining hall, which contained a glass cage quite similar to the one in the gambling den. Even before he approached the cage, Zot could smell the beast. There was a musty, humid stench in the air, like the jungles of Hammerstroke after heavy rain.

Zot joined Neheb, bending forward over the glass cage, looking down at the tangle of branches that had been organized inside to simulate the scolopendra's natural environment. Wane kept his distance, glaring at the glass cage.

"How many are in there?" Zot asked.

"One," the prince said, eyes glittering. "But a very special one. In fact, this specimen was sent to me for tonight's occasion. I have been assured by my father's personal poisoner that only a dozen scolopendrae were caught in the oasis where this one was found. The venom of each was tested for potency on a series of mammoth calves. They assured me that a single drop of this one's venom paralyzed a year-old mammoth for over a month. It never walked again.

"So we can both trust that tonight's stakes will be suitably high. Exciting, don't you think?" Neheb grinned, baring a row of long teeth.

There was hunger in his face, similar to the expression he'd worn when choosing his warrior in the arena the last time they had met. Zot recognized that look, having seen it in many of the men and women he'd employed in the past. Some people, having experienced excitement in quantities far greater than most people ever did, developed an appetite for the thrill.

It was a fever that could only be quelled by increasingly stimulating undertakings. Zot had much preferred people like that in the past when he'd needed dangerous jobs done, as one could be sure that they would launch themselves at the problem head-on, praying for a hit of adrenaline.

CHAPTER 62

Zot could even feel it in himself—the growing desire to do something great, something he could always remember and point back to and say, "I did that."

They left the room containing the cage and sat down for dinner in the dining hall. While Zot and the prince ate large helpings of grilled meats and rice with spicy vegetables, Wane refused to so much as touch a bowl of stew. He didn't speak the entire time and didn't respond when the prince asked him for his name.

The only time he spoke was to excuse himself to go to the bathroom, where he stayed a long time.

"Something wrong with your servant?" Neheb asked, brow furrowed as he watched Wane stride from the dining hall. "He looks stressed."

"It's nothing," Zot assured Neheb. "You know how teenage boys can be. You were once one of them."

"As were you," the prince remarked. They shared a laugh at that. Zot remembered how he'd been around Wane's age when he first became malcontent with the life his parents were laying out for him—a daily struggle. His father had been a fisherman all his life, and while he could afford the minor luxury of living inside Mallion's Depth's mighty stoneward, he'd been treated as a glorified servant.

He sailed out into the wildest storms and harshest weather, praying each time to return with full nets, knowing full well that Zot, his four siblings, and his mother were one week's poor catch away from hunger.

Zot had been about Wane's age when he decided that living on the street couldn't be that much worse than the constant threat of ending up there. He had kept the decision to himself and snuck out of his home in the dead of night. Half a year passed before he ran into one of his siblings at a market, where they grudgingly admitted that his absence had relieved some of the monstrous financial burden that rested on the family's back.

"Anyway," Zot concluded, "the boy is just finding his feet as a man in this world, that's all. I'm teaching him everything I know. Soon enough, he'll understand."

"Why go through the trouble?" The prince raised an eyebrow. "There are plenty of servants on the market who are docile and accommodating already. Personally, I don't tolerate any cheek from my staff. I don't understand why anyone else would."

Zot felt a stab of anger at the repeated term "servant." The way the prince talked about Wane was like he was a piece of cattle, something to be bought and sold at a whim, but there was no way to counter the prince without the risk of offending him. So instead, he shrugged and drank what was left in his third goblet of wine.

"His bloodline has served my family for many generations now. I know what they grow into. So if a few years of growing pain is what it takes..." Zot shrugged again.

The prince looked as though he was going to offer another rebuttal, but then the door opened and Wane re-entered. He glared straight ahead as he marched back to his seat and sat down with a heavy thud. The prince shrugged and gestured at the table, which was still laden with enough food to feed an army.

"Is there anything else either of you want to partake in? If not, I'll have my servants clear the room so we can proceed to our entertainment for the evening."

Zot looked at Wane, who hadn't eaten anything, with an inquisitive expression.

"I'm not hungry." The boy stared at his own reflection in his silver plate, refusing to meet Zot's eyes.

"In that case, I think we can proceed to the fun, my prince."

"Excellent."

CHAPTER 63

Neheb led the way into the chamber containing the cage and sat down on a decorated mahogany chair on the far side of the cage. It occurred to Zot that since Neheb had designated a specific seat for him to take, it would be all too easy for him to cheat. Especially in a game where the stakes were as high as this one, neither man was above tilting the odds in his favor.

Zot sat down on his side of the cage, trying to read the prince's expression, but there was only genuine excitement there.

The prince beckoned for a servant, and a woman strode over at once, carrying a heavy pouch that jangled with every step she took. The prince took it from her and raised it to show how full it was.

"I assume you have brought your own as well?"

"I did," Zot said. He motioned for Wane to bring over their pouch. It jangled in much the same manner as the prince's, but Zot's was filled with chunks of polished glass. He prayed to everything that was holy that the prince wouldn't insist on checking the contents of his pouch before the game. If he lost, it wouldn't matter if his ruse was discovered. His life would be over, regardless. *But if I win, Neheb needn't know a thing.*

Wane raised the pouch over the cage, drawing a broad smile from Neheb. Just like last time, the money seemed to be an afterthought for him. Something to spice up an already dangerous game.

"Very well," the prince said, "I have instructed my servant"—he pointed a finger at the woman who had returned to her post in the room's corner—"to hand you your winnings in case the bite incapacitates me before I can do so myself. I suspect you have a similar arrangement with yours?"

"That seems reasonable." Though he hid it well, Zot's anxiety spiked. He hadn't thought about that scenario. If the bite took him out, he would leave Wane alone to hand the prince counterfeit money. Would Neheb blame Wane once he discovered the deceit? With the way he looked at servants, it seemed likely. Zot cast a look over his shoulder at Wane, whose face was set into a determined scowl.

"I'll hand it over if you lose," Wane said.

"Thank you," Zot muttered. For the first time tonight, he felt nervous. Not because he was about to stick his hand into a cage with one of the most venomous creatures in existence, but because he risked placing Wane into a lethal situation. He should have known this upfront and refused to take the boy with him. *Winners don't think about what could go wrong*, he chastised himself. *Winners look ahead at what needs to be done.*

"Are we doing standard inspections?" he asked.

The prince shook his head. "In a match between gentlemen, that doesn't seem necessary. Wouldn't you agree?"

Zot remained silent, contemplating the possibility that the prince had every opportunity to cheat.

"I could have my servant fetch a sniffsel somewhere in the city if that puts you more at ease, but I'm afraid it would keep us from our game for at least another hour."

"That won't be necessary." Zot aimed for a smile and missed. "Like you said, in a game amongst gentlemen, trust ought to be present."

The prince nodded. "Well, let the best man win, and may our predecessors carry us to a better place if that is our fate."

Zot thumped a fist on top of the glass cage in approval, then shoved his hand into the cage. He could see the prince's servant slide over so she could monitor his hand, ensuring that it was, in fact, inside the cage. On the other side of the table, he saw the prince mimic his movement, a hungry expression on his face.

Silence fell in the room as both men stared into the cage, looking for any sign of a stirring leaf or a trembling branch. Wherever the creature was, it was hiding well. Zot could feel the rush of adrenaline in his veins as he realized just what was on the line. He could either go home tonight as a winner, carrying more riches than they'd ever dared imagine when they first set foot on the island, or he could be imprisoned in the prince's dungeon, or worse. Over the years, he'd seen a good many players being carried away from the scolopendra table, but he'd never given much thought to what happened after a bite. Would it be painful, or would the venom take him out before he even realized what was happening?

Maybe I'll find out what it's like soon enough. He cursed himself. *Not a chance. You're Dimimzy Zot. A winner. If that beast comes near you, you*

CHAPTER 63

know what to do.

A common tactic in scolopendra was to dig your hand into the soil at the bottom of the cage as deep as it would go, so that the scolopendra had as small an object as possible to detect in its environment. Zot's fingers dug into the loose ground, and he could feel the moist soil squelch as he forced his hand into it as deep as it would go. Only the back of his hand now stood out, a light brown against the almost pitch-black soil.

A branch rattled about a foot away from him, to his left, near the top of the three-foot-high cage. It was gaining height. He realized the scolopendra had spotted his hand first. The question was, would it go for it?

He pushed his hand down to fight the human urge to pull back his arm and get to safety. To distract himself from the dread of impending doom, he stared at the prince, who sat opposite him. There was a distant look in the man's eye, as though he'd disengaged from reality and tumbled into a trance.

Finding no connection there, Zot looked over his shoulder at Wane, who was standing a handful of feet behind him, leaning against the wall. When the boy returned his gaze, Zot looked away at once. He shouldn't make this harder on the boy than it needed to be. Besides, he didn't think he could stomach the disapproval he knew he would see there.

The boy had warned him time and time again that he was being overconfident and overplaying his hand. Victory had seemed certain to Zot until now. The beast emerged, hanging from a branch near the top of the cage. He could see its many legs skittering across the branch as it positioned itself for a strike. Beads of sweat formed on Zot's forehead.

Just stay calm, he thought. *There's no other option but winning.* The scolopendra's red and black scales glittered in the glow of the jelly lanterns that hung from the ceiling. It slithered down, skulking between the foliage of a low-hanging branch.

It was getting ready now, Zot could tell. A rush of anger came over him. He wouldn't—couldn't—lose. He was one game away from regaining the wealth and honor that was due to him, and there was no way he was going to give that up.

Zot pulled his hand from the leafy soil, exposing its full extent, and flipped it upside down, the back of his hand pressing into the sand.

This was foolish under most circumstances. His wriggling fingers only tantalized the scolopendra into striking, as they looked like smaller, separate targets. But he was no longer interested in avoiding a strike. He was trying to bait one on his terms. If the beast wanted to bite him, so be it, but he would make sure it wasn't a free shot. He took a deep breath and focused on every skittering move as the critter positioned itself.

You may be fast, you stinkbug, but I'm faster.

It was on him before he could move a muscle. Hundreds of sticky, barbed legs curled around his hand, prickling into his skin as he tried to gain a hold of the scolopendra's head. He reached for it with his thumb, then watched in horror as both of the creature's venomous pincers sank into his flesh.

It was over. It didn't even sting, and yet, the scolopendra had just taken everything Zot had left to lose.

His mouth fell open with a gasp. Everything they had worked for was gone, and once the pouch in Wane's hands was opened, the game would be up. He looked over his shoulder at the boy and mouthed, "I'm sorry."

Zot steeled himself, waiting for the first wave of nausea to hit. He was going to keep his hand in that cage until he passed out. Every second he could hold on was one more second he could stave off defeat.

"You were right," he said to Wane over his shoulder, who looked into his eyes with a straight face, betraying no emotion. "You were right. We should have left when we had the chance."

The boy jerked his head, drawing Zot's attention to something happening on the other side of the room. He snapped around and watched as Prince Neheb slumped out of his chair, sagged sideways, and thumped onto the stone floor.

The servant standing in the corner rang a bell. Two surgeons dressed in leather aprons rushed into the room. They wasted no time in treating the prince, pouring potions down his throat and monitoring his wrist for a pulse.

Zot withdrew his hand from the cage in utter shock. He had been the last to withdraw his hand. He was the indisputable winner. Even if the bite incapacitated him now, the money was theirs. It rightfully belonged to them.

He jumped to his feet. "I won," he declared, walking over to the servant, who was more concerned with her fallen master than the money that stood abandoned on top of the cage.

"I won," Zot repeated, pointing at Neheb's pouch. He wanted to have that bag in his hand when the venom hit.

"Here," the servant said, dropping the heavy pile of gems into Zot's open hand. "I will escort you out. My master needs rest."

Zot's skin seemed to tingle where it touched the pouch of money. When the servant let go of it, the weight of it sparked a tear of joy.

The pain Zot was awaiting didn't come. On the contrary, he felt great.

CHAPTER 63

Amazing. Was that the rush of victory or the onset of the venom penetrating his nervous system?

He had done it. Against Wane's warnings, against his own misgivings, and against the odds, Dimimzy Zot had rebuilt himself from nothing. He was back where he was supposed to be. At the top of the food chain.

He looked down at his hand and found that he couldn't spot any puncture marks on it. The beast had bitten him, and yet he felt wonderful. If that wasn't a good omen, then what could be?

He held out the bag of money to Wane, who had already tucked away their own pouch containing glass beads.

"Look at this." Zot held up his thumb for Wane to see. "The thing bit me, and I'm unscathed. Explain that."

"You got lucky." Wane shrugged. Before Zot could say another word, the boy marched out of the open door that led back to the dinner hall. Zot followed him, casting a backward glance at the incapacitated prince who lay on his back on the marble floor, surrounded by servants placing iced rags on his forehead and bare chest. He would have felt bad for the man if he didn't feel so delighted for himself.

"See," Zot said as they walked through the long hallways back to the outer gate of the palace, "I told you I would do it and I did it." He grinned wider than he had in years, feeling just like he had when he pulled off his first score.

Zot hadn't just waited around for the universe to reinstate him. He had reached out and grabbed what he wanted, and it felt more satisfying than a hit of the best kelp rum. Wane ignored him.

Sore loser.

"You have nothing to say now, do you?" Zot couldn't help himself from jangling the large pouch of money at the boy. "We're rich. By morning, we'll have tickets to get out of here on the most luxurious ship we can find. When we reach Metten, we will be heroes. Heroes."

He repeated the word just to hear it echo through the long hallway. When they reached the gatehouse, four guards rushed to open the steel gates. Zot reached inside the pouch of money, grabbed a handful of shards, and thrust them into one guard's hands.

"Here," he said, "for your excellent service." He winked as the man's mouth fell open.

"You just handed him what could very well have been multiple months' wages. Don't go giving it away," Wane muttered. "We need that money."

"I'll give away however much I want to whomever I want," Zot said, anger rising. "I don't recall you putting it all on the line to make this happen. I risked my life, and I won it fair and square."

"No," Wane answered with a glance over his shoulders. As soon as they were out of earshot of the guards, Wane leaned in closer to him. "You risked nothing."

Zot opened his mouth, ready to call the boy every name he could think of.

Then the boy reached into his pockets and pulled out something that made him stop dead in his tracks. Two inch-long black pincers.

"You were never bitten. You couldn't have been bitten, because I made it so." Wane's voice grew low with fury.

The boy seemed to age ten years right in front of him. *No*, Zot corrected himself, *he's not a boy anymore, he's a man. An angry man.*

"You would've lost it all," Wane said. "I prevented that. I made sure you couldn't get us both killed, and as much as I hate to break it to you, it cost quite a bit."

"What are you talking about?" Zot asked. He hated the surprised tone in his own voice. This was his moment, and he shouldn't be worried about what some gutless twerp thought about it.

"I rigged the game."

"Wait," Zot said out loud, realizing the implications of what Wane had just shown. "If the scolopendra had its fangs removed, then how did the prince get bitten?"

Wane's face hardened.

"He didn't get bitten. That's the whole point. I poisoned him."

"You what?" Zot asked, mouth dropping open. He almost dropped the pouch of money, aghast.

"That's right," Wane said. "I went to Sachrya. I figured if there was anyone who could help me out of this situation, it was her. She concocted a special poison designed to mimic scolopendra venom. All I had to do was ensure that the prince would touch it. That's why, when you two idiots were stuffing your faces, I went into the room that held the cage. I clipped the scolopendra's fangs with this"—he retrieved a pair of tongs from his pocket— "and then I smeared poison all over the cage on the prince's side. I knew he would have to put his hand in there, and all it would take was for his bare skin to touch the poison. He won't remember a thing," Wane said, "so don't worry, everything's taken care of. When he wakes up, he'll think he's been bitten, and he'll feel like he's been bitten. By which time, you will be long gone with his money."

"You mean *we* will be long gone?"

CHAPTER 63

"No. It will just be you."

"What's that supposed to mean?" Zot asked. "We came here together; we're leaving together. Besides, the others would kill me if I didn't bring you back."

"Then that'll be the end of you. Because Sachrya's services didn't come cheap."

Zot groaned. "No, no, no. What did you promise her?"

"One year of my undivided service. That was the price I had to pay to prevent you from driving us both into the ground, and the rebellion right along with it."

He withdrew his shirt sleeve, showing a bruised puncture mark on his forearm.

"The poison is already in me."

"And only she has the antidote," Zot concluded.

"That's right," Wane said. "So don't you dare talk to me about who sacrificed what to make sure the rebellion got its funding."

Zot felt the world closing in around him. He stumbled to the side of the street and sank down against the white facade of the nearest house. A cloud of dust rose as he hit the ground. "No," he said, "that can't be. We have money now, we'll..."

"We will do nothing," Wane said, his voice hollow. "I already tried that. She wants me. To be more specific, she wants my use of the sigils. She has some plans that only I can help her realize. So it was this, or you would've just lost everything. We would've been in the prince's dungeon at this very moment."

Fear swelled in Zot's throat. "No," he said, "I will take your place. I'll do whatever. We will go there right now."

Wane shook his head. "We will do no such thing. She's made it quite clear what would happen if I go back on a done deal. Besides, I agreed to it. I had every choice not to take it, but I did because I knew it was necessary."

Zot closed his eyes and felt his throat close with grief. "This can't be happening. I can't leave you here. I'll stay here. I'll work the rest of the year. We will rent a place somewhere together, whatever it takes, but I won't leave you here."

Wane shook his head. "The others need that money. That's what all of this was for. If you don't return to Metten with a shipload of weapons and rations, the others will be fighting a dragon with a stick. You need to make sure that we have a fighting chance. All of us will have to make sacrifices before the end. This is mine. When the year is up, if I'm still alive, I will find you guys. But for the next twelve months, this is where I'll be."

CHAPTER 64

Brina was enveloped in the grip of a heavy steel chain, suspended in darkness. Immeasurable force pulled her limbs in opposite directions. She tried to scream, but the pressure on her throat was so immense that the only sound that came out was a panicked squeak. She kicked and struggled, but found herself immobilized, eyes unblinking, forced to stare into a tunnel that extended downward into eternity.

This is it. This is what the end looks like. A distant burning sensation reminded her of where she was and why she was here. The venom. The ammitarach venom had made its way through her system, pumped around dutifully by a heart that struggled to survive, and in doing so had ensured its own demise.

Finally, a distant voice in the back of her mind said. She was done struggling. Done fighting. She had taken a stinger to the leg in battle, and now she was allowed to walk away. Life had been laborious, but now she was allowed to return home to a warm hearth after a day of toiling in the fields. No one could say she had died without honor. It was a blessing.

"What kind of cowardly bullshit is that?" a low, grumbling voice said behind her. She found herself sitting on a grassy meadow atop a grave hill overlooking a vast tapestry of blue. She realized where she was: Barrow's Perch. Beside her sat a dark-skinned man, whose face was slashed with thick strips of white scars, making him look like a walking spider's web. After all, that's what they had always called Acheron: the Spider of Rothmoor.

"What did you just say to me?" Brina snapped.

"You heard me, kid. That's some cowardly bullshit, and you know it."

Brina was torn between flinging herself around Acheron's neck and punching him in the teeth. So she settled for a disgruntled glare. "Says a lot, coming from you." That ought to hit him where it hurt. Acheron smiled.

"I've missed that," he said. "Someone who isn't afraid to get in my face and tell me how it is. I think we all need that from time to time. And the friends who grant us that honor are rarer than those who would share a cup

CHAPTER 64

of rum with us."

Brina stretched herself out onto the ground, feeling a tangle of dried grass prickling the back of her neck. "So this is it?" she asked. "The afterlife?"

Acheron shrugged. "Call it whatever you want. But it isn't half bad, I can tell you that."

Brina exhaled, feeling the tension she had been storing for months leave her body.

"No, it's not," she agreed. "And it's been a long time coming."

"So, you're planning on staying here, then?" Acheron asked. He stared straight ahead, watching an immovable sun sink into the Sundered Sea. Brina could tell something bothered him.

"Yes," she said. "I'm done. I continued for as long as anyone could expect me to, and now I'm taking a well-deserved rest. Forever."

"You almost sound relieved to be here," Acheron said. "As though you were waiting for an excuse to kick the bucket and leave the physical world behind."

"So what if I was?"

Acheron scoffed. "That's a cop-out. You were one of the most valuable assets the rebellion had. Without you, an uphill battle has just become a little steeper."

"You were the one who always insisted on the uselessness of rebellion," Brina said, pushing herself up on her elbows. "You kept telling me how pointless it was to stand up to the empire. I came around to your way of thinking, that's all. When we first met, I was naïve. I believed things could be different. Then I saw what happened to you."

A long silence stretched out after this statement. The old wound had reopened. Almost a year ago, Brina had watched Acheron launch himself off of Locktower A at God's Maul prison, limbs entangled with Solana's. She had survived the fall. He had not. If any more evidence was needed of the sick and twisted nature of the world, that was it. Solana had wormed her way into the expedition that ought to have been Acheron's.

"That's when I knew that it's all pointless," Brina said. "You were safe until we met. And I forced you out into the world, convinced you to give resistance one more try. And seeing from a front-row seat what you got in return—that guilt has never left me. I might as well have hanged you with my own hands."

"That's a lie," Acheron said. His dark eyes locked on to hers. Tears were forming in the corners of them, heavy, threatening to roll down his face like a boulder down a mountainside, ravaging everything in its wake. "I didn't die before we met because I was already dead. You helped me give meaning to a wasted life. It was always a matter of time before I would've huffed myself to death in the dark. Instead, I got a far greater end. I lived. I existed, and every day, the consequences of that resonate in you and Abrasax. It wasn't much, perhaps. But Acheron of Rothmoor served his part in history. For that, I am grateful beyond what I can express."

When Brina didn't speak, Acheron went on. "What do you think I felt after I launched myself over the edge and saw that cliff hurtling toward me?"

"I don't even want to think about it," Brina said.

"I felt giddy," Acheron said. "The demons and the guilt I had accumulated over a lifetime of failure dissipated like mist in a morning breeze. For those few glorious seconds, I was alive. And I felt it in every fiber of my body in a way I had never felt before. Those few seconds made all the difference."

Brina swallowed. She may not have been hiding in a barrow the way Acheron had. And it wasn't cloud she was using to dull her nerves. But tucking herself away in her ship's cabin and downing an army's ration worth of rum every night came pretty damn close.

"So, was this it for you?" Acheron asked. "That one moment where it all came together when you saw with absolute clarity that you had given everything you were born to give and made your ultimate sacrifice for your friends, family, and people?" Acheron stared straight ahead, toying with a blade of grass before ripping it out.

Brina stayed silent. He was right. She hadn't given everything she had to give. The last thing she felt before the venom took her was fear. Panic. She had been so scared of going through another traumatic injury that she had untied the cloth keeping the venom in her lower leg.

"The last thing I ever felt was terror," she admitted. As that thought sank in, she leaped to her feet, digging her heels into the ground atop the barrow. "No," she said, feeling the same panic that had caused her to untie the cloth. "I didn't give it all. I'm not ready. I shouldn't be here."

The corners of Acheron's mouth curled into a smile.

"That's what I thought. When the time comes for you to lay it all down and join me at the top of this eternal barrow, you will know. It will feel like coming home. It will feel not like escaping, but like arriving."

"What do I do?" Brina asked. "I can't stay here. There are too many dark-helms left for me to kill. Too many people are still counting on me."

"Then I guess you'd better run," Acheron said with that same smile. "Because the veil will be here any minute to sweep us both away." He pointed off into the distant tree line, where a cloud of mist was descending on

CHAPTER 64

Barrow's Perch. "Once it reaches us, the choice is made."

"Come on, then," Brina shouted, extending a hand toward Acheron, who was still sitting atop his barrow.

He shook his head. "You know that's not how it works."

"But if it did," Brina asked, taking in every crevice of her godfather's face for what she knew would be the last time, "if it worked like that, would you run with me?"

Acheron smiled and lay back in the grass. "If I could do it all again, I would run like the wind, kid."

***

Brina awoke with a gasp, her heart pounding. Sweat and tears intermingled on her face. She sat up straight, then was overcome with a wave of nausea that caused her to lean over the side of her bunk and throw up liquid she didn't remember ingesting. She peered out of the small window of her cabin, only to see a thick veil of fog in the distance.

Brina tried to stand up but found the rocking of the ship too treacherous an opponent. She would have to wait until someone came to check on her. Thick bandages were wrapped around her lower leg. Dark stains on them promised a gruesome discovery underneath. She reached around her neck for the pyramid and found it missing. Instead, it lay on her bedside table, tucked away in a wooden box that was new to her.

Before she could explore her situation further, however, the usual stomping and shouting above her head exploded into something far more vicious. Harsh words were exchanged, and the stamping on the deck took on a fervent quality.

Groups of people shouted at each other, and though she couldn't hear what they were saying, her father's voice was one of the loudest among them. Gripping her bedside table, Brina forced herself to her feet and, clutching at the walls and furniture as she went, she exited the cabin and struggled up to the main deck. It was there she heard the words: "Your word was death. You've doomed us."

CHAPTER 65

Brina fought her way up to the main deck, where she collapsed against the mainmast. No one seemed to notice or care. They were far too preoccupied with the shouting match atop the quarterdeck. Beyond the deck's railing, ragged stone pillars loomed up in the mist all around them, towering over them. It was like sailing into the maw of a giant beast.

"It's as though this entire place is cursed!" Samok shouted, thumping his fist against the ship's wheel. "We've been floating in circles for days. According to my calculations, we should have exited the strait yesterday; it's like the current is pushing us backward. Strange forces are at play here. Something is working against us."

Abrasax stared straight ahead, mouth twitching. Two dozen crew members stood staring at him. Mutiny was written across their faces.

"Someone," he muttered.

"What?" Samok asked.

"It's not something that's poised against us," Abrasax said. "But someone."

Then, almost to himself, he muttered, "I must have angered him even worse than I thought."

"Who?" Samok asked.

"Wiley," Abrasax said. "He's sometimes called the Keeper of the Strait."

"What do you mean "Keeper of the Strait"?"

"It is said, amongst those in the know, that Wily Walter, the Keeper of the Strait, is so in tune with its climate that he can influence its currents and weather patterns."

Brina forced herself to her feet and staggered her way up the steps leading to the quarterdeck. For a moment, all eyes turned on her as they realized she had made it out of bed. Bron ran down the steps to support Brina, a gesture she accepted with a grateful smile.

"That's impossible," Samok said. "No one can control the weather."

CHAPTER 65

"It isn't," Solana replied. She had been listening in on the conversation from a distance. A peculiar look adorned her pallid face. "At Everberg, there was talk about a specific section of heretics who had developed their own brands of rituals to draw upon the Keeper's power—"

"Sigilists, you mean?" Brina said.

Solana's mouth tightened into a fine line. "Welcome back, Sabrina. Of course, sigilists. My apologies." She rubbed her hands together before she went on. "Anyway, it is not unthinkable that one of these people from our scripture exists. They were supposed to see over long distances, hear things yet to be whispered, and plead with the Keeper to turn a thunderstorm into a mild drizzle."

Abrasax sighed. "Yes, that's what I just said. He's real. I've met him before. Given the circumstances, I thought he'd be at least somewhat accommodating to our presence here, but it seems that the years of isolation are taking their toll on his sanity." Abrasax looked up into the surrounding mist with an annoyed expression, as though daring the wisps of white to transform into a human person he could shout at.

"And you think this Keeper of the Strait is foiling my attempts to navigate?" Samok asked. He looked from Abrasax to Solana, then to Brina, with an expression of astonishment. "What is it with you people? Don't get me wrong—it's useful to have a little extra power here and there. But messing with the weather? Driving currents?" He pursed his lips. "That's just wrong."

"We knew it," one of the crewmembers shouted. The one who had spoken, a tall Hawqallian with waist-long dreadlocks named Sennach, stood at the front of the pack, shaking his head. "We were just talking about that," he said. "We knew something wasn't right here. You"—he pointed a finger at Abrasax—"you sent us in here knowing that this demon, whom you had angered, calls this place his home?

"For days, we've been double-checking every adjustment we make to the sails, ensuring that we are going as straight as possible. Rundale has been sitting in that crow's nest for two full days without a break because she didn't want to risk missing a glimpse of land if it could save us. But now all is revealed. You might as well have sacrificed us to the underworld yourself."

A murmur of assent rippled through the crew. Brina hobbled to the staircase, positioning herself between the enraged crew and Abrasax. Behind her, Samok looked like a man perched on the edge of an abyss, torn between his allegiances to his crew and to the mission.

"It makes sense," one of the other crew members yelled. "The only way to appease the demon is to get rid of the one who angered him." His gnarled finger pointed at Abrasax.

Rage flared in Abrasax's eyes. "Indeed? And which of you is going to come get me?"

It was the wrong thing to say.

Sennach stormed up the stairs. Brina stretched out her arm to block him. "That's a fight you won't win, my friend. Don't make him hurt you."

Sennach halted. His eyes narrowed as his gaze found Brina's.

"Look, we're all stressed," Brina said, "but the only way we're going to make it out of this is by staying calm and working together. Nobody is being thrown overboard or sacrificed to any demons. If someone is messing with us, I guarantee they've underestimated us." She raised her voice to ensure everyone aboard the *Chimera* would hear.

"We've got the best captain this side of Hawqal on board." Brina jabbed her thumb at Samok, who shrank back, still unsure which way the situation would go and what side he'd choose if forced. "We've got a crew that has carried us through many dangers, and we've got the power of sigils on our side."

She underscored the last sentence with a hint of *Consol*. She descended the stairs, clutching at the banister. Sennach stepped back, permitting her to pass. "Who among you can truthfully claim they weren't told beforehand that we'd face dangers?"

A hush fell.

"Didn't all of us agree that, no matter what happened, we'd do whatever was needed for this mission to be a success?"

"But you didn't meet your side of the bargain," a man with gnarled stumps for fingers called out. "We were supposed to build an army, yet we were forced to flee from Onderheem like thieves in the night. They tricked us. They're not coming to help us. And neither are the Morassians, are they?"

Brina sighed. Though the failure at Morassia hadn't been communicated to the crew, they hadn't lied about what a success it had been. She found herself at a turning point: She could lie, hoping to appease the crew, or she could be honest and retain a far more valuable resource—trust.

"No," Brina called. "They are not coming to help us. We have done all that we could do to persuade the other free peoples of the Sundered Isles to come to our aid, to come to Bior's aid. They have refused the call. Because they are scared, because they are weak, and because they lack the courage that each of us possesses.

"But I guarantee this," she said, her voice rising. "When we make it back

CHAPTER 65

to Metten, you will be heroes. The cowardice of others casts no shadow upon you. The sacrifices you have each made for the rebellion will be remembered for years to come. Now let us face this challenge head-on. We will take an hour's break, and when that time is up, we will sit down right here on the main deck and discuss a plan of action. If there is a way out of this accursed strait, we will find it together."

"She's right," Samok's first mate, Alhela, said. "Drawing blood amongst ourselves won't get us out of this mess. But our collective wits just might. Are we sailors or superstitious geezers?"

"Well, that's one crisis averted," Sneak muttered as the crew scattered, taking their seats along the deck. Abrasax vanished to his cabin, still fuming. Brina left him to it. His anger had almost sparked a full-on fight. And given the extent of his powers, that was something a man of his stature ought to be above.

"For now, I suppose," Brina said. "There's food and water on board for a few more weeks, but when it runs out..."

"Aye," Bron grunted, leaning on the ship's railing. "Then we will see who is made of stone and who is mere clay."

"I love your quaint little sayings," Sneak said. He ruffled a hand through the Biori's long beard, causing the metal skulls that were woven into it to tinkle. Bron seized Sneak's wrist and twisted it, drawing a yelp.

"Can you two knock it off for one second?" Brina's annoyance spiked. "Help me figure this out, or else we'll soon be at each other's throats again."

Sneak shrugged. "I'm out of ideas."

"And you?" Brina looked at Bron.

The man shrugged. "Maybe if we wait long enough, the mist will lighten up enough to see the stars."

"And if that doesn't happen?"

"Then I guess you can season me with some cinnamon and roast me above a wood fire."

Brina threw her head back and laughed. As she looked up, a ball of light appeared in the sky above her. She blinked, and the cluster of light split open like a geode struck by a hammer, unfolding into a curtain of light leading off into the distance, cutting a trail through the mist.

"There," Brina said, pointing at the sheet of light unfurling in front of her. As it snaked its way through the mists, its colors changed from different hues of starburst to light blue, purple, and back again. It was like watching a rainbow unfold before her eyes.

Sneak frowned. "I only see the same damned mist we've been seeing all day."

Brina called over Samok and pointed at the sheet of color once more. "Please tell me you see that, and I'm not going crazy."

There was some nervous shuffling as those around shook their heads.

"Well, it's there," Brina said, "and if what my father said is true, then maybe the same person who has been messing with us is now trying to help us."

"Why would they do that?" Sennach asked, his face contorted into a scowl.

"No idea," Brina said, "but we're already sailing in circles. I say we see where it leads us."

"You want to follow it?" Samok asked, scratching his head. "Seems suspect."

"What's the worst that could happen? We're already lost." Brina shrugged.

"Very well," Samok said. It was a testament to their growing despair that following lights nobody else could see had become a viable course of action. As they trailed the light, avoiding jagged rocks and navigating shallow reefs through shouts from the crow's nest and Solana's whispers in Samok's ear, Brina realized just how easily a trap set like this could end their miserable journey.

But even if that were the case, would it matter? They were drowning, and here was something resembling a rope—they had to pull it.

The fog grew so dense that the only thing distinguishing any sort of direction was the shimmering curtain of light ahead.

At one point, the ship's hull brushed against something hard in the water, and everyone on board drew in a collective gasp, but somehow they squeaked by without disaster striking.

Brina stood on the bow, watching the light's movements and then calling out to Samok to adjust course.

After what felt like at least an hour, she shouted, "Coming up ahead—it's gonna be a tight squeeze!"

The light snaked in between two immense walls of stone, which loomed up from the mist at the very last second. They were so close by the time Brina saw them that even if they had wanted to avoid the tight fit, they wouldn't have been able to. Brina fought the urge to run away to the back of the ship, so she wouldn't have to look at the imminent collision, but she had steered them this way and should be the first to suffer the consequences.

She needn't have worried. Samok steered the ship through the narrow passage between the stone walls and into a circular cove, where the mist seemed lighter. Ahead, a huge stone spire came into view. It rose from the water and ascended up into the mist, its peak invisible.

CHAPTER 65

At the base of this monstrosity, a wooden pontoon was affixed to the rock. The trail of light they'd been following converged just above the pontoon.

"It wants us to moor the ship," Brina said.

"It wants?" Samok asked, looking uncomfortable. "The light wants things now? How do you know?"

"I just do," Brina replied. "Lower the anchor. I will use a boat to cover the final stretch."

As they did so, Abrasax approached Brina, face drawn.

"This is it," he said. "This is where he lives."

"The guardian of the strait, you mean?" Brina had suspected that the light had been his doing, though she could only guess at why she was the only one who could see it.

"I'll come with you," he said. "Walter can be quite a character—temperamental if you catch him in a bad mood." He peered at the distant pontoon with a look of nostalgia on his face.

CHAPTER 66

hen the boat tapped against a wooden pontoon, Brina jumped over the side, staggering as the platform wobbled under her feet. Abrasax followed.

"Not you," a high-pitched voice snapped overhead. Brina looked up, but all she saw was a blanket of fog.

Abrasax, who still had one leg in the boat, scowled. "Come on, Wiley, I thought we left our differences behind us years ago. I spent the last decade of my life in prison. I might be rehabilitated."

"Our last conversation was enough to last me a lifetime, thank you," the voice called back. "If you lot want to find your way out of here, I suggest you get back in that boat."

Brina opened her mouth to speak, but Abrasax held up a hand and called back. "What about my daughter? How will she get back?"

"She'll find a way," Wiley said. Abrasax looked at Brina, an apologetic look on his face. "I told you he could be temperamental."

"I heard that," Wiley boomed. "Now, what will it be? You can drift out there for the rest of your lives if you want to. No skin off my teeth."

"Just go." Brina put a hand on Abrasax's shoulder. "It'll be fine."

"Are you sure you're up to it?"

Brina shrugged. "We're lost and running out of supplies. How much worse could things get?"

"Fair enough." Abrasax sighed. He got back in the boat and began pulling at the oars. A giggle echoed overhead.

"That's right, little viper, row away now."

As soon as Abrasax had disappeared from sight, a rope ladder tumbled down from the skies, clattering against the cliff. Brina sighed and began the long climb. With every step, her wounded leg burned. Once she was far enough off the ground to see the wooden pontoon disappear in the shroud of mist, her pulse quickened. The ropes that made up the ladder were old and

CHAPTER 66

moldy. With every step, the wooden slats creaked ominously. How long had it been since this ladder had last been used? Not to mention the numbness that was spreading through her injured leg. It felt like it could buckle at any moment. At this height, falling into the sea would be the same as slamming onto a stone slab. Brina shuddered.

Keep it together, Springtide. How much further can it be?

After climbing into the mist for what felt like a mile, Brina reached a wooden platform with an open trapdoor.

She couldn't stifle a gasp of surprise as she clambered into Wiley Walter's hut. It was a cozy little room hewn out of the rock. The floor was covered with a blue rug. Atop the only piece of furniture in the room—an oversized green armchair—sat a tiny man, peering through a dusty window. Though only mist was visible outside, he seemed to gaze at something in the distance.

Tufts of white hair sprouted from Walter's wrinkled ears, like stalks of leek protruding from soil. His head was the size of a coconut, which made his nose and ears look too big, as though his head had been shrunk while his features retained their original size. If he hadn't been so old, Brina might've mistaken him for a child. His dark skin hung loosely over a bony frame.

"Welcome," he croaked without turning around. "Close that door, will you? The cold gets into my bones, and it flares up my arthritis something fierce."

Brina did as he asked, and when she stood up to her full height, she first heard it—the low hum of dozens of tiny devices that hung against the cabin's walls. The effect wasn't quite musical, though there was a soothing quality to the coming together of multiple harmonizing frequencies.

"They are beautiful, are they not?" Walter asked.

Brina shrugged. This elicited a wheezy giggle from the small man.

"Take a seat," Walter said. He jumped up from the chair and offered it to Brina.

"I couldn't take your chair." Brina waved him off. "I'll sit on the floor."

"No, no, I insist. It's an excellent seat. You'll notice that one has a magnificent view from up here."

Once again, Brina peered out through the large window and saw nothing but clouds of white. Remembering what she had heard about Wiley Walter from her father, however, she decided that offending his hospitality was a poor choice, so she sat down without further comment. As she sank into the soft filling of the armchair, the humming of the machines grew louder. It buzzed all around her, coalescing into something like a choir, droning in her head.

"See," Walter remarked, "it's a pleasant spot, isn't it?"

Brina nodded, and as she stared straight ahead, she noticed that the fog seemed somehow thinner from where she sat. Walter sat down cross-legged at her feet and peered up at her. "You must be wondering why my waves guided you here?"

Brina nodded, unable to tear her eyes away from the window.

"I am going to answer your question in the fashion of those annoying babblers, the philosophers, with a question of my own. What brought you here?"

Brina thought about how they had sailed into the mist, hoping to elude the darkhelms. In doing so, they may have risked the secrecy of Walter's hideout. Was it safe to tell him that? Or should she tell him they got lost instead? Or perhaps she should make up a third reason. She looked down at Walter, who sat with his eyes closed and his wrists resting on his crossed legs, palms turned upward. He looked at ease, and Brina wondered for a moment how long he would sit there in silence if she never replied. He seemed content just sitting, a modest smile on his face. Brina decided that lying to this man was a very poor idea indeed.

"We were being pursued by the Heilinist fleet," she said. "The Mist Strait was our only avenue of escape. It worked, but we got lost."

Walter giggled. "Yes," he said, "it is remarkable how easy most of us get lost once we lose sight of our surroundings, is it not? We think we chart our own course, and yet without an outside frame of reference, we find ourselves dreadfully lacking."

Brina didn't reply, unsure what to make of this.

"I will ask you again, what brought you here?"

"You did. Because you were done playing games with us, and we were on the verge of murdering each other."

"Oh no," Wiley said, with the casual demeanor of a man asked whether it will rain later. "Besides, to me, it didn't sound like you were in trouble at all. In fact, it sounded like you had things under control."

"What do you mean?" Brina asked, frowning.

"You turned a deadly situation into renewed vigor to find a way out of here. When others stood nose to nose, knives drawn, you remained calm and made sure that no energy was wasted. That is a rare gift."

The question that had been gnawing at Brina ever since the conversation had begun now burst from her lips. "How do you know all this? You speak like you were there."

"That's a reasonable question with a complicated answer," Wiley said.

CHAPTER 66

"How about this? I shall go for a nap, and when I wake up, I want to remember promising to teach you everything I know. The memory should feel so real that I believe that I myself have decided that you are worthy of my teachings. I gather you are capable of such trickery."

Brina was getting sketched out. "No. I don't want to manipulate you."

"It's not manipulation if one asks for it, is it? Consider it a test. I have a theory that I would very much like to put to the test."

Brina looked out of the window once again and found that she had almost stopped noticing the droning harmonies around her. Instead, she felt at ease, not at all perturbed by the strange company she found herself in. Outside, the mists receded. She could now make out the *Chimera*'s mast and Rundale sitting in the crow's nest with her spyglass, peering around fruitlessly.

"Fine," she said. "I'll try. I've only done it once before, though."

"Once is infinitely more than never," Wiley said. Brina wondered how the little man was going to get to sleep with her staring at him, but when she leaned over to look at what he was doing, she heard the low rumble of snoring. He was already gone.

Brina took a deep breath, then folded her fingers into the complicated sign Solana had taught her. Last time she'd gotten lucky to find the darkhelm officer willing to submit to her influence. Panic reached for Brina's throat as she peered down at the sleeping figure. She got up from the armchair, knelt in front of Wiley, and attempted to clear her mind to make room for the shape's power.

"A young woman will visit you today," Brina said, attuning to the prayer of dreams. "She needs to know what you have learned. It is of the utmost importance that you aid her in her pursuit of justice for all." Brina continued whispering in Walter's ear until she had tried just about every variation on a similar theme. She felt rather silly, speaking into a sleeping man's ear, and still wasn't convinced that Wiley wasn't tricking her somehow. When she was done, she grabbed Wiley's shoulder and shook him. The little man awoke with a start.

"Wait," he smiled, "I had a dream about you."

"I know you did," Brina said. "You summoned me here to learn from you, and I'm ready."

Wiley Walter smiled a toothy grin. "Right you are, so I did."

Brina wondered whether he was just playing along or whether Solana's shape had worked. For all his oddities, Walter seemed to be a powerful man, and the thought that she could mislead him was laughable. And yet, he got up, walked over to a trinket standing nearby, and beckoned her to join him.

"You know," he said, "I don't think I've ever met someone who was capable of two branches of sigilism."

"Excuse me?" Brina said.

Wiley smiled. "My child," he said, "of course, I can tell my own memories from an artificial one. They are like old friends to me. I notice when they suddenly sprout a boil from the tip of their noses." He twisted his ear hair around a bony finger. "Even so, it's there. You implanted a memory in me, as real as though I was there. That counts for something. Did you know that, aside from what we call sparkgazing and sense surging, a third art exists?"

A ripple of excitement coursed through Brina. She shook her head.

"Well, there is, and if I might be so arrogant, it's by far the most refined of the three branches. I call it wave watching. It consists of inducing a trance, during which our natural attunement to the world grows. It isn't as sudden as the sigils you burn behind your eyes, nor is it as brutally powerful as the finger contortions of the sense surger. No, wave watching requires time and finesse. It requires a total commitment to feeling what is going on around oneself. And those who want to do it right are best to spend their days in isolation."

"How does it work?" Brina asked, looking at the devices in front of Wiley.

"All one has to do," he said, "is listen. I constructed these devices myself, using a refined silver in which grains of fine quartz have been embedded. Quartzite hammers drag along the sounding plate, creating a perfect wave." He gestured for her to listen.

Now that Brina had gotten up from Wiley's chair, it was hard to hear anything at all. She strained to pick up the faintest trace of sound with *Auris*.

"Tut," Walter chided. "Those banal tricks will do little to help. You are supposed to listen. No more, no less."

Brina let go of *Auris*, and the clutter of noise that had swelled in her ears died down again.

"You're not alone," Walter said, a smirk creasing his lips. "Once we try, most of us find it harder than expected to listen. We are a species built on dialogue—giving and taking, acting and reacting. But I assure you, the universe has plenty to give, and she expects nothing in return."

Brina clenched her teeth. She still heard no sound emanating from the device and found herself distracted by Wiley, who was standing beside her with his eyes closed, bobbing his head up and down as though listening to a favorite tune. She opened her mouth to ask for more instructions, but the tiny man shook his head, eyes still closed.

CHAPTER 66

"Give it time," he said. "Most of us spend our entire lives missing things that are right in front of us because we couldn't be bothered to take the time."

Trying not to think about everyone waiting for her outside, Brina closed her own eyes and listened. *This is stupid. This guy's a lunatic.* She pushed the thoughts away. Every time similar thoughts arose, she fought the urge to open one eye and see what Wiley was doing.

The man probably spent most of his time up here, seated in his chair, listening to his trinkets. He had all the time in the world, and meanwhile, all the pressure in the world was bearing down on Brina's shoulders.

Her jaw tensed. She grew frustrated with herself for interrupting the experiment. It was clear Wiley expected something to happen. If it didn't, would he still help her find a way out of the Mist Strait? Could she lie to him and convince him she had heard something, even if she hadn't?

Next, Brina's thoughts wandered to the ship outside and the heavy winds that raged there. How was it that perfect silence reigned inside this tiny house, while the outside world battered its walls with rushing storms, cascading waves, and shouting sailors? Realizing that she was once again lost in thought, she let out a roar of frustration.

Beside her, Wiley chuckled.

"It can be tricky at first to quiet one's mind, even for practiced sigilists. The techniques you sparkgazers use require only superficial focus when compared to the fine art of wave watching. It will take time, but I don't doubt that you will figure it out."

"And why is that?" Brina sounded petulant even to her own ears. Her frustration with her lack of focus was shifting into annoyance toward the wispy man standing beside her, who seemed to only speak in riddles.

Wiley shrugged. "Some things one knows."

Then it hit Brina. If Wiley was aware of all the intricacies of what was going on in the outside world and spoke as though predicting the outcome of situations was a mere trifle to him, what else did he know? Maybe there was something he could foresee that could give the rebellion an edge in Bior. "Have you—"

"Foreseen what you are planning?" he asked, a twinkle in his eye.

Brina swallowed, then nodded.

Wiley sighed. Silence regained its grip on the cabin.

"Events have not unfolded in your favor. Every day, the balance in the Sundered Isles tilts further and further away from equilibrium. Dark times lay ahead."

He knows, Brina thought. *He knows what we're planning.* "So the empire will win the war. Is that what you are saying?"

Wiley shook his head. "That is not for me to say," he muttered. "But what I know is this: Though the cards have not fallen in your favor, you have one thing going in the right direction."

"And what is that?" Brina asked. At the moment, she didn't feel like anything was moving in the right direction.

"Aboard that very ship, lying in the bay below, are the Viper of Barangia and an agent of the Abbey of Everberg."

Brina tried her hardest not to show the disgust she felt at the mention of Solana.

"Sure," Wiley said, correctly guessing her sentiment. "You stand on opposite sides of the political and ideological struggle that is set to consume these lands. And yet, your ship remains whole. It has not been torn apart by the clash between the great powers that your father, the priestess, and you yourself carry. Despite all of that tension, you are still afloat. That means something."

"It's a matter of necessity, nothing more," Brina said.

Wiley shrugged. "Of course it is. When else have diametrically opposed people ever found common ground if not in the face of shared hardships?"

Brina sighed. She was growing tired of this.

"But what about Bior? What about the invasion? You must have sensed the movement of the Cardinal's troops and felt the nervous energy in the air. What have you foreseen about the clash that will happen on Bior?"

"So you still intend to fight?" Wiley asked.

Brina stared at him through narrowed eyes. "What else would we do?"

"You come here fleeing for your lives after the king of the Heemians tried to sell you to Mallion's Depth. I already know you were unsuccessful with the Morassians too," he said. He held up a hand when Brina started to ask questions. "Yes, I am aware of that, too. And unless I'm very much mistaken, you have just run out of options. The Cardinal's taxes and patrols weigh down every nation in the Sundered Isles. They haven't got so much as an inch of breathing room, and the only two peoples who could have been of any use to your purposes have chosen to maintain equilibrium for a few moments longer, instead of risking it all for a win. You must realize by now that if you choose to fight at Bior, you will fight alone. You will stand unsupported against a power far greater and, beg your pardon, far better trained."

"So you have seen the outcome, then?" Brina asked. There was a hollow feeling in her gut. Wiley was telling her, without so many words, that they

CHAPTER 66

were going like lambs to the slaughter.

"Surely, my child, I am telling you nothing you did not already guess? When two forces meet in a clash of arms, and the measure of their numbers is so unbalanced, there's very little that can be done. But," he said, "not all victories are military in nature."

"What does that mean?" Brina asked. "If we get slaughtered, we get slaughtered. There's no gray area when it comes to cold steel cutting through flesh."

"Sometimes the fact that a battle occurred at all is a victory in itself."

"Is that what we are supposed to tell the recruits? That they will be slaughtered, but that there is victory in death?" Brina asked.

Walter sighed. "Such trifles are not for me to decide. I have said all I can on the subject, I'm afraid."

"And what will you do?" Brina asked the old man, her temper flaring. "You're telling me I should walk into an unwinnable battle, to prove some kind of point? Will you join me? Will you die by my side? Or will you hide out here, surrounded by mist and treacherous waters?"

"Someone has to keep watch," Wiley said. Brina scoffed, then made her way back to the trapdoor from which she'd come. She had had enough of the old man and his babbling. It was all nonsense anyway.

As the trapdoor opened and Brina had her feet on the first rung of the rope ladder, Wiley's voice carried after her. "And here I thought you would ask me how to find your way out of my strait."

Brina's heart dropped, as though she'd missed a couple of steps striding down the stairs. Of course, that had been the whole point of her coming here. Wiley had made her head spin with his predictions. She had almost gone back down to the ship, just as empty-handed as when she had crawled up here.

She nodded, unable to bandy one more word with the old man. His prophecies had made her sick to her stomach. Until this point, she had believed that there would be some miracle, a stroke of genius, or the sheer strength of courage that could turn the tide of war at Bior. But now she had heard it, right out of the mouth of the only man who could foresee the unforeseeable. Their doom was already written in the stars.

"Here," Wiley said. He kneeled down beside the trapdoor and handed Brina the device she had tried fruitlessly to hear.

"What is this?" she asked.

"And here I thought you'd been listening to an old man's mutterings," Wiley replied.

"No, I'm sorry. I mean, I know what it is, but how will it help me lead the ship out of the mists?" Brina asked.

"All you need to do is listen," Wiley said. There was a last flash of grinning yellow teeth, then the trapdoor closed overhead.

CHAPTER 67

Early the next morning, a knock sounded at the door. Brina rolled out of bed as quickly as her injured leg allowed, rubbing her face. She couldn't recall falling asleep. Wiley Walter's device lay on the floor. In the light of day it looked innocent, but last night Brina had learned its true nature.

"Go away," Brina barked, "I'm working."

"Come on," Sneak's voice called from the other side of the door. "The least you could do is talk to us. People are growing restless. If you could just tell us what's going on, maybe…"

Brina yanked the door open. Sneak took a quick step backward. His face drained of color as he saw her. "You look terrible. Did you just wake up?" His eyes narrowed.

"Like I said," Brina grunted, "I was busy."

"Fine," Sneak said, "I get it. But you can't blame the crew for worrying. All we saw was you returning empty-handed from a ladder reaching high into the sky, looking furious. We didn't know what to think. You can't expect people to sit around wondering whether they'll live or starve. So, which is it going to be?"

Brina sighed, scratching at her tangled black hair. "I'm trying to figure that out myself."

"So he didn't help you? The Keeper of the Strait?"

Brina shrugged. "I believe he thinks he did. It's just that he should've given me a map instead of whatever this is." She picked up the device from the floor and waved it in Sneak's face. "It's supposed to help me get us out of here. But so far, no luck."

Sneak's face lit up. "That's excellent. We've got the key to our problem. The only thing we need now is to…"

"Give me some time," Brina said.

"But surely, Solana or Abrasax could know something about this, too?

Why do you have to do it alone?"

For a moment, Brina contemplated telling him the truth—of how the device had tormented her through the previous night, the pain it induced when she attempted to tune into its vibrations, but that would entail telling him about Wiley Walter's grim predictions as well. She couldn't bear to say those words out loud. So instead, she lied.

"Wiley Walter said it's my problem and mine alone. He'll know if I seek help, he'll sabotage us again. I think this is his idea of a twisted joke."

Sneak blinked. "He told you all that?"

Brina shrugged. "He's been up there all alone for all those years. Gives a man a lot of time to go insane."

"I suppose." He put a hand on her shoulder. "You'll figure it out. I'll go up and tell the others we're making progress, but we're not there yet. That should keep them busy for another day or so. Buys you a little peace to work on this thing. And remember, if there's anything any of us can do, all you need to do is ask."

Brina attempted a smile and failed. Instead, she closed the door in Sneak's face. As soon as she heard his footsteps receding in the hallway beyond, she sat back down at her writing desk, the humming device placed in front of her. Even before she attempted to listen to its low hum, she winced. It would happen again. She was sure of it. And what if this time, she failed to snap out of it?

So be it.

For the briefest instant, a clear chime resonated throughout the ship's cabin. Brina could almost see the mist lift beyond her small window. Then it struck. The cabin whirled away around her. She sank through the wooden floor and found herself trudging through a swampy forest. She sank into a patch of mud down to her waist.

Bron hung from a branch high above, arms outstretched, quivering with the effort of holding on. "You said you would help me!" He growled in between heaving breaths. "You said you wouldn't let me fall."

"I'm trying," Brina responded, pulling against the suction of the mud. "But everything's working against me."

Something moved to her left. Brina raised an instinctive arm to shield her face just in time as a giant anaconda clamped its massive jaws down on her arm. It pulled her down with immense force. With one desperate look at Bron, she watched the Biori tumble down, falling head over heels toward the forest floor.

CHAPTER 67

Then the mud closed over her head. Pulled lower and lower, unable to breathe, Brina writhed and struggled against the serpent's grip on her arm. It was futile. Suddenly, her feet struck solid ground. The mud cleared around her, and when she opened her eyes, she was standing on a mound of armored corpses. They were adrift on a river of blood. The surrounding countryside was scorched black. Smoke and ash littered the ground where grass had once grown, and huge blackened stumps were all that remained of the trees. The corpses beneath her feet wailed and groaned, their armor creaking as the ghastly flotsam was carried down the bloody river.

"Why did you bring us here?" a woman near the top of the pile cried out at Brina. Her head was detached from her body, which lay lower on the pile. The helmet framing her face was dented and streaked with blood. "We believed you would lead us to victory. Instead, you led us into the abyss."

Brina kneeled down, her knees scraping on the heavy armor. "I promised my friends we would help. It was the right thing to do. We fought to halt the empire's advance."

"We fought," a man below her feet growled, "and we died. And you knew!" The other corpses in the pile joined in the chant, "You knew! You knew! You knew!"

With a jolt, Brina was sitting behind her desk once more. Hot blood trickled down her face. She shook herself. They were tears. Not blood. Simple human tears. The vision was gone. *It's gone,* she told herself. *It's over.* When she realized the device on her desk had triggered another round of gruesome hallucinations without giving up any of its secrets, she flung it against the far wall, screaming at the top of her lungs.

Why had Wiley Walter done this to her? He could've lifted the fog and allowed them to exit. Instead, he had given her a cursed gift—the responsibility of leading her crew out of the Mist Strait, and the reality that she couldn't do so. Somewhere in this tangle of jumbled desires, fears, and worries was a lesson, Brina was sure of it. It was just the type of thing a crooked old bastard like Walter would come up with. But she didn't want wisdom, she wanted answers.

She picked up the device and placed it in front of her on the desk once more. What did it mean? Walter had said that even lost battles were worth fighting. Why then was the device showing her all of this? Were these visions the future, or her own fears?

Think, Springtide, think.

Did it make a difference? That was the question that pushed itself to the forefront of her mind. If the images that the device was showing her were the future, would she abandon her resolve to defend Bior? The harsh truths of Archdruidess Evanna's refusal and King Krocht's cowardice would not dissuade her from helping those who would soon feel the empire's wrath. She stared out into the mist outside, watching the rise and fall of the sea.

She sat there for a long time, contemplating the question and its implications. If what she was seeing horrified her, did that mean that she would look away from it? The answer came to her as easily as the exhalation of her next breath. Of course, it didn't matter. Even if she had to go alone, she would set sail for Bior and she would be there when the Cardinal's troops landed. If certain death was the price of resistance, that was fine by Brina.

She remembered Acheron's words when she was in the throes of the venom's embrace. It all came down to one moment of absolute resistance. Of showing that she was free and that the empire did not control her. What did it matter that the Morassians and Heemians had refused the call? What did an old man's predictions matter? She knew now, as she had known months ago, what needed to be done. She had known it as soon as she unfurled the scrap of parchment she'd stolen from the guard tower in Doorstep's Ditch. There was no question if there was only one answer. It didn't matter.

She slunk back in her chair, relief washing over her. The agonizing weight of the responsibility she felt toward everyone around her gave way. She knew in her heart what the right thing to do was. And that was all that mattered. A ringing rose in Brina's ears as the device whirred away on her desktop. This time, when the images of horror rose, she pushed them away with a light touch. They were irrelevant. They were nightmares evaporating in the dawn. She knew she would do what needed to be done, no matter what.

Outside, the mist lightened, until the vast peaks of the rocky spires that littered the Mist Strait came into view. Far off in the distance, she could see the canyon give way to open sea.

CHAPTER 68

"We made it," Sneak called from the top of the crow's nest. The mast creaked as the ship bobbed up and down amidst the heaving swells of the sea. Brina ran over to the starboard side, eager to catch a first glimpse of the rippling jungle and crumbling walls of Metten.

"Blood of my mothers," Bron said beside her, his huge hands clasping at the wooden railing. "I didn't think we'd ever see those towers again." His round face appeared sunken underneath a mass of ginger beard.

The dressing gown Brina had worn since their escape from Onderheem hung loosely from her diminished frame. She felt like a child wearing an older sibling's hand-me-downs. Just yesterday, she'd been forced to add yet another hole to her belt.

With nothing but seawater to bathe themselves, her hair was hard and crusted with salt, sticking out in unruly tufts.

As the shoreline of Metten drew closer, Brina salivated, as though the nearing promise of fresh water had already cascaded from her mind into her leathery mouth.

"What's the first thing you're going to do when we land?" Brina asked Bron, who stood beside her. He ran a hand through his scraggly beard, then said, "Find Bahov, and have him make me another spear."

There was sadness in his voice. He had lost his weapon in the commotion during their escape from Onderheem. And though Brina didn't understand the ceremonial value of it fully, Bron hadn't quite been the same ever since.

"I doubt we'll be doing much fighting soon," Brina replied.

"It's not about that. I feel naked without it, like a boar who's lost his tusks. We are to carry our spear with us at all times. Our first one is granted to us when we become adults. Traditionally, they are made by our direct ancestor. A daughter's weapon is made by her mother, and so mine was made by my father. He carved the tip out of the bone of a mighty erymanthian he'd slain. Its haft was constructed with wood from a tree planted the day of my birth." He paused and cleared his throat. "It was irreplaceable. Losing it is a great shame."

"Couldn't we visit your father when we sail for Bior?" Brina asked. Bron looked up at her. The look in his eyes said it all.

"I'm sorry for your loss. When did he...?"

"Bay of Bones," Bron muttered. "Very first day of Estav's invasion. We weren't ready for it. Many soldiers died that day. Most who were old enough to bear arms. I was sent away with my younger brothers and sisters to watch over them and guide them to the safety of Mother's Mount, our capital. Neither my mother nor my father survived that first wave of the invasion."

"That's horrible," Brina said.

Bron's eyes lingered on the slanted ruin of the central donjon of Metten's fortress.

"They had a good death," he said. "They fell defending our nation's honor. Our forebears will welcome them in the eternal village with open arms. I do not weep for them. I weep for myself, and for the fact that I was not there to die alongside them. It would've been my greatest honor. Instead, I ran halfway across the Sundered Isles to Barangia, looking to join one of the mercenary crews of my people for gem dust. In the end, I chose an employer that pays me little by comparison." He chuckled.

"You mean Saf?" Brina smiled.

Bron nodded. "Once I realized that most mercenaries go where the money is, which is the empire, it was hard to pass up an offer to join someone willing to risk it all to kill as many of those darkhelmed bastards as possible."

"And with any luck," Brina said, a sly smile creeping on her face, "we'll get to kill many more soon."

"Aye," Bron said. "Let's hope so."

When they arrived at Metten, Brina was embarrassed to find over a hundred new recruits lined up along the makeshift docks in a formal salute. She lifted her arm to return the greeting, caught a whiff of her own armpits, and winced.

Cheers erupted from the crowd as they staggered across the gangplank. The effects of malnutrition and poor sleep made their legs unsteady. As the recruits parted to form an aisle of honor, Brina caught sight of the Biori war leader, Bahov, who was prodding the recruits with a wooden stick, pushing them to straighten their backs and lift their spears.

At the end of the line, in between both rows, stood Saf, beaming, arms outstretched.

CHAPTER 68

"Welcome back," she said. "I assume there is much to talk about?"

"More than you'd like," Sneak muttered under his breath, drawing a chuckle from Brina. The group had been on the verge of drawing straws to see who would be the unfortunate miscreant to inform Saf that their mission—their last-ditch effort to prevent the empire from seizing Bior and the resources that it held—had been a fatal disaster.

It was a bleak summary. Brina was torn between laughter and tears as she trailed behind Saf and Abrasax, who led the group up the broken steps toward the donjon inside the fortress. First, they had almost been eaten by the Morassians' hydra-god, after which Archdruidess Evanna had told Abrasax she planned on hiding away in the swampy jungle of her homeland. Then, circumstance had forced them to take on a church-affiliated fugitive, whose loyalties were, as far as Brina was concerned, dubious at best. To top it all off, King Krocht of Onderheem had tried to use them as a bargaining chip in his own negotiations with the empire, causing them to plunge the Shimmering City and the harbor town of Cordwain into chaos on their way out.

Brina ran a hand through her salt-crusted hair and stifled a groan. Yes, things had gone just about as poorly as they could have. And she hadn't even found the courage to tell the others what Wiley Walter had revealed to her in the foggy confines of his cabin atop the stone spire in the Mist Strait. If Walter's predictions were accurate, they were doomed.

CHAPTER 69

o neither of them will come?" Saf asked, her thin fingers clamped upon the white sandstone windowsill like a crow's claws digging into a carcass.

"I'm afraid so," Abrasax replied. He was the only one who had gotten up from his seat at the long, polished marble table at which all of them sat.

Samok, at the far end of the table, looked from one end to the other, his wide eyes tracing every movement in the room, as though he still wasn't sure where he was and whether he was even supposed to be here. The rest of the crew were enjoying a few well-earned comforts after the voyage, but since Samok had captained their journey aboard the *Chimera*, Brina had dragged him along with her.

"I thought you said you could handle this assignment," Saf told Abrasax, not bothering to whisper. "What happened?"

Abrasax opened his mouth to speak, but Saf interrupted, her voice soaked in despair. "Did you explain to the archdruidess just how much she stands to lose?"

"Obviously," Abrasax said. "We did everything we could, but I'm afraid there are very few arguments that can convince a mole to stop burrowing."

"That mole has an entire nation's worth of sickles at her command," Saf said. Her nails raked across her forearms, leaving shallow scratches.

Abrasax let out a tired sigh. "It's how the Morassians have always dealt with crises. When things get too hot for them on the beaches of their lands, they retreat into the shade of the forest until times change. In the year 378, Archdruid Nichlay retreated to Sunken Spire, after which no Morassian was seen for two hundred years."

Saf waved an impatient hand. "I know, I know. I have eyes. I can read."

"Then you know that this strategy has served them well in the past, and they hope it will do so again."

"Except it won't," Saf spat. "The church has changed. They aren't content

CHAPTER 69

to send a handful of preachers around the continent or to seize the resources they deem favorable. We now suffer from a Cardinal who aims for total subjugation. He desires control of every living soul. There is no hiding from a person like that. He will uproot every tree on that island if he has to."

"You're right," Abrasax said. The muscles in his jaws clenched. "I tried to convince Evanna of that very fact, but I'm afraid my counsel is worth little in the face of imminent destruction."

"So it would seem," Saf snapped. "And Onderheem?"

"That bastard Krocht set us up," Bron grunted, his fist slamming into the tabletop. "He sold us out to save his own stinking skin."

Saf's face paled. "What do you mean 'sold you out'?"

"Exactly what it sounds like," Brina said. "He threw us a feast to make sure we would be where he wanted us, and then he traded the freedom of his people for ours."

Saf let out a low groan. "I take it your departure from the mountain was less than quiet?"

"Well, it wasn't subtle," Sneak said. "I can tell you that much. Though I suppose on the bright side, there's a couple dozen fewer darkhelms to worry about."

A silence fell in the room as the magnitude of their failure hung in the air. They hadn't just failed to gain allies; they had made a bunch of new enemies.

"Let's focus on the one thing that's still in our control," Saf said. She strode over to the table and bent down to pick up a scroll of parchment. As she unfurled it, an entire world blossomed on the wooden tabletop. The horseshoe-shaped Isle of Bior was drawn in great detail. Every individual fortification and village was noted down. "Does this seem accurate to you? "

"It looks old," Bron said.

"And yet it is very new. Your mentor, Bahov, helped me make this. We used a handful of existing documents and his own remembrance of the place."

Bron nodded at the mention of Bahov's name. "I'm afraid some of the fortification data are out of date," he said. "For example, the west wall, here, has been pushed back almost a mile in this direction." His finger prodded at the parchment. "Some watchtowers on it are gone as well. I can help you correct it, though."

"That's what I was counting on. In the meantime, we ought to prepare for the oncoming assault," Saf said. She pointed at a dark section of the map. "This area near the Bay of Bones is still in the empire's hands, I take it?"

Bron nodded, then spat on the smooth sandstone floor underneath the table.

"Bastards. They keep about two hundred of my brothers and sisters as prisoners," he said. "They force them to work on their whaling ships."

"Ah, yes," Abrasax interjected, "the whale pods. That'll be one resource the church will be loath to let go off."

"Resource?" Bron asked with disgust. "They are gods. Breathing remnants of a time far more ancient than any church or empire dreamed up by humans. But we remember; we Biori remember where life came from, and these bastards... they go out with their ships year-round, forcing my brothers and sisters to wrench that which is not freely given from the grasp of our ancestors. It's not right. They must be so disappointed in us." His voice was choked with emotion.

"Whalebone arrows are about the sharpest anyone can manufacture," Abrasax said. "Do it right, and the very tip breaks off in an opponent's flesh, making it almost impossible for anyone less than a skilled surgeon to remove. Combine that with depriving your people of an important food source, and the strategic value becomes enormous."

Bron shot him a look that could have melted steel.

Saf smiled. "Good."

"How is any of that good?" Sneak exclaimed, shaking his head. "Honestly, Saf, sometimes I worry."

"It's good because it means that our most important ally is already within the walls. Two hundred Biori, already inside the empire's fortifications, could be the difference between victory and crushing defeat."

She turned toward Bron. "Am I right in assuming that these people will help us if we can get word to them?"

"Any of them would kill a darkhelm as soon as they got the chance," Bron said.

"Perfect," Saf said. "Now let's consider what offensive strategies the church has at its disposal." She pointed down at a section of land between the western wall of Bior and the Bay of Bones fortifications the empire had built. "Bahov tells me that the strip of land between both settlements is a swamp during dry season, a lake during the wet months."

Bron nodded. "Aye, it's what saved my people in the end. When what remained of our army after the initial invasion was retreating deeper toward the center of the island, the darkhelms, stomping through areas they knew nothing about, got themselves stuck. Many drowned, and those who didn't met with our wrath. The marshes are only traversable by those who've spent a lifetime navigating them. Some of the darkhelms may have learned by now,

CHAPTER 69

but not the ones they're importing for this assault. I doubt they will try to come through there. It would be too obvious and too difficult."

"My thoughts exactly," Saf said. "Then where else could they land?"

Bron shrugged. "The center of the island is guarded well. And the cliffs near the water are steep. It would be hard to land there. We could reach them with a barrage of quarrels, stones, and boiling oil while they were still on the beach."

"Right," Saf said, "and if we assume our enemies are no fools, they will have come to similar conclusions. Which leaves the far tip of the horseshoe, the eastern side of the island. Bahov tells me that the mountains level out near Antler's Grove, where the country turns into level plains surrounded by sea."

Bron nodded. "Only hunters dwell there," he said, "collecting erymanthian when they are in season, or pronghorn when there's no other choice. It would be hard to keep the darkhelms from landing there. There must be close to thirty miles of clean coastline with no real defenses in place. "

"I agree," Abrasax said. "If I were them, that would be my choice. Even though we will see them coming a long way away, it'll be impossible to prevent them from getting boots on the ground. After that, their superior numbers will do the rest."

"That is what I feared." Saf tapped a long nail against the marble tabletop.

Brina stared at her own hands, twisting together in her lap. Deep creases of doubt were forming in her stomach. She had to tell them. The others were still struggling to find a solution, when Brina already knew it was hopeless. Wiley Walter had told her as much. She ground her teeth, staving off the moment she would have to interrupt their plotting and set fire to the entire undertaking.

She reached for a bottle of kelp rum she had hidden away underneath the table months ago and was glad to find it still there. The liquid sloshed around as she struggled with the cork. Saf threw her a sideways glance, but was too deep in argument with Abrasax to say anything. Brina removed the stopper with her teeth and drank. She didn't stop. As soon as the bottle touched the table, she would have to speak up. After weeks of privation, the liquor ran down her throat like molten lead.

Her nerves jangled for a moment, then she felt the comforting numbness set in. She thought of Acheron. That man had had a way of saying the grimmest things with a smile on his face. He did it so casually you almost didn't register what you'd heard. It was a skill Brina did not possess, and she wouldn't have time to learn.

She set down the bottle, rubbed her fingers in her tired eyes, and waved a hand at Saf and Abrasax, whose voices were rising in volume with every passing moment.

"What I'm saying," Abrasax yelled, "is that we ought to hide our troops as far outside of the walls as possible. We could ambush them while they're still in travel mode. Their column will be long and vulnerable. They will expect us to wait behind the walls of Mother's Mount. I say we go for the surprise."

"That's the most foolish thing I've heard all day, and you've said quite a lot," Saf replied. "Those walls were built for a purpose. We could..."

"We could do whatever we wanted, and it still wouldn't matter," Brina said. All eyes in the room turned toward her.

"What do you mean?" Abrasax asked. "Of course it matters; we have limited pawns, sure, but where we place them could make all the difference in the world."

"You're not listening," Brina repeated. "When I was with Walter, he told me something."

"Who is this?" Saf interjected.

"The Keeper of the Mist Strait," Abrasax said out of the corner of his mouth. "Now, what did he say?"

Brina spoke slowly, dreading every word. "He has been watching the waves for months, trying to predict the future of the Sundered Isles. According to him, there can be no victory at Bior."

Silence lingered, broken only by the nervous shuffling of feet against the wooden floor and the creaking of chairs as people slumped where they sat.

"You spoke with the Keeper of the Strait?" Saf's eyes narrowed as she regarded Brina. "In what form did he appear to you?"

Taken aback, Brina took another sip of rum. "A man," she said with a shrug, "an old, skinny man. There wasn't anything special about him."

"Oh, but there is," Saf said. "The wave watcher of the Mist Strait has been regarding all goings-on in this part of the world for centuries now. He knows how every leaf will fall, even before the tree has bloomed. He sees what is inside us, even if we ourselves do not."

"Wiley said that while us putting up a fight will be a victory in itself, we will not win this war on Bior. I don't want to believe it, but somehow I do." Brina looked out the window at the blue skies beyond. "There was something about the way he said it, as though he was reading his own journal entries from days yet to happen."

"Yes." A prolonged sigh escaped Saf. "They say he can be quite convincing."

CHAPTER 70

rina sat back in her chair. She had expected to be relieved once the burden of Wiley Walter's prediction was no longer hers to carry alone. Instead, she felt hollow. Where moments prior the room had been filled with talk of strategy, ambushes and charges, there was now only a despondent vacancy. A crater left by the newfound knowledge that hope was folly. The map of Bior in the table's center seemed to grow blood red in the light of the setting sun.

"This cannot leave this room," Saf said. Everyone looked at her in disbelief. "If the recruits catch so much as a whiff of this, no cause on this earth will get them onto those ships. And I do not intend to let the Biori die alone. Even if we lose the battle, a shared sacrifice might convince their fiercest warriors to resist being drafted into De Leliard's hordes."

"So you suggest we lie?" Samok interjected. It was the first time he'd spoken, and his words fell like a hammer.

"It's not lying if we neglect to inform them of something." Saf began pacing along the donjon's circular wall. "And what is there to tell? That some old fool says we can't win? The watcher of the strait has no more knowledge of the future than any of us do."

"You know that's not true," Abrasax said. "You've looked for him. I saw it in your eyes earlier. Just like me, you tried to find him, but he wouldn't appear to you."

"I don't see how that matters," Saf said.

"It matters," Abrasax said, "because you, just like me and Brina, realize what kind of power he possesses. He may not have the future written out word for word, but he has a feel for things. And if he feels that defeat is imminent, we would do well to heed his words."

Saf's mouth moved, but she didn't reply.

"Brina," Abrasax said, his voice lower than when he addressed Saf, "what did he say exactly? Every word matters when it comes to the watcher."

"He said not all victories are military in nature, that sometimes the fact that a battle occurred at all is a victory in itself." Brina shook her head as she spoke. The memory of those words was a brick in her stomach.

"See," Saf said, extending an arm toward Brina, "how are we going to sell that to an army of recruits who have never set foot on a battlefield? 'Oh, don't worry, we're going to lose, but the battle has value of its own.'" She shook her head. "If we want to send even one full ship to Bior, we need to keep our mouths shut."

"That amounts to murder." Abrasax stood up. His thin frame reached almost to the room's ceiling. With his back straight and chin raised, he towered over all of them. His scraggly beard quivered with anger as he looked down at Saf. "Our enemies may scoff at the notion of freedom, but I will not send even a single soldier into the fray based on lies."

"Do you want to abandon all hope of defending our one remaining ally, on the word of one old man?" Saf turned around and leaned on the windowsill, her outline ink black against the last light of the sun.

"That's not what I said," Abrasax countered, his voice growing colder. "I said we should let the recruits choose for themselves which path they want to take. They are not our prisoners or our mercenaries. They are volunteers—"

"Who joined a cause, knowing in advance it could end in death," Saf shouted. "If we want to play the game, we need pawns. And I tell you now, none of those pawns will voluntarily board our ships if they hear that prophecy."

"Then so be it." Abrasax threw up his arms.

"I shall lead by example." Brina took a swig from the bottle of rum and stood up, facing Saf. She'd had just about enough of this talk of deceit. They were talking about people, not cattle. Saf had sunken so deep in her tallies of rations and ledgers of weaponry, armor, and tools that she had forgotten the essence of what made them different from the Heilinists. "I promised you if you helped me free my father, I would do whatever it took to help the rebellion succeed. I will keep my word, but I won't drag anyone into death with me based on lies. These are the options. You can detain me, or I will walk out and inform everyone of what we know."

Saf's face grew pale. "You wouldn't."

"Yes, I would. And you will thank me for it once you realize the weight of what you are proposing. This is not who we are. Our recruits are just as important as we are. If we get to make a decision, they get to make one too."

"Hear, hear," Bron said. "I won't fight alongside those who lose their courage when they see just how long the arm of the church has grown. I aim for

CHAPTER 70

a good death, one fighting alongside those with lion hearts, not whimpering cowards surprised to find themselves in water too deep for them."

Brina raised the almost empty bottle of kelp toward him, took one final swig, then stood up and marched out of the room.

***

"It's a miracle even this many showed up," Bron grunted as he and Brina watched the assembled recruits split up into three squads of a hundred each.

Even though Wiley Walters's prophecy had scared off almost half of the rebel warriors, the other half was as determined as ever to fight and not give up another inch of territory to the scepter unchallenged.

"True warriors, no doubt about it," Brina said.

"Yes, but there aren't enough of them," a voice rang out behind her. She turned to find Saf standing on the ship's main deck, leaning against the mast. "These numbers will be little more than an annoyance to the darkhelms."

"What'll happen to those who stay here?" Brina asked, nodding toward an uneasy-looking mass of recruits, who stood at the edge of the citadel's walls, shifting uncomfortably as their compatriots finished loading up the last of the three ships.

"Bahov is coming with you," Saf said. "So, I've agreed to keep training them and oversee the new arrivals. We've spent too much time forming this motley band into something resembling an army to stop now."

"Does that mean you're staying?" Brina could feel her face flushing. Though rationally, she knew someone ought to stay behind and manage the rebellion's next steps, she was growing frustrated with Saf's hands-off approach. It reeked of something the Cardinal would do: shifting pawns on a map, drawing up plans, but never getting his own boots dirty.

That's not fair. Someone has to do it. Saf's put in her time already, and when the time is right, she will do so again. Or at least that's what Brina wanted to believe. Staring into the woman's expressionless face, it was hard to discern any certainties.

"So, you're not coming, huh?" Brina kept her eyes fixed on a cluster of seagulls fighting over half a fish on the shoreline.

"You know I want to," Saf said, her mouth twitching. Bron walked away, ostensibly to check on Samok, who was tallying barrels of water, but Brina wasn't fooled.

"If I leave," Saf said, "and all of us are killed, what then?"

Brina gave a mirthless chuckle as the biggest of the gulls swallowed the remainder of the fish's tail whole. "There'd be close to three hundred leaderless recruits in a ruin in the jungle."

"That about sums it up." Saf sighed. "As long as I'm here, we can keep things on track. Word of mouth is still spreading. Our allies in Doorstep's Ditch are campaigning as we speak. We need to make use of that momentum, no matter the outcome of the assault on Bior. Dark times lie ahead, and people aren't ready for them. Through happenstance, we've just filtered out the bravest half of our supporters. The others need a leader. They need me to keep them focused."

"Politics." It was all Brina could think to say.

"It's a compromise. I know how you feel about those," Saf said, a faint smile curling her lips. "But that is what this all comes down to in the end. Our opponent is playing the game, and flipping over the table won't change the fact that we're losing."

Brina shook her head; there was always an explanation, always a logical argument. "When you see the enemy, you fight them. That's always been my motto. Everything else is just playing for time."

Saf took a step closer and took both of Brina's hands in her own. Brina fought the desire to jerk them back, but in the end, she allowed it.

"That's what I've always admired about you, you know," Saf said. "You know what you stand for, and you take the most direct route to get there. There is beauty in that. Once you start strategizing and weighing the costs and benefits of fighting back and when to do so, you lose that sense of urgency. It becomes almost like a game."

She stared off into the distance, and for a moment, they both watched the shoreline of Bior appearing and vanishing as the swells of the ocean rose and fell.

"Sometimes I think I can see a flicker of light on the horizon still," Saf said. "Other days, I wake up, to find myself at the helm of a vast rudderless ship, jerking the wheel back and forth, while a vast cliff rushes to meet me. No matter which way I turn, catastrophe seems inevitable."

"You carry your own weight," Brina said, squeezing Saf's hands.

"It will haunt me forever, I'm afraid," Saf said, her voice sinking to a drone. "Looking at these soldiers and knowing that we could've doubled their number, and in doing so, have given them a fair shot at victory, no matter how slim. Informing them of the prophecy was the right thing to do. And yet, it made it even more likely that none of these soldiers will live free lives.

CHAPTER 70

"Those are the things I think about before I go to sleep at night," Saf continued. "The realization that a clean conscience is a luxury that comes at a cost. Do you understand what I mean?"

Brina nodded. It was painfully similar to something Acheron had told her over a year ago now, which had always stuck with her. *We do what we do for the cause, and that is the weight we bear.*

Until now, Brina had considered the implications of that for how she'd treated enemies as she slit throats and cracked skulls, finding it easier and easier as time went on. Perhaps too easy. But now, with a dizzying swirl of realization, she realized it applied to their allies all the same.

It had been Brina who had insisted the prophecy be shared. And if it was nonsense, an accusatory voice in her head droned, *you may have just turned a victory into a defeat and sent hundreds to the slaughter.*

She removed her hands from Saf's grip, clenching the muscles in her jaw. For better or worse, they had made their choice, and just across the narrow gangplank, a small army of men and women willing to die for their beliefs stood waiting for her command.

"A clean conscience is a luxury indeed," she murmured, turning away from Saf. Unable to look the woman in the eye, she raised her voice, addressing the gathered recruits. "Eat and drink while you still can. We embark at noon."

She turned on her heel and walked away from Saf, across the gangplank, to have one last meal alone, before she faced the great unknown.

CHAPTER 71

The palisade wall of Bior's capital, Mother's Mount, rose from the mountainside like a jagged hydra's tail. Built in multiple tiers, the city stretched from the base all the way to the top of a steep hill. At the very top, the headmother's palace towered over them, one of the few buildings constructed out of stone. Its limestone roof glittered in the afternoon sun.

As they marched through the open gate and into a maze of narrow, muddy streets lined with hundreds of curious onlookers, Brina couldn't help but feel that the wooden fortifications of the city looked flimsy compared to the mighty stoneward in whose shadow she had grown up.

Marching between Bahov and Bron at the head of the column, she was introduced to various acquaintances and family members of both men. People waved at her everywhere she looked. Brina couldn't remember the last time anyone had been glad to see her, not to mention a crowd.

The wooden single-story houses crowded together closer and closer as they ascended the tiers of the city.

"The buildings at the top are the oldest," Bron said, pointing out a crest that swung from an inn's entrance, noting the opening year as 126 of the Mother's Birth. At least five hundred years old, if Brina's translation to the common Heilinist time reckoning was correct.

"As the city grew, we added ever more tiers," Bahov said, stroking his beard and waving left and right like a benevolent king. "They're like the rings of life on a tree; each of them marks an era of growth for our people."

"And let us hope we get to add a few more," Bron grunted. "Things look sorrier here than I remember."

Brina realized what he meant. The handful of merchants that lined the houses on a small cobbled square had lackluster assortments of wares. Remnants of fruit, much of it already sporting the dark stains of rot, lay at the bottom of crates as flies buzzed around. The fish offered by a stinking saleswoman at the very end of the square were small and sickly looking. Even in dire straits, most fishermen would have tossed them into the chum bucket.

As they wound their way up the hill, the crowds thinned like trees on a mountainside.

"It's mostly the nobles and elders up here these days," Bron said. "Only the oldest families have property in the deepest two circles. There are no real homes up here, only status symbols maintained by the wealthy. The closer you are to the headmother, the more important you are. Or so they say."

The dwellings beside the road had shifted from daub-and-wattle shacks with straw roofs to opulent wooden facades with pillars carved to resemble snarling bears, regal wolves, and breaching whales. Raw gemstones were set over doorways like glaring eyes.

"My parents—I mean, we used to live near the back of that hamlet over there." Bron pointed out a U-shaped street surrounded by elegant wooden houses. In the middle of the street stood a bronze statue of a fierce warrior, holding her broken spear over her head in both hands. Her expression was something between rage and ecstasy. "I moved to a dosshouse in the lower tiers when I turned thirteen. My mother thought it would—"

His voice died in his throat as they passed underneath a gatehouse and stumbled upon the headmother's palace. Though Bron and Bahov had called it a palace, Brina thought it was more of a fortress. It was a utilitarian block of stone, chiseled from vast blocks of limestone. Countless towers, with gaping murder holes, loomed over the courtyard and the lower tiers of the city. The palace was surrounded by a wide moat and atop its exterior wall, dozens of guards carrying long spears patrolled. Brina's confidence in the city's fortifications rose at once.

Biori warriors, carrying the traditional two-handed spear, bowed as they entered through a vaulted stone gate into the palace's courtyard, which was soon filled with the recruits trailing behind them. Stone steps on the far end of the courtyard led to an inner hall, between whose open doors stood Gavitt Akt, the current Biori headmother and a distant relation to Bahov. She was short, but broad. Two ginger braids fell across her gleaming steel chest plate. Her spear lay on a long velvet pillow carried by two servants who stood at her side.

As they approached, Gavitt lowered her forehead in a gesture Brina had seen Bron make on countless occasions. Bahov approached the headmother, grabbed her head in both of his hands as she did the same, and slammed his forehead into hers. There was a loud thunk, after which the headmother grabbed his forearm and spoke. "Well met, we are glad to have you back. We were much pleased when word reached us about your renewed freedom."

"Those bastards are gonna be sorry they ever kept me on that damn island," Bahov grunted. He wiped his hands on his breeches, as though the very memory of it made him feel dirty.

"Make it so," Gavitt said.

Bron followed. His forehead clashed with the headmother's with such force that Brina couldn't help but wince. As Bron passed by the woman to enter the hall, Brina stood in front of her awkwardly, unsure of what was expected of her. Then, Gavitt Akt lowered her head and grabbed Brina by the sides of her head. Brina had no choice but to follow through. She considered if she could get away with using a touch of *Forte* to soften the impact, but before she could decide whether this would be considered rude, their foreheads collided with such staggering force that she momentarily forgot where she was. Stars popped in front of her vision.

Gavitt Akt grabbed her by the shoulders and held her upright. "Sorry," she said, her voice deep. "I forget you flatlanders are not used to our ways."

"I'm fine," Brina muttered through tearing eyes, unable to stifle a chuckle. "I feel very welcome in your hall indeed."

"Good," Gavitt Akt said, leading them into the hall. "It is much preferable to fight alongside a friend."

***

After a heavy meal of fried snake, dried fish, and a dessert of cinnamon cakes, the company was herded to their feet and out into the courtyard. From there, a mixed procession of Biori warriors and the Metten rebels made its way to a square in the second tier of the city, where rows of wooden seats had been erected that could seat a few hundred. Mud squished under their boots as they slopped across the unpaved square to take their places. Brina was seated right beside the headmother, a great honor.

"So," Brina asked, "what have you got planned for us?"

She gestured to a group of Biori, clad in colorful tunics, who were busying themselves with coils of rope next to a low building that resembled a stable on the opposite side of the square. Compared to the other houses in the vicinity, it looked sturdier. A series of five wooden gates were reinforced with thick oak beams, and there were no windows to be seen anywhere.

"It's a contest," the headmother said, baring stubby teeth in a broad grin.

CHAPTER 71

"The highest form of entertainment in all the horseshoe. It's rather costly, so we keep it for the most special of occasions. What better time than now?"

Brina gave a nod that turned into a half bow. "That's very gracious of you."

"I've been looking for an excuse for a while." Gavitt grinned, playing with the ends of her braids. "People are growing uneasy. News of the oncoming invasion has leaked, and most fear that the end of our great nation as we know it may be upon us. I'm afraid I do not disagree. It seemed fitting to go all out now, while we still have a chance. One pleasure now is worth a hundred in the afterlife."

"So it is," Brina agreed.

Before she could ask any more questions, a horn rang out from the stands. The fortified building opposite them held five doors in total. Two Biori stood on either side of each one, holding ropes that were tied to the latches in the center of the doors. When the horn rang out a second time, they all pulled at the same time.

The doors flew open with a crash. Enraged squeals filled the air as five huge erymanthian boars skidded out, slipping and sliding in the muck as they charged. Their tusks were as long as Brina's forearms, and a layer of foam crusted their jaws. They rounded the corner and sprinted down the muddy street leading to the lower tiers of the city. They had almost gone from view when Brina noticed the riders. Atop each erymanthian, strapped down to a leather saddle, were five riders clad from head to toe in boiled leather armor, pulling on the beasts' bridles to keep them on track. The Biori in the stands whooped and shouted, a cry that rang out through the city in a cacophony as the erymanthian riders passed through the streets.

"Follow me." The headmother stood up and extended an arm toward Brina, who took it and was pulled to her feet. She followed Gavitt to the top of the stands, where a narrow wooden tower had been constructed for the occasion. "After you." The woman stood back so Brina could ascend a creaky ladder to the top of the tower. As soon as she reached the top, she realized what they were doing there: It was a perfect vantage point from which to watch the carnage unfold in the lower tiers of the city.

A spray of mud spattered the streets as the beasts and their riders hurtled through the city. Somewhere on the course, the race intersected with a market square. One of the erymanthians, trying to pass another contestant, slammed headlong into a fruit stall, causing a shower of splintering wood and pulped fruit to spray everywhere. Whoops and jeers rose from the crowd.

"My money's on yellow," Gavitt said, indicating a rider near the front of the race, whose leather armor was trimmed with yellow stripes visible even from this distance. Yellow was close on the heels of Red, who led the race. Brina squinted and noticed how Yellow, though riding one of the stronger beasts, was fighting to keep the forceful creature on course. Behind Yellow, the blue and green riders jockeyed for position. Limping all the way at the back, only just now exiting the market square a full ten or fifteen seconds after the others, was the purple rider.

"How many laps?" Brina asked.

"Two," Gavitt replied. "The main gate and the palace are the turn-around points."

Brina grinned. "I pick purple."

Gavitt gave her an incredulous look. "Purple? Not a chance."

"Want to make things interesting?" Brina raised an eyebrow.

"You're on," the headmother said with a grin. "What have you got?"

"If I lose," Brina said, "you can have any sigil from my script collection. How does that sound?"

The head woman let out a low whistle. "That's a dangerous game you're playing."

"What have you got in return?" Brina asked.

"For those stakes, you can enter my treasury and take with you all you can carry in your hands. What do you think?"

"You've got yourself a deal."

When the riders reached the lower section of the city and turned around to go back up, Brina and the head woman descended back to the stands to catch the arrival of the riders at the palace.

One by one, the erymanthian boars came pounding up the street, passing in front of the stands before making a skidding turn at the palace wall. Each rider was careful to brush their fingertips along the outer stone wall before turning. Purple was the last to make the turn, and with a gnawing sense of dread, Brina watched as the four other riders passed from view as Purple made its way back to the stands and down into the lower tiers of the city. Brina had counted on a gap to bridge, but this was a ravine.

As the rider passed the stands, she stood up on her seat and launched herself into a fortified jump. She sailed in a clean arc toward her moving target and landed right behind the purple rider. The jostle of the beast threatened to shake Brina off. Only a last-minute grasp for the leather straps holding the rider in the saddle kept her on.

"Blood of my mothers! What are you doing?" the rider shouted.

CHAPTER 71

"Winning!" Brina's shout was drowned by the rush of the wind.

"Get off," the rider shouted. "The two of us will be too heavy."

"I doubt that'll be a problem," Brina said. "What are the rules of this thing?"

The rider barked a laugh. "Rules? What rules? The first one across the finish line wins. Those are the rules."

"Excellent." Brina grinned. She bent low over the creature's neck and used *Consol* to urge it onward. The erymanthian gave a fierce snort, then broke into a sprint. They skidded around a corner, just barely making it sideways through the gate leading into the city's third tier when the first of their opponents came into view.

"Get us next to him," Brina shouted to the purple rider. The rider's heels jabbed into the erymanthian's sides. With a jolt, the beast leaped forward, drawing level with the blue rider's mount.

"Close enough." Brina hooked her foot behind the leather strap of the saddle, and, leaning sideways, she extended her dagger. The tip of it sliced through the leather straps holding Blue's saddle in place. There was a ripping sound, and the blue rider tilted sideways off the beast's back and crashed into the ground.

"Sorry!" Brina shouted. Without its rider, the erymanthian went berserk. It bucked and kicked, spinning in circles. Blue leaped up from the mud and managed to get the slipping and sliding erymanthian under control again by pulling its bridle. But by the time he had done so, Brina and the purple rider were long past him. They whirled past the green rider, whose erymanthian had stopped in the middle of the road to chomp away at a basket of apples someone had left in the street. Though its rider kicked, screamed, and tugged at the leather bridles, the creature hardly seemed to notice.

They reached the second tier of the city just as the red rider, now in second place, skidded through the gate. His erymanthian slipped, hooves clawing at the muddy ground. They crashed sideways into a house on the opposite side of the street. Windows shattered, exposing the houses' horrified inhabitants. Desperate to correct its course, the creature clawed at the ground. Its legs slipped, and it tumbled sideways. The rider just avoided being crushed by cutting himself loose from the saddle at the very last moment.

"Three down, one to go."

Ahead of them, Yellow had taken up the leading position. Her fierce mount plowed straight ahead, bristling and foaming. She maneuvered through the throng of onlookers that spilled out into the street, taking care not to get trapped in the human tangle of drunken limbs and shouts.

Brina had no time for such subtlety. She raised her voice using *Consol* and bellowed, "Move! Get out of the way, idiots."

"Spur it," she whispered to the rider.

"But there are people down there," the purple rider said.

"They'll move. Trust me. Spur it." Once again, the spurs dug into the erymanthian's sides, and the beast lurched forward. With a hailstorm of terrified shrieks, people leaped aside just in time to create an open space for them to pass unhindered.

Surprised, the rider in first position looked over her shoulder and found Brina and the purple rider right on her heels.

"Surprise!" Brina yelled. She let go of the purple rider's saddle, stood up on the erymanthian's heaving back, and leaped straight on top of the other rider, covering her eyes with her hands. Blinded, the woman was forced to jerk the reins back, causing her beast to skid to a stop. Brina smiled as she watched the purple rider cross the finish line in the distance.

"Get off me," the other rider shouted, punching and pushing at Brina's weight. Every bruise was worth it. Brina descended with a broad smile on her face. "Sorry about that. Better luck next time."

A series of well-timed fortified jumps from rooftop to rooftop brought her back up to the second highest tier of the city, where Gavitt Akt was waiting in the stands.

Even before Brina could push her way through the rest of the onlookers to reach her, one of the Biori pushed a drinking horn full of smokewater into her hands. She took a big gulp of it, then raised the horn in celebration.

"Now that was something!" the headmother shouted, clapping her on the back. "Completely outrageous, of course, and an affront to the very notion of sportsmanship. That's what we like to see." Laughter and shouts went up all around her, and Brina couldn't help but join in. At least for tonight, there would be drink, food, and laughter. Tonight, life was good.

CHAPTER 72

"They are on our flanks! They are..." The soldier's cry was stifled as a wind-up quarrel caught him in the throat.

He looked at Brina, hands clutching weakly at the feathers sticking out of his trachea. He drew instinctive breaths which came out in gurgling rasps. "Help," he croaked. But Brina knew there was nothing to be done. The man sank to his knees, choking. All around them, Biori war cries clashed with menacing shouts as armored darkhelms advanced through the nighttime streets of Mother's Mount.

When they had least expected it, the enemy had found its way into the very heart of the city. They had waited until the welcome festivities had ended and all soldiers had sunken deep in the grasp of alcohol-infused sleep. Then they had struck. The full invasion force was still a multiple days' journey away, but the darkhelms stationed at the Bay of Bones colony had filtered their way through the swampy marshes to assault the fortifications to the west. Leaderless, the Biori had filtered through the palace's main gate in loose units to drive them back. It had worked until a second group of darkhelms appeared out of nowhere in the second tier of the city.

Now they were stuck amidst a barrage of bolts coming from nowhere and everywhere. At Brina's feet, Beranek, a young recruit, was convulsing. The kid's lips turned blue as he drowned in his own blood, getting just enough air not to suffocate quickly.

"I'm sorry. You did well," Brina said as she kneeled down beside the boy and reached for her dagger. She showed it to him in an unspoken question. There was terror in Beranek's eyes, but then he nodded. It seemed to take all his strength.

"You did well," Brina repeated. Then, with a burst of strength fueled by *Forte*, she jammed her dagger down into his heart. The man let out a groan, and it was over. Brina jumped to her feet, ignoring the crushing sensation in her chest at what she had just done. All she knew was that Beranek's death needed to be avenged. Bodies lay strewn throughout the city's second tier. Covered in mud and gore, it was impossible to tell who belonged to which side.

Brina climbed up the nearest rooftop to get an overview of the situation. On a nearby rooftop, a darkhelm sniper sat reloading his windup. Brina's throwing star flashed in the air and hit him straight in his helmet's eye slit. He went down without a sound as the star sank into his eye socket.

The darkhelm toppled forward, rolling down the thatched roof and impacting the muddy streets with a wet squelch. Brina launched herself into a fortified jump. Wind-up quarrels whizzed through the darkness below her, missing her by inches. She spotted one of her assailants lying prone on a roof near the tier wall. She ended him with a long-distance star shot that would have made Acheron proud.

Brina landed in a crouch and sprinted toward the noises of battle ringing out from the lower tiers of the city. She had no time to keep playing hide and seek with cowardly bowmen. The church's troops were inside the walls. Somehow, they had breached the city even before an assault had begun. Brina slipped and skidded down the road, sprinting on sheer adrenaline.

When she reached the tier gate, she found a trail of bodies lying below the raised metal grate. A handful of them were Biori; the others were her own Metten soldiers.

A circle of dead darkhelms lay around them. They had fought like lions to keep the darkhelms out of the city's higher tiers. But in the end, their efforts had failed in the face of the darkhelms' overwhelming numbers.

A horn blew, and with another series of jumps, Brina traced its origin to the market square on the third tier of the city, where fighting was still intense. Two platoons of darkhelms in rectangular formations advanced on a group of Biori soldiers who stood clustered in a disorderly heap, hyping each other up with war cries. A small group of Metten recruits formed a tentative spear wall, trying to fend off the second darkhelm platoon. They were terrified, and as soon as the darkhelms made contact, the formation would break.

Brina skidded to a halt in the middle of both groups and, seizing *Rhetoris*, yelled, "Merge! We'll force them into a chokepoint!" At once, the group of Metten recruits fell back, establishing a hold on the road between two large houses. Covered by the houses, they would be impossible to flank there, and the darkhelms would have to break formation to fit in the narrow gap. The Biori followed suit. Like a cork plugging a bottle, both groups closed off the road to the higher tier.

CHAPTER 72

"Brace yourselves! Whatever you do, do not turn, do not flee. Your brothers and sisters are counting on you. If we hold the line, they cannot and they will not get through." Almost as if the darkhelms' commander had made a similar calculation, the shield formations began retreating, marching backward across the square, further away from the remaining defenders of the city. Brina's pulse quickened.

"You," she asked the nearest Biori soldier, who clutched his spear in trembling hands, "where does that road lead?"

"It leads to the first tier, just inside of the city wall."

"Is that the only place they could go?"

The man nodded.

"Are there any of us down there?" Brina asked. Even as the man replied, his own eyes widened in horror as a realization dawned.

"No soldiers," he said. "Only citizens live there."

"Surely not even a Heilinist would..." another Biori soldier began.

Brina, who still saw the burning of Doorstep's Ditch every time she closed her eyes, had no time to tell this man just how deeply he was underestimating Heilinist ruthlessness.

"After them!" Brina shouted. She led by example, running across the square on her own strength. Her breath stabbed at her side. How long had it been since she'd run without the aid of *Forte*? She couldn't remember, but her heart did. She fought through the pain. If she was to lead the soldiers, she needed to have a realistic grasp of the exertion she was putting them through. She couldn't demand more of them than an unfortified body could handle.

When the darkhelms spotted their pursuers storming down the second-tier street toward the first-tier gate, they broke formation and ran for it.

"The enemy routs!" a recruit to Brina's left yelled. "We have them now. If we can catch up..."

Brina raised a hand to call for calm. "Maintain marching speed," she called. "Nobody runs, nobody rushes."

Her eyes flickered left and right to the rooftops. Something was fishy. A well-disciplined platoon breaking at the sight of the very enemy they were marching down on moments prior? It didn't add up.

The rooftops were deserted. No wind-up bows twanged. No spears soared through the night. There was only silence and the drumming of boots against the cobbled streets. When the routing darkhelms reached the northern gate of the first tier, Brina was surprised to find it closed and locked. A half-circle of Biori spearmen was formed in front of it, determined not to let the enemy open the gates to the city.

But the darkhelms weren't interested in the gate. Instead, they ran in a wide circle around the spearmen, casting no backward glances, running west along the city wall. Left and right, Biori warriors and novice recruits were passing Brina, their patience wearing thin and their pace quickening.

"Halt!" Brina repeated as the ill feeling in her gut intensified. "If we're out of breath when we catch them, tomorrow's funeral could still be our own."

"Mother Springtide," one of the Biori called, charging to keep up with her, "we can cut through the alley on the left side here and cut them off. If they're headed for the western gate, we'll get there first."

"Excellent." Brina clapped a hand to the woman's armored shoulder, causing the thin sheets of metal plating to rattle against each other. She directed her squad left, and they stretched out into a narrow column to fit between both rows of houses. With the alley only wide enough to march two abreast, progress was slow, but if the Biori woman was right, it could be just the edge they needed.

Besides, it forced the soldiers to slow down, allowing them to recover. Brina was first out of the alley. Her heart leaped as she saw the escaping darkhelms appear in the distance to her right, running along the tier road at full speed. Most of them had even dropped their shields.

The Seven be praised, she thought. They may have suffered casualties, but the darkhelms were about to receive a crushing blow. Then the first of them vanished.

Brina blinked, confused. Behind her, the rest of her squad was flowing from the alley like blood from a wound. Then another darkhelm vanished, and another, and another. They seemed to melt into the very earth, as though they were made of sand.

A tunnel. The bastards had dug a tunnel underneath the western fortifications. The one place where the wall was poorly defended because of the swampy terrain just outside of it.

"Charge!" Brina raised the spear she had picked up earlier and sprinted toward the disappearing darkhelms. "Don't let them get away!" The last group of the darkhelms turned to face their attackers, assembling into a tight battle formation around the tunnel entrance. Even as they formed up, the last ranks of the formation continued filing away through the tunnel.

"Spears up front!" Brina shouted. "They don't have enough shields; their wall is compromised!"

The impact was brutal. Biori spears slammed into weak spots in the dark-

CHAPTER 72

helms' shield wall, while heavy mace blows rained down upon them. Spears shattered, skulls cracked, helmets were dented, and the mud at Brina's feet turned red. Soon, both sides were standing atop bodies, tripping and sliding as they wrestled for control of the tunnel's entrance. Only a fourth of the darkhelms remained, and Brina noticed a sudden shift in their demeanor.

The very first ranks rotated backward, filing into the tunnel, leaving only an armored subsection behind. These warriors were not going anywhere. Brina could see it in the plant of their feet and their close-knit formation. They had come to buy time, to fight till death. And their short, stocky frames left no question as to their identity. Skullbeard mercenaries—the very same who had razed Doorstep's Ditch—now stood face to face with their own kin.

The Biori component of Brina's force stepped backward. The Skullbeard mercenaries lowered their own spears, spear wall against spear wall. Brina saw through the slits in their fierce helmets the same doubt and anguish she sensed in the warriors around her. The Metten recruits, who comprised a smattering of peoples from all across the Sundered Isles, felt no hesitation to charge. Brina held out an arm to keep them back. Would she really lead the charge of brother against brother, sister against sister?

"It's not too late," Brina called out to a woman on the second row of the formation. Her ornate metal armor was encrusted with rubies set in the top of her helmet—a clear mark of an officer. "Why spill the blood of your own when you could join us and fight for the freedom of your people?"

"These aren't my people," the woman spat. "When the Bay of Bones was overrun, we pleaded with the headmother for support."

"And she sent it!" a woman behind Brina shouted.

"Not enough," the officer replied. "Not enough to keep our families out of slavery, not enough to prevent my own parents from having to sail out in cold and heat to work."

"So now you're going to fight for those who enslaved them?" Brina demanded.

"I know where my bread is buttered," the woman said. "The Cardinal will reward us. Their freedom, for our service. And we intend to hold up our end."

"And you believe he will not betray you? That he will just let all those workers walk free out of the goodness of his heart?"

"He swore it on the Keeper," the Skullbeard mercenary spat. "He swore it on all that is holy. There is no renouncing such a vow."

"The Keeper is a tool to them!" Brina shouted back over the uneasy rustling of armor as troops on both sides readied themselves for the fight they knew was imminent. "He uses his god to get what he wants when he wants it. You must have seen this by now."

A flicker of doubt passed over those shadowed eyes. The officer looked down, her face obscured by the ornate helmet. Brina saw it a second before it came. The officer stooped down and flung her own spear with tremendous force, aiming straight for Brina. It was the knee-jerk move of a woman standing atop a cliff who shuts her eyes and jumps because she feels she is losing the courage to dive.

Brina's arm struck out, but without *Veloce* to slow down reality, her timing was off. The spear passed just over her shoulder and struck a Biori warrior in the crook of his shoulder. He staggered backward, strands of scarlet blossoming on his metal armor. With a unified roar of rage, the Biori and Metten recruits swarmed forward. The first line of Skullbeard mercenaries toppled backward into those behind them.

Brina burned *Forte* and advanced with her own spear, swiping it left and right, and using its blunt shaft as a club to make her way to the officer with the rich armor. Then she saw her—a glint of sapphires falling backward into the open hole of the tunnel as the Skullbeards were driven back. More and more of them slipped and fell into the tunnel's steep entrance, cascading down. Some lay still where they had fallen, others crawled on broken bones into the darkness.

Biori were trained to fight to the death and not yield under any circumstances. Life as mercenaries hadn't stripped the Skullbeards of this principle. Those Skullbeards who could stand pushed forward, trading fierce jabs of their spears.

Brina clutched the shaft of her spear, burned *Gnis*, and as the spear burst into flame, she threw it with all her might straight into the center of the Skullbeard formation. It sliced straight through one of the soldiers' chest plates, as though it were made of fall leaves. Panicked, the woman clutched at the burning wood jutting out of her shoulder, turning left and right, screaming in agony. Her frantic movements caused the flame to spill over, catching cloaks on fire and burning exposed limbs. The circle broke. The Biori defenders exploited this sudden weakness.

"Come on," Brina shouted, looking away from the twitching woman she had turned into a torch. "We've got to collapse this thing, or they'll just send reinforcements." She jumped down into the dark tunnel, landing atop the officer. The woman let out a groan. Still alive, Brina thought.

She stooped and seized the woman under the arms, carrying her upright.

CHAPTER 72

"Why are you sparing me," the woman croaked, "when I intended to kill you?"

"I'm not sparing you," Brina said. "You're going to show me the way."

***

Brina dragged the wounded officer through the passage. Wooden beams creaked overhead, straining to keep the unstable soil at bay. At the very entrance, the tunnel had only been wide enough to fit two soldiers abreast, but the deeper they penetrated, the larger it became.

"How long have they been working on this?" Brina asked, squeezing the woman's chest. Her suspicion that she would have at least broken or bruised ribs during her fall was confirmed by the woman's scream of pain.

"Months," she said, "perhaps longer. I don't know."

"Where does it lead?"

The woman winced, preparing for a fresh jolt of pain. But Brina held back. It wasn't necessary. She hadn't arrived at the hard questions yet.

"The tunnel surfaces half a mile inside the swamp. They had us show them the safest path through. Once we reached the edge of the swamp, just far enough to be outside of view with a spyglass when standing atop the western fortification, they began digging. Most of the work was done by the enslaved."

Brina shook her head. "You may have just doomed your own people to an age of slavery and oppression. And the rest of the free lands with it."

The woman remained silent. "What good is another's freedom when my own family walks in chains? If you had the power to reverse that scenario, you would do the same."

Brina remained silent. The woman was right. But Brina's blind hatred for the church and all those sided with it was at an all-time high after tonight's events.

"Besides," Brina went on, the temptation of cruelty overcoming her, "what will they do to you when they realize you've failed?"

The officer let out a strange giggle. "I didn't fail."

"You may have killed some of us," Brina said, "but we cut down plenty of yours. And now we know where the tunnel is. You won't fool us a second time."

The woman shook with heaving laughter, and Brina let go of her, disgusted. The woman sank to the ground, her legs giving way. Then she raised her fingers to her lips and let out a shrill whistle. Brina knew that it was trouble. The point of her spear lashed out, stifling the whistle in the woman's throat.

As her last moments slipped away, the officer's eyes found Brina's, a smirk etched on her face.

"We should go back," Brina called.

"Back?" one recruit called out. "After we made it this far? They were running. We could still catch a fair few of them."

"Something is wrong." Brina's jaws clenched. She felt like a hare in a noose.

Then a rumbling sound reverberated through the tunnel. Something shifted deep inside the earth. Brina flared *Lux* to penetrate the darkness. A wave of roiling green and brown water and mud was hurtling toward them, filling the tunnel as it went, ripping away stones and wooden supports. Brina looked back at the Biori warriors, the recruits she had led on the pursuit. Over a hundred good soldiers in total.

"I've doomed us," she whispered to herself. Then, finding her courage, she screamed, "Turn back. Run for your lives!"

CHAPTER 73

rina's mind was awash with faint fragments of memory. Her body felt weightless. It drifted up and down with the breath of the ocean. She was thirteen again, scavenging for clams along the rocky outcroppings of Crab's Cove during low tide. She was seventeen, crouching on an elm branch, aiming a wind-up bow at an oversized night eater as it sat on a bait carcass. She was twenty, descending into the dark depths of the elder mine, in search of a pack of wampyr.

She was... lying on a straw mattress, in a sun-filled room with a white vaulted ceiling. The weightlessness vanished. Her limbs felt heavy, brittle, and sore. Then she remembered.

"How many?" she asked nobody in particular.

A hand landed on her forehead, and an unfamiliar woman's face drifted in and out of focus above her. "What did you say, dear?"

"How many dead?"

The woman's face contracted, as though she had drunk something sour. "I... I don't know. You need to rest."

Brina pushed herself up on the mattress. Two hands pressed down on her collarbones, forcing her back down. She tried to resist, but the effort exhausted her. She sank back into the mattress, defeated.

"How many? Damn you." Brina's voice was harsh and faint at the same time. "You must know something. You're not stupid, are you?"

The woman's face disappeared. "I'll summon someone. In the meantime, you stay where you are."

Brina would have liked to protest, but she didn't have the strength. She drifted in and out of consciousness until Bron's face appeared above her.

She opened her mouth to repeat her question, but Bron held up a hand.

"One hundred and fifty-two as last count," he said. The words sank into Brina's chest like a knife. "Fifty in the city, the rest..."

Brina's knuckles whitened as she grasped at her sheets. Her right eye flooded with tears. "How many of ours, from Metten, I mean?"

Bron shrugged. "Does it matter?"

"It's my fault," Brina whispered. "I led them right into that trap."

Bron's calloused hand closed around her forearm. "We both know whose fault this is, and it's not yours. The rescuers are still at work. Every few minutes, they uncover someone. Found some of them alive too, the Allmother be blessed. We also found this."

Bron's hand reached for a pouch in his pocket. He opened it and poured the contents onto Brina's bed. Golden skulls with ruby eyes, made to be woven into a warrior's hair or beard.

"They had these on them as well?" Brina asked, propping herself up on her elbow.

"Looks like it," Bron said, his face neutral. "Damn morons, they insisted on betraying their own blood, and look where it got them. The darkhelms sacrificed the lot of them, just hoping to catch a few more of us. They were worth nothing to them." Brina closed her eyes and once again saw the Skullbeard officer glaring at her.

"The Skullbeards in the tunnel were all related to those working the whaling boats in the Bay of Bones," Brina said. "They were promised freedom for themselves and their families if they helped with yesterday's raid. That's why they couldn't be persuaded to join us."

Bron shook his head and turned away. He cleared his throat, and when his gaze returned to Brina, she could see that his eyes had grown red.

"We could still ensure their deaths weren't in vain," Brina said.

"Weren't in vain?" Bron roared. "They tried to put the entire city to the torch in the dead of night!"

"Yes, but think of why they were willing to go that far. I bet there are hundreds of captives in the western colony who feel betrayed right about now. And once they learn what happened to their family members, which side do you think they'll choose?"

Bron shook his head. "I see where you're going with this, and the answer is no. For one, it's not up to us to decide their fate. That's the headmother's prerogative. Besides, you're in no shape to be raiding any colonies right about now."

"Watch me," Brina said. She pushed herself up and withdrew her leather satchel filled with scripts from her bedside table, and began preparing.

CHAPTER 74

rina crouched low against the underbrush. The acrid smell of sulfuric swamp water mixed with the scent of fresh grass to form an intoxicating cocktail. She held up a hand, and the column of Biori warriors and Metten rebels came to a halt. As the thrumming of footfalls and the murmurs amongst the warriors died down, Brina burned *Auris*.

The swamp was silent. Water trickling down from one pool into the next clattered in her ears like bricks impacting on solid steel. The heartbeats of the warriors behind her formed a low hum in the background of her hearing. They were nervous. They were right to be. Brina reached for a rock and flung it as far away as she could. It thumped against a tree trunk some hundred yards away. Silence.

"They either have great scouts out here, or none," she told Bahov, who kneeled beside her. "I can't detect any movement anywhere. Not even an exhalation of breath."

"Let's make haste either way," Bahov replied. "I've got a bad feeling about this."

They covered the last mile of the march with urgency, reaching the western colony just as the second chariot stood highest in the firmament. They were still an hour or three away from the dark window. Timing was of the essence. Use the light of the moon to fight, then disappear into the dark. That had been the crux of the plan Brina had sold the headmother. And she wasn't about to disappoint herself or her soldiers again.

The outskirts of the colony were populated with farms and fishermen's huts, which covered a broad swath of land around the central fortified town of Marencrest.

Everything was eerily quiet. Brina crossed a pumpkin patch behind a large farmhouse while the soldiers crouched down behind a hedgerow, waiting for her signal. She slipped underneath the windowsill and peeked inside. Empty. Her quick glance showed a deserted living room. A dining room table lay upside down on the earthen floor, the ground around it littered with shards of broken porcelain.

When she made it to the other side of the house, she spotted a pot hanging above the cold hearth in the kitchen. Sliced fruits and chunks of fish lay on a cutting board on a table beside it, ready to be added to a stew that was never finished. Something was wrong. Brina gestured for her soldiers to follow her, and together they swept through the colony like ghosts carried on the wind. If the darkhelms had stationed sentries, Brina neither saw nor heard them.

Her instincts had never been this sharp. The life-and-death struggle against water, mud, and wooden beams as the tunnel had collapsed behind them had triggered something inside her. It was as if she was in survival-mode around the clock. She could have heard a twig snap a mile away.

"Let's pick up the pace," she hissed at Bahov, who gestured for his troops to move forward. Staying low, Brina rushed from house to house, ducking behind hedgerows, trees, and bushes wherever she could. Contrasted like a black shadow against the moonlight was the hill town of Marencrest. It rose from the surrounding dwellings like a pustule on a giant's back. It hadn't been this fortified years prior when Cardinal Estav's troops had landed in the Bay of Bones to establish a foothold on the island.

In the years since, whale hunting expeditions set out weekly from Marencrest, manned by captive Biori. Aside from their meat and bones, it was especially the substance ambergris which was used in high end perfumes and medicines that made them valuable to the empire. Those Biori who stayed behind on land were made to either farm or to add layers upon layers of fortification around the storehouses placed on the hill.

Intelligence about Marencrest Brina had received from the headmother, Bron, Bahov, and half a dozen spies hadn't quite prepared her for the sight that greeted her as she approached the hill. Half a dozen rows of spiked logs were dug into the ground, interspersed with short, pointed branches and caltrops buried just deep enough to be practically invisible to the naked eye. When taking fire from the walls at the end of the defensive line, these layers alone would be enough to dissuade even the most determined of attackers. Somehow, Brina couldn't spy so much as a glint of a helmet on top of the walls. No torches were lit anywhere, and not even *Lux* could reveal so much as a protruding spear tip or the stock of a wind-up bow over the battlements of the town's walls.

"I don't know what is going on here," she told Bahov, "but I don't like this one bit."

CHAPTER 74

"Agreed," the warlord replied. "Give me a volley of quarrels over silence any day. I prefer an honest bloodbath over this cloak-and-dagger nonsense."

"Wait for my signal." Brina began the slow and arduous process of crossing the defensive line. She didn't dare use a fortified jump to cross it, for fear of jumping into a hidden pit or landing on one of the many buried spikes. Instead, she burned *Lux*, and prodded at every foot of soil with the tip of her boot. She squeezed past sharpened stakes, and edged past hidden pits, kicking away the branches and leaves so they would be exposed to those following behind her. As she cleared a safe path for her troops, still no reaction could be heard or seen from the city.

Every so often, Brina flared *Auris* as brightly as she could, hoping to catch any mutterings from the defenders or even the scrape of a boot against a stone floor. But all she heard were the quick and shallow breaths of her own terrified soldiers waiting on her mark before advancing on the wall. When she reached the end of the field, she looked back at Bahov, who was craning his neck, squinting against the moonlight, waiting for her signal. She shook her head, making a large X with her forearms.

Turning to the outer wall of the city, she made her way to the gatehouse, the only way in or out of the town. She was growing more unnerved with every passing moment. It was one thing to be outnumbered, another to be surrounded by blood and screams. But silence? That was the last thing Brina wanted to face.

When she reached the gatehouse, her mouth dropped open. The heavy wooden gate, comprising two steel halves with five deadbolts made of oak logs, stood ajar. She nudged one of the gates with her boot, making the hinges squeak. She switched to *Auris*, scanning for any reaction. Nothing. She suppressed a roar of frustration. *This is how you're going to play it, huh? Cowards.*

She made another X gesture to Bahov, indicating that he ought to stay right where he was. With a deep breath, Brina slipped through the gate and into the town. The cobbled streets were abandoned. The houses along the edge of the wall seemed deserted, too. There were no lights, no sounds, not even the smells of human waste in the streets or the smoke of hearth fires escaping chimneys. She tiptoed in the shadows, up the inclined hill deeper into the city. That's when she heard it: muttering, shuffling of feet, clinking of chains.

"Someone's there," she heard a man mutter in a Biori accent.

"Silence," a woman replied. "They told us not to breathe a word, remember?"

"What do I care what they told us?" the man responded. "They've told me to do one too many things. They've been gone on their boats for hours."

Brina's heart raced inside her chest. By the sounds of it, the darkhelms had rounded up all the Biori living in the area and locked them up in a handful of storage barns along the main road of the fortified town core. Her immediate desire to free them was superseded by a gnawing question: Why?

It made no sense. To strike at Mother's Mount in the night and then abandon a profitable colony one week later. *Unless,* a small voice in her head told her, *they expect to gain a lot of ground soon.* Maybe they thought it was only a matter of time before not only Marencrest but the entirety of Bior was theirs. Perhaps they hoped to spread out the defenders by giving up the western colony. If that was the plan, it might just work. How many would be necessary to defend not only the capital city but the western colony as well? It would dilute the defenders. Trading stealth for speed, Brina broke into a run. If she kept Bahov and his men waiting much longer outside the city limits, they might get ideas of their own and rush in without a signal.

The central fortification of Marencrest wasn't so much a keep as a single tower surrounded by a ring wall of stone. Here too, the gates were left open. The stables were empty. The servants' quarters in the lower section of the tower were empty, and there wasn't so much as the tremor of a drawn breath audible on the floors above when she burned *Auris.* Using *Leve* to keep her feet as light as possible on the cobbled street, Brina listened in on the conversations going on inside the barns.

"When are we going to eat, Mother?" a high-pitched voice asked, followed by shushing noises.

"We'll find a way. We'll find a way out."

When she passed the first barn's double doors, she noticed heavy stones, of the kind used to build a wall, stacked in front of the door, with a thick layer of cement poured on top. Brina poked a finger at it. It was still wet. She ran back down the cobbled street and gestured for Bahov to approach.

Meanwhile, she circled the barn, looking for the weakest point of entry. The roof was a contender. It was covered in thatch and clay. If they could find a ladder to get up there, they might be able to create a hole large enough for people to pass through. But it would take a long time to get everyone out, and some of the oldest and youngest trapped inside might not have the strength to climb out.

The doors themselves weren't an option. The blockade of cement and stone had made sure of that. Perhaps they ought to take a leaf from the darkhelms' own playbook and try to tunnel underneath the walls. Brina kicked at the heavy stone walls. Perhaps there was a cellar of some kind with a weakness

CHAPTER 74

they could exploit.

Bahov and his recruits entered the city gates moments later, confused and suspicious.

"The Biori are in here." Brina thumped a fist against the barn wall. "Tell your soldiers to look around for anything they can use to dig. We'll have to dig under the wall."

Bahov hesitated for a moment as though he might argue, but then set to work, commanding his recruits to search the surrounding houses. Brina herself scaled the side of the building, reached the thatch roof, and began plucking pieces of thatch out to make a hole. Once she had created enough space to see through, she called down, "Stay calm, we're coming to get you."

"The Allmother be praised," an elderly man, huddled atop the hayloft, called. "They left us here. They wanted us to starve. We were forced to load their boats. All the grain, the whalebone, the dried fish, all of it is gone."

"We'll worry about that later," Brina said. "Is there anything in there you can use to help us dig you out?"

"Our hands, perhaps, but we won't make much progress with those alone."

"Use them," Brina said. "We're digging underneath that wall." She pointed at the ground on the opposite side of the barn. "Every inch helps."

"Of course," the man called. He scrambled to get down a rickety wooden ladder from the loft and began chattering to the other Biori, whose faces darted from Brina to the place where they were supposed to dig. The desperation on their faces made Brina's heart sink. It would be a long night to get them out, and depending on how deep the foundations ran, they would have to endure many more hours of deprivation and a long march back to Mother's Mount before they could eat or drink anything. Many of them already looked on the brink of passing out.

There was a thump beside Brina, followed by a stinging pain in her left arm. She looked aside and yelled out in horror. A flaming arrow was lodged in the thatch roof, which was catching on fire. Angry red blisters sprang up across Brina's hand and forearm. As she rolled over, a sticky substance clung to her arms. Tar and oil. The roof had been soaked with them, priming it to go up at the first spark.

A second arrow whizzed by her neck. Brina whirled around and saw an archer on the second-floor window of the house across the street. She cursed.

"Ambush!" Brina's scream came too late. Arrows rained down from slits in windows as the roof of the barn turned into an inferno. Anguished shrieks reverberated from inside. There wouldn't be time to clear the houses and free the Biori before the fire got to them.

"Platoon one, split up in groups of three and clear those houses," she yelled, pointing at two houses where she could spot archers raining down death on the soldiers below. "Second platoon, get to the other side of the barn and hack, smash, wrench at that wall. I don't care how you do it, but get those people out of there."

Brina launched herself from the burning roof to the opposite side of the street. She burned *Grave* as she landed, making herself so heavy that she smashed through the roof with a crash, landing beside two archers who were taking aim at troops in the street below. She grabbed both of them by the hair, flared *Forte*, and forced their heads through the glass windows, slicing their necks as they went. The momentum carried them forward, and they tumbled head over heels to the cobbles below.

Brina slithered out through the broken window, looking left and right, then spotted a group of a dozen darkhelms clambering out of a cellar hatch on the backside of the house. They were hoping to strike at the rescuers, who were trying to bring down the barn's back wall. Brina slid down the roof, feet first. She collided with one of the darkhelms, breaking his neck. Before the others could react, she flared *Forte* and plunged her dagger into a second darkhelm's chest. He stumbled backward, bowling over his four remaining companions. He lay on the ground clutching at his chest, heaving. The four others regained their composure and spread out to encircle Brina in the narrow alley. With her first dagger gone, she reached for the second one in her ankle holster.

Even amongst spears and maces, the dagger had always been her weapon of choice. She had to get up close and personal, looking the enemy in the eyes as she finished them. It was what they deserved. One of them was foolish enough to lunge for her. Brina sidestepped the strike of his mace, allowing the momentum of his own blow to carry the darkhelm off balance. She lashed out and dragged her dagger across his neck. Blood spurted everywhere.

The three others came for her in a coordinated attack. She was forced backward. With her eyes focused on her assailants, she missed the rain barrel standing right behind her. It caught her lower legs, and she flipped over backward, hitting the ground head first. Her neck landed at an awkward angle. Her limbs spasmed as the alley grew blurry around her.

"General's going to be happy about this one," the nearest darkhelm said with relish as he lifted his mace above his head with both hands, poised to strike at Brina's exposed head. She tried to roll out of the way, but her body

CHAPTER 74

failed to obey her commands.

Brina watched in slow motion as the mace reached the apex of its swing, ready to come down.

"Urgh." The darkhelm groaned.

Feathers sprouted from the eye socket of his helmet. He toppled over with a gurgle.

"Thought I lost you," Sneak said as he threw aside the windup bow and sprinted forward, drawing a short sword. The remaining darkhelms fled as they caught the blue glare in his eyes.

Brina blinked, rolled over, and forced herself to her feet, shaking off the daze that had settled over her. She stumbled over to the wall of the barn where the second platoon was doing everything it could to free those trapped inside the burning building.

"Come on," Brina snapped at one of the Biori warriors who had gotten his hands on a rusty pickaxe and was swinging it against a crumbling section of the barn's stone wall with desperate fervor.

Brina had untapped *Forte* left, and she was angry. Very angry. She snatched the pickaxe and noticed Bron and Sneak moving through the throng of soldiers, each grabbing whatever tool they could to join her. Brina channeled her strength and swung the pickaxe against the stone. It landed with a crunch. The tremor shook through her entire body. She swung again.

"I. Have. Had. It. With. These. Bastards."

Each word was stressed by a strike from the pickaxe against the stone. A crack appeared, followed by the first layer of stone crumbling. Once there was a hole, the three of them battered at its weakened edges. The heat from the burning roof radiated down upon them as though the sun had been pulled closer to the earth, scorching them.

"Cowards!" Brina screamed. "Cursed cowards!" This was the second time the Heilinists had set up unwinnable scenarios for themselves, just to do as much damage to Bior as possible. Though they outweighed the Biori resistance forces in both numbers and equipment, they were too cowardly to face them directly. They had the upper hand in every conceivable way and yet they insisted on playing these games, not caring that they were consigning their own soldiers to die after inflicting as much damage as possible.

A hole appeared, and a face was visible on the other end.

"Stand back," Brina called as the pickaxe came down once more, scattering sharp fragments of stone.

"Hurry," she called. "The roof beams are about to fall." Through the tiny hole, Brina could see tufts of burning thatch raining down on the captives inside. Thick smoke hung like fog in the barn and began leaking from the hole like blood from a wound.

Feeling a stab of panic, Brina flared *Forte* as brightly as she could. There was a heavy clank, and the head of the pickaxe bent over, followed by the snap of the handle. Brina swore and cast it to the ground.

"Another," she called. "Someone hand me another!"

Someone thrust a spade into her hands, and she began chipping away at the mortar seams between the rocks. Beside her, Bron looked furious. He was silent except for grunts of effort with each stroke of the hatchet he had already blunted against the sides of the hole. There was a mad look in his eyes—half rage, half fear. He wasn't just angry. He was beside himself.

Brina had never seen him lose control like this before. When the hole was large enough for a head and shoulders to fit through, they began pulling out the Biori one by one. The young and old came first, while the strongest stayed behind, tolerating the smoke for as long as possible. At one point, the captives began pushing unconscious people through the hole. Brina grabbed their arms and handed them off to soldiers, not thinking about who was alive and who was dead, not thinking about just how many more might be on the floor inside at that very moment.

Brina's hands closed around the wrists of a ginger-haired Biori woman, whose face was blackened with soot, her eyes bloodshot but void of tears. She jerked back her arms with surprising force. "I've got it," she said, worming herself through the hole and pushing herself up as her legs slid out.

"I was the last one on my feet," she said. "The smoke was too thick to see how many were left behind, but I'm afraid that whoever is still in there has long sailed for the beyond world."

Brina nodded. "You did well," she said. "Now go rest."

Fits of coughing from the freed echoed through the street like thunder.

"Water," many of them called. "Please, water."

"My throat," an elderly woman called, clutching at her neck. "My throat."

Brina gestured for a handful of soldiers to spread out in search of a barrel of rainwater or any stores the darkhelms hadn't taken with them.

She then called Sneak and Bron to join her in clearing Marencrest's central tower. She was determined to root out every last darkhelm that had been left behind.

CHAPTER 75

"Careful," Bron muttered as he stepped into the central tower of the village. "If those mud-breeched scoundrels were cowardly enough to hide in the shadows, they might have left more surprises in here. It's what I would've done. Just wait until I get my hands on those..." He trailed off. None of the curses in any of the tongues he'd learned in his years overseas were sufficient to describe what he had seen here tonight.

He, Springtide, and Sneak circled the inner side of the wall, methodically clearing spaces as they went. Springtide had reloaded one of the bows that Bahov had brought, and Sneak had a shortsword at the ready. Bron just had his gloved fists balled. The first darkhelm he caught was going to wish they'd been attacked with a weapon.

The stables were empty. The stench of soiled hay rushed up his nostrils, sharp and pungent. All horses were gone. Bron strode into the next section of the stables, where the other animals were kept. The buzzing was all he needed to hear. Even before he looked over the low walls into the muddy pigpen, he knew what he would find. The pigs' carcasses were bloated, their blackened blood staining the mud below them. Thousands of flies swarmed the deep gashes in the beasts' necks, laying eggs, and multiplying. Dozens of headless chickens lay on one side of the coop, their heads littered throughout the stable. A dozen sheep, their luscious wool still clinging to their backs, lay in the last quarter of the stables.

"They did this days ago," he spat into the hay. "Unbelievable. The lengths these people would go to. The depths to which they would sink. They'd rather waste all those souls, all the meat on their bones, than risk so much as a pound of flesh falling into Biori hands—into hands to whom the fruits of these lands rightfully belong."

He kicked at a pile of hay, spraying it everywhere as he left the stables. He thumped his fist against the wooden wall, flaring *Forte* as he did so. The blue shape flashed in front of his eyes. Fueled by his rage, his fist went clean through the wooden panel. He let out a roar as he stepped back into the courtyard.

"Come out, you bastards! Come out and let me show you how a real warrior handles business!"

Sneak raised a hand and let out a hushing sound, the way a mother would soothe a crying baby. Bron whirled around, mouth working. He held his tongue, not wanting to debase himself by dishonoring his brother-in-arms. The spindly Sneak got the point well enough. He fell quiet, hands raised in apology. Springtide's eyes narrowed, scanning the windows of the tower up above. She clearly felt the same way he did. Whoever was in there was going to pay.

They cleared the kitchen first, followed by the servants' quarters, then up the stairs into a gaudy office, where only dusty squares on the stone walls betrayed the presence of portraits that had hung there not long ago. Everything of value had been stripped from the place. Not so much as half a bottle of gods damned kelp was left.

Bron stomped up the wooden stairs into the first sleeping hall, not bothering to silence himself. He felt like he could eat a windup quarrel whole. He could chew up a spear right now and spit out a bar of pure steel. The sleeping quarters were empty, too. Before he knew it, they stood atop the tower, where nothing remained except two damp fire pits. Ashes and charred wood littered the floor.

They had gone. The darkhelms had left a few dozen suicide fighters to ambush them as they tried to prevent three hundred captives from burning alive. They had killed both loyal workers and their own soldiers and left. He let out a roar like a wounded bear and flung one of the fire beacons over the edge of the tower. He leaned over the battlements and watched it tumble and explode onto the cobbles below with a clang. It wasn't enough. He reached for the second beacon but stopped as he saw Springtide and Sneak staring off into the distance, mouths agape in horror.

At first, he didn't see it. Then he remembered to burn *Lux*.

"No, no, no, no," Springtide muttered under her breath. In the distance, not one but two Heilinist fleets were visible. The first was making for the eastern shore, as they had expected. The second, comprising more than half of the total amount of redsails, was headed for Metten.

CHAPTER 76

"You swore no one knew the island's location," Brina told Abrasax. They were standing in the headmother's audience room, lining the circular walls, while the headmother's calloused fingers pattered against the wooden armrests of a crude throne.

"Its location was secret," Abrasax replied, striding back and forth in the center of the room. "But a secret is only as strong as the weakest person who knows it."

"None of the recruits themselves knew how to get there," Brina said. "Not until they were on the island, and none of them have left the island since beginning their training. The only people who were aware of the location were the recruiters who brought them to the island and us."

Abrasax let out a deep sigh that filled the room like a howling wind. He waved an irritated hand. "We can't do anything about that now. The point is, they know we are there, and they have put us in an impossible position."

"What are the developments on the eastern shore? About as dire as we expected?" the headmother asked. She looked at her military advisor, who stood to her right, dressed in a long black robe.

The man scowled. "Three dozen ships have moored near the edges of the island. They have set up a base camp at the very tip of the horseshoe and are now taking their time unloading supplies, horses, and equipment. We expect the process to be complete within forty-eight hours."

"Excellent," Bron grunted from a dark corner of the room. He stood there, looking straight ahead, arms like tree trunks folded. "We'll hit them right now. While they're still up to their necks in logistics, we'll march them down and sweep them back into the sea."

The headmother gave a sad smile. "Your ardor is, as always, admirable, Bron Brokenspear. But I'm afraid we are past that. We have traded significant casualties for the corpses of a few dozen enemy soldiers. Our forces are spread thin, and the western colonies' workers are all but incapacitated for the foreseeable future."

"We are outnumbered," the advisor croaked in summary. "Marching down on the enemy is nothing short of steering a ship into a cliff, hoping the cliff will yield."

"Then what?" Brina snapped, pushing herself up from her chair near the far end of the wall. Her anger spiked. Twice now, the church had tricked her, forced her to watch as those under her command fell to dishonorable low blows. They were not playing the same game she was. They had no principles, no mercy, and no regard for their own troops. But they had their eyes on the prize. There was no doubt in Brina's mind that, as soon as the full army could unfurl itself, the darkhelms would become an unstoppable force.

"They have all the time in the world," she continued. "As soon as they have deployed, they can advance across the land at a leisurely pace. We won't be able to attack them directly, as you have already stated, while they can take the time to forage, pillage the outskirts of your lands, and then lay siege to your city. If that happens, we could be trapped in here for months. How long will your rations last?"

The headmother waved an impatient hand at a woman standing off to the left near the exit of the room.

Her hands clasped together as she stepped forward into the light, clearing her throat before speaking. "It seems as though, given the loss of all the resources in the western colony, and the extra mouths to feed, we can hold out a maximum of six weeks. Of course," she added, "any foraging we can do, nighttime hunting expeditions or fishing boats the enemy cannot reach might prolong such a situation."

"Let's round up and make it eight," Brina said, striding into the center of the room. Her anger had washed away any anxiety she felt at being the center of attention. More than ever, she knew what she wanted, and it wasn't to hurt the Heilinists. It was to outmaneuver them, to humiliate them, to beat them at their own game and watch them look dumbfounded as their superior hand was beaten by a superior mind. "If we give them two months, Metten's defenses will be worn thin. They will pick us off slowly."

"Outlasting them is our only option," the military advisor said, his eyes flaring wide. He looked angry, but Brina sensed he was scared.

"Fine," Brina shouted out, looking around the room. "Tell me, if we take this so-called optimal path, what are our chances of victory? What are the chances we can outlast the Heilinists while trapped within these city walls?"

Nobody spoke.

CHAPTER 76

"I know you and your people are fond of the Galleon's Table," Brina went on, unable to suppress a smile as the memory of Acheron flooded back to her. "If you have the lesser hand, what is your best chance of winning?"

"Going all in early," Bron shouted, pumping his fist, "before the opponent with the better hand gets to play all his cards and push you out of the round on value alone."

"That's right," Brina said, pointing a finger at Bron. "I do not doubt the wisdom of your counsel," she told the advisor, "but that would be playing to avoid losing now, not playing to win. If we are to lose, what does it matter if it happens two months sooner rather than later? I say we roll the dice, take the gamble, and play to win."

The military advisor paled, threw up his hands, and said, "Listen, I understand what you're saying. What you propose is a gamble that, in the best scenario—if everything lines up in our favor—could pay off, but it's risky. Going into a siege is the safest option. But I admit, even then, the outlook is dire."

"All I hear," Brina said, "is that you would rather lose a foot every day and end up with nothing than give up the entire field in a day. If we lose, we lose. The outcome is the same, and frankly, if I am to die, I'd rather it be one fell stroke to the neck than a thousand cuts administered over a thousand days."

There was a murmur of assent in the room now. Brina was gaining their confidence.

"If we were talking about a game of cards, I would say you were right," the advisor said, "but we are talking about hundreds of lives. If we do what you propose, everyone old or young enough to carry an axe, spade, or fishing harpoon will need to be placed in that field, and if things play out as they are likely to, all of them will perish between the rise of the sun and the sinking of the chariots. Would you be able to live with that?"

"My only response is this," Brina said. "Within the last ten days, we have seen how these people operate. First, they drowned an entire squad of their own mercenaries just to avoid freeing your people who have been working for them for two decades. Then, they were prepared to kill hundreds of your people stacked like cattle in a barn just to get a few of our warriors off the playing field." She looked around the room, staring into eyes, searching for a connection. "What do you think they will do once they breach the gates of your city?"

***

"Some speech that was," Sneak said as they exited the room last, shaking his head. "You rattled a few cages in there."

"Needed to be done," Brina said. The rush of anger that had been circulating through her system for days now was turning into a baseline. She felt like someone who had jumped off a cliff and was watching the rocks grow closer and closer below her. She enjoyed the feeling. "The only way we're going to win is if we put it all on the line now, in time to support Metten. You know the rabble left behind there. They're the ones who didn't dare join us here. What makes you think they will hold up under siege?"

Bron shook his head and lobbed a glob of phlegm out a nearby window. "Whether they want it or not, that's what's headed their way," he grunted. "For our part, I thank the Allmother that we had you in that room." He looked around in disgust at the elders disappearing around the corner of the corridor ahead of them. "These gray hairs have seen too many cycles and grown too comfortable in their chairs in this cushy palace. They have forgotten the feeling of sweat burning on calloused hands, have forgotten the thump of the war drum pulsing through their chests. They have forgotten all they were trained to stand for. We are Biori, not flatlander rabble or Heilinist snakes. We stand. If a boulder rolls our way, we stand. If an avalanche comes rushing down at us, we stand. And this is no force of nature we're faced with. These are men, far more brittle than stone and ice."

He looked out the window in the distance, where tiny black dots signified ships unloading. "If it were up to me," Bron said, "we'd hit them by sunrise. Roll over their flimsy barricades, fling them away. They may have a few hardened soldiers in their midst, but I bet most of them have gotten so used to having superior numbers and equipment that they won't know what to do when faced with a foe who cares about neither."

Brina looked over her shoulder and saw Abrasax shuffling out of the headmother's room, looking pale and anxious. "Give me a moment, lads," she said as she strode over to him. "Father…"

"Let's take a walk," Abrasax said.

CHAPTER 77

They drifted through the headmother's palace, trudging up endless winding staircases until they reached the top of the central tower. Abrasax flared *Consol* to convince half a dozen guards who were stationed there that they should take an early break and that they would keep things under control for a while. It was easy. Influencing others had once come as naturally to him as taking his next breath. As soon as they had disappeared down the trapdoor, Abrasax closed it. He sat down on the battlements with his back to the deep drop to the courtyard below and gestured for Brina to do the same.

Abrasax stared out into the distance. He touched *Claritas*. The shape burned so smoothly that it felt as though spyglasses were built into his skull. Even with the enhancement, he could only make out a line of ants near the far end of the horseshoe island. They traipsed back and forth from ship to shore, carrying barrels, crates, and racks stacked with glittering weaponry.

"Are you okay?" Brina asked. Her intense demeanor from before had shifted. There was genuine concern in her voice, which broke Abrasax's heart. No daughter ought to worry about her father's courage in situations like these.

During his days spent in the darkness of God's Maul, he had lived a parallel life in his own head. Day after day, he had imagined living the life the church had taken from them. In that fantasy life, he had been strong. He had picked Sabrina up when she fell, dusted her off, and told her it would be all right. He had taught her all he knew so that she could be stronger than he ever was. In his own mind, he had told her proudly of the dozens of raids he and the Signum had conducted. Of the tight gaps they had squeezed through, the insurmountable odds they had conquered without blinking.

Now that she was sitting right in front of him, he didn't have it in himself to be proud of all that bloodshed. Instead of feeling strong, feeling like he could show her the way in these dark times, he felt broken. When he tore his gaze away from the distant green fields and the seam between land and azure sea, he spoke in a hoarse voice that would have embarrassed his former self.

"I really thought that we could escape this."

When she gave him a questioning look, he gestured at the distant fleet anchored before Metten and the one on the east coast of the horseshoe. "I've had my fill of suffering. Both my own and that of others.

"When Saf pestered me day in and day out to involve myself in the recruits' training, to offer words of encouragement, I refused. I didn't want to be that person anymore. The one who inspired struggle, the one to fan the flames of strife and war. I deluded myself into thinking that my part was done. I should've known better."

In his head, he watched Cardinal De Leliard's pudgy face loom over him as he slammed the casket shut, condemning him to another week in the narrow, sweltering darkness of his prison. He scratched at the puckered scars that covered his arms and legs, felt his hands crawling underneath his tunic like parasites digging for deep cuts that had never quite healed. "I should've known," he repeated.

Brina sighed, combing her fingers through her scraggy black hair, and rubbing a knuckle at the scar tissue where her left eye had once been.

"It's not your fault," she said. "I won't lie. At the beginning of all this, I didn't understand why you wouldn't want to take revenge on those who had imprisoned you and murdered your friends. I get it now. I have killed many more darkhelms this past year than I could've ever imagined. All their spilled blood combined hasn't laid Acheron's memory to rest in my mind. It hasn't restored Doorstep's Ditch from its ashes, and it hasn't made either of us younger, so we could live the lives that were taken from us. To tell you the truth, it's only made me callous."

"And now..." She stared into the distance, swallowing. "We're about to enter a world of pain. No matter the outcome, all we'll have when the sun has risen and fallen twice more are grieving families and hearts turned to manure for soil no hands will be left to till." She laughed, her voice hollow. "Perhaps," she said, "I should have accepted your offer back in Morassia. We could've spent a pleasant year roasting fish caught with our own hands and drinking water from coconuts gathered by our own sweat."

"That was only a dream," Abrasax said. "It was my mind giving me a brief reprieve from that which I knew needed to be done. It's not in our blood to let the world pass us by and to hide in the dark crevices of the world. Nor, for all he tried to prove the opposite, was it in your godfather's blood."

"We would've turned into him, wouldn't we?" Brina asked. Abrasax gave

CHAPTER 77

her a sad smile. A lightness was pushing away the mixture of guilt, horror, and dread that had been building up in his chest for months.

"You know what?" he said. "Now that the end of the road lies in front of us, I wouldn't change a single thing. This last year, I spent hiding from who I was meant to be. When the sun rises tomorrow, I will leave that in the past. If we are to walk on solid ground for the very last time tomorrow, we will make sure that our legacy lives on."

Brina nodded, one corner of her mouth twitching into a wry smile. "Yes, we will," she said.

"It was you who showed me that," Abrasax said, nodding toward the staircase, thinking about what had gone down in the throne room, how his daughter had spoken the words he ought to have spoken. Words he'd like to imagine he would have spoken, but they had caught in his throat.

"I didn't get a chance to teach you half as much as I wanted to," he said, "but you have taught me more than I had ever dreamed."

Brina got up, and he did the same. For the first time since they had been reunited, she hugged him. He put his arms around her shoulders and squeezed. Whatever came tomorrow, he had never felt more at peace.

CHAPTER 78

"Faster!" Saf yelled as her fellow rebels moved around heavy stones to rebuild the most brittle sections of the citadel's wall. "They could be upon us as soon as tomorrow. We need to get this done now." With every word she spoke, she flared *Consol*, putting urgency in every syllable. If they were to withstand a siege for more than a handful of hours, she needed to squeeze every drop of energy out of these people.

She made her way down to the temple, which lay outside of the citadel's walls, where most of the loose stones were being collected. A young woman, no older than fifteen, stumbled and fell behind the heavy cart she was pushing. The road was sandy, and the cart's wheels had sunk into the ground. Saf picked the girl up and set her down atop the enormous stone block she was transporting.

"Take a rest," she said. With a little help from *Forte*, she grabbed the handles of the cart and pushed it up the slope as the girl lay flat on her back on the stone slab.

"I'm sorry," the girl muttered. "It's just so heavy. So heavy."

Part of Saf wanted to tell her to harden up, that worse days lay ahead, but it wasn't the right move. Tough love would only get her so far. Instead, she lowered her voice. "I know times are tough. Rest for a while, and when you can, get back on your feet. Try going for smaller blocks. I'd rather have you working at a pace you can maintain than burning yourself out."

The girl nodded. When they reached the top of the hill, where the wall was being reconstructed, Saf handed the girl her canteen, full of fresh spring water from this morning. Another thing to worry about.

Potable water had never been a problem on Metten. A spring in the center of the island flowed down in a winding river, providing crystal-clear water just half a mile's march away. Now that was half a mile too far outside the citadel's walls. As soon as the Heilinists gained ground, water would become inaccessible.

CHAPTER 78

Saf noted it down on her mental list of concerns and began walking down the hillside again, yelling out encouragements to those faltering during the work and spitting admonishments at those who were slacking. Even now, some recruits found time to sit in the sand, casting dice and betting what remained of their meager rations. She crouched down beside two older men who sat in the shade with their backs against a thick tree and neglected to burn *Consol*. She wanted to encourage herself to choose every word with precision.

"If you do not earn your keep, you will sleep outside of the keep. Do I make myself clear?"

One man looked like he wanted to make a snarky remark, but Saf jabbed a finger over her shoulder toward the bay where, in the distance, the approaching fleet was visible. "Who would you rather be accountable to? Me or them?"

This got them back on their feet.

"Looks like she still got the golden touch," a voice drawled behind her. Saf turned around and found two figures in long black leather coats, wearing black helmets, staring in her direction. They were already drawing attention from the working recruits.

"You are distracting my people," Saf said. She activated a low burn of *Testudo*, closing off her mind to any emotions. Agents of the weavers obscured their eyes for a reason. "We will talk in my office."

The taller and bulkier of the two, Methuselah, waved his hand toward the gatehouse as though to say, "After you."

***

"Now? Of all times?" Saf flung the door shut behind her. Methuselah and Felix had already taken up seats at the far end of the long conference table.

"Of course," Felix said.

"When else?" the other continued as though reciting a practiced routine.

"When my work is done," Saf snapped. "That was the agreement."

"Your work is done," Felix said.

"More than done, one could argue," Methuselah said.

Saf wandered over to the open, glass window on the far end, and gestured with both hands at the redsails fleet that was drawing closer with every passing minute. "Does this look done to you? Has the empire been destroyed?"

"Ah," Felix said, with the polite tone of one inquiring about the time. "I thought we might hit this little snag." He withdrew a scroll of parchment from the inside of his robes. An icy hand squeezed Saf's heart. She recognized the blood red parchment at once and, with a stab of regret and shame, saw her own curly signature at the bottom.

"I, Saphara Al Noor, solemnly promise to uphold the following agreement with the Order of the Weavers." Felix skimmed through the document, lips moving as he read, ""Yada yada... Possession of my eternal soul... Yada yada... Service until death..." Ah, here we are." Felix raised a finger. ""In exchange for the power of the weavers, and the privilege of using it to take revenge on those who captured, enslaved, and abused me in every way imaginable.""

Felix rolled up the scroll. It disappeared with a flourish into his inside pocket.

For one insane moment, Saf wanted to lunge at Felix, twist his head so it faced the opposite way, and tear that scroll into a thousand pieces, burn it and cast what remained to the sea, but it wouldn't work that way. She knew it, and they knew it. It wasn't the parchment that held power. It was the order.

"As my fair colleague has just read, the terms of your agreement state that we were to offer you the opportunity for revenge. Mistress Weavess trained you in the sparkgazing arts to grant you the power to manipulate, coerce, and destroy those who have enslaved you, as per the agreement. Subsequently, the order granted you over five years' time to achieve this objective. We were delighted to hear that on the tenth day of the first cycle of last year, the entire slave colony on Snake Island was burned to the ground after their metal works exploded. According to our sources, all slaves were freed. I think you will find that this constitutes revenge under the contract's terms, and that our end of the deal has now been completed."

"Which leaves," Felix added with a simpering smile, "your end of the deal."

"You are to be evacuated from the island today," Methuselah stated, "to return to the order's headquarters and await assignment. We have trained you, shared our secrets with you, and indeed, provided you with the very scripts that are in your possession right now." Methuselah's eyes, shaded by the black helmet he wore, roved over Saf's body as though determining where she kept her pouch of scripts. "It is only just that you now turn these powers to the good of the organization who gave them to you."

"Wait," Saf said. "That's impossible. Without me, these people stand no chance, they would be rudderless. I swore to them when they began training with us that I would guide them until the very end in this matter. I cannot desert them now, right before they face the full might of the empire. We are outnumbered as it is."

CHAPTER 78

"I'm afraid the terms are not up for debate," Felix said. "We must protect our asset. In this case, you. If you were to be destroyed, you can imagine the loss of value to our employer."

"It is only fair," Methuselah added.

"And if I refuse?" Saf said. Though she could feel the power of their influence, the constant burn of *Testudo* prevented the venom in their voices from reaching its full effect. She knew full well what the alternative was. Both Felix and Methuselah were accomplished sparkgazers. She would not win a fight against both of them at once. *Then again,* Saf reasoned, *if they kill me, they have no asset. Leverage, that is what I need.*

"How about this?" she said. "In exchange for more time, I will return my pouch of scripts to you, including all the ones I have added during my own journeys, as collateral. After the siege of the island is over, I will voluntarily return to the order's headquarters and serve."

"I'm afraid we are not at liberty to negotiate," Felix said.

"The terms of the agreement are quite clear," Methuselah added. "The mistress wants us to hold you to the terms you yourself have signed."

"Then I want an appeal," Saf said. "I would argue that the terms of the contract have not been reached. Revenge is only obtained when the very institution that enslaved me has been ruined."

"That is not in the mistress's interests," Methuselah said. "She stands to lose much if the internal strife between the free states and the Heilinists were to come to an end. Many of our agents have been driven by motives similar to yours. It is too valuable a source of assets to give up. You are done fighting."

Saf took a deep breath, then held the pouch of scripts out of the window with her outstretched arm and put her leg on the windowsill. One move and both she and the scripts would cascade into the sea, lost forever.

"Stop!" Felix's voice rang out at once, followed by Methuselah's. Saf was ready. She flared *Testudo* with all her might. The force of their combined commands pulled at her muscles in a vain attempt to keep her rooted to the spot. She lifted her other foot off the ground and stood on the windowsill with both feet, staring at the men in defiance.

"I have grown stronger than you imagined. Stronger than the mistress imagined. I will serve my end of the deal, but not until I have received what is rightfully mine."

"Get down from there." The both of them spoke mechanically, and this time, the combined efforts of their wills were enough to make Saf wobble toward the inside of the room. She held her protective shape, aided by the knowledge that if she failed this test of wills, everyone remaining on this island, who counted on her, would suffer a gruesome future. Saf would be damned if she allowed one more person to fall prey to the slavery machine that was the Heilinist church.

"You don't control me," she said. "Nobody controls me. That was why I trained. That was why I joined. I will hold up my end of the deal. But I will not be carted away from this place like a slave in chains, never again."

Just like that, Felix and Methuselah's hold on her mind slipped. She sat down on the windowsill, glaring at them, demonstrating that her movements were still free and smooth and determined by no one but herself.

"Here." She strode over to the table and dropped her entire pouch of sigils on the table. "Here is my collateral. All the Weavess stands to lose now is the beating of my heart. And I'm afraid that is mine to give or take." The two black figures swept up the pouch of scripts, tucked it away in an inside pocket, and strode from the room. As they disappeared down the hallway, Saf was reminded of crows taking flight as they realized the carcass they had landed on was still alive.

CHAPTER 79

he darkhelms had established a temporary fortification on the last stretch of plain before the coastal region of Bior transitioned into the mountain range that dominated the island. They had spent the entire day felling trees, raising palisades, and digging trenches. They knew they had time on their side, and they clearly intended to use it. From a distance, it appeared there were about two thousand of them. Compared to the eight hundred Biori warriors and rebel recruits, the church held overwhelming numbers.

As dusk fell, Brina, Bron, Abrasax, and Solana descended from the foothills where the Biori had set up their boar's hide tents. Under the veil of darkness, they crept toward the darkhelm camp. They lay flat on their bellies in the low brush and waited.

"How long until the dark window?" Sneak whispered.

Brina looked up at the heavens. The first chariot had vanished into the sea, while the second sat atop the horizon like a tumbleweed rolling down a vacant street.

"Handful of minutes. Ten at the most." Brina's heart pounded in her ears as she looked around at her compatriots. If there had ever been a time to execute a plan flawlessly, it was now. There was no room for error. The defenders' slim hopes rested on their shoulders. They had to do a lot of damage quickly. If they were caught, Bior was a major step closer to becoming a Heilinist province.

"Listen up," Solana said. "They're likely to keep the food and water toward the back of the camp, as those would have been in the back of the caravan as the army marched. We'll have to sneak around the camp and find an entrance near the back. From there, I'll handle the distractions while you ensure that their food and water turn to ash and mud. Are we clear?"

They all nodded.

The moment the second chariot dove into the Sundered Sea, they jumped to their feet and ran. Racing across the dark plain with a low burn of *Lux* to guide her, Brina could smell the fresh grass underfoot, mingling with the first flowers of the season. It would have been a beautiful night, like those she had loved in the wilds of Hammerstroke, had it not been for the dark cloud of danger overhead. It was strange to think that such a peaceful landscape would soon be drenched in blood. Two cultures would clash until only one remained, while nature, oblivious to the machinations of humanity, bloomed and ripened at its own immutable pace.

"Here we go," Solana whispered. "Leave this part to me." She donned the same officer's helmet they had stolen at the Port of Cordwain, and approached two sentries posted near an opening in the palisade wall.

"Excellent work, recruits," she snarled. Brina recoiled. The effects of Solana's unnatural influence were awe-inspiring. Even though Brina knew it was a trick, every word sliced through her like a razor. "You let me sneak right past you twice. I knew by the looks of you two that you weren't up to the task. Follow me." Solana strode past them and into the camp.

"But surely, Your Purity," one of them began, "we shouldn't abandon—"

Solana cut him off. "It doesn't matter if you abandon your post, you imbecile, because you are as blind as a monk of Everberg, without the skills to make up for it. You're relieved for the night, and be sure that tomorrow morning there will be consequences." As she strolled off, the guards followed her.

Seizing the moment, Brina and the others scurried into the camp, using *Leve* to muffle their footsteps. It didn't take long for them to discover an enormous pile of crates and barrels stacked together between a pavilion and multiple tents.

"Damn it," Brina hissed. "They've surrounded the supplies with tents. If we make so much as a noise, we'll be surrounded."

"Let's get on with it," Bron growled, his eyes gleamed with excitement as he placed both hands on the first pile of crates and then the second. Working in tandem, they ignited one crate after the other until the entire pile of supplies blazed like a bonfire. For good measure, they brushed their fingertips along the tents, setting them alight too.

Bron let out a low laugh. "Unbelievable. They're almost making it too easy. Let's get out of here before they realize we were here." He turned around, and his face fell open in a gape of horror. Behind them, in the walkway between two burning tents, stood Solana, backed by fifty darkhelm archers.

Solana raised an arm. "Surrender now, heathens! We've got you outnumbered and surrounded. Come quietly and you shall live. You have three

CHAPTER 79

heartbeats to decide." Brina froze, gazing at the tiny slits in Solana's helmet, searching for the woman's eyes. It had happened. After all the pleading and discussions, this was the moment it all came down to: Solana, backed by fifty of her former associates, standing against them at the most crucial of moments.

"One," Solana raised a single finger in the air. None of them spoke, dumbstruck by what was happening.

"Two."

"Come on!" Abrasax called out, always the voice of reason. "We can talk about this."

"Three." Solana's arm swung downward.

"Get down!" Brina shouted. There was the rattle of dozens of bowstrings being unleashed. An ominous buzz, like a hive of angry wasps, filled the air. Brina hit the mud face-first, caught between the heat of the flames beside her and the rain of death above.

Beside her, Bron and Abrasax did the same. Sneak, however, seemed to have frozen. He stood there, staring at Solana, frozen in terror. His eyes were wide as one, two, three of the windup quarrels struck him in the chest. He toppled backward like a puppet with its strings cut, tumbling into the mud. Abrasax let out a roar, eyes burning blue with *Forte*, and charged straight at Solana. The last thing Brina heard him say was, "Get Sneak out of here; I'll hold them off."

He launched himself into the air, landed amidst a cluster of darkhelms, and fought like a lion. Armored bodies went flying, windups were cast aside, and the other soldiers beat a hasty retreat. They dispersed with a shout from Solana: "I'll deal with him! You make sure the others don't escape. Get reinforcements! Wake as many as you can."

Brina and Bron, both burning *Forte*, charged into the darkness, each carrying one arm of Sneak's limp body. Though their stamina had been boosted by the sigil, carrying the unresponsive Sneak between them slowed them down. Boots thumped in the mud behind them, and though they were gaining a small lead, Brina knew in her heart that they couldn't maintain this pace as long as a well-trained army of darkhelms could.

They ran out of the camp, back toward the hillside where the Biori's camp lay hidden. They sprinted for what felt like fifteen minutes, the throng of pursuers growing heavier and heavier behind them. As their numbers swelled, the darkhelms slowed down, but there were dozens, perhaps hundreds of them, right on Brina's heels. To add insult to injury, the first chariot chose that moment to reemerge from the Sundered Sea, ending the dark window and casting a dim glow on the plains where Bron, Brina, and Sneak were making their escape, making them visible once more.

When they reached the hillside, they laid Sneak down on a boulder. Glancing behind them to gauge the distance, Brina's stomach dropped. A sea of torches was approaching. The darkhelm camp had emptied, and every awakened soldier in the camp was marching in their direction.

"This is it," Sneak groaned. "Just leave me here and return to the camp. It's not worth it. You can't drag me all the way."

"Don't be stupid," Bron grunted. Branches and twigs snapped underfoot, announcing the presence of booted feet. The first group of darkhelms was only a hundred yards away. "They're here."

"Well, in that case," Sneak announced, "I suggest we crack some skulls." He reached down the front of his leather tunic, undid the bindings, revealing the thick steel plate he was wearing underneath. All three darkhelm quarrels had barely dented the surface.

On both sides of the darkhelms, groups of Biori warriors emerged from the tree line. The darkhelms were surrounded.

"Tricked you, you morons!" Sneak jumped to his feet, grinning from ear to ear.

In the distance, Brina could see Abrasax and Solana sneaking out of the darkhelm camp amid the commotion. Brina's jaw clenched. Solana had kept her word, after all. She had created total chaos, allowing them to drag the darkhelms out of their camp when they were least prepared.

The trap had sprung.

CHAPTER 80

"Captain, they're following us!" The cry shattered the stillness of the night.

Zot turned to gaze over the stern of the ship's quarterdeck, confirming the lookout's call from the crow's nest. A dozen red-sailed ships, lit by the celestial chariots above, edged across the horizon, growing larger. At least five were galleons—full-sized vessels ready for battle—while the remainder were smaller support craft. Their exact number was hard to guess at this distance, but one thing was certain: Metten was in trouble.

At the helm, Captain Burke—a man with a voice as slick as his black hair and a beard so unkempt it might house relics predating the Heilinist era—tensed. His plump fingers drummed against the wooden wheel as he, too, glanced over his shoulder at the approaching threat.

"It's okay," Zot reassured him in a soothing tone, as though he were talking to a skittish horse. "They're after the island, not you or your crew."

"Is that so?" Burke shot back. "That'll be small comfort when they find me with a cargo full of weapons and enough provisions to sustain an army for weeks. Whatever you've got planned, it incriminates us."

Zot flashed a grin, revealing a row of sharp teeth. "You worry too much, Captain. By dawn, you'll be long gone, and your crew will be richer than ever. Steer left here," Zot instructed, pointing at the stone pillars jutting out from the water around Metten. "It's a direct path to the docks. The fleet won't risk crossing at night. Without knowing these waters, they couldn't."

It took some persuasion and the sound of jingling shards, but in the end, Zot convinced the captain to stay on course toward Metten.

As the docks appeared in the distance, Zot's shoulders tensed. This was the moment he'd been waiting for. It had been months in the making, but now that it had arrived, everything felt off. He'd left behind the boy in Sachrya's clutches, and it had all been his fault. His stinking greed had brought disaster down right on top of their heads.

As they approached the bay, two dozen points of light poured from the citadel's gates. Even from several hundred yards out, nervous chatter carried over the wind to the ship.

Captain Burke navigated the maze of stone pillars and brought the vessel into the bay near the citadel with apparent ease. The ship nudged against the dock, where two crew members set to work securing heavy ropes to begin the mooring process.

A spear whizzed overhead, embedding itself in the mainmast with a resounding thwack. Zot rushed to the ship's edge to identify the source of the weapon and saw a hundred rebel recruits positioned in battle formation along the shore. An officer was reprimanding a young man who was lacking his own spear, yet the front lines held firm, spears pointed outward and makeshift shields raised.

"It's me, you fools! Dimimzy Zot!" He jumped up and down, waving his arms in exasperation. "I've brought weapons and food, as I promised," Zot shouted, raising his hands above his head as the anxious eyes of the crew scanned the night for more stray spears.

"Zot?" A low, smooth voice resonated from the crowd. Those silky tones could only belong to one woman. The ranks of recruits parted down the center, allowing Saphara Al Noor, clad in reinforced leather armor, to step forward. At a mere whisper from her, all the spears in formation shifted upward into a relaxed stance. Murmuring broke out behind Saf as the tension eased.

"It's safe, lads," Zot told the sailors holding the mooring ropes. "Go ahead."

Once the gangplank was positioned, Zot sauntered down to the docks, extending his arms as though ready to envelop both Saf and her army in a grand embrace.

"You came," Saf said. Her expression remained neutral, but a spark ignited in her eyes.

"I did," Zot confirmed. "And judging by the situation, my arrival is timely. I'm sure you've noticed your impending visitors."

"We have," Saf said. "That's why we were so quick to assemble this little welcoming committee for you. We thought the enemy was upon us."

"Not yet," Zot responded, smiling. He gestured to the crew, who began unloading crates from the ship's hold onto the dock. Before Saf could respond, the recruits erupted in cheers, their crooked spears pounding against improvised shields.

It was only now, up close, that Zot noticed just how primitive their weapons were. Many recruits wielded what amounted to knives tied to sticks,

CHAPTER 80

and their shields were an assortment of random items cobbled together into circular shapes. Their armor was a mishmash of leather studded with rusty nails and small sections of worn metal plates. It was pathetic.

As more goods were unloaded, the recruits began chanting his name: "Zot, Zot, Zot!"

For a fleeting moment, a wave of euphoria swept over Zot. He'd fulfilled his promises. He'd proven that he could still get things done. As quickly as the feeling came, it extinguished like a candle in a gust. Wane's face haunted him. They had started this journey together, vowing to support the rebellion as a duo. Now Zot was alone. Without the boy, there was no true victory.

He remembered the sting of the boy's bravery, as piercing as a scorpion's sting into his flesh. Now, weeks later, the poison of that moment finally overwhelmed him. He had been arrogant and dismissive. And yet, against all odds, the boy had secured a win for the rebellion. Now he was back in Sachrya's grasp, bearing the consequences of Zot's hubris. With each cheer of Zot's name, a piece of him wilted. He was a fraud and a loser.

Sensing his distress, Saf leaned in and murmured, "Where's the boy?"

She glanced over her shoulder to confirm that the recruits, now helping to unload the ship, hadn't overheard.

"It's a long story," Zot answered. Noticing the concern on Saf's face, he added, "He's alive. He's safe, in a way, but we had to make sacrifices to get these supplies here in time."

"Master Zot," a sailor called from behind him. Grateful for the interruption from Saf's penetrating gaze, Zot swiveled around. "You instructed me to deliver this to you—and only you—upon arrival. Remember?"

The sailor presented a mahogany box that reeked of jungle underbrush.

"Ah, yes," Zot responded, smiling. "Thank you, Dorian." He delved into his pouch and handed the kid a few shards for his troubles.

As they started back toward the keep, a line of recruits hoisting bundles of spears and shields trailing behind them, Saf inquired, "What's in there?"

"A secret weapon," Zot replied, his lips curling into a smirk.

"Good," Saf responded. "We'll need it."

CHAPTER 81

"Forward! Get them!" Brina, clutching a heavy metal shield, charged like a bull. Darkhelm maces thundered down on her shield, but aided by *Forte*, she didn't feel a thing as she rushed into the fray. Behind her, cries and screams intertwined in a bloodcurdling symphony of slaughter. For every foot of ground Brina wrested from the enemy, a legion of Biori warriors and Metten rebels filled the space. Together, they formed a battering ram, a spear driving deep into the enemy's ranks.

Brina slammed an approaching darkhelm in the face with her shield. His head spun with a crunch. She raised her spear to halt an oncoming darkhelm officer on the other side. The officer hesitated, staying just out of reach of Brina's spear. Things were going well. Though outnumbered, Brina and Bron had formed a spearhead formation that kept the darkhelms on the back foot.

As the officer continued to dance around the outskirts of Brina's range, Brina, tired of waiting, leaped forward. Her spear lashed out at the officer's helmet. At the very last moment, the woman's hand shot upward. There was a glint of silver against the moonlight, followed by a blinding flash of white. *Forte*'s power vanished.

Brina's shield became a millstone tied to her arm, pulling her to the ground with its abrupt weight. Exhaustion washed over her as hands grabbed at her from all sides. Blinded and disoriented, Brina kicked and swung her arms, trying to fend off whoever was reaching for her.

"It's Springtide!" two soldiers with heavy Biori accents shouted to each other. "Grab her! We need to move her behind the lines." Two pairs of muscular arms pulled Brina backward. She was dragged across the ground for a few yards, then hoisted onto their shoulders and carried away from the battlefield. "It's going to be okay," one of the Biori soldiers said. "Our brothers and sisters are holding the line. We won't let them get to you."

By the time her vision cleared, Brina lay among a row of wounded soldiers being treated by Biori shamans in muddy white robes. They smeared herbal

CHAPTER 81

salves on bleeding wounds and applied pressure to gashes to stem blood loss. Brina crawled onto her knees, stood up, and stumbled into the largest tent she could find, one with a mounted erymanthian's head above the entrance. This, she knew, housed the mobile war room where the warlords were discussing battle strategy. Guards moved aside to let her in, casting terrified glances at her worn face.

"What happened?" she asked. "What's the status on the field?"

"It's not good."

***

The headmother sat hunched over a parchment map, flanked by Hammer the Younger and Drauz, both of her senior military advisers. "The darkhelms are gaining a lot of ground," Hammer said. "Soon we will have to decide whether to break camp and retreat further back toward the capital. We risk losing the advantage of high ground if they push us across this hilltop." His finger tapped down at the approximate location where they were positioned. "When you were injured, there was a lot of shuffling on the battlefield, and it seems like the darkhelms are taking the time to regroup for an oncoming push. We have precious little time to decide our next move."

Brina rubbed her temples. It was a lot to take in all at once, and the aftereffects of the flash still burned every time she blinked. "What are our options?"

"The most sensible thing to do," Drauz said, "is to break camp, push the darkhelms one last time, and then execute an organized retreat. It's the only way to ensure our soldiers don't break into a rout. Should we face a rout, the consequences would be devastating, and the slaughter awe-inspiring. We could retreat to the capital, where we would at least have the comfort of walls between ourselves and the enemy."

"And then what?" A lower, hoarse voice spoke from the corner of the tent.

Brina looked over her shoulder to see Bahov, the ancient warlord, leaning against the tent wall. His head was bandaged, and he was applying pressure to a nasty cut on one of his forearms with a bandage. "If we retreat, what will happen next? That is the question we need to consider."

"What will happen if we don't suffer defeat somewhere in the following hours?" Drauz said. "Because that's what we're headed toward right now. We could reinforce the walls, keep them out for as long as possible."

Bahov gave a sad smile. "Realistically," he said, "what is your outlook on this scenario, Hammer?" He looked at the other man. Hammer closed his eyes as though reliving a most painful memory.

"They will starve us out," he said. "It's the only outcome. They have superiority at sea, and if we cede land to them, they will have superiority on land. They will have all the space to forage and hunt for as many supplies as they need while we're trapped in a cage of our own making."

"But we could get the civilians to help," Drauz urged. "We could use them to swell our numbers."

"I will not turn noncombatants into soldiers," the headmother said. "Everyone able to bear arms rode out with us. What's left in the city are those too old, too young, or too frail to hold spear and shield. I will not force them into harm's way. And I do not believe, evil though they may be, that the darkhelms would give up a labor force like that. If we keep them away from the fighting, at least they will be safe."

"You call that safe?" Drauz asked, his tone rising. "To be considered a labor force too valuable to be slaughtered on the spot? They're better off dead."

A silence fell, heavy enough to shatter limbs, deep enough to cleave flesh from bone.

"In times like this," the headmother said, "when there are no winning options on the table, we have to return to the essence of what it means to be Biori. The very nature of what is in our blood. So what does your sense of honor tell you to do? Is forcing the elderly and weak to fight, because we could not hold the line, what your honor dictates us to do?" she asked Drauz.

"No." Drauz stared straight ahead. "It is not."

"Then I ask all of you present," the headmother said, "if the options are to fight and to die, or to cower and to die, what the Allmother would have us choose. I consider everyone's opinion in this room, including yours, Miss Springtide, of high importance in deciding this matter."

Brina, stunned to be addressed, stood frozen on the spot.

"What does your honor tell you?" the headmother asked again.

Brina dug deep, rummaging through her hatred of all things empire, past the anguish she had felt when she realized she had sent many soldiers to their deaths a mere week ago. To the feeling she had had when Doorstep's Ditch burned, and she stood by and did nothing. Her gut told her all options were terrible. The thought of leading recruits who had joined their cause believing victory was possible to a certain death was agonizing. And the thought of retreating, and allowing the darkhelms to take their sweet time to destroy Metten and Bior in one fell stroke, tasted just as sour in her mouth.

When she spoke, she surprised even herself. "What it comes down to is math," she said. "If we die regardless of what we choose, how do we ensure there are the fewest of these empire rats left to infest our lands once they are through with us? If we allow them to starve us, we won't have the strength left to decimate their numbers. I say if every one of us can drag two of them with us to the below world, that's as close to a victory as we will come." She rubbed her face with her hands, trying to regain control of her trembling limbs. "However, it would weigh on me," she concluded, "to command such a thing. It is not mine or anyone's right to dictate how and when another should die."

"But it is not we who decide to command such things," the Headmother said. "Honor commands it. Dignity commands it. History commands it."

"Honor commands it," Hammer agreed.

"Honor commands it." Drauz nodded.

"Then it is decided," Bahov said. He closed his eyes as though reliving a memory from long ago. "We will push one last time, two shields colliding until one of them shatters."

Brina looked at Abrasax. "Do you have that *Sonorus* script with you?"

A faint smile crept over Abrasax's face as he nodded.

"What's there to smirk about?" Brina narrowed her eyes at him.

"A father's pride. Nothing more, nothing less." He put a hand on her shoulder and handed her the script with the other. "Do you realize what we just agreed to? The true ramifications of it?"

"Death by dawn," Brina said. Inexplicably, she felt herself grinning. Rather than fear, an exhilarating rage filled her body as the words left her mouth. She felt like Acheron, leaning over the edge of the tower and peering into the void. *The eternal barrow awaits.*

"Death by dawn." Abrasax repeated the words slowly, as though he were trying to taste them. "The journey draws to a close at last."

"Death by dawn!" Bahov pushed himself to his feet, eyes wide with renewed vigor. "By the Allmother, we will give them a fight to resonate through the ages. These bastards have no idea of the storm that's about to descend on them."

CHAPTER 82

Brina lined up what remained of the Metten rebels on the hilltop. Though the tide of war had eaten away at their number already, a solid one hundred and fifty remained. She split them up into three groups of fifty, one to be led by herself, one by Abrasax and a third by Sneak. Brina paced back and forth before their ranks, like a sheikan, cornered and ready to pounce. The faces before her were bloodied, terrified, and drained from exhaustion.

Shields lay shattered, spears broken. Every single one of them looked ready to fold. Brina's gut churned as she realized how much they had gone through already, and how much more she was about to ask of them. The words spoken in the headmother's tent threatened to flit away into the dark like fireflies. It had been easy to strategize and draw a conclusion about what needed to be done. To look someone in the eye, and tell them that tomorrow would never come, was a different beast. *Death by dawn*, she repeated to herself. With every repetition, the mantra fueled her anger until she found the courage to speak.

"My friends," Brina shouted, her voice amplified to unnatural levels by *Sonorus*, "I want you to take a moment and think back to everything the empire has taken from you over a lifetime.

"I want you to remember the long hard days of forced labor, the murder of friends and family, the blaze as everything you owned was put to the torch."

She glared at the soldiers as she passed them, head held high. Her blood rose as she remembered the hanging of Azaria Oldenbreeze and Acheron tumbling head over heels down Locktower A at God's Maul. The empire had forced her to grow up in the muck, and from the dirt, the filth, and the blood, a monster had risen. Tonight, that monster was ready to devour as many darkhelms as it could on its way to the afterlife.

"What have they taken from us?" Brina screamed.

"Everything!" the recruits chorused back.

CHAPTER 82

"How much more are you willing to give them?"

"Nothing!"

Brina nodded at them, jaw clenching and unclenching. The time was now to tell them just how badly the deck was stacked against them.

"My friends, tonight we stand before a beast unleashed. The Cardinal, from his comfortable halls, has sent his lapdogs to subdue us. He seeks to overwhelm us with numbers and to forcefully return us to the forges, and the mines, and the mud before the stoneward. He thinks we will bow down and allow ourselves to become his prisoners once more.

"The truth is this. The darkhelms outnumber us, and they know it. They intend to seize Bior, our freedom, and our way of life while risking nothing. They expect us to cower behind the capital's walls until they can starve us out.

"We cannot allow this. All we have left is our lives. I intend to choose the time and place where I lay mine down, rather than wait for the empire to decide for me."

Silence followed as the reality of the situation sank in. Brina waited for disparate murmurs to simmer down before continuing.

"I'm not here to tell anyone what to do," she said, "but I know one thing. I know that when, in a handful of minutes, the Biori sound their war horns to launch a frontal assault down the hillside, I will be right beside them. And I will not let up until my strength gives way and my body crumples in on itself. I will not run anymore. I will not let the church gain another foot of ground. Tonight, I will draw the final line here on this hilltop. Who is with me?"

At first, only a handful shouted their approval. Many faces looked tense, terrified. Then the first of the Biori war horns resounded in the distance, signaling the start of the assault.

"For the last time," Brina said, "I ask you, who is with me?" The roar was deafening.

Spear and shield raised above her head, Brina turned around and took off at a jog down the hillside, meeting up with the Biori forces near a vast boulder atop which the headmother stood. Only two, perhaps three hundred yards away, the first lines of darkhelms were reforming. They crept up the hillside, gaining ground.

The Biori division to Brina's left was led by Bron, while to her right, two more divisions of Metten rebels were led by Sneak and Abrasax. The four of them formed the vanguard of the assault. Distributing the sparkgazers across as many units as possible had been as much a tactical decision as it was focused on morale. Not only would it boost the soldiers' confidence to have a sigilist by their side as they stormed the darkhelms' positions, but in case of another flash being deployed, they didn't risk all four sparkgazers being hit at the same time.

Of course, Solana wasn't vulnerable to the flashes, which gave her the unenviable task of guarding the headmother. The two were never to separate throughout the battle. The Biori would give their all for as long as their headmother was there to witness their efforts. To lose the head of the snake would be to lose all control over the battle, and that was to be avoided at all costs.

Heart pounding, Brina waited for the double blast of the horns that was the agreed-upon signal for the rush to commence.

***

Before Brina's ears had registered the second blast of the horn, she was swept away by her own momentum. Charging down the hillside, she thought of just how useful her *Veloce*-script might have been that night. She hoped the little girl in the swamps of Morassia, who now possessed it, practiced daily and had caught as many fish as her heart desired. *If I am to die, at least I left behind one thing not defined by blood and death.* That thought put a smile on her face as they neared the darkhelms' ranks.

Brina prepared for the night to fill with windup quarrels as the darkhelms' archers took position. By charging ahead of the pack, Brina hoped to make the first volley as awkward as possible. The darkhelms would want to aim for her, to take out a high-value target, but to do so they would have to shoot while most of the rebels were still out of range. If they waited until the entire depth of the rebel platoons was in range, Brina would already be upon them, making it impossible to shoot her for fear of hitting their own soldiers.

When she heard the thwack of the first bowstring, Brina shouted, "Shields!" Her voice boomed in the dark, amplified by *Sonorus*. A second later, she made a fortified jump straight up into the air. As dozens of windup quarrels sailed beneath her feet, Brina spotted a detachment of archers stationed on a ledge to her right. They would be out of reach for most common foot soldiers, and the lack of throwing spears in the rebels' hands would make them an irritating force that could harass them with windup quarrels again and again while being almost untouchable.

Brina switched into *Grave* and plummeted like a rock, landing straight on the outcropping amidst the confused archers.

"Hello and goodbye." She grinned as she kicked one archer squarely in the

CHAPTER 82

chest. The force of the blow caused him to fly backward into his companions, half a dozen of whom toppled over the ledge, tumbling down the cliff.

Brina whirled around with her spear and shield outstretched, like a farmer scything down ripe grain. In a matter of seconds, the ledge was empty. Windups and ammunition lay scattered all around her. Brina picked up one of the weapons, used *Forte* to rewind it, and began picking off targets below.

Further down the battlefield, she could spot Bron and his regiment of Biori, carving a path through the darkhelms who parted before them like the sea at low tide. He almost didn't need his sigil power as he stood at the head of the spear wall. The triangular formation carved an opening in the darkhelm lines, which was instantly filled with more Biori warriors.

Brina's own squad of rebels made contact on the right flank of the battlefield right below her. Brina leaped down from the ledge, burning *Grave*. With the force of a boulder crashing into loose sand, she slammed into the darkhelms from above. None of them had seen it coming, their eyes trained on their adversaries who were jabbing spears and raising shields right ahead of them. The surprise attack was enough to disrupt their line, providing an opportunity for Brina to join up with her platoon once more.

As they drove the darkhelms back down the hillside, Brina's exhilaration surged. Their plan was working. They were gaining ground. The darkhelms, overconfident in their impending victory, had underestimated the fight remaining in their opponents. Now, they were suffering the consequences. The ground was churned into mud beneath their booted feet as both armies grappled and clawed at each other. To Brina's left, Abrasax's and Sneak's troops had joined forces. Both of the sparkgazers were at the forefront of their columns, dodging mace swings and disrupting the enemy's defensive line with powerful, *Forte*-infused blows.

Brina spotted an officer, observing in slow motion as the woman's hand dipped into her pocket. She whirled around just in time as a blinding white flash hit her in the back.

"Missed me," Brina taunted. She touched *Forte* and charged forward like an enraged bull. She shoved aside a handful of intervening soldiers to reach the officer, who was fumbling with a capsule of magnesium powder. Brina snatched the flasher from her and used it as a blunt instrument, beating the woman onto her knees. Other soldiers behind her rushed to drag the woman away, but not before Brina's spear had found its mark between the narrow slits of the officer's helmet. Crimson blood gushed over black metal as the officer was hauled away.

As the battle wore on, Brina felt the momentum they had initially generated dissipate like a puddle under the rising sun. The mud deepened as blood saturated the ground, turning the soil into quicksand.

A dozen yards to Brina's right, a recruit lunged forward to finish a stumbling enemy, but slipped in the mud. His shield arm was trapped, and he was pummeled by darkhelm maces until his twitching body fell still.

Brina called out, gesturing for more soldiers to help, but it was too late. In their rage, the recruits surged forward, yanking off helmets and exposing the darkhelms' bare faces. They pulled at their hair, forcing them into the bloodied mud, while the darkhelms swung their maces indiscriminately, smashing everything in their path. Jaws were broken, eyes gouged out, teeth rained onto the battlefield. The fighting grew brutal as the positions became more entrenched.

While the Biori warriors and Metten rebels were losing stamina, the darkhelms rotated their frontline every so often with fresh soldiers from the back of their ranks. It was an unfair advantage granted by their superior numbers, and it was showing. Though the darkhelms couldn't match the resistance's ferocity, the cold, calculated strategy of their officers ensured that at the end of this bloodbath, their side would be the one left standing.

Brina fought like a wild beast, making fortified jumps across the frontline to aid those sections that seemed to weaken under the relentless pressure. Using her shield as a battering ram, she flared *Forte*, charging forward, forcing the darkhelms back, knocking them over, and leading a stampede of rebels to trample them in the mud. As the battle wore on, Brina could feel her energy reserves dwindling, exhaustion seeping into her sigil-enhanced muscles. For a moment, she pulled back, allowing a disorganized mass of rebel soldiers to fill the gap she had left. Clutching a stitch in her side, she looked up. Her blood froze in her veins when she saw them.

In the tree line to her right, a fresh battalion of darkhelms had advanced through the forest and had flanked the resistance army. Soon they would be encircled and trapped, and then the back-and-forth would turn into a massacre.

A distress call sounded from the headmother's war horn as the trap sprung shut. For the first time since they had launched the assault, the attackers had become the defenders. Brina swore under her breath. Though she had known victory was impossible, the impending defeat was bitter. The empire was spitting in her face one last time.

"Come on," she rallied the soldiers nearest to her. "To the flank! We have

CHAPTER 82

to break out before they can surround us." She led a small group of two dozen toward the spot where the darkhelms were emerging from the tree line. There was a whizzing sound in her ears as an unexpected volley of windup quarrels found their marks in those around her. With a series of dull thuds, half a dozen of her compatriots sank into the mud, crimson roses blooming from holes in their leather armor. It was an unlikely stroke of luck that none of the projectiles had hit Brina, who was at the head of the group. The close call drained her spirit. It could have been over right then, right there. She wouldn't have known what hit her. In minutes, she would have bled out, and all this suffering would have ended.

"No such luck," she mumbled to herself, thinking again of her *Veloce*-script and the little girl who owned it. Oh, how she hoped the girl would experience one more peaceful summer before the empire's inevitable conquest of Morassia. Brina launched herself forward with yet another fortified leap, crashing into the first rows of darkhelms. Her spear snapped as a well-timed mace blow landed in the middle of it. She struck the darkhelm who had broken it with her shield. The darkhelm went down, and three of her comrades surrounded Brina, their maces thundering down on her shield.

Brina whirled around, burning what little *Forte* she had left. However, the further she advanced, the more ranks of darkhelms became visible in the darkness. Their torches lit up the forest edge like stars in the firmament. Brina came to a stop as more and more lights flickered on.

"There's just too many," she muttered to herself.

"Mother Springtide," one of the Biori warriors behind her shouted, "look!" Brina glanced over her shoulder and, as she did so, she spotted the first rays of dawn as the sun poked its head out of the Sundered Sea. In the faint gloom of the early light, she saw hundreds of tiny figures marching toward the bottom of the hillside. Divided into what looked like half a dozen legions, each a hundred strong, they marched a quarter-mile or so off to the start of the hillside. "How many more are there?" Brina shook her head, almost disbelieving what she was seeing.

Then the darkhelms near the back of their ranks began turning around. Horns resounded in the valley below, three distinct sounds unlike any she had heard all night. These were not Biori and certainly not darkhelms. The darkhelms in the tree line, responding to a blast of their own horn, retreated to support their comrades in the valley below. As they turned their backs, Brina tried to use her remaining *Forte* to mount a pursuit. But her sigil store had run out. As she landed face-first in the mud, the world went black around her.

CHAPTER 83

The walls of the citadel were lined with ashen-faced recruits. Saf gritted her teeth as she watched red-sailed ships maneuver their way through the forest of stone pillars in front of Metten's coast. It was like watching water seep through the hull of a ship. With every passing moment, doom approached.

The iron wyvern stayed just behind this natural barrier, bobbing up and down in the open water. In the light of dawn, it looked like a floating jewel. The metal plates that covered it glittered and gleamed in the rising sun. It moved slowly, constantly making tiny adjustments to its position relative to the citadel. No sails or masts were visible on the outside, and the oars on its side moved with a mechanical precision that Saf had never seen in a human crew. Whoever had engineered the thing had been both a genius and a madman.

The thought of who had leaked Metten's location irked at the back of Saf's mind. Though she had known it would only be a matter of time before the empire found out—the growing number of recruits making it impossible to ensure secrecy—there seemed to be a link between events that was eluding her. The timing of it all was suspect. Someone had waited until half of Metten's defenders had set out for Bior before telling the empire exactly where it lay. Was there a spy among them? Or was there a third party out there with an agenda of its own?

A hatch atop the iron wyvern opened. A long barrel appeared through the opening. Saf hadn't seen the monstrous machine in action herself, but she remembered all too well how little had remained of Zot's galleon when she'd picked up the survivors of the wyvern's bombardment last year. *Let's hope stone fares better than wood.* The wyvern gave a lurch, as though it were about to belch.

"Everyone on the ground now!" Saf shouted.

A thunderclap echoed across the water. Moments later, the citadel's wall

CHAPTER 83

quaked. The shock of the impact rattled through Saf's rib cage, causing her to gasp for breath. Terrified whispers arose from the recruits, interspersed with the splashes of rubble tumbling into the sea.

"Stay low. We will make it through this."

The impact of *Consol* was immediate. The recruits calmed down, lulled into silence by her words. When a second impact rocked the wall, none of them broke out in nervous chattering. Rubble toppled backward off the wall and exploded on the courtyard of the citadel behind them. A third cannonball whizzed overhead, missed the wall, and hit the barracks on the opposite side of the courtyard. It smashed through the wall, shattering windows and timber beams alike.

"Miss Saphara!" someone called in the distance. "They're at the docks!" Atop the gatehouse, a young captain named Jane Morris waved to draw Saf's attention. Saf launched into a fortified jump. As she floated across the courtyard, yet another cannonball sailed below her feet. It knocked down a section of the battlements, spraying shards of stone at the defenders. Saf landed atop the gatehouse with a grunt of frustration.

Below, two of the red-sailed ships had moored. A first group of darkhelms was trudging their way up the steep path toward the central gate. They carried wooden ladders equipped with iron hooks at the top to secure them to the parapet.

"Prepare your stones and spears," Saf yelled, running past the soldiers atop the wall. "As soon as they're within reach, rain down death on them. Pace yourselves. They're likely just testing our defenses. We can't run out of projectiles before they begin their actual assault."

As the attackers neared the wall, rocks the size of human heads flew down from the citadel's wall, wreaking havoc on their formation. Saf watched as one hit a woman straight in the face, knocking her backward, her head tilted in an unnatural position. The first ladder hit the wall moments later, its iron hooks clamping down on the parapet.

Using *Forte*, Saf tore the hooks from the stone. Heart thumping, she waited until she could see the top of the first darkhelm's helmet. With another flash of *Forte*, she gave the ladder a jolting push, causing it to topple backward. The heavy ladder and half a dozen darkhelms clinging to it crashed down on the attackers' ranks, breaking and shattering as they went. More ladders went up. The defenders pushed each back as soon as it touched the wall. A smirk broke across Saf's face. "You won't get in that easily, you bastards."

"What's that on the docks?" Captain Morris called.

A giant battering ram, with an iron griffin's head at the top, was being assembled on the beach. It was large enough to house two dozen darkhelms to push it up the hill. Inside, they'd be impervious to arrows, spears, and other projectiles. Saf looked down at the shoddy wooden gates reinforced with rusty strips of steel and knew that they were in trouble.

"Get down into the courtyard and begin stacking the rubble from the wyvern's blows against the gate," she yelled at the nearest cluster of defenders. "I'll deal with the ladders."

"But we'll be locked in," one of the recruits said, his eyes wide.

"Let's hope for all our sakes that we will be. Now go."

CHAPTER 84

Brina awoke with her face in the mud. A weight bore down on her back, forcing her face into the sludge of soil and dew. The weight lifted, followed by two hands gripping her by the shoulders and rolling her over onto her back. Her headache spiked as sunlight seared her face. She felt worse than she ever had after a night's drinking. Depleting her sigil stores had left her exhausted and nauseated.

"By the gods, you're alive!"

Brina rubbed her eyes with bloody hands and forced them open.

"I don't believe it," Brina muttered. "You're..."

The man holding her by the shoulders was Silas, the Morassian. Clutched in his hand was a golden compass. Its needle pointed straight at her. Silas kneeled down and helped Brina to her feet. Though every muscle in her body protested, her legs hesitantly agreed to carry her weight.

"Where did you come from?" Brina shook her head, convinced she was suffering from hallucinations. Silas smiled, extending his left arm for support while holding up the compass with his right.

"This thing," he said, holding up the glimmering instrument in the sunlight. "It came to me tied to the legs of a sea eagle almost four weeks ago."

"What?" Brina blinked.

"I know. I couldn't believe it myself. The only thing that came with it was a note that said:

"In a world of darkness, a spark becomes the center of the universe. Heed the call or watch what you love fall to the void."

It's a strange thing. When things get quiet, it's almost as though it's humming to itself."

Brina swallowed. "Wiley," she said.

"Who?"

Brina shook her head. "It's a long story. He's an old man, or at least I think he is a man, who dwells in the Mist Strait. He has many strange powers. This sounds like something he would do."

Silas nodded and began escorting her down the hillside. They passed through a landscape torn up by war. The soil had been trampled to a mush. Blood intermingled with the mud to make a paste that clung to Brina's shoes and legs. Darkhelm corpses littered the ground. Here and there, groups dragging behind them carts or wheelbarrows made their way across the battleground, picking up Biori wounded, and occasionally soldiers Brina did not recognize. Yet others traversed the field to strip the deceased darkhelms of their heavy armor, loading it onto carts while leaving the bodies in the sun.

"Cleanup is still underway," Silas said. "It was almost impossible to find you, and if the needle of this compass hadn't been pointing straight at you, I might have missed you underneath those bodies," he said, pointing back up the hill to the spot where she had lain. "They thought you were dead. Felled by a windup quarrel. A handful of soldiers from your group swore to seeing it happen, describing how you toppled face-first into the mud after being struck."

"I fell," Brina confirmed, "but luckily, it was my own stupidity that caused it rather than an arrow."

As they strode onto the plain toward the imperial camp, Brina noticed groups of Morassian warriors intermingled with Biori rebel recruits, aiding in the campsite's reorganization. "Where did the darkhelms go? What happened?"

"It was fortuitous that you guys had made a large enough dent in their forces for us to swoop in and clean them up. They routed straight away when we showed up, and after that it was..." His voice trailed off. "It was unlike anything I've ever seen. Slaughter on such a scale flies in the face of the divine. But what else were we to do? We couldn't allow them to regain their formations."

"They got what was coming to them," Brina said, clapping a hand to Silas's shoulder. "And I, for one, am grateful you arrived when you did. Things were looking dire. Worse than dire."

They marched into the camp, and Brina found her eyes drawn to a space between two tents on the left, where two figures sat hunched on a pile of crates. One of them was Solana, and the other was a demonic creature with green skin and horns sprouting from its cheekbones. Brina blinked, shaking some of the exhaustion out of her eyes, and realized it was a mask. Versa.

"Well, if it isn't Springtide," a voice called out. A head of golden hair flashed in the sunlight as Mattheus leaped up from a nearby tent, raising his

CHAPTER 84

hand to shake hers. Brina let go of Silas and felt her legs turn to jelly. She shook Mattheus's hand, then returned to clutching the Morassian's shoulder.

"You're here?" Brina asked.

"Wouldn't miss it for the world," Mattheus said, flashing a pearly white smile at her. "Besides, this thing..." He held up a golden compass identical to the one Silas had wielded. "Wouldn't let me get so much as an ounce of sleep. I tried to ignore it at first, but the humming just became louder and louder until, frankly, I didn't see what else I could do. That it led here was a lucky coincidence. Or maybe that's not entirely true—we've been awaiting your call for some time. But we never heard from you, so we assumed something had gone wrong."

He glanced at the compass, then scowled. "Would you look at that? I think we found out what the needle is pointing at." He walked around Brina in a half circle, watching in amazement as the needle stayed pinpointed at her. "Swallowed any metals recently?"

"Hilarious," Brina said. "Now, where is the war room? There is much to discuss."

Mattheus grinned. "Still not done with war yet? Anyway, I was just headed over there myself. Apparently, we need to 'talk strategy.'"

Supported by both Silas and Mattheus, Brina stumbled to a large tent in the center of the camp. As she stepped inside, she spotted a third familiar face.

Eleanora, the Heemian noble lady, sat draped in silver armor studded with sapphires and emeralds at the table. Her helmet stood on a separate bench beside her, the top of which was dented. Dark bruising protruded from her hairline, but she seemed full of life.

Before Brina could ask her how she had gotten here, Abrasax leaped up from a corner of the tent and swept her into a hug. "I thought I'd lost you," he said. "All morning I was out there, searching for you. I must've walked that hill up and down half a dozen times before my sigil stores wore out, and I was forced to sit down."

"It's okay," Brina said. "I'm not injured. I overdid it with the sparkgazing and collapsed. They all thought I was dead, so they left me alone."

"Do you have your compass with you?" Mattheus strode over to her, addressing Eleanora.

"Yes," she said. "Why?"

"We found out what it's pointing at. It's Springtide." He held up his compass on one side of Brina, and got Silas to hold his up on the other side. They watched in amazement as both of the needles pointed in opposite directions, straight at Brina.

"That's how I found her," Silas said, his voice sounding like a whisper in the tent. "She was lying beneath darkhelm corpses. I wouldn't have spotted her if it hadn't been for..." He wiggled the compass.

Eleanora smirked. "Well, well. Turns out I was right. There is something about you. I thought it the moment I met you at King Krocht's banquet under the mountain. But look at this, now you're magnetic over long distances as well."

"How did you get here?" Brina asked.

"I'll skip the part about how the compass came to me delivered by a giant eagle, as I'm sure you've grown tired of that tidbit already. Truth is, we had been planning a rebellion already. When the foilfaces began lowering their presence on the island, we saw our chance. We rushed through the front gates into the city of Cordwain and slaughtered every last one of the enemy. Then we went from town to town, expunging what little was left. I think the Cardinal never in a million years would have believed that we would rebel. He left a paltry number of foilfaces to keep us subdued. Frankly, I think he believed he had us in his pocket so deeply that the very thought of armed resistance was laughable in his mind. He was right about one thing: Krocht had fallen to the empire's influence. But we, fortunately, had not.

"We were cleaning up the last of them when that eagle showed up with the compass. That's when I realized what I must do. It was an embarrassment, the way we forced you out of our city. And now that we had taken the leap into fighting for what was ours, it seemed only fair that we help the Biori do the same for their island. We only hoped that we got here in time."

"Well, I'm glad you did," Brina said. She sank down into a nearby chair, which was much too comfortable for a field camp.

"Well," Eleanora said, "next time I'd rather we didn't cut it so close. You lot were surrounded and dying by the time we arrived. Many more could have been spared terrible ends had we arrived just a day sooner."

"How many lost?"

"Two thirds," Gavitt, the headmother of the Biori, marched into the tent. "Though we haven't counted the Metten rebels, we expect something similar on your end," she said. "They are with the Allmother now. And they have honored her greatly in their conduct. If it can provide a little solace, I know for a fact that each of them would do it again in a heartbeat."

Brina frowned. The idea of honoring a deity by dying for it had never sat well with her. But if it helped the Biori make sense of the slaughter, who was she to argue?

"Anyway," Gavitt said, gesturing for all of them to sit down on similar mahogany chairs surrounding the map of Bior she had laid out in front of her. "We haven't won yet. There is still the fleet in the distance."

"The siege of Metten will have begun by now," Abrasax said. "We have very little time. Though the citadel is well fortified, and the cleverest woman I know is leading the defense, it's only a matter of time before they collapse. If the Darkhelms gain entry to the fortress, we have no hope of retaking it. They will have a permanent outpost here."

"Then we must make sure they don't," Brina said, her jaw clenched. "I, for one, have a few more darkhelms left to reckon with."

CHAPTER 85

ot let out an involuntary yelp as the steel griffin's head smashed a hole in the front gate. It wouldn't be long before they were through.

"Whatever's behind that gate," he called, "we have to hold. If we lose the inner courtyard, we'll be trapped in the donjon, and from there, they'll starve us out."

The griffin's head crashed into the gate a second time. There was a groan of steel as the gate's frame bent toward its breaking point. "Shouldn't you have a weapon?" a recruit nearby asked him, scowling. The boy stuck out his spear, offering it to Zot.

Zot looked down and remembered that he was still clutching the wooden box that smelled of jungle. He'd been waiting for the perfect moment. And now was as good a time as any. He rushed forward, opening the intricate lock, and right as the third crash enlarged the hole in the gate, Zot threw the entire box through. He could see a few of the scolopendrae on the inside, flying this way and that as they landed underneath the battering ram.

It took a few moments before the screaming began. The battering ceased as the darkhelms struggled to get out from under the ram. As soon as they did so, they were pelted from above with rocks and spears thrown by Zot's guards near the top.

"I don't believe it," Zot said, as much to himself as to anyone else. He looked over his shoulder at the recruit. "Did you see that? It worked."

A few of them looked excited by this news. "Forward," he shouted. "Close that hole with whatever you can find!"

Beside himself with glee, Zot began piling more rubble against the gate. Much of it had been forced aside by the griffin's hammer blows, but they had a brief window of opportunity and he would use it well. Together, they stacked the rubble higher so that it covered the holes in the gate once more.

Good thing it opens inward, Zot thought. Even if they shattered the gates,

CHAPTER 85

the darkhelms would have one hell of a time stumbling over a solid five feet of stone and debris.

"They're retreating!" The call came from overhead. Zot whooped. "Man, who said rebelling was stupid? Not this guy!" He thumped a fist into his own chest and whooped again.

A moment later, the world shattered. The iron wyvern struck the gatehouse. Stone exploded, raining down sharp shards on the defenders. Bodies toppled off the battlements back into the courtyard. One of them fell on top of Zot, and he smashed into the ground. He tasted blood—whether his own, or from the boy who'd fallen a good fifteen feet onto the stone courtyard, was unclear.

He crawled out from underneath the kid and saw by the glassiness of his eyes that he was gone.

A second blast rocked the world, and what was left of the gate flew from its hinges, shattering inward. Now the small dike of rubble was all that stood between the darkhelms and the courtyard. They seized their opportunity at once, storming back up the hillside and braving the rain of projectiles from above. The iron wyvern ceased its barking as dozens of darkhelms clambered over the stone barricade and into the courtyard.

Zot ran backward, feeling very naked without a weapon or shield to defend himself. The recruits rushed forward around him. He stooped to grab a spear from one of the fallen defenders, and it was only when he felt the clumsy haft in both his hands that he realized he'd never so much as held a spear.

Unsure of what to do, he staggered forward along with the other recruits. "Forward," he called. "Let's get them!" And as they charged, Zot hung back, trying to blend into the crowd.

It was no use; the gatehouse had become an oozing wound, spewing the vanguard of the darkhelms' invasion into the courtyard. They were swept back toward the donjon. Zot looked with desperation at the small door that led to the fortified tower in the center of the courtyard, then ran inside, past the defenders who were holding the door open, and up a winding staircase to escape the siege.

They were trapped; it was as good as over.

When he reached the third floor, he stormed into the war room and looked through the windows over the scene. The courtyard had turned black, like a rotting wound. The darkhelms crowded around the donjon, kicking and clawing at the front door where the last of the defenders remained.

Saf was on the battlements of the outer wall, leading her troops around the keep and to safety through the bridge on the third floor. Zot put his head in his hands. "Stupid, stupid, stupid!" he berated himself. He could've had it all. He was rich, had wormed his way back into the ranks of high society. He could've gone anywhere and done anything. Instead, he'd come here, just in time to die.

CHAPTER 86

rina placed her forehead against Razorwing's, petting the griffin behind the ears. The improvised rebel camp had gone quiet as most of the soldiers were marching toward the coastline, where they would embark on the fleet headed for Metten. Razorwing's hooves clawed at the churned-up mud.

"I tried to make him stay in Doorstep's Ditch at first," Versa said. The smile behind the mask was almost audible in their voice. "But it was as if he knew where I was going, and he wouldn't leave me. When the ship departed, at first he just circled overhead. By nightfall, he got tired and landed on the ship. Ever since then, he's been with us. But don't worry, I kept him out of the fighting. I wasn't going to be the one to tell you your pet griffin had died."

Brina chuckled.

"Very touching," she said, "but we're not out of the woods yet."

"Are we clear on the plan?" Mattheus strode over, brushing back his sleek blond hair from his eyes. "I wouldn't blame you if you want to bow out. You look awful."

"Thanks," Brina snapped. "But I've recovered enough to fight. Besides, your ships aren't equipped for naval warfare. If we attempt to land at the docks, they'll ram us and board us before we reach shore. But if we land the ships on the opposite side of the peninsula, near the temple, they won't see us coming. The march will be a half-hour trudge through the jungle to reach the dockside. It'll be like we've appeared from thin air."

"I agree with that part," Mattheus said, "but it's the iron wyvern that concerns me. Have you seen what that ship is doing to the citadel?" He pointed a finger off in the distance, where the gatehouse to Metten stood. Even at this distance, the damage was visible—a dark gash in a white wall. "That thing is vicious. And feathers don't stop bombs."

"And they don't need to," Brina said, still brushing Razorwing behind the ears. "The thing can't shoot straight up. Don't worry about us. You can get on your boats, me and Razorwing will do the rest."

"Fine," Mattheus grumbled. "See you there?"

"See you there."

Before she mounted the griffin, Brina turned to Versa, put both hands on the innkeeper's shoulders and said, "Look, I know she's your sister." She nodded toward Solana. "But don't forget where she came from. And don't forget what she did to you. I would hate to see you in such a horrible state ever again."

"Sometimes," Versa replied with a chuckle, "it's almost like you've forgotten I'm a sparkgazer as well."

"Of course," Brina smirked, "you can take care of yourself. I don't doubt that for a second."

She mounted Razorwing, then bent low and whispered in the creature's ear, "Up."

***

As they soared over the Sundered Sea, a peculiar calm came over Brina. The rush of the wind in her ears was like a bucket of icy water to the face. Brina felt more awake than she had all day. Though she'd had some time to rest and imprint, she was forced to maintain a low burn of *Forte* to stay alert. The exhaustion from last night lingered in her bones. Today, she wouldn't be able to power through everything in her way. She would have to be conservative, monitoring her stores at all times.

They ascended above the clouds, only dipping down now and then to gain their bearings. The four-nation army she had left behind was visible in the distance, miniature figures drifting across the horizon, while the darkhelms' fleet grew ever larger beneath her. The iron wyvern lay in front of the citadel. It hadn't fired in a while, but whether that was good news or bad, Brina did not know. One thing remained clear—once the rebel army appeared from the jungle to defend the citadel, they needed to ensure that their numbers wouldn't be decimated by the wyvern's bombs.

When the wyvern was below them, Brina pulled on Razorwing's feathers. "Time to dive, buddy."

The griffin rose for a moment, then dipped down in a sleek vertical descent. Brina whooped as her stomach lurched with the sudden drop—it was like free-falling while tied to a millstone. The griffin's weight pulled Brina down with it. Brina touched *Forte*, locking her knees behind the griffin's wing joints. At the last second, the beast pulled up, its claws skimming across the top of

CHAPTER 86

a wave. Then, both of them landed atop the iron wyvern, right behind the hatch where the turret's steel barrel was mounted. It had retracted into the hatch, lurking just below the surface of the deck like a shark waiting for a bird to land above it.

Brina crept toward the hatch, clutching what little *Forte* she had stocked up on during a brief session of imprintation on Razorwing's back. She reached for the steel hatch and tried to close it through sheer force. At first, the heavy steel wouldn't budge under her touch. She strained and clasped *Forte* with all her might, pressing down on the hatch.

"What's going on?" she heard a call from below deck.

"Come on," Brina whispered. "Come on."

Finally, the steel gave way beneath her touch. The hatch closed. Burning *Gnis* she touched one of its hinges. It smeared apart like thick clay. Then, she touched the second set of hinges and melted them too, cementing the trapdoor shut. There was a thumping on the hatch as the engineers below tried to force it open again, but the wind cooled the metal, holding the hatch in place.

A second, smaller hole opened beside her, and an engineer in a brown leather apron and thick wooden goggles peered out over the edge of the deck. He didn't spot her at once.

Brina tapped the man on the shoulder. He turned around, gasped, and dropped his wrench down the hole. Curses followed from below.

"My foot, you moron! Why does it always have to be me?"

Brina grabbed the engineer by the front of his apron. "How do I fire this thing?"

"What?" the man sputtered.

"You heard me. How do I fire this thing?"

"It's a complicated mechanism," he replied. "Besides, we can't fire with the hatch closed—the thing would explode."

"That's the idea."

"I can't," the engineer protested, "I wouldn't. Besides, the wyvern would take all of us with it."

"How about you hop in this nice little sloop"—she pointed at the boat carried on a complex system of pulleys on the side of the wyvern—"and tell me how I fire this thing?"

The burn of *Consol*, made her words sound reasonable, trustworthy even. "I can't. It would be treason," the engineer refused.

Brina sighed. "You're no fun." With a low touch of *Forte*, she pushed the man over the railing, where he tumbled head over heels into the boat.

Another head appeared—one belonging to a second engineer. Her head popped above the deck.

"Look, lady," Brina said, "let's not do this again. You heard what I said—how do I fire this thing?"

She seized onto *Consol*, and the woman's eyes turned glassy.

"First you push the lever, locking in your target, then turn the wheel clockwise. Once you pull the lever a second time, it takes thirty seconds for the mechanism to heat up enough to fire."

"Perfect. You will do this for me right now."

"But the sig—"

"You will do this now." Brina held onto *Consol* with ease as the adrenaline urged her on.

"Very well." The woman's voice sounded dull and emotionless as she lowered herself below deck once more. There were rattling pops and clicks below, and lastly, the screech of metal on metal as the woman pulled a large lever. "There," she said, "we are ready to fire."

"Then I suggest you get out of here," Brina said with a smirk. She hopped onto Razorwing's back, patted the griffin's neck, and they shot up into the air like an arrow.

Before they reached the low-hanging deck of clouds, there was a roar as the wyvern turned itself into the largest hunk of scrap metal ever seen. Brina looked down just in time to see a gout of flame protruding from the manhole where the engineers had been moments prior. The heavy ship overturned and sank. Step one was complete.

CHAPTER 87

Leaving the flaming wreckage of the iron wyvern to plummet to the depths, Brina urged Razorwing on as they soared toward the Citadel of Metten. Flying just below the clouds, the world became a tapestry of blue and green beneath the griffin's mighty wings. As they neared the shore, Brina spurred Razorwing into a dive, causing them to pass low over the fortress.

Brina gasped as the scene below came into view. The citadel's courtyard was teeming with darkhelms. Heavy fighting was taking place on the bridge leading to the tower's third floor, which served as the only entrance to the donjon—the central fortified tower and the citadel's last stronghold. The defenders had been driven back to their last bastion of resistance. Even though they were holding the narrow chokepoint of the bridge, the rest of the citadel had fallen. It would only be a matter of time before the darkhelms could leverage their overwhelming numbers against the exhausted defenders.

For a brief, crazed moment, Brina contemplated swooping down over the bridge and sending the darkhelms tumbling to the cobbles below. The risk was too great. A single well-aimed windup quarrel could end her—or worse, Razorwing. Besides, the element of surprise was vital. The darkhelms had hemmed themselves in. If the allied army of the four nations could arrive while most of the darkhelm forces were packed together in the citadel's courtyard and narrow hallways, the enemy would lack the space to leverage their superior numbers.

Departing from the citadel, Brina landed in the jungle, where Razorwing transitioned from flight to a galop. Weaving through the trees, the creature carried Brina onward to reach the point where the four-nation army would break from the tree line to assault Metten's makeshift docks.

Whether five minutes or half an hour passed was difficult to guess. Brina's pulse pounded in her ears, and the exhaustion of the previous day lay heavy on her shoulders. When she heard the thumping of boots on the jungle floor,

Brina jumped up in alarm, rubbing her eyes. Mattheus raised a hand in salute. He marched at the head of a long column that made up the four-nation army.

"There is little time," Brina breathed, looking over Mattheus' shoulder as Eleanora, Silas, Bahov, Abrasax jogged over to greet her. "The citadel's defense is on its last legs."

"Then it is as I feared," Abrasax said, rubbing his temples. "We saw the darkhelms streaming in through the main gate from aboard Samok's Chimera. I knew then that it was only a matter of time before all was lost."

"Well, it's not over yet." Brina slid off Razorwing's back and drew level with the others. "If we attack soon, we can force the darkhelms to fight on two fronts. They won't expect an army of this size to spring up at their backs. There will be a moment of confusion. We need to exploit that to the maximum."

"And the crews of those redsails moored at the docks?" Mattheus twirled a lock of golden hair around his finger. "If they sound the alarm, the game's up."

"Leave them to me," Silas said. His eyes flickered toward the tree line, where the afternoon sun carved slits into the shadowy jungle floor. "My troops are trained to be silent and deadly like jaguars. Our blowpipes will take them out before they know what hit them."

Bahov grinned and clapped the Morassian on the back. "You are an honor to your people. If you can buy us enough time to reach the gates, I promise we shall not squander the opportunity."

Eleanora nodded. "We'd best make haste. Every second spent dawdling here could be enough for the foilfaces to break the defense."

"Agreed." Brina turned around and made to get on Razorwing's back once more.

"Where will you go?" Mattheus asked.

"I've got to go up there," Brina said, pointing at the top of the donjon, which was visible over the citadel's outer wall. "The defenders are holed up in there, but if we can somehow clear the bridge and push the darkhelms out from inside the tower, we'll be fighting on two fronts. They'll never know what hit them until it's too late."

Mattheus licked his lips, his gaze darting between Razorwing and Brina. The former roamer had never grown comfortable with the griffin, especially after it had killed his accomplice and almost claimed his life the previous year. If it hadn't been for Brina's timely intervention, Mattheus would have ended up as one of Razorwing's meals. "Do you think you can make it? If they've got even close to as many archers as they had on the field at Bior..." His voice trailed off, the conclusion self-evident.

CHAPTER 87

"Only one way to find out," Brina replied with a smirk. "Are you up for it?" she asked Razorwing, patting its saddle. Whether or not the creature understood her words, the tension in its muscles proved one thing to Brina—it was still full of energy, ready to take off at her command.

With an explosive lurch, Razorwing shot straight up into the air, its muscular wings beating against the soft ocean breeze wafting in from the Sundered Sea. The fortress shrank below them. Brina circled its perimeter once, steeling her nerves. Landing atop the donjon wouldn't be an issue under normal circumstances, but now, she would have to stick the landing and hide as quickly as possible.

"Don't land, Razorwing," Brina instructed. "Not this time. Just drop me off and get yourself to safety. I'll be fine. I can enter the tower, but there's not enough room on the staircase for you. And once they rain down arrows..."

On their third lap around the citadel, Brina tugged at Razorwing's feathers to guide the creature into a low swoop. As the donjon passed underneath her, she released her grip on the creature's neck and seized *Forte*.

Her freefall came to an abrupt halt as her feet collided with the donjon's top level. The defenders had vacated this section of the tower—and for good reason. The top was littered with broken quarrels and feathers sticking out from the cracks in the cement. Brina absorbed the impact of her landing with her knees and rolled across the tower toward a heavy wooden trapdoor. She took a beat to watch Razorwing make a narrow escape over the citadel's far wall, before she lifted the trapdoor and crawled into the spiral staircase below.

"What is this?" came Saf's voice. Even under duress, it chimed like crystals clanking against each other on a lazy afternoon breeze. "Brina Springtide, how is it you always know where to be just when everything seems hopeless?"

A radiant smile, ill-suited to the circumstances, bloomed on Saf's face. A series of heavy thumps followed as the trapdoor above was peppered with falling quarrels. "Was Razorwing...?"

Brina shook her head. "I jumped off. It was quite the adventure, but I'm afraid the tale will have to wait."

"It will," Saf agreed. "I assume you didn't risk your neck for nothing, did you?"

"I did not," Brina confirmed. "We had some unexpected help. Turns out, some of our allies still dare to fight for freedom. It's a long story, but we've got a force a few hundred strong. They will knock at the front gate of the citadel at any moment. If you've got any energy left, now would be the time to force the darkhelms off the bridge and retake the barracks. We could open a front on two sides and take advantage of how cramped the darkhelms have packed themselves into the citadel."

"Now this is excellent news." Saf beamed. She beckoned for Brina to follow her from the top of the tower down to the fourth floor. Just one floor below, the clangor of battle filled the air. Nervous soldiers stood ready near a wooden staircase, taking turns with their exhausted comrades.

"Miss Springtide has just arrived bearing tidings of hope," Saf called out. Her voice glimmered with *Rhetoris*, fanning the flames of Brina's resolve. "An army is marching up to the citadel right now. Our allies have gathered under one banner, and they are willing to fight for your freedom and their own. That bridge out there needs to become ours again." Saf jabbed a finger at a small barred window. "We need to make headway into the gallery above the barracks, to spread out the enemy. Who here still has the strength and courage to follow me and Miss Springtide in an assault worthy of history?"

Saf raised her fist in the air, and a dozen recruits responded in kind. A roar of excitement filled the room.

"We will set the example, and the rest of you," Saf gestured at the cramped room which was filled with three or four dozen bloodied and shivering recruits. "Once we launch the attack, we will need every man and woman we can get to ensure that bridge stays ours. Do I make myself clear?"

Murmurs of assent rippled through those still standing.

Saf turned around to look Brina in the eye. "Do you have it in you?"

Brina took inventory of her reserves. *Forte* was low. Dangerously so. She'd had little time to recharge after yesterday's exhaustion, and what little she had left she needed to keep exhaustion at bay. Of *Leve* and *Grave*, however, she had enough. Her psycho-sigils were untouched.

"I'll think of something," Brina said. It was the look in the soldiers' eyes more than anything that made her want to keep going. By reason, she shouldn't be going back out there into the fray. Her strength was on the verge of failure. But such is life, she thought. The thought forced a smile onto her lips. She should have died yesterday. Every extra minute was a luxury she didn't deserve.

Saf and Brina descended the wooden staircase side-by-side, the recruits parting to let them through.

"You," Brina said to a terrified-looking soldier who couldn't have been much older than sixteen or seventeen. "Give me that and get yourself upstairs." She snatched a wooden spear from the girl's hands and grabbed another from a second recruit further down the line. She grinned as she twirled the weapons around in her hands.

"Showtime."

***

Brandishing the two spears in her hands, Brina muscled her way to the front line. When she reached the edge of the conflict, she burned *Gnis*, lighting the spears like torches. Flames licked at the spear points, casting erratic shadows onto the battle-worn faces of her companions. Brina pushed her way to the front line and swept at the opposing darkhelms with the burning spears. Sparks flew as she thrust the spear in front of her. The darkhelms hesitated, raising hands to shield their faces from the heat.

Brina burned *Forte* and charged. She hit one of the darkhelms in the chest, knocking him off balance. He toppled backward into his companions, who stumbled. Brina pressed her advantage, forcing the darkhelms back.

From behind, Saf vaulted over Brina, landing among the retreating darkhelms. With a fierce yell, she shoved half a dozen of them off the bridge. Their screams penetrated the din of battle as they tumbled to the cobbles below. The rebels behind Brina seized the opportunity and pressed forward to force the darkhelms off the bridge.

Brina rushed after the darkhelms, storming into the gallery on the far side of the bridge. As she crossed the threshold, she came face to face with an officer attempting to rally her troops and retake the bridgehead. Brina's heart hammered in her chest as she hurled one of her burning spears. It flew true, finding its mark in the narrow gap between the officer's chest plate and helmet. The woman let out a desperate gurgle, arms flailing as her cloak caught fire. The blaze spread, catching onto the cloaks of the nearby darkhelms and inciting a stampede.

Fortunes were shifting. More recruits surged across the bridge, challenging the darkhelms' hold on the gallery. Archers positioned themselves on the bridge, raining down quarrels on the tightly packed enemy below. Some recruits hurled rubble down at the attackers. Chaos reigned as the darkhelms in the courtyard trampled each other to get away from the rain of projectiles. The Citadel of Metten reverberated with the scream of bloodshed, but for the first time that night, there was a glimmer of hope.

"Step aside, you cowards, I shall deal with them. We must reclaim that bridge. Now."

A harsh croak sliced through the din of battle like a knife through skin. A tall, thin figure, hunched and cloaked, marched through the sea of darkhelms, parting them like blades of grass in a storm. His hands were covered in steel gauntlets studded with spikes. Below his hood, a gilded mask glimmered.

Brina stepped forward to meet the intruder and crumpled. Fear squeezed her throat shut. It was like she could sense the man's power on the air. There was no doubt in Brina's mind that she stood face to face with a sense surger. With her stores low, and the exhaustion of battle weighing on her like a leaden cloak, entering a duel with a sense surger was the last thing she wanted to do. She remembered how easily Solana had swept her aside and cursed.

"Give it up!" Brina winced as the words left her throat. She could hear the fear in her own voice. "You're losing. Why spill more blood? Stand down, and we will allow you to retreat."

"Stand down? Retreat?" There was a derisive cackle of a laugh. "Funny, coming from a fire-eyes. I remember when I was a boy. You lot hid in the dark corners of the world. Every town used to have its section of your followers until we rooted you out like weeds. We've gathered and destroyed your effigies by the thousands. You cannot recharge your powers. What little you have left is but an exhalation of breath compared to the storm we can conjure up. I would sooner toss myself into the deepest well on this earth than surrender to the likes of you."

"Have it your way," Saf replied as half a dozen sigilist stars sliced through the air.

Brina jumped aside just in time. The sense surger's gauntlets sprang up, defending his face. He moved quicker than human eyes could capture, knocking each of the projectiles aside as though they were flies.

"You'll have to do better than that," he taunted, holding the last of the stars. He flicked it in Brina's direction.

Caught off guard, all Brina could do was throw herself to the ground. The star nicked her upper arm, tearing through armor and flesh alike. Hot blood spurted from the wound. Her scream caught in her throat as a wave of cold engulfed her. Remembering how Solana had incapacitated her by freezing her muscles, Brina rolled over, flaring *Gnis* in response. There was a sizzle as ice met fire.

Saf sprang forward. Her face was impassive, but her eyes burned blue.

Peppering the sense surger with fortified punches, Saf forced him backward. Seizing this moment, Brina reached for a chunk of rubble on the ground. Seizing her dwindling store of *Forte*, she hurled it in the priest's direction with the force of a trebuchet shot. As the stone left her hands, she

CHAPTER 87

gasped for air. Bright spots filled her vision. The sense surger punched the incoming stone, which shattered.

Brina staggered, held up by a recruit who ran forward to support her. The fight for the bridge was still in full swing. Saf and the sense surger were locked in tight combat, while the world spun around Brina.

No, Brina thought. *No, no, no. Just a little more. I need just a little more.*

Brina steadied herself, reducing *Forte* to the lowest burn she could maintain, just enough to keep her on her feet but not enough to enhance her power in any meaningful way. Her back was against the wall, she was out of options.

Saf jumped back as the sense surger unleashed another wave of cold. She landed on the edge of the gallery, her back to the three-story plunge to the courtyard. Her enemy closed in on her with amazing speed. They began trading blows, dancing on the edge of the drop-off. They moved so fast they became a blur to Brina's eyes. She dared not attack from a distance, for fear of hitting Saf, and without *Forte* she would be useless in a hand-to-hand struggle.

Scrambling, Brina reached for a windup one of the darkhelms had dropped. She searched the floor for a quarrel, found one, and began loading the weapon. Maybe she could end it all with one well-aimed shot. She just needed an opening in the melee. The gallery was emptying. The darkhelms had retreated to the floor below, allowing rebel forces to stream from the donjon and chase them down. A group of them stopped, staring at the struggle between sparkgazer and sense surger.

"Should we help her?" a woman at their head asked Brina, panting.

"Keep pushing the enemy backward," Brina replied, peering down the windup's sight. "We'll handle this."

Saf put her back against one of the gallery's pillars and mule kicked the sense surger in the chest. Although the priest lifted his forearms in an X-shaped pattern to block the blow, the force of the attack caused him to stumble backward.

Now, Brina thought. She pulled the windup's trigger. The bolt plunged straight through the sense surger's armor and into his side. Blood burst from the wound like a hot spring. Thrown off balance by the impact, he let out a roar and reached forward to grab Saf by the neck. As he tumbled sideways into the courtyard, Saf struggled against his iron grip. A moment later, they disappeared over the edge.

Brina screamed. She rushed to the edge just in time to watch Saf and the sense surger land fifteen feet below, a heap of limbs on the cobblestones.

Brina launched herself after them. As the ground rushed up to meet her, her dwindling store of *Forte* flickered. Her legs buckled on impact, forcing her knees into her chest. She didn't have enough air to scream as she felt her legs break. Everything went black as *Forte* winked out. Depleted. She clung to consciousness through sheer will, digging her nails into the courtyard's cobblestone floor. Brina forced her eyes open. She couldn't pass out. It all came down to this moment. Four nations stood together against the empire's might. The die had been cast, and Brina would either see the rebels victorious or she would die with her eyes open.

Saf and the sense surger were already upright and trading blows again.

The priest released a wave of cold, which Saf countered. In response, he lashed out with his spike-studded gauntlets in a series of furious blows. Saf dodged each, as elegantly as if they were engaging in a leisurely afternoon of sparring.

The fighting in the courtyard below had escalated to a crescendo. The rebel army had gained the gate and was now pushing inward, faced with a front of frantic darkhelms. There seemed to be no strategy to the darkhelms' fighting, as if the concept of facing an equal opponent hadn't been considered during preparations. Shouts of conflicting instructions echoed back and forth, causing confusion among the ranks and heightening the sense of panic.

A circle formed around the sigilists as they battled. Soldiers from neither side dared intervene as the duelists traded lightning quick blows. Brina felt useless, lying there with broken legs as the sense surger wore Saf down.

She crawled toward a wayward spear and hurled it at the sense surger, who froze it midair with a lazy flick of his wrist. With his other hand, he struck Saf in the chest. She hadn't seen it coming. Her face contorted in a grimace as she sank to her knees. Brina screamed as the priest's gauntleted fist drew back for a killing blow.

"No!" She put every ounce of *Consol* she could muster into that single syllable. If she couldn't fight, her only option was to assault the sense surger's mind. Her shout was enough to make the sense surger turn around. "Leave her alone."

The sense surger laughed. Something about that high-pitched noise made Brina's guts churn.

"You think you can influence me?" he cackled. "You think I am some empty vessel waiting to be filled with your hollow words? I am the puppet master. And I will cut your strings. Lie still."

Brina felt her limbs lock up. The sense surger stepped forward, towering

CHAPTER 87

over her. Blood dripped from his spiked gauntlets onto Brina's forehead. She struggled against her invisible bonds, but she felt as though she'd been cast in concrete. Her muscles refused to budge. The priest knelt beside her, his gilded masked leering down at her.

"Let me tell you one thing, Springtide. You may have thrown a temporary stick in our wheels. But this"—he waved his hand around at the chaos unfolding around them—"is but a temporary setback. A necessary sacrifice before our inevitable victory. You sparkgazers couldn't convince a drop of water to flow down a hillside, let alone push back the tides. Now, I will show you true power. Get up."

Brina felt her broken legs move against her will. She tried to scream but couldn't speak. An explosion of agony overwhelmed her as her legs buckled beneath her, unable to carry her weight. She fell onto the cobbles, tears streaming from her eyes.

"Again." The sense surger's command was soft yet cruel, like a pillow pressed over an infant's face.

Brina's legs tried desperately to force her upward. Along with the pain, Brina's hatred for the priest grew with each pathetic attempt her broken legs made to hold her up. She dug deep and forced her lips to move. "This is a fire you can't put out, old man." She spat at the sense surger's feet. "With or without me, the stoneward will fall. Mark my words."

The sense surger kicked Brina in the ribs, then turned away from her. While she writhed in pain, the sense surger reached down and picked up Saf's motionless body from the courtyard's cobbles. He forced Saf's head in Brina's direction with a bloody hand.

"One push, and her neck will twist past its breaking point. What will you do now, Miss Springtide? If you are so very convinced that you can stand against the might of Heil, then do something."

Tears streaked down Brina's cheeks; she thrashed against the bonds of her flesh cage, but found the priest's control over her was unyielding.

The sense surger tilted Saf's head back, preparing to snap her neck. Suddenly, his gilded mask turned white as a wave of frost spread over it. Two hands, bare and unprotected, clasped his head on both sides, forcing icy cold through the slits toward the sense surger's head. He let go of Saf, steam rising from his helmet as he whirled around.

"What in the..." he croaked.

Solana stood behind him, panting, bloody hands raised. "Hello, Reynziel Methusal," she said, her mouth twisting into a snarl. "Nice to see you again."

***

Solana panted as she stood face to face with Methusal. She had revealed herself, and now the only way forward was for Methusal to die. If he lived to report back to Mallion's Depth about Solana having joined forces with the rebels, the consequences for her mother would be catastrophic. As yet, her mother lived under the protection of the faulty belief that Solana had died a martyr—a protected status even to one as wicked as Cardinal De Leliard. If Methusal made it back to De Leliard, her mother would be outwalled, which, in her condition, was as good as a death sentence.

Methusal's eyes widened behind his gilded mask. "You would betray your brothers and sisters for this filth?"

"I was taught to maintain balance," Solana said. Her heart forced its way into her throat. "I know a spreading disease when I see one."

Methusal let out a roar of anger. His hands flicked upward. A scorching heatwave raged across the courtyard. Soldiers of both sides abandoned their weapons and ran to avoid the blaze. Solana's feet remained planted. She recited the prayer of frost. The air sizzled and bubbled where heat met cold. Solana groaned as Methusal stepped forward, forcing her back. A foul stench filled the air as the hairs on her arms were singed off by the boiling air. Methusal's power was awe-inspiring. It was like fighting the sun itself.

Solana strained to maintain the prayer of frost. *Heil, don't abandon me,* she thought. *You know it's always been you in my heart. You and your creation.* It felt wrong to call upon the Keeper while Solana battled one of her high priests, but it was all she'd ever known. She may have abandoned the church, but Solana would never turn her back on Her. It would be like denouncing the very air she breathed.

Suddenly, the heat evaporated. There was a rush of wind as Methusal surged toward her with unnatural speed. Solana sidestepped. Too late. Methusal's boot landed in her stomach, sending her sprawling on the cobbles. Solana rolled with the momentum and attuned to the prayer of speed. Methusal was on her in a heartbeat.

Solana echolocation couldn't keep up with where Methusal's blows were coming from, but she felt the displacement of air on her skin, giving her a fraction of a second to respond each time. She danced backward, then struck out with her leg, sweeping Methusal to the ground. Before she could press the advantage, the old priest leaped back to his feet.

"And to think we wrote your name on the wall of the fallen," Methusal

CHAPTER 87

spat. "I will scratch it off myself."

"Heil stands for balance, not domination." Solana took a deep breath as Methusal circled around her. "You have recited the tenets so often that they have become mere words to you, but I remember them."

She took a step toward Methusal. Her fear was turning into rage.

"Number one. 'You shall not kill or cause grievous harm to another.'" Solana swept an arm out as to embrace the slaughter going around them. "Guess you and De Leliard have forgotten about that one.

"Number two, 'All living creatures are of the Keeper and the Keeper is of them.' Yet you would seek to oppress countless souls in her name."

"This is sophistry. Intellectual poison." Methusal's voice sank to a whisper, and yet it carried over the cries of battle like smoke on the wind. "You have allowed these heretics to cloud your mind."

A seed of doubt sprouted in the back of Solana's mind. What if he was right? What if her judgment turned out to be wrong? *You're already in too deep. You've made your choice, and it's up to Heil to decide who is worthy and who is not.* With an unhinged scream, she launched herself at Methusal.

Methusal sent out a wave of cold to keep her at a distance. Solana countered with a wave of cold of her own. The very moisture in the air crackled and froze, raining chunks of ice down on the crowd of onlookers that was forming around them. The fighting in the courtyard seemed to slow as the pair of dueling sense surgers made their way to the center of the battleground. Rebel soldiers had taken firm control of the courtyard and the Enlightened Watch, exhausted by the long siege, was grinding to a halt.

Solana struggled to maintain her grip on the prayer of frost as Methusal strolled toward her as though he were out for a walk on the beach. Solana's skin burned and cracked as a layer of hoarfrost covered her arms and face. The cold seeped into her very bones, causing her hands to tremble. She struggled to hold the shape, but felt it weaken as Methusal neared.

"Rule number one," the old Reynziel said with glee, "never match the opponent's element unless you are certain you have to strongest connection to Heil. You should have known that I would be most worthy."

Solana's chest froze. She felt herself curl up into a ball on the floor, desperate to hold on to what little body warmth she had left. *Don't forsake me,* Solana prayed to the Keeper. *I have lived for you, I will die for you, but please, not here, not like this.*

"Never in a million years," Methusal said, "would I have believed that I would face one of our own here tonight. You were blessed by Heil's light, and you have defiled the powers granted to you by using them to further a wicked cause."

He loomed over Solana, a specter in the black and gray world she had inhabited since her vision was taken from her.

"You might very well be the first blind sister on record to defy the Cardinal's will. A new low for the church, and a disgrace to all who have come before you. But worry not. I shall expunge you, your family, and the very memory of your name from history. I will erase you."

Tears bloomed in Solana's hollow sockets and froze on her cheeks. Family. All her life she had worked to make her family proud, and now she would prove their undoing. She thought of Luna and all things she'd never said. They had suffered so much for her. They suffered a fate worse than death to protect Solana and their mother. For all these years, they had lived just outside the stoneward, a shell of their former self, and all Solana had cast their way were filthy looks and violence. Solana would never have a chance to make that right. She had waited too long, and time had just run out.

There was a clang of stone hitting metal. Methusal whipped around, distracted. "Who threw that?"

"Me, you pathetic sack of wampyr dung," Brina Springtide shouted from a distance. "Look around. Your army is losing. With or without me, your entire church is coming down. Mark my words."

Methusal growled, too incensed to speak.

A second. That was all Solana needed. She seized onto the prayer of heat, felt Heil's light echo through every fiber of her body. With a lurch, she seized Methusal's head like a drowning woman seizes a rope. The hood of his cloak caught first. He struggled against her grip, trying to maintain his hold on the prayer of frost. Solana forced her fingers into the slits of his mask, digging for the hollow sockets she knew would be there. The gold of the mask melted and bubbled underneath her palms as they fought.

Methusal let out a bestial screech of agony. His fingers closed around Solana's throat, squeezing with immense force. Lights popped in the black and gray of Solana's world, but she couldn't and wouldn't let go. *Let us both die*, she thought. *Let it be over.* The stench of burning flesh filled her nose as Methusal strangled her. She could feel the strength in her limbs give way. Just a little bit more. Just a little. Bright light enveloped her. She was ascending. Soon, the pain would end.

Methusal grip slackened, and the light receded just enough for Solana to form a clear image of Luna and her mother standing side by side. It was

CHAPTER 87

still possible. Everything could still be made right, if only she hold on to her prayer for a little longer.

As Solana poured the grief of a lifetime into the prayer, Methusal sank to his knees, twitching.

"You will burn in the next life," Methusal croaked through burned lips. "Heil will reward me…"

"We shall see." Solana's face twisted into a wry grin.

She stomped down on Methusal's chest, attuning to the prayer of strength. His chest plate caved in. Solana grimaced as the breaking of ribs clawed at her eardrums. Blood welled up from the cracked armor in slow bursts. Carried onward by adrenaline and terror, she kneeled down and seized Methusal's head in both of her hands. The battle's climax came not with a roar, but with a soft snap, followed by silence. Methusal's blood ran in rivulets across the citadel's courtyard, staining the boots of his horrified darkhelms.

As if waking from a spell, the surrounding darkhelms, witnessing the fall of their leader, dropped their weapons in a clatter of surrender. The sound resonated through the courtyard like the tolling of a bell.

The tense silence was broken by a lone voice behind Solana.

"Rebellion one, Mallion's Depth zero."

Solana smiled. She recognized that voice. Turning on her heel, she marched over to a gray outline she knew to be Brina Springtide. She tried to lift to woman up off the ground. Brina struggled under her grip.

"I can stand," Brina barked.

"No, you can't," Solana said, poking a delicate finger at Brina's legs. Springtide recoiled in agony. "Please. Let me help you."

"Fine. But don't get used to it."

Solana raised Brina in her arms.

"We won," Brina said, her voice thick with emotion. "I can't believe it. We won."

"Yes, we did," Solana replied, blinking away a tear.

She stood amidst the chaos, Brina Springtide clutched in her arms. All around them, the rebels were rounding up the remaining soldiers of the Enlightened Watch. Here and there, lonely cheers erupted, but mostly there was silence. Today had been a costly victory. Countless dead lay in the courtyard, staring at the blue sky with unseeing eyes. In the distance, the whooshing of rolling waves intermingled with the cries of the wounded and dying.

Heil's creation was beautiful, yet cruel and brutal at the same time. Loss and celebration. Pain and joy. Honor and cowardice. Exhilarating adrenaline and the numbness of death. They were all just a hairsbreadth apart from each other. It was hard to grasp, and yet as self-evident as the air they breathed.

Solana felt the breeze on her bare face and smiled. For the first time, she felt truly free.

CHAPTER 88

"And so the sun rises on a new world," Abrasax muttered, staring out of the meeting room's window as starburst hues colored the Sundered Sea. Brina thought he looked awful. His voice was hoarse and quiet. There were dark bags under his eyes and his skin had taken on an ashy quality. "History will remember yesterday's battle as the dividing line between two eras."

Brina fidgeted with the cork of a bottle of kelp rum she had stolen off a darkhelm's corpse in the courtyard below. She pulled at it with her teeth, grinning as the harsh liquid inside reached her nostrils. A buzz of activity floated into the donjon through the open windows. Already, rebel soldiers were hard at work, separating the dead and retrieving weapons and armor that could be reused. Brina yearned to be out there with them. Another round of strategy chatter sounded hollow when compared to the painful work those outside were doing.

Last night had been part funeral, part celebration. Every one of the survivors had lost friends, family, or both. And yet there was the unbridled exhilaration of having faced death and living to see another day. The rebels had been victorious, but it had cost them a great deal.

"At least give us one day to enjoy this," Mattheus groaned. His blond hair was matted and disheveled, and his hands trembled as he reached for Brina's bottle of rum. "Please give us a single day without more premonitions of doom heaped upon our shoulders."

"Abrasax is right," Saf said. "Some darkhelms escaped. They're on their way to Mallion's Depth right now. When the Cardinal finds out the siege has failed, he will be furious."

Brina took a gulp of kelp rum and sloshed it around in her mouth. Somehow, it didn't taste as good as it usually did. "Good," she muttered. "At least now he knows he can't just walk all over us."

"Which is precisely the problem," Abrasax said. "De Leliard underestimated us. He will not make that mistake again. Whether or not we intended to, we have declared open war on the Heilinists."

Brina scratched at the table, desperate to keep her hands occupied. Images of fallen rebel soldiers forced their way into her mind's eye. She had trained with them. Had led them. Or, in the case of the Heemians and Morassians, she had convinced them to join her battle against the empire. None of them would have been here if it hadn't been for the rebellion she and the others had started. And now she sat huddled in a warm tower, while they were out there cleaning up what remained of their comrades. It was wrong. She needed to be out there with them, sharing their burden. She put the cork back in the bottle and rolled it toward Mattheus, who reached for it with a grin.

"We need to keep the pressure up," Eleonora said. Her pale face looked white in the light of the rising sun. "My people are in grave danger. Those left behind on Heem are made weaker by the absence of the warriors I brought with me on this campaign. We need to make sure the Cardinal's eye remains on us, lest we lose again that which we fought so hard for."

"Agreed," Silas said. "My people can hide out in the jungle for a while, but they are no match for a legion of trained darkhelms. We started something yesterday, and we had better finish it."

When Saf unrolled a vast parchment map of the Sundered Isles and began placing wooden figurines on top of it, Brina realized she'd had just about enough. Today was not a day for sitting around, shoving tokens across a table. Today was a day for doing. She ignored the others' questioning stares as she got up. She didn't want to speak another word.

As she stepped out onto the third floor bridge, she got a view of the courtyard below. The cobbles were black with dried blood. Corpses lay everywhere, some still clutching their spears in death. Dozens of rebel soldiers were busy loading carts with armor, weapons, and the dead. Many of them wore bloody bandages. Brina was embarrassed to feel a tear rolling down her cheek. So much suffering. So much destruction. All because they had wanted to live in freedom.

Brina's hatred for the empire, the church, and the Cardinal rose into her throat like bile. She looked at the darkhelmed bodies sprawled out below her and fought the overwhelming urge to spit on them. How could anyone stand at the side of such evil?

She entered the gallery, then descended bloody steps into the barracks below. The first floor had been torched by the iron wyvern, leaving only blackened walls and the charred remnants of bunk beds. As she stepped out onto the cobbled courtyard, she spotted two figures bent over the body of a fallen darkhelm.

As she approached, one of them looked up. Versa. They wore an ebony mask devoid of all features under a black cloak, making them look somehow ethereal and shapeless, like a wraith walking in the daylight. Beside them sat Solana. Her face was covered in bandages, and the exposed skin of her neck was covered in painful looking blisters.

"Someone has to tend to them," Versa said, answering Brina's unspoken question. "The other soldiers won't touch them, except to strip their armor and take their weapons." They nodded at a cart loaded with blackened armor on the other side of the courtyard. "But these were people, too. They deserve a proper burial."

Brina's jaw tensed. She looked down at the body with disgust. The armor had been stripped away, but the woman was still wearing that ghastly black helmet.

"I made them leave the helmets," Solana said. "It's the respectful thing to do. Exposing their faces to the world would dishonor them, even in death."

"Then why have you been walking around barefaced for months?" Brina snapped. As far as she was concerned, not taking a perfectly good helmet was a waste.

"I am not one of them anymore," Solana said, getting to her feet. "I gave up the traditions of the church, but I still have love for those that adhere to them."

"After all they have done to you? And to Versa?" Brina struggled to unclench her fists. "Methusal would have squashed you like a bug yesterday. Heil is not on your side. How many times must they prove it to you before you learn?"

"The church is my enemy, but Heil remains my Keeper. She granted me the strength to survive. This has all been part of my given path, laid out before I was born. I just didn't see it yet. My purpose is not to serve the church, but to prune it back to its essentials, to root out this imperialist disease that has seized something I once loved."

Brina opened her mouth to begin shouting, then remembered how close Methusal had come to finishing both her and Saf. If it hadn't been for Solana, neither of them would have survived, and the outcome of the battle might have looked different. It was a hard truth to swallow. She owed Solana a life debt. The least she could do was to hear her out.

"These people fought for what they were taught was right," Versa said with a sigh. "They had families, dreams, and aspirations. De Leliard took all of that from them, just as he took it from us."

"Growing up inside the stoneward, we are forced into their way of thinking from birth. They make it sound so common sense that many don't realize they never had a choice." Solana bit her lip. "All of these people died believing they were doing the right thing. That doesn't make them evil. It makes them naïve."

Brina stared at the dead woman at her feet. Did she have a lover, waiting in Mallion's Depth for news of what had become of her? Maybe she had wanted to make her parents proud. Brina would never know, and in the end, it didn't matter. What mattered was that yet another human life had ended to fuel De Leliard's war machine.

She kneeled down and grabbed the woman's legs. "Come on, let's bury her."

Together, the three of them spent the rest of the day tending to the empire's dead. Rebel soldiers and darkhelms were buried side by side, and each grave was marked with the same wooden stakes.

When they were done, they sat on Metten's docks, their feet resting in the cool water. The Sundered Sea turned gold as the sun descended beneath the horizon.

"Soon everything will be different, won't it?" Versa said. "War is coming."

"We've been at war our entire lives," Brina said. "What's one more?"

CHAPTER 88

THANK YOU!

Hello there, friend. Glad to see you made it out the other side. After yapping at you for 175,000 straight words, I only have one thing left to say to you:

THANK YOU.

Thank you for giving my work a chance. Thank you for sticking with it until the very end. Thank you for your time and attention.

These days, there are a thousand entertainment options barking for your engagement, and yet you took the time to sit down with this book. I cannot overstate what a blessing that is.

If you enjoyed your renewed stay in the Sundered Isles, you could do me a huge favor by leaving a review. As a small author, your reviews help me find more readers who would enjoy my books.

On the next page you will find links to my various listings. Leaving a review on one (or more) of these websites would go a long way towards helping me along in my career as an author.

If you are busy, even leaving just a star rating would make a world of difference.

To get the inside scoop on my upcoming projects, join my newsletter at www.danfswinnen.com.

Scan this code to review on Goodreads.

Scan this code to review on all major retailers.

If you want to dive further into
the life of Brina Springtide:
Get the FREE novella Springtide at
www.danfswinnen.com

THE SPARKGAZER SAGA BOOK 3:

THE SHATTERED SCEPTER

AVAILABLE FROM THE 5TH OF JULY 2025

www.ingramcontent.com/pod-product-compliance
Lightning Source LLC
LaVergne TN
LVHW091653070526
838199LV00050B/2162